CHASING DIFFERENT

LOVING DIFFERENT SERIES

STAND ALONE BOOK 1

COLETTE R. HARRELL

Library of Congress Control Number: 2024913317
ISBN: 979-8-9862851-2-2 (e-book)
ISBN: 979-8-9862851-3-9 (Paperback)

Book Cover by 100 Covers
First edition 2025
www.coletteharrell.com

To all the Baby Boomers,
We're still here! And to everyone pursuing their dreams despite the
obstacles, keep going. Even an inch is progress.

To all the libraries in the world,
Thank you for offering us a window into the marvelous people, places,
and things that inspire us to be better and the lessons that guide us
away from negativity's grasp.

**Please note: This book took fictional liberties with the layout
of the Columbus Metropolitan Library for storyline
purposes. Please visit this bastion of excellence and explore its
treasures.**

Acknowledgments

This inspirational thriller is my love letter to my neurodivergent family members and to an omnipotent, omniscient, and omnipresent God who makes no mistakes.

You are all incredible individuals who navigate life with unique perceptions, strengths, and challenges that deserve recognition and celebration. My novel pays homage to the idea that neurodivergent individuals have the right to their own love stories, filled with the same complexities, joys, and heartbreaks as any other. I hope these stories are considered valid and vital, offering a glimpse into the myriad ways love can develop and thrive.

As depicted through the characters in this book, love knows no bounds and respects no labels. It flourishes in understanding, patience, and mutual respect, no matter how unconventional it may appear to the outside world.

I've intentionally chosen not to assign a specific diagnosis to my main character, Deacon. This decision allowed Deacon to embody his own experiences, as many individuals on the spectrum (a term debated by many neurodivergent support groups—my family uses it; therefore, I employ it sparingly). Rather than focusing on the clinical aspects of a specific diagnosis, this story emphasizes the emotional and societal journey of navigating life while being "different" and the complex dynamics of acceptance and nonacceptance accompanying it.

This is a work of fiction and is intended for entertainment

purposes only. Deacon is just one of a million stories yet to be told and should not be used to depict any living or deceased individual(s). This book is a work of fiction and is intended for entertainment purposes only. It should not be used as a guide or recommendation for medical treatment.

Content warnings for this book are under the Content Warnings section on my website. www.coletteharrell.com

Prologue

The Reign—15 Years Before

Somewhere in Finland . . .

The scream came first—sharp, raw, slicing through the frigid night like a blade severing flesh. It ricocheted off the towering stone walls of the castle before vanishing into the oppressive silence.

Death had arrived. It prowled behind the tinted windows of four black luxury cars as they crawled up the icy road, their snow-tread tires crunching in unison. The only light in the oppressive darkness came from the castle on the hill, its windows glowing like predatory eyes, watchful and unblinking.

Inside one car, Eric of New America shifted in his seat, the leather creaking under his weight. He leaned forward and glared out the frosted window.

"Finally," he muttered, his nasal whine breaking the silence. "Ridiculous how long this took. Do they expect us to act as trained dogs?"

The driver ignored him. High in the castle tower, General listened to every word through hidden microphones embedded in the vehicle. He smirked, his severe features hardening with amusement. A meticulous man, he thrived on control, and he never left anything to chance. Bugging his guests was a necessity, and it also provided entertainment.

Ragnar Alstead, known by all as General, didn't earn his title through military rank but instead inherited it from a father who believed his son would lead not with vision but with brute strength and force. That flawed prophecy—equal parts admiration and indictment—fueled Ragnar's hunger for absolute domination.

"The newbie will bear watching," he thought, narrowing his pale icy-blue eyes at the convoy below.

Eric's impatience didn't surprise him. Puppets often forget they have strings until the moment someone yanks them.

The procession of cars halted in perfect synchronization. Tires crunched one last time before silence fell. General observed from his perch as the drivers stepped out, their dark coats blending into the night. They opened the car doors, and, one by one, the heads of the world's most powerful families emerged.

Each leader carried a single vote—one decision that could reshape the entire world's trajectory. General had orchestrated their arrival with meticulous detail: the secluded location, the pageantry of the journey, the deliberate isolation. Every element was designed to humble them before they stepped into his fortress.

The formidable castle did its job as it loomed over the visitors like a grave marker.

The town surrounding the castle wasn't much better. Its inhabitants lived in shadow—both literal and figurative—bound by invisible threads of submission. The Council, led by General and his handpicked allies, didn't govern the people; they enslaved them. Every decision, every rule, every breath they took was calculated and imposed. Obedience wasn't requested—it was demanded. Generations of manipulation had warped morality and survival, leaving the townspeople hollow and compliant. They didn't question the Council's decrees. Questioning only led to one place: the castle, and few who involuntarily entered ever left.

In the depths of the fortress, another scene unfolded. A man strapped to a steel table gasped for air, his brown skin gleaming with sweat and streaked with crimson. Blood dripped from his neck and pooled beneath him. A scalpel's jagged edge carved deeply into his flesh as he writhed against his restraints. The metallic stench of blood hung thick in the chamber. His screams had long faded, leaving only ragged breaths.

General flicked his hand into the air, and the servant beside him gave a slight nod. "Da, General."

The servant, Geoff, wielded the blade's final thrust. The prisoner gurgled, blood bubbling at the corners of his mouth. His head slumped to the side, but he did not remain silent. Using what strength he had left, he whispered, his voice faint but deliberate: "Father, deliver me; vengeance is yours."

General stilled. He then swiveled, his nostrils flaring at the audacity of one so beneath him. But a faint shiver ran down his spine as the whispered prayer lingered in the room, heavy and unwelcome. For a fleeting moment, the words settled like mist, curling into the cracks of the stone walls, clinging as if they had substance.

He dismissed them with a sharp breath and arrogant thoughts. *Words are meaningless. Power is all that matters, and prayer has none.*

He turned from the scene, his thoughts shifting to why he had brought these family heads to his doorstep—the *Book of Disasters*. A tome filled with prophecies used to manipulate the world for over 250 years. It had served as both a guide and a promise of destruction for generations. But General didn't believe in using it sparingly.

Unlike his ancestors, he hadn't stopped at a single copy. General had recently created four duplicates, each of which had been locked away until now. The books weren't just tools—they were weapons waiting to be used. Together, they would sow chaos on a scale the world had never known. General smiled at the thought. He alone held the keys, and he would be the architect of the world's total surrender.

He watched from the window as guards ushered the family heads into the castle, their breaths visible as puffs curling into cursive letters against the darkened sky. His jaw tightened, and he turned sharply, his boots striking the polished floor with each step.

The time for games was over. It was time to move forward and claim it all.

Chapter One

Nia

Grafenwöhr, Germany—2013

Nia Lewis despised parties.

To her, they were like a fat fart in a packed elevator, suffocating and inescapable.

She scowled, refusing to look at her reflection in the full-length mirror, her hands planted on her hips, shoulders hunched like a prisoner bracing for sentencing. Behind her, Sincere rummaged through her overstuffed makeup kit, muttering under her breath as she pulled out powders, brushes, and what looked like medieval torture devices disguised as beauty tools.

Nia sat in the straight-backed chair, stiff as a mannequin, while Sin worked, her mind was elsewhere. Thoughts popped like cartoon bubbles above her head.

Ugh, makeup. Stupid parties. Shoot, this entire situation.

Her face shifted with every calculated sweep of Sin's hand—an inch to the right, then the left—dusting, patting, painting.

I swear if she hits my nose one more time, I'm gonna—too late . . . "Achoo!"

Sin stumbled back with a dramatic gasp, one hand over her heart, the other clutching a compact like a lifeline. "Girl! Can you at least *warn* me?"

Nia sniffled, fanning away the lingering puff of blush clouding the air. "My bad," she muttered, though she wasn't sorry in the slightest.

Sin sighed, as though exasperated, and tilted Nia's chin up with a practiced flick of her fingers. "It's a dance, not a freakin' dental appointment. Lighten up, ladybug! A hint of blush makes your caramel complexion really pop. You're looking sooo cute."

Nia grunted, finally risking a small peck of her reflection staring, she was totally unimpressed. Her cheeks looked too pink, her nose too powdered, her entire self too unfamiliar.

Why am I letting her do this?

Because Sin was undeterred, and that side of Sin was relentless. She grinned and ran a hand through Nia's thick curls, letting them tumble over her shoulders. She then gathered them on top of her head in a curly bun, tendrils flying around her temples. "Keeping the hair out of your face frames these beautiful features. You have Daddy's doe eyes and Mama's bow lips. Girls out here paying good money for lips like yours."

Remaining unconvinced, Nia mumbled something unintelligible.

She perched at the edge of the chair, her arms crossed, feet tapping against the floorboards, waiting for Sin's inevitable next move.

Sin exhaled loudly, dragging a hand down her face like the sheer burden of Nia's resistance exhausted her.

Nia arched an eyebrow. She wanted to ask so badly what Sin's problem was when she was the one who trussed like some throwback Kewpie doll.

Then Sin did what Sin does. She launched into her usual "*I know more than you*" speech. "Baby girl, we're on a base in Germany. New enlisted people show up all the time."

Nia snorted. "Yeah? And? You're an extrovert. I prefer books to people, remember?" She dropped her gaze to the floor, biting the inside of her cheek. *Sin doesn't get it. She never will.*

Nia's mind swirled with memories. The awkward encounters. Standing at the edge of crowds, feeling like a misplaced puzzle piece. The way even the other wallflowers ignored her, as if sensing she wasn't even worth saving a spot on the outskirts.

"I don't want to go," she said, her voice low, developing into a plea. "I'd rather stay home and read."

Ignoring her, Sin plucked a lip brush from her bag, smirking like she held the secret to the universe. "Uh-huh. Nonsense. Just go this *one* time. You might mess around and have *fun*."

Nia gave her a flat look.

Sin pressed her cheek against Nia's, their faces reflected their heritage—Sin's skin deep and rich like dark chocolate, Nia's golden and warm like honey. The contrast was striking, like twilight spilling into a sunlit field. And yet, their kinship was unmistakable—same tilted eyes, same angular chins, same stubborn set to their mouths.

"What if you meet other book lovers? Maybe some fellow introverts who also hate parties?"

Nia's skepticism deepened. "So . . . people who hate parties will be *at* the party to meet other people who hate parties? You hear yourself, right?"

Sin groaned, rolling her eyes so hard they nearly spun out of her head. "Little one, I'm trying to break you out of this self-imposed prison—"

Before she could finish, their mother's voice sliced through the door like a gavel slamming down in court.

"Don't you dare, Sincere Monica Lewis! If she doesn't want to go, leave her alone."

Nia clapped a hand over her mouth, snickering. "Ooooh, you in trouble. Mama used your whole government name."

Sin raised her hands in surrender, wagging her fingers at Nia in a warning. "Oh, I'm *gon'* get you for that."

Victory couldn't feel sweeter.

Grinning wide, Nia kicked off the chair, shaking her curls free of their elastic prison. She flopped backward onto her bed, a weight lifting off her chest. Winning against Sin? Unheard of.

She reached for her book, the familiar weight of it comforting, grounding.

Sin lingered in the doorway, makeup bag in hand. "Sis, I'm glad you let me teach you how to defend yourself," she breathed. "Maybe one day, you'll wish you'd let me teach you some girly stuff too."

Nia waved her off. "Martial arts? Cool. Giggly girly things? Hard pass. Bye-bye, Sin."

Sin huffed, slamming the door.

From the hall, their mother's muffled voice floated back. "And stop calling your sister Sin! Her name is Sincere. Lord 'ave mercy. Jesus, take the wheel and drive me away from both my daughters' foolishness."

Nia frowned. Mama always made a big deal about Sin's nickname. The last thing she heard made her stomach twist.

". . . And the wages of sin is death. Y'all gon' fool around and connect that spirit to your sister."

A chill slid down Nia's spine.

She tried to shake it off, pushing to focus on the words in her book. But the letters blurred, and something in her chest ached.

Despite her earlier complaints, Sin was her best friend. The girl everyone on base wanted to be, especially Nia. She was vibrant, social, and the "It Factor" at every gathering. But, Nia wasn't her sister, and she wasn't just losing interest in parties—lately, she felt like she was fading altogether.

Her book forgotten, she hunched deeper into her mattress and curled into herself.

With each passing year, she felt smaller.

More insignificant.

And the terrifying thought that kept her up at night?

One day, she might just . . . disappear. *Poof.*

* * *

Deacon

Columbus, Ohio—15 Years Ago

"Punch him back, Deacon."

Jonesy's voice throttled out like the rattle of Mr. Kelly's old Chevy, the one that woke the neighborhood every morning with a cough, a sputter, and a defiant roar. Nobody liked it. But nobody said a word. Mr. Kelly was huge.

And like the Chevy, Jonesy wasn't holding his peace while he watched his little brother get punked. Wind whipped through his loose blond locks, the green kerchief on his forehead sliding back as he leaned in—too close—hovering over Deacon like an executioner instead of a savior. "Get up," he hissed.

But Deacon liked the ground. The dark grit cool against his light-colored cheek. The dull throb where Curtis's fist had landed. The earth was steady, solid—a good place to think, to wait it out.

But Curtis Jackson wasn't one for waiting.

Standing over him, sneakers planted wide, his breath coming in hot and ragged bursts, Curtis spat every insult a boy like him could master—words learned in the street. Words passed down like hand-me-down fists and inherited rage.

Deacon burrowed into the dirt, wondering if there was a *Handbook for Thugs*, a syllabus of slurs and beatdowns. If so, Curtis was an A student.

But the time for wondering ran out fast. The air snapped with kinetic energy. Deacon felt it in his slender bones—something was about to give.

His head flicked from one person to the other. While Deacon pondered, Curtis was still spewing filth. Jonesy, fists curled into cannons, was watching Curtis like a hunter with a clear shot. And then Deacon watched both pairs of eyes go molten.

The WWE Royal Rumble had just begun. No starter bell needed.

Deacon would've laughed if Curtis hadn't lifted his size eleven Jordans, his foot hovering over his ribs, ready—no, *eager*—to strike.

Deacon didn't flinch.

Because he knew his brother.

Jonesy had had enough.

A roar ripped from Jonesy's chest, raw, untamed. Then he was there, ripping Curtis away, his bandanna hitting the dirt like a discarded flag of truce. It's green color signaling, go.

"Monkey!"

The word landed like a grenade. Too late to take it back. Too heavy to ignore.

Curtis stiffened. Deacon's breath hitched, his tawny brown face tightening. Words had power—hitting even the unintended victim.

And then chaos.

Jonesy was already on Curtis, fingers locked around his neck, dragging him away from Deacon like a lion defending its wounded cub.

Deacon scrambled up, his hands shaking and his mind screaming. Jonesy always did this. Always throwing himself between Deacon and the world, violence was his go-to answer.

Curtis shook him off and swung first. Jonesy ducked and swung harder. Curtis staggered back, caught himself, then lunged again. They collided like falling buildings, fists flying, rolling into the street.

"Fight! Fight! Fight!"

The chant rose, hungry for more violence. The street held its collective breath.

Jonesy's caustic word had sealed the deal. Nobody was rooting for him now.

They punched until their arms were heavy, and their breaths came in ragged gasps. Battled until it wasn't a fight —just two exhausted boys sprawled on the grass, staring up at the sky, wondering what happened.

Dusk loomed. Deacon stood over them, his hands in his pockets. "We have to get home, Jonesy."

Jonesy sat up slowly, blinking at his watch. "Yeah. Yeah, we do."

Curtis, still wheezing in the dirt, taunted, "That's right. Run."

Jonesy sighed. But Deacon shook his head. Nobody argues with a cornered dog. He wasn't about to go a third round.

Jonesy stood, and they fell into step, walking in silence.

Jonesy's lip was split, his knuckles raw, but he grinned, slinging an arm over Deacon's shoulders. "What'd you even say to him, little man?"

Deacon shrugged away, shifting under the weight. "Too much."

Jonesy let go. "Sorry."

Deacon avoided his gaze, knowing lately, he was constantly ducking away from things too big to name. "I just told him he smelled like Auntie's cabbage."

Jonesy froze midstep. "You told him what?"

Deacon's expression didn't shift. "I said, 'You smell like my auntie's cabbage.' Then he flipped out."

Jonesy smacked his forehead, then winced when the bruised skin protested. "Deacon . . . man. We talked about this. You can't just say whatever pops into your head. You're thirteen. You gotta learn."

Deacon's brow furrowed. "I don't get it. Why can't we just call it what it is?"

Jonesy groaned. "Mama Linette explained this already. And you—little genius that you are—never forget anything. So act like it."

The smells of home-cooked meals drifted from open windows. Safe. Familiar.

"Hey, Jonesy?"

Jonesy loudly exhaled, as though he was already bracing. "Yeah?"

Deacon didn't look at him. He couldn't. "You're sixteen. By now, you should know you can't call Black people monkeys. That's not just some word. It's a drumroll of hate, filled with a painful history. It's something you don't get to say."

Jonesy tensed.

Deacon pressed onward. "Mom and Dad say it's because of how you were raised. That separatist camp. But it's been a year, Jonesy. You've had time to learn. So I'm telling you—stop."

Jonesy's jaw clenched. "Easy for you to say." His voice was sharp, then cracked. "People here see my face and assume I'm the enemy like I asked to be part of this. Like I did something to change this neighborhood. And Curtis messing with you? It just tipped me over the edge."

Deacon didn't reply.

Because he understood.

The King-Lincoln neighborhood had changed under gentrification. It started small: a lone family fixing up a house with good bones but bad cosmetics. Then word spread. Soon, like an infestation, more came—buying, renovating, conquering, and absent landlords evicting to make room.

Families like Curtis Jackson's, living just a few streets over, knew they'd be next. Some tried to hold on, but money ruled everything. Property values soared, taxes rose, and they were forced out, one by one.

The neighborhood's complexion was changing, and it wasn't about race. It was about green. And money was king.

Deacon's parents bought their home when it was falling apart —termites and neglect eating at its bones. But they worked and restored it. Five years later, it gleamed, standing strong, validating their belief in home.

A year ago, Deacon's father, Jones, came home and found Jonesy curled up on their porch—starved, beaten, a runaway. His cheap clothes were torn, his face mottled with bruises that had gone untreated long enough to yellow at the edges. His lip was cracked, and his knuckles bore the raw scrapes of a boy who had fought back—but lost.

Jonesy had run. Run until his feet bled, until the road blurred, until he could no longer feel the weight of Alice's slaps or Jeffrey's belt buckle.

When Ms. Alice banged on their door two days later, her voice was shrill, her rage curdled with a bitterness that had been festering long before Jonesy was even born.

"Bring my son out here, you race traitor!" she shrieked. "Jonesy Everette, bring your whiny tail out of there. Boy, you don't need a mammy at this point in your life! You hear me?"

Beside her, Jeffrey, her husband, stood taut, his small frame vibrating with hate. He was a petty, wiry man who didn't command fear on his own, but let his venom seep into others, poisoning them until they struck for him.

Everyone knew that Jeffrey had always hated Jones. After Jones left the camp, Jeffrey despised his memory and resented the ghost of him that haunted their camp, as though he had been a legend who had once walked among them.

Deacon watched as his father glared back, he was smart enough to understand that for this small man, the reality of Jones—the towering, broad-shouldered, six-foot-four man who had dared to walk away and become something more—helped to fuel the hatred.

And now, here stood Jones' son, Jonesy, and he was healing. His stance was somehow bigger than their memory, and the whispers of the camp elders who had warned Alice never to let her boy look up to his father.

Because Jones was proof of their greatest fear. That their bloodline wasn't superior. If given the chance, nurtured instead of poisoned, a boy like Jonesy could outgrow their hate.

Jeffrey spat on the porch, his eyes flicking toward Jonesy, who stood behind Jones., He was no longer peeking through the doorway but standing boldly. "Boy, you best get out here. You know where you belong."

Deacon and his mother, Linette, stood behind the curtains. On this perfectly positioned chessboard, Jones prepared to checkmate. He didn't yell. Jones didn't curse. He just stood firm, his presence enough to make the ground feel unsteady beneath a cowardly Alice and Jeffrey. There was an authority in Jones that was unshakable.

"You've had him for fifteen years, Alice," Jones said, his voice even. "And the boy looked half-dead. I left him with a woman I thought could love him enough for both of us. To my infinite regret, I was wrong."

Alice's face twisted, something between fury and wounded pride. "You can't take him!"

Jones let the silence settle before he spoke. "I didn't. He left. The decision's over."

Jeffrey clenched his fists, his beady eyes squinting, but he didn't step forward. He knew better.

Jonesy later told Deacon that moment was his first lesson in true strength. That strength didn't always mean shouting or swinging fists. Sometimes, strength was being—a quiet, immovable force that said, *Try me if you want to.*

Neither Alice nor Jeffrey tried him. Even stupid people have a radar for survival. So, they slunk away back to the wreckage of their hate-filled lives.

Jonesy had been home ever since. Deacon knew Jonesy was happy with his address change, even if, at first, he had not seen Black people as people. He had to unlearn all the garbage stuffed inside, a bit at a time. Deacon got tired of it sometimes. It could be a lot.

That's when he realized his mother was a saint. She had taken the time to gently remold Jonesy and guide him into a life he had hard-earned. She had done the same with him. Because of her caring hand, Deacon was okay with those who didn't get him.

He wasn't a people pleaser. He just wished that Jonesy didn't feel that he had to take care of him. He honestly could take care of himself. His father had taught him how to defend himself when he was only three years old, and other kids on the playground tried to bully him.

Deacon had a hard time wrapping his mind around the fact that the kind, loving giant that he knew as Daddy could once have been a racist. His further bombardment of questions led to the discovery that his father came from a long line of racists. Was it in the genes? His genes? It had kept him up at night, the question of how and why.

But love had changed Jones. Love had reeducated him.

The turbulence of other people's biases sparked Deacon's curiosity, leading him to study his own skin. He was fascinated by the power of melanin and promised himself that one day, he'd understand it all.

And his brother's racist taunt had brought it all back. Jonesy stared up at the sky, his hands in his pockets. His voice was achingly low. "Yeah. I get what you're saying, little man. Sometimes, my past sneaks up before I can shut it down. But I'm working on it."

Jonesy let out a shaky breath, the kind that carried years. "I ain't proud of the words I sometimes let slip. Truth is, they're ghosts—passed down, worn in. I don't want to carry 'em any more. I see now . . . They don't just haunt me. They haunt the family. They haunt you."

Jonesy's eyes never left the clouds, but the silence that followed was heavy—like the truth had finally settled between them.

He glanced at Deacon, smiled, bruised and tired. "We both got our fair share of baggage. Like, I shouldn't have pulled you close like that. Sorry. You know I love you, right?"

Deacon nodded. "Words hurt, Jonesy. Love shouldn't hurt."

Hearing that honesty, Jonesy dropped his head.

But they were blood-bonded. Together, they stepped inside, separate but finally in sync.

Brothers in a family with a past, in a city that didn't quite know what to do with either of them. Both were bound to silent vows they had made to each other.

Jonesy would always have Deacon's back. And Deacon?

He'd spend his life figuring it all out. One day.

Chapter Two

General

Present Day—Finland

Miles away from the routine of Nia and Deacon's lives, the world had already shifted—and the tentacles from a small Scandinavian town were reaching for them.

General stepped out of the stone cottage with the iron-reinforced door and ancient symbols carved into its crossbeams. The chill bit through his heavy coat, but he felt restored.

Every week, without fail, he visited a local woman whose skilled hands and quiet expertise melted away any tautness from his body. Her touch aroused him, then left him soothed and invigorated—each night in her company was a celebration, and then come morning, a promise of renewed strength.

Witch.

General stopped and stretched his long, muscular arms in languid satisfaction, but the thought concerning his mistress hovered. How else could one woman hold his attention for more than a few nights? In his black-and-white world, such a feat defied logic.

She had to be a witch. Maybe a Siren.

As usual, the morning fog was thick, coiling around the village of Henkilöjärvi like a living thing. Four Halti Hounds flanked him —named centuries before from the mountain looming behind— massive beasts, their black fur blending into the shadows, their eyes glinting like molten steel. He removed his glove and ran his hand down the spine of the nearest hound, savoring the ripple of restrained power beneath the fur. The air was heavy with quiet, broken only by the wind's distant howl and the hounds' low growls.

"Hiljainen," he commanded, placing his glove back on.

Instant silence. The hounds calmed, and even the wind complied.

Nodding, he moved through the winding paths, past shuttered cottages whose curtains fluttered. Their occupants peered out with relief. Another night survived after watching his hounds stalk freely through the town. Another morning, they weren't his pets' dessert.

General preferred walking to and from the village. It kept him sharp. Softness was a liability. The gym might keep a man fit, but nature forged steel.

Beyond the village, the terrain grew treacherous. Mount Halti loomed above; its summit was swallowed by fog. He inhaled deeply, the frigid air burning his lungs. This was *his* kingdom. From Henkilöjärvi, the Council ran its operations. From here, the world bent and kissed his ring.

But lately, he had felt a ripple in his subconscious, and he couldn't put his finger on the disquiet. Not knowing its source, he was getting frustrated. Every step he took away from the witch brought him further from peace and deeper into the void.

His mind raced through his strategic three-year blueprint: destabilize the USA economy, incite chaos between allies, and tighten the Council's grip on world leaders. By keeping them all so busy reacting, no one would have time to plan a viable offense. Nations would be brought to their knees. Allies would become enemies—enemies now friends. Leaders would be bought and then broken. He relished it. Power was a game, and he was a master at it.

But going through his blueprint didn't give him the comfort he sought; instead, his unease grew.

Something is off.

One hound stiffened, his nose twitching like he'd caught a scent on the wind. General's lips curved into a cold smile; this favorite hound, his baby, was always in tune with his moods. "Patience," he murmured for himself and the hound.

He pressed on, climbing higher. The fog began to thin, and his fortress rose before him.

Almost home, at the edge of an overlook, General paused. The hounds panted beside him, their hot breaths rising like steam. As the mist swirled before him, his face stilled. This was his favorite place to think. Standing here, clearing his mind, usually brought answers to even complex questions. He didn't like the lump in the center of his stomach. He needed to retrace his steps, stand in the open air, and analyze his gut feeling that something was going wrong. He inhaled with his eyes closed and allowed his mind to drift.

* * *

Henkilöjärvi—2013 (The Day of the Gathering)

. . .

I stood at the towering rectangular window, my gaze sharp, cutting through the falling snow as I observed the activity below. There were black luxury cars lined like dominoes, ready to topple, releasing thick clouds of exhaust. Chauffeurs moved with the precision of clockwork, their practiced hands opening doors to release passengers who strode forward with a quiet urgency. Even the elders—usually deliberate in their movements—walked with rare haste.

They were hungry for what I had promised.

Behind me, a man's final breath rattled out.

Crimson trails seeped from the slashed-open brown body on the gurney. It had now ceased its struggle. For twenty-four hours, his captive fought. He whispered prayers, his white teeth clenched in defiance. And yet, his spirit never broke.

Almost admirable. Almost. But admiration was a weakness I couldn't afford.

Was it true, then?

Could these people withstand such torment because they were built to endure suffering? I asked myself this, already priming my conscience with an excuse to justify my actions. In my sense of the world, it seemed plausible—some being destined to carry the weight of others, their legacy reduced to nothing more than beasts of burden.

But what got me? The man had prayed continuously. It was not my expectation, even though he had been taken from a church. People faked being pious; they didn't actually live it.

"Geoff." My voice cut through the stillness.

"Da, General."

"Do you know why some are born to lead and others to kneel?" I straightened, not hiding my facial expression, sneering as I continued. "Of course you don't."

Geoff's pause was barely noticeable. "I'm at your service, sir."

I shook my head at his mindless obedience. "Quite right. Why?

Because you've always been a sheep. Ba-aaa." I had to chuckle at my little joke.

Sobering, I leaned back in, my cheek connecting with the corpse's. I breathed in slowly, then released solemn, almost tender words, "You fought hard . . . But in the end, the world still took its due. It always does."

I stood, my fingers tracing the edge of the gurney. It was cold metal, refreshing. "Ah, such is life, is it not? Cruel. Beautiful. Final."

The round table near the gurney now held five ornate silver goblets, each half-filled with dark liquid—my tribute to the future.

Nodding to Geoff, I pointed at the goblets. "Deliver these downstairs—do not spill one precious drop."

Striding toward the door, pausing to strip the disposable covers from my blood-smeared boots, I discarded them with practiced ease. The hallway lighting caught the full-length mirror ahead, and I knew if I looked at my reflection, it would be crisp and clear. But, I didn't need validation that I was tall, broad-shouldered, and my ash-blond hair streaked with gray was cut to perfection. Outfitted in a tailored suit hugging my robust frame, I had dressed that morning with the upcoming celebration in mind. As such, I was the image of a man in absolute control, my features chiseled by time and privilege. I was not an insecure man.

I was untouchable.

My smirk deepened.

Excitement bubbled through my veins. Today, I will make history. I would shift the balance of a centuries-old war.

Good versus evil.

And to think, it had almost unraveled.

My expression soured at the thought. Geoff had returned just over a day ago with the wrong specimen, a mistake that could have cost us everything.

* * *

The hounds' sudden howls yanked General back to the present, their voices slicing through the mist like a warning. They had felt his agitation, the sour edge of the memory trying to claw its way free. Just the memory of that weekend long ago, when his team almost failed him, made his blood heat.

Crouching, he pressed a steady hand to each flank, murmuring low until they quieted. Their breaths slowed, but their eyes—watchful and uneasy—remained locked on him.

He understood. The past had teeth.

He'd been so close to an answer . . . He could feel it. There had been something there, just beneath the surface of his recollection. A flicker of insight. A sliver of truth. Whatever was wrong was somehow connected to that weekend. If he could just grasp it . . .

Pulling his collar tighter against the cold, he tilted his face to the sky. The thick air wrapped around him again like a veil, and he leaned into the weight of memory.

He wasn't done with the past. Not yet.

* * *

2013 (The Day before the Gathering)

I barely glanced as Geoff entered my office, his usually steady gait carrying an air of unease.

"Is the sacrifice here?"

Geoff cleared his throat. "Somewhat."

My temperature instantly spiked. I slowly rose, my voice deadly calm. "Explain the meaning of 'somewhat.'"

"We have everything you required—except for one detail. It's a man. Not a woman."

Geoff's fear thickened the air, and I almost choked on it.

My fists curled, but I kept my voice light. "I specifically requested a woman. The feminine energy is crucial to taming the aggression that the books may stir. If we move too fast, the world will notice. Aggression is never silent. These simpletons think they are in control with their partisan politics weaving here and there, dividing their countrymen so that they can conquer—only for them to be pawns on our chessboard. Our goal is for them to stay greedy, self-righteous, convinced they are in control."

I growled in suppressed fury. "Only feminine energy can finesse that. Therefore, when I give you an assignment, you follow it to the letter!"

Geoff exhaled, but I knew he knew me well enough to brace himself. "I take full responsibility. The team followed all your specifications until they arrived, and our team leader thought his childhood nanny resembled the target, and he didn't have the stomach for it. Instead of abandoning his mission, he brought us someone else."

General's jaw tightened. "At least tell me the right church was selected."

"Yes. A congregation of the faithful, unshaken by any media manipulation. The true remnant—those who love instead of hate, who forgive instead of condemning. The ones who understand what it means to stand in the gap."

Waiting, I pressed my lips into a thin line. "And why couldn't he pick another woman?"

Geoff fidgeted, clearly aware that his explanation was testing my patience. "The women weren't alone. They were escorted to their cars by strong, alert men. My team—already . . . hesitant—balked at drawing too much attention with a battle. So they waited until they saw a single vehicle left in the parking lot. Then they made their move."

I couldn't believe what I was hearing. My brows lifted in mocking disbelief, and I snapped, "For the love—"

"—as I was saying, he was male. A deacon, we believe. And for all the praying he's doing, his faith runs deep. Will he do, sir?"

A long pause.

I exhaled. The sharp sting of disappointment was acrid in my nostrils. "Where would we find another at this hour? The ritual must proceed. The gathering is tomorrow." I looked down, moving papers across my desk, a sign to Geoff that he had been dismissed. "Prepare the way."

"Da, General."

* * *

Twenty-Four Hours Later, The Council's Arrival

The Council arrived, and I left the stiffening body laid out on a slab. Anticipation increased my pace. I reached the hidden panel in the wall, slid it open, and stepped into the elevator. I descended four stories into the depths of the fortress. On the main floor, the grand chamber awaited. And I was almost giddy as the air sweetened.

The massive fireplace crackled, flames casting flickering shadows across opulent brocade wallpaper. Heavy French furniture, thick imported carpets—wealth dripped from every detail.

Four men sat in high-backed chairs, brandy snifters in hand, each carrying a vote capable of restructuring the world.

I strode to the center of the room, the weight of the moment pressing down like a vice.

This was it.

The next phase.

In my hands, I held the future—leather-bound, filigree-lettered, glowing faintly in the dim light.

The Book of Disasters.

A collective breath stilled as I turned the tome, letting each man glimpse its flawless perfection.

"General, is that it?" The secret, genuine Emir of Turkey's voice trembled, his walker wobbling as he leaned forward.

"It is life," James of Russia murmured, folding his hands as though in prayer.

Eric of New America rose, tall and polished, his auburn-streaked hair impeccably styled. "Gentlemen," he declared, his voice ringing with misplaced authority, "we are reclaiming what is ours. We will not *be replaced."*

I knew he was going to be a problem—an upstart. "You're what? Thirty-five? A mere child among us." I watched my words peel away Eric's self-importance like weathered paint. "Your father's death rushed your ascension, but you have yet to earn your seat at this table. And mimicking archaic dribble like 'We will not be replaced' is beneath us."

A quiet cough masked an amused chuckle from one of the men. Eric stiffened, his face reddening.

I ignored him.

With deliberate care, I placed the book on the mantel. The room seemed to tighten around it.

"There are four copies," I said, my voice low and measured. "Each identical. For over 250 years, this tome has guided the world's course. Never copied. Never duplicated—until now." My gaze swept over them. "The cost was high. Paid in blood. But it is time."

A hush ricocheted through the group.

Then Elias of Finland, the eldest among them, stirred. Slowly, he pushed himself upright, his cane groaning under his weight. His voice was gravelly, aged, yet sure.

"We have ensured this battle is ours," he said. "This book has been our guiding light since our ancestors first revealed its power. A prophetic tome that predicted the catastrophic China Flood, where two million souls were lost. As our guide, we thrived and prospered, knowing it was better to be the lender than the borrower. When Black Wall Street flourished in Tulsa, the book revealed the town's power structure's jealousy against them and, as a result, Black Wall Street's inevitable downfall. And indeed, we paid attention and used the information not only to prosper but also to ensure that no similar haven has arisen for those people since. And now, through careful manipulation of a too-proud nation and its people, we are commanding the ruling party to what we now have coined as New America." Those listening leaned forward, his voice resonating through the room like an old-time preacher who had witnessed a divine revelation. "No more waiting. The Serpent shall reign as the Dragon, and all will be as foretold."

A servant appeared, setting five silver goblets on the table—each brimmed red.

I snapped my fingers for Geoff to hurry and leave. "Let's begin."

The men stood. They grabbed a goblet and lifted it.

Power pumped through my veins, and I roared. "Pour!"

Dark liquid spilled onto the books. Instead of soaking the pages, it vanished, absorbed instantly.

A collective awe descended as each book filled with script across its pages.

Then, in unison, our voices rose in a forbidden chant, words never meant to leave our bloodlines.

"Nachalo, Nachalo, Nachalo."

The word echoed, its meaning filling the room.

Beginning. Outbreak. Origin.

I exhaled deeply, my chest swelling with triumph.

I felt exhilarated; after years of clandestine planning, the five books were in each leader's hand. We were now four hundred percent more powerful, which made me euphoric. I wanted to beat my chest. My father and I disagreed; he demanded that the Book of Disasters *never be duplicated. I believed he didn't have the mettle needed to maximize its potential. He repeatedly said my thirst for more would be the Council's downfall. He stated that the original book was for the original head family to control. I was never worried because, as the leader, I led the Council with an iron hand. Allowing each of them to have a book was a sacred trust never to be broken. Only death could break it.*

Theirs!

* * *

There was a gust of wind, and then one of the hounds growled deep in his chest, the memories slipping away like smoke, and General returned to the now. Alert, he looked around, blinking, and noted a hare burrowing into a crevice. At least, this time, something concrete had disturbed his hounds.

"Go."

His hounds bounded off in glee in full pursuit of the hare. He resumed his walk up to his home's entrance. He hadn't figured anything out yet, but he knew this feeling of anxiety had something to do with that weekend long ago. There was a reason his thoughts were full of 2013.

What was it?

That spooky prayer? He shook his head. Naw, he wasn't a believer.

The doors swung open before his hand could touch the doorknob.

"There is news," Geoff said as he took General's coat and scarf.

A pounding sound like horses' hooves could be heard coming up the porch. A butler appeared through a sliding paneled door, and each hound flew through the opening.

"Steak for each of my babies today, Charles."

"Da, General." And the paneled door slid closed with a click.

"First, I'll have my morning tea and breakfast. Then at 9 a.m., you may bring me this news."

"It is a he, Sir. A very nervous Eric of New America," Geoff said, promptly leaving.

General didn't rush; he took his time going to the sunroom as he had anticipated a sumptuous breakfast after such a rousing night of pleasure. His peak performance took stamina; now he hungered for food. Geoff's announcement that Eric of New America had come to see him made him smile, because with the announcement of his visitor, everything had clicked into place. Eric was the source of his unease. General's emotions settled, and he stretched and exhaled with comfort. He would eat slowly; he liked the idea of making Eric wait. Like a rooster in a barnyard, the young upstart's puffed-out chest was a clear product of overindulgence on his nanny's part. The waiting would do him good. He was pampered and spoiled by a life of privilege. The weekend Eric came to the leaders' meeting, he showed General his true character. Eric's overblown sense of self would be his weakness. It could not be the Council's.

Whatever the pup wanted, he would handle it.

Like his father before him, he was built to rule.

Forever.

* * *

Across the ocean, Nia Lewis and Deacon Everette lived in ignorant bliss. They had no idea the currents of fate were shifting, inching them toward an inevitable collision.

Checkers was child's play.

Chapter Three

Nia

The Present

Nia hustled through the automatic doors of the Columbus Metropolitan Library's Main Branch, her heart hammering against her ribs.

Weaving between colleagues, she slurped her drink, a few drops escaping, hitting her chin, and landing on her sweater. To anyone watching, it seemed inevitable the way she lurched through the morning foot traffic.

Glancing down at the small wet spots, she cringed. And the award for clumsy goes to . . .

The weight of her backpack—pressing on her shoulder, thudding with her every sudden movement—signaled the start of the workday, and both she and her soiled sweater needed to get a move on.

Late again.

She already knew the script. Mary, her boss, would cross her arms and arch an unimpressed brow. "Do you not know what time your workday starts?"

A rhetorical question. A ritual, even.

And like clockwork, Nia would counter with saccharin-coated sarcasm. "Yes, Mary. The time got away from me this morning, Mary. I'll try to do better, Mary."

"Mary," she snickered, dragging the name out just like Saundra from *227*, that old sitcom from the '80s. Honestly, it was involuntary at this point—her brain was hardwired to deliver it with the same dramatic flair as if she were about to lean over a balcony and spill some messy tea.

But this was routine. Nia would be late. Mary would scold. And then the world would keep spinning. Because when it came down to it, Nia was the best at her job. Tardiness was her Achilles' heel, her kryptonite. Punctuality? Not her thing. It wasn't that she didn't try—she did. She just got too tangled in the now to worry about the next.

Today, the culprit was her sister, Sin. As always, she didn't care that she was calling right when Nia was getting ready for work. And, as usual, the conversation wrapped up with a list of things Nia needed to fix about herself.

* * *

"I have to go, Sin. I'm going to be late for work," Nia panted, hopping into one leg of her pants.

"Okay, quick update. I sent the money to Mom and Dad for their anniversary cruise. They'll be off in less than a week, with Dad finally experiencing a country as a tourist, not a soldier."

All Sin got in response was the sound of heavy breathing.

"Nia! What are you doing?"

Rolling her eyes, Nia yanked up her pants. "Why? Dang, girl, I'm putting on my pants."

"Why? Why? Because you sound like you're running a marathon. When was the last time you went to the dojo? Martial arts is about discipline, Nia. Where's your discipline?"

"Next to the cheesecake I ate yesterday on the second shelf of my fridge."

"Girl, how many times have I told you? You indulge as a reward, not as a lifestyle. You go to the dojo, you get cheesecake. You go to work on time, you get cheesecake. See how that works?"

Instead of answering, her cell phone tucked against her cheek, Nia threw on her jacket, then pulled it away to glance at the time. "Not today, Satan!"

She grabbed her thermos and backpack, rushing out the door.

Sin's voice flickered in and out as Nia sprinted down the walkway. "So, you're going to be late? I read somewhere that chronically late people use it as a passive-aggressive control tactic."

"Said the sister, trying to control me from thousands of miles away." Nia started her car, checked the rearview camera, and peeled off. "Gotta go. Thanks for handling the money. It means they can enjoy their trip without worrying."

"Yeah, since they leave Monday, I didn't mind fronting it until your payday on Friday."

"Thanks, I got you. I'll call them on my break. And Sin . . . You're good, right?" Nia always checked to be sure her Black Ops Agent sister was safe. Even if she wasn't sure Sin was telling her the truth.

"I'm golden, baby. Later."

A relieved Nia glanced at the clock on her dashboard. "Dang it, Sin, I'm late."

* * *

Now, she was paying the price.

Deacon Everette, not her supervisor, Mary, was already waiting at the front desk when Nia arrived, his presence an undeniable fixture in her mornings. He stood with the careful stillness of someone measuring the space around him, his movements deliberate, almost too controlled. As someone who practiced making herself small, she understood. His caramel-toned skin was smooth, his short, twisted locks neatly arranged across his forehead. His sharp cheekbones, strong jawline, and long lashes framed eyes flecked with gold and green, making him almost painfully gorgeous. But there was an awkwardness about him, a hesitance in how he held himself—six feet of wiry muscle wound tight as if bracing himself against the world.

"Hello, Nia Lewis. You're late again." His voice was loud, more like a public service announcement than a greeting.

Nia exhaled, trying to shake the lingering tension of her rushed morning. "Library voice, please. And I'm not late late," she countered, arching a brow. "Just fashionably tardy."

Deacon blinked, his head tilting slightly, his voice lowered. "That's late, Nia. Maybe try using an alarm clock."

Her lips pressed together. "Why can't you just say good morning?"

His fingers twitched at his sides before disappearing into his pockets, his shoulders rising just a fraction. "Because . . . A person should help their friends be better," he announced, his gaze flickering from her face to the floor, then back again. A sigh slipped past his lips, rolling into a groan. "I did it again, didn't I, Nia?"

Recognizing the uncertainty in his voice, Nia softened. "No, you just told a fact, Deacon. I was late. I'll work on it."

His body's stiffness eased slightly as if absorbing her words for safekeeping. Yet he lingered, shifting his weight, his fingers twitching lightly against his jeans. She knew he was anxious when his fidget rings appeared, and he began to rotate them from one finger to the next, almost hypnotizing Nia as they effortlessly flowed over and under his fingers. To refocus, Nia bent over her work, effectively dismissing him. Getting the message, he turned and headed to his table.

His absence allowed the tension in Nia's shoulders to release; her muscles relaxed for a moment before she felt a shadow cast over her, an unmistakable presence at her back. It was her coworker, Serena, whose footsteps were loud and whose attitude was blunt, always finding amusement in Nia's interactions with Deacon.

Nia had liked the bubbly, overweight young woman, but lately, her rude comments about Deacon got on her nerves. It was nobody's business if Nia found Deacon attractive—or if Deacon liked her back. What mattered was that he showed up every day, consistently and intentionally. And Nia appreciated that. His honesty, though often clunky, was refreshing.

Most of the time.

"I see your pet met you at the door again," Serena said, sarcasm slick as oil. "Oh wait, is he still whining for scraps of your attention? Did you rub his tummy?"

Nia took a slow, measured breath, the kind that kept her from saying too much. She turned to Serena, whose sweet face never matched her tongue's acerbic bite. "*Seriously?*" Nia said, weary but steady. "He's a customer. Can we be decent for once?"

Serena rolled her eyes. "Girl, *you* be decent 'cause that man ain't here for no one else but you. You betta go ahead and let him take you out. Get y'all a little white picket fence and have little awkward babies." She cackled loud enough to draw attention.

Deacon had already turned to leave, but not far enough. His steps, never quick to begin with, dragged—slowing to a crawl. His fidget rings, pulled from his pocket, gave him away, flowing between his fingers like water. He'd heard Serena—every snide word.

Nia's jaw clenched. She fought the urge to slap a hand over Serena's mouth—anything to shut her up. He wasn't deaf or dense. And his body language screamed hurt.

Heat surged up Nia's neck. "No one said he was obsessed with me," she hissed, her voice clipped and tight. "Stop being messy. You're doing too much."

Serena snapped back, loud enough for anyone nearby to hear. "Too much? Before you got here, he told me I didn't need the donut I was eating because I was already overweight. Then he asked me if I didn't want to live better."

Midsip, liquid spurted out of Nia's mouth. She quickly grabbed napkins and blotted furiously. "Girl, he doesn't mean anything by it. I'm pretty sure he's just one of those people that doesn't have a filter. Not mean, just blunt. I have a great-aunt like that—"

"No! That doesn't make it right, Nia. Why should I care about hurting him when he clearly doesn't care about hurting me? I'm a tit-for-tat person. You want me to take it on the chin? I'm going to punch you in your throat." She cozied closer, "And I can tell you're falling for him. But where you gonna take a man who says anything to anybody at any time? You'll be a pariah—and for good reason. I hate he hangs around here because of you. Dang."

Nia didn't respond. What could she say?

Serena moaned. "Look, I don't mean I hate the guy. I just . . ." Her eyes flickered toward Deacon, who had returned to where they were standing.

Deacon's interruption was a loud blast. "You shouldn't talk about people like they aren't present."

Serena scoffed, caught off guard. "Listen, I didn't—"

"You did," Deacon said plainly. "I *heard* you."

Upset at herself, Nia's stomach twisted. Just that quickly, she had forgotten he was listening. "Deacon—"

But he was already in motion, backpedaling and settling at his table. His back was straight, and his fingers were tapping in a rhythm against his laptop, each tap precise and continuous as he resumed working with quiet intensity.

At a loss for words, both Nia and Serena stood there. Then Nia slinked off when a young woman came up asking for a book recommendation. Nia welcomed the distraction. When the girl walked away, hugging her new YA read, Nia glanced up to see a beautiful blonde striding toward Deacon.

Of course. He was handsome, clean, and mysterious. His black shirt and jeans were paired with expensive tech and a gleaming silver cross that looked too sentimental to have been self-purchased.

As Nia hurried and wheeled a cart past, she watched the woman stop at Deacon's table. He didn't look up. Still typing, mumbling.

She tapped his shoulder. "Hi! I'm Jennifer."

He closed his laptop and looked up. "Hi, Jennifer."

She flinched under the intensity of his stare. "You looked lonely . . . I thought I'd say hello."

"I'm not lonely. I'm here to be near Nia. She's right behind us, waiting to see if I want to talk to you." He turned, locking eyes with Nia. "I'm interested in Nia."

Jennifer's eyes widened, and her face flushed pink before she bolted for the elevators. Embarrassed, Nia ditched her cart and sprinted to her desk.

Moments later, the cart rolled up. "Here, Nia," Deacon said.

"Uhh . . . y-yeah. I mean—yes." She cleared her throat, still not meeting his gaze. "Th-thank you."

"You're really pretty. Even when your face turns pink." He tugged at the band of rings on his finger, his eyes flicking to hers and then away. "I, uh—I like you. A lot. Jonesy said I've been pussyfooting around—his words, not mine—and I should just jump in the lake and swim."

He exhaled, quick and shaky. "So . . . I'm jumping. I've been coming here for six months. Since that day I needed a book on quantum physics and AI game immersion. And you smiled."

He looked at her, finally holding her gaze. "That's when it started."

Nia grasped for something to say. *Am I ready for him to ask me out?* "Did you ever find what you were looking for? The book?"

Deacon raised his voice again. "Do you need to change the subject? I want to please you. So, if you need me to, I will. Jonesy said when you really like someone, pleasing them becomes second nature."

Nia tugged at her collar. Flushed. Flustered.

"Lower your voice, please. Some people are reading. And as I said, I need to get back to work."

"Not yet, Nia. Would you go out with me? For coffee? I have to stop beating around the bush. I'm finally in the lake. I'm swimming."

She chuckled despite her reservations. *Be brave, girl.* "Okay, Deacon. We can go for coffee."

He grinned. Big. Wide. All sunshine and gleaming teeth. "Thank you. I'll meet you right outside at six p.m."

He left with his grin beaming so hard a blind man could see it.

"Why is he wearing that intense grin? It's scary. Should I call security?" Serena asked, walking up.

"No. I handled it. You need something?"

"Slow morning. Quiet bores me. I'm sorry if I offended you earlier. Want help with these books?"

Nia glanced toward Deacon. "It's not me you offended. But I'll accept your help. Thanks."

Serena's face shifted. Her lips thinned. She stared over at Deacon, her look hard and cold.

Nia turned to see what had changed.

Deacon was totally focused on her, riveted, Serena not even a thought.

Dog meet bone.

Then something she would have sworn wasn't possible . . . He gave her a slow, intimate wink.

Nia gasped. *Oh my.*

Chapter Four

Nia

Nia shook her head in disbelief as she curled her thick sweater coat around her neck. The evening air was nippy as fall trees lost their leaves. Just two days ago, the thermostat had read seventy-seven. Crazy weather, crazy world, and even crazier that she was outside waiting for a man who she should have said no to.

What am I doing?

Nia took a steadying breath, then gingerly made her way down the library steps, careful not to trip. Earlier, she'd gone to her car and changed into a pair of low kitten heels, definitely not because I wanted to impress Deacon. That would be ridiculous.

She just didn't like the flats she'd worn that day. Reaching the sidewalk, she glanced around.

No sign of him.

She walked to the corner, where she'd be easy to spot. Not that she was eager. She was just . . . being efficient.

"How you doing, sweet thang?" a man slurred, slowing down as he walked by her. Then he had the nerve to walk backward as he continued to flirt. "You lookin' too good to be standing on somebody's corner, mama. Come take this walk with me."

Nia swung her head away from him and sucked her teeth, a bad family habit. "Drunk fool," she mumbled under her breath.

Looking around, Nia grimaced. She had told Deacon yes when he asked her out, and here, he had her waiting in nippy weather, being accosted by men she didn't know.

McDonald's was right down the street; she thought it would be a quick walk they could take together. She chose the spot because it was nearby, and she didn't think he had a lot of money. Although his laptop looked expensive, she had never pried into the type of work he did. She always thought his parents or brother might have bought it for him the way his brother always seemed to hover around in protective mode.

Where is this man?

Nia heard the deep hum of the Jeep Wagoneer's engine before she saw it. The all-black ride rolled up close, and when the passenger door opened, Deacon emerged like a glossy *GQ* magazine cover. His black ribbed turtleneck stretched against his broad shoulders, and his dark jeans hung snugly on his waist. His hair was styled in neat twists, glistening in the sun, with one lone twisted curl hanging over his forehead. The scent of Tom Ford's Tuscan Leather wafted through the air, evoking memories of an old crush who used to wear it. She felt a chill of anticipation run down her spine.

Cheesing, Deacon enthusiastically offered a firm embrace, then quickly released her. "Hello, Nia," he said, his voice shaky.

Nia could feel her heart rev its motor as she gently stepped back after the tight hug. "Hey, Deacon. I thought you might have stood me up." She pushed his shirt up his arm and glanced at his watch, emphasizing her point. "Glad you made it."

Deacon looked at his watch. "It's 6:00 p.m. on the nose, Nia.

And you were early, and you're never early. So, maybe you were anxious to see me, too."

Outdone, Nia opened her mouth to respond when the Jeep's window rolled down, and Deacon waved the driver away.

Instead of leaving, the driver leaned forward, and the ruggedly handsome blond man shook his head. In a teasing tone, he said, "My brother sometimes forgets the little social niceties that make us the civilized society we live in today." Nodding to Deacon with a smirk, he said, "I'm Deacon's handsome older brother."

"Good to meet—"

Slapping his hand against the side of the car, Deacon interrupted their introduction and bent to the window. "Hey, man, we talked about this. You promised to keep it brief."

"I am, but if I hadn't brought you, you would have been late, so a 'Hello, how are you?' is the least a brother could do," Jonesy argued.

"Naw, I would have been late because I was waiting for you. When I told you I was ready to go, you said I would look pressed coming in early. Nia thinks I was late, and you're making unnecessary small talk."

Nia's head swung right to left as the two brothers went back and forth, their argument transporting her back to her many similar tiffs with Sin. And Deacon sounded like anyone else while talking to his brother. She felt right at home.

"Not late," Nia said. "Maybe I was early?" She didn't want to stand out there debating when the temperature was dropping with every sentence.

Jonesy looked at her as she noticeably shivered. "Deacon, maybe you should both get in, and I can drive you down to McDonald's."

Deacon shook his head firmly before grasping Nia's hand and pulling her up the street opposite Jonesy's car.

As they moved away from the vehicle, Jonesy backed up and yelled through the open window, "Text me when you're ready!"

Nia tugged on Deacon's arm, and he slowed his steps.

"Sorry." They could see the golden arches ahead, and Deacon again increased his pace. "Jonesy said you're a keeper, Nia."

Grinning, Nia chuckled, "That's nice."

"He said, 'Any girl who is satisfied with a Big Mac has got to be easy to please. You better keep that one.'"

Nia blinked hard, her steps faltering. Deacon, moving instinctively, steadied her, his hand tightening around hers like he wasn't letting go.

She looked at him, her brows knitting, trying to mask the sting in her voice. "Deacon," she said carefully, "that's not a nice thing to say. I'm not easy."

"What? I didn't say you were easy. It took me months to ask you out for coffee, Nia."

"But you said that your brother said that I . . . You know what? Never mind."

Right before they crossed the street into the McDonald's parking lot, Deacon abruptly stopped.

"May I kiss you, Nia?" He appeared anxious, moving from one foot to the other.

Taken aback, Nia parroted, "Kiss me?"

"Yes, I've wanted to forever, and my stomach won't stop tossing until I do it. I want to enjoy my hamburger and you, Nia."

"Ummm, okay." Nia turned her cheek and leaned forward for Deacon to peck her there.

Instead, Deacon reached around her and turned her whole body into his. He pulled her into him and kissed her with a passion that Nia had never experienced.

Where has this man learned to kiss?

Pulling back, touching her lips in wonder, feel-good tingles flowed through her body. Nia whispered, "I was permitting a peck on the cheek for a coffee date, Deacon. Not what you gave me."

Contrite, Deacon shook his head. "Then I apologize, Nia. But I kiss my mama on the cheek. I didn't want to kiss you the way I kiss my mama. And I like real touches, Nia. Again, if I was out of line. I apologize, but you kinda kissed me back."

"All touches are real, Deacon, and I don't think I kissed you back. You're imagining things."

Okay, I kissed you back because it was the best kiss I've never wanted. Deacon Everette, you have just made walking away from you so much harder!

While she was all in her head, Deacon appeared to ignore her denial. "I like firm, intentional touches where I can feel your pressure against me. I don't like to be closed in, though. If we hug, it shouldn't be where I can't breathe. But maybe you don't need to know all that right now. I'll wait for your permission to kiss you again and not on your cheek, Nia."

Exasperated, Nia started across the street. She was overwhelmed with the feelings Deacon had stirred up without even trying, and his demands concerning how to touch him had her disconcerted.

He started humming.

No, he's not *humming. The nerve of him!*

She couldn't believe he was acting as though all was well in his world when he had just blown hers away with the most toe-curling kiss of her life.

When they reached McDonald's, Deacon bumped her while scrambling across her to open the door. He then admonished, "I'm a gentleman, Nia. My father taught me chivalry when I was six years old."

"Oh." Nia ducked under his arm as she stepped through the door because Deacon failed to move out of the way.

People turned as a jovial Deacon shouted, "What do you want?" as they approached the counter.

Nia took a deep breath as the butterflies in her stomach settled, and uncomfortableness crept in. Her eyes drifted as she wondered if everyone stared at them, the scorching kiss forgotten.

Maybe this wasn't such a good idea.

One of the teen cashiers, whose name tag read "Tim," snickered, and another jabbed Tim with her elbow. "Not cool," the cashier whispered to him.

Definitely not a good idea.

Nia mouthed, "Thank you" to the nicer teen.

"I'll have a large tea with honey and a Danish." She spoke low to give Deacon a hint to lower his voice.

Deacon did not take the hint. "I can't hear you, Nia. A tea with honey and a Danish? Don't be easy, Nia."

Nia nodded to the teen to get what she ordered, mumbling, "I'm not that hungry."

"All right. But I'll have a Big Mac meal, with an upsize of everything." Deacon's voice stayed on ten.

Her cheeks felt as though they were on fire. She nervously fiddled with her hands, avoiding eye contact as she muttered, her voice trembling slightly, "Let me go grab us a table," she said, and then skittered away.

She found a table near the back and kept her head down, feeling people were staring at her.

They're probably thinking I'm a loser to be with him.

Nia's knee did double time under the table . . . up and down, up and down.

And he kissed me. The best kiss I've ever had.

Nia's thoughts were interrupted when Deacon returned.

"I do that too," he roared as he slid into the booth and placed their food tray on the table, motioning to her knee, bouncing up and down. "It makes my mother nervous when I fidget. Sometimes, I sit on my hands to stop it, Nia."

"Is that why you have those rings? You're pretty good at maneuvering them."

"My mama gave them to me when I was about eight. It stopped her from telling me to stop fidgeting during my lessons."

"You were homeschooled?"

"Yeah, till I could go to high school with my brother."

Nia remembered the times she saw him pound away on his laptop and then slide his hands under his thighs as he sat. She thought he was cold, but now, he indicated that he was aware of some of his tics and mannerisms.

Nia cradled her hot tea between her hands, warming them. "It sounds like maybe fidgeting is something we have in common."

"See? We could work, Nia," Deacon said in a surprisingly softer tone.

Nia didn't know how to answer, so she remained quiet, using the silence to take a small bite of her Danish.

"What do you like to do, Nia?" Deacon took a large bite of his burger, then gulped some of his drink.

Watching the mayo smeared on the corner of his mouth move with each word he spoke, Nia shivered.

Uh, uh, this will never work. How do I let him down without hurting his feelings?

Making her decision, Nia started her journey of letting Deacon down in the most painless way she could. "I like to read. I keep to myself a lot. I prefer it that way. I came on this outing to let you know that, Deacon."

"Outing? This is a date, Nia. Our first date," he said, still broadcasting their business to everyone in the restaurant.

At that point, the teen who had held off laughing before was now falling over, guffawing, and slapping the counter in mirth.

The pimpled teen bawled between his gasps, "They're on a date —a date!"

Feeling her face warm, Nia glowered but spoke with deliberate resolve.

"What I'm saying, Deacon, is I don't date. But I wanted to thank you for the compliment of inviting me."

She paused, swallowing the lump in her throat. "I won't be seeing you anymore. Please don't let it be awkward between us when you come in for your books . . . or to work."

Her voice softened at the end, a quiet attempt to spare him the same embarrassment burning through her.

"Why, Nia? What did I do?" Deacon said, lowering his voice somberly. "I haven't liked someone in a long time. Do you think I won't make a good boyfriend, Nia?"

"It's not that, Deacon. You're a very nice person. I just don't date."

Rubbing his hands back and forth on his thighs, Deacon leaned forward. "I can kiss well, and I know how to have sex. Jonesy taught me."

Nia scooted backward. Her eyes shot open, and her mouth shaped in an O.

A crimson flush crept up Deacon's neck and cheeks. "Come on, Nia! I don't mean I had sex with my brother. Jonesy hired a lady to teach me how to make love. She still calls me, but I told her no more, even when she tried to return my brother's money. My mom reminded me that I should want to be in love and get married first. My mom's a Christian. Don't you want to be loved, Nia?"

This had always been her hesitation in accepting a date from Deacon. From the moment she met him, he had been extra— unpredictable and always willing to say what others wouldn't. He made it clear to everyone at her workplace that he was interested in her, broadcasting his intentions without hesitation. It was a lot. He was a lot. And it left her feeling both flattered and uneasy, unsure if she could handle the intensity that came with being around him. The truth was, she didn't want to deal with this level of intensity. Not now. Probably not ever.

If she could get anyone to take her bet, Nia would place one that her face had gone from pink-warm to a five-alarm red blaze. She twisted the scarf around her neck back and forth, wishing she had listened to Serena this once. Deacon was too . . . something. She could never do this.

Exhaling, Nia spoke from her heart. "You're a good guy, Deacon. I like you, but I'm not looking to be loved by you or anyone right now. I thought maybe I was—something—so I accepted this dinner outing. But it's not going to happen. People do this kind of thing to see if they're compatible; if they aren't, no harm done."

She breathed deeply, feeling satisfied with how she had handled a difficult situation. "Yes, no harm done," she murmured.

Deacon sat like a stone. The shift in him was quiet but absolute —like someone had closed a door behind his eyes. His face was unreadable, but something in him had clearly stepped back. He pulled out his phone and sent a text, not looking up, not saying a word.

Silence reigned between them. Nia had no idea how to break the tension. She was not well-versed in this kind of thing, and her anxiety had her winding her scarf around her neck until it was choking her. Deacon had somehow left the room while still sitting directly before her.

Whatever SOS he texted, his brother pulled up within five excruciating minutes of Nia staring at the ceiling, the floor, and the ribbon stitching on the bottom of her sweater. The only thing that made sense to her was that his brother must have waited nearby.

Shoot, how did he know I couldn't handle a date with Deacon? Okay, I admit it, if only to myself. Yes, it was a date.

Like monks at a monastery, they rose and walked out of the restaurant. No Deacon chirping on volume ten. He wasn't even whispering on volume one. The silence was stifling, and Nia didn't know how to bridge the enormous gulf she had created. She wished she could materialize magic powers and blink her eyes, and . . . Kazam, be gone, or click her heels twice and disappear.

Jonesy's face held no welcoming warmth as he reached over and pushed her door open. It was the same expression she remembered him giving to everyone whenever he had previously accompanied Deacon to the library. There was no greeting, no small talk, as he raced them back to the library, gunning his engine. When he screeched to a halt, she saw that he had at least let her out near the doors closest to the inner garage where she had parked her car.

Nia jumped out almost as soon as the car had come to a complete stop. "I just, ah—"

Midsentence, Jonesy peeled off.

"Well, that didn't go well," Nia grumbled, watching the car fly up the street. She hoisted her satchel over her arm and stepped methodically as though noisy footsteps would highlight that this evening was a fiasco.

Well, maybe not that kiss.

She entered the building, quivering from the cold in her spirit and the nip in the air. Woodenly waving at coworkers she encountered, she took the garage elevator to her level and then made it to her car. Opening the door and sliding in, she finally let go and cried.

Remorsefully, she dabbed her eyes with her scarf, then sobbed fresh tears. Nia squeezed her lids shut, willing her mind to erase the wounded look on Deacon's face. She did like him. She thought she was up to the task of being with someone with all his tics and quirks. She wasn't a social butterfly herself, and she could get things wrong.

But . . .

Inhaling and exhaling deeply, she placed her foot on the brake and hit the button to start her car. A jarring thought pierced her heart.

It's easier to think of yourself as a hero than to actually be one.

Chapter Five

General

"You stupid, little boy. Tell me you're not the idiot you've turned out to be," General thundered as he threw a glass snow globe against the wall. He was so angry that he could have killed the fool where he sat. But he needed information, and ending his life now would be counterproductive.

Heavy footsteps pounded toward the door, which swung open. "Are you all right, General?" the blond giant inquired, his hand on his sidearm and his posture military. Two additional men, equally broad and blond, stood behind him.

"Yes, yes, Geoff. Close the door, please," General said as he shooed him away as though he were a pesky fly. Then, removing his reading glasses, he rubbed the indent they had left and studied the scene outside his window to calm himself. It had been a good breakfast, but now, knowing what Eric had let happen, he was two seconds from having him flogged.

In his purview, he could see Eric physically tremble. General understood that this act of fear was foreign to Eric because his youthful arrogance had not yet been tempered by wisdom and guidance. The pup had never known fear before, but General would ensure he tasted it today.

Speaking concisely, General turned and placed his hands behind his back to ensure he wouldn't strangle the fool. "Explain it to me. Leave out no detail."

Eric Rothwell laid his manicured hands on the three-hundred-year-old desk. He leaned forward, his voice quivering as he stuttered what he had practiced in his private jet on his way over. "Her name is Ariel. I-I-I met her a year ago at Henricks, our j-j-jeweler. She was buying an expensive necklace for her grandmother's birthday. She was lovely, y-y-you see. And—"

"Spare me your simpering romantics, boy, and that insufferable stutter. Spit it out!" he gritted.

Eric took a large gulp of air as though he had finally understood that breathing was a precious gift. "Uh, yes. Well—" He breathed deeply and then spoke slowly, hesitantly. "She asked for my opinion, and I told her I thought it was quite fitting. I was late for a meeting, so I grabbed my watch. It's a platinum Patek Philippe Calatrava Astronomic Minute Repeater with a perpetual calendar. It took nine years to create in 1939." He held out his arm in triumph but snatched it down when his eyes met the scorn in General.

"I am aware of the watch and its origins, Eric. What I do not know is how you lost your copy of the book." The iciness of his voice made Eric visibly gag. "I will not ask you again to reflect on the past year. I repeat, leave nothing out."

Swallowing, Eric wiped his forehead. "I left the store. Later in the week, I went to Buffie Heatherton's for dinner. It was a small affair, with fewer than forty people. Ariel was there. She was b-b-b-breathtakingly beautiful—" Stopping, he cleared his throat, pulled his collar away from his neck, and continued. "We struck up a conversation. She was on the arm of Senator Balter, a staunch conservative and friend to the cause, as is Buffie. I felt it safe to pursue her. And before you continue, I did have her checked out. She cleared."

"Did you have her checked out through the consortium?" he spat.

"I did not. I didn't want to bother anyone when I have perfectly good people," Eric stressed.

"You are already falling into your old habit of not reading the room. Did I ask you what you thought, or did I ask you for the facts of what took place?" General's jaw clenched, his eyes sparking fire into Eric's. "I set up the perfect marriage for you with the perfect family. A mistress, two or even three, is more than acceptable. What is *not* acceptable is leaving our group uncovered to wallow in your own sense of self-importance."

General slithered behind Eric. He then placed a hand on each of Eric's shoulders. Eric panted, his breath shallow and rapid.

General squeezed until Eric slumped in his seat, avoiding the red-hot pain.

"I am disappointed in you, son." The General stepped away while Eric rubbed one shoulder and then the other.

Closing his eyes, Eric sniffled contritely, "I regret my actions. I will retrieve the book. I know her habits, favorite places, and schedule."

"Did you meet her grandmother, the one for whom she supposedly bought the necklace?"

"No. Since I am engaged, I thought it would be best if she didn't introduce me to her family. She complied."

General stood at the window once again. "Come look at this splendid view."

Eric rose and inched toward the window, keeping more than an arm's length away.

"It is lovely. But if all you see is loveliness, you fail to see beneath its cover. Like a beautiful woman who seems content to serve and then, instead, commands, this scene is deceptive. You need to understand that two things can be true at once. Take note, pup. This is an estate, *and* it is a fortress. There are one thousand acres of hard, rugged soil between us and any other property. There is only one way out, and I have over two hundred men patrolling the area unseen, along with a surveillance tech team of five people providing 24-hour scrutiny of the house and grounds. If I called the tower, they would tell me how many breaths you have taken in the last twenty seconds. On top of that, if you run and we don't find you, the bitter cold, terrain, or wolves will kill you. And that's if I don't send out my hounds."

General could see Eric's mind ticking. He still believed he was smarter and better. It was a shame he truly could have been shaped into something extraordinary.

"I see your mind going clickety-clack. The villagers won't help you either. You are alone."

General sat down, studying Eric. "You have failed me. You have failed the cause. Your younger brother is a Harvard graduate, has made the right contacts, and has even pledged to step in and marry your fiancée if today does not go as I hope. I ask you for the last time . . . Give me every minute detail of the last year."

Eric paled. He stumbled to his chair and poured out day after day of his time with Ariel . . . down to her favorite lingerie and her obsession with a small, stinky hamburger hailing from its headquarters in Columbus, Ohio, known as a White Castle. When he was done and spent, Geoff quietly entered the room. He grabbed the arm of a quaking Eric and escorted him from the room. At the door, Geoff paused but did not look back.

General groused, "No. Not now. We may need him later."

Bowing his head, Geoff yanked Eric, who was now weeping, through the door and closed it softly behind him with a click.

"Did you get all of that, Victor?" General spoke into the air.

A voice emerged from hidden speakers. "Yes, my people are already on it. I'm reviewing Eric's file, and it appears he had another mistress on the side to distract us. The consortium sanctioned this mistress. According to our intel, he stopped seeing her eight months ago but kept her in the condo in the same building we were aware of. When we thought he was visiting her, he paid the doorman to let him out through the servant's entrance at the back and walked to the high-rise behind that building. This is where he stashed Ariel Sutton, a woman whose death certificate places her in Mount Greenwood Cemetery in Chicago, Illinois."

"Find her! And find out who she works for and how they got this close to our inner circle."

"Roger that, sir."

Hearing the intercom click off, Ragnar Alstead demonstrated why he was referred to as General; he didn't rage; his demeanor held a calculating gleam in his eye. He and his family had flown under every political, social, and royal radar for over a century. At times, modern technology made it challenging to remain incognito. The internet, social media, and private sleuths made it crucial to confront all challenges ruthlessly. If anyone even caught a soft whisper of their presence . . . they vanished, suffered an "accident," or were publicly discredited as crackpots. However, those in law enforcement, journalists, or wronged business associates never got close enough to know why something had happened to them.

They should have heeded their own intuition. The blaring warning inside signaled, "Be careful of the doors you peek in and the questions you ask."

In less than ten years of having the book, Eric of New America had lost it. General believed Eric was a good representative of how New America was . . . a country filled with privileged people. People who felt they knew everything tired him. And he was never wrong. He was confident they would retrieve the *Book of Disasters* —in time. They had to because they were close to taking over everything and everyone.

A scorched-earth policy would be put in play until Ariel and the book were in his hands.

Then, although regretful, the General would ascend Eric's brother to the New American throne due to the vacancy.

Chapter Six

Deacon

Deacon stared blankly at the wall in his condo.

"Hey, buddy, you're not shutting down, are you?" Jonesy sat with his feet on the coffee table.

"Get your feet off my table, Jonesy," Deacon said without looking away from the wall.

He lifted his feet off the table and stared at Deacon. "You'll feel better if you talk about it."

Deacon glanced over, frowned, and turned back to the wall.

"Aw, come on, man. It's a blank wall."

Groaning, Deacon spoke softly. "I did what I do. I talked too loud and embarrassed her. I tried to stop myself, Jonesy, but I was too excited. Some stupid kid laughed at me. Now, she doesn't want to date me."

"I've told you before that if you add some of that ghetto bass to your tone, throw in some curse words, and hold your junk as you talk, nobody will pay attention even when you speak too loud."

Deacon shook his head. "You know that's racist, right?"

Jonesy laughed. "Yeah, but at least you're looking at me now. And you gotta admit, some of that was true."

Deacon turned back around, his head hung low.

Jonesy opened his mouth and then shut it. He hesitated, leaned back, and folded his arms.

"What, Jonesy?" he demanded. "I can hear you thinking."

"She's not the one. When someone needs you to change to be with them, ghost them."

Deacon's arm flew into the air as he became more agitated, standing and pacing back and forth. "Nia is a good person." Realizing his actions, he clutched his arm to his chest and sat. Then he exhaled and folded his hands together to keep himself from gesturing wildly. "Man, you think I don't realize I get loud, and my arms flail around when I get excited—that's not sexy—but I'm a good person. I earn a good living. It's crazy how I can see people's eyes roll away after I speak when I enter a room. It never mattered so much before, though." He then paused, and his eyes widened. "You should have let me tell her I've made a lot of money."

Jonesy jumped to his feet. "No, I shouldn't have. Remember Rhonda?"

"Rhonda's not Nia. Rhonda tried to scam me, and her feelings got hurt. I can take care of myself. And Nia would never be after my money. I bet it would impress her if I told her how smart I was —that I graduated from high school at sixteen and had my doctorate at twenty-two. She's a librarian; they like smart people."

"Yet, with all those degrees, you can be naive to people's greed. You should want her to like you for who you are."

"This is who I am. I'm the one who got paid for these research projects, and now I have a lot of money. I think Nia needs to know this."

"I think you're being naive, Li'l Brother . . ."

"Enough with the naive!"

"Okay then, how about how I've always looked out for you? When you were under so much stress, who got you laid?"

"I told her about that, Jonesy. She wasn't impressed."

"If she had let you kiss her, she would have. I've heard you have mad skills. Remember that girl—"

"Man, forget any other girl. I kissed Nia and felt the tingles throughout my body flow to hers." He jumped up and paced. "Man, it was magical." A despondent Deacon moaned, "But she doesn't want me, Jonesy. That's why I have to show her I can take care of her. Nia is fragile. I've noticed she cares about what people think of her."

"A people pleaser?"

"Yeah, so maybe I shouldn't hide who I am. It will make others feel better; she's with me."

"You can't. You know that your geneticist role could attract the wrong kind of attention. People are cautious about individuals tampering with and manipulating genes. Then there are the conspiracy theorists, government watchdogs, and nefarious groups seeking to steal the next big breakthrough. After all the precautions Dad and I took to ensure that everything you accomplished was done under an alias, you can't simply share everything with everyone. It's already concerning that some leaders in third-world countries are aware. Things can turn dangerous quickly, bro. It's not just about the money. You already understand this. Don't let a big butt and a smile distract you."

Deacon's eyes glazed with old and new pain. He was still, a quiet intensity surrounding him. "I need to help people, Jonesy. When you and Dad wouldn't reach out to the leaders I wanted to work with, I had to do it alone. I decide who I help."

"You've made that clear. Since you were a kid, you've been super focused on whatever fascinated you. Now, it's underdeveloped populations. Man, I remember you putting our arms together and studying the skin. Our differing complexions bothered you."

"No, it bothered *you*! You were filled with so much hate against Black people. I needed to understand why you were angry with people who hadn't done anything to you, but you never talked about your mother with anything but affection when we both know she abused you."

"'Cause that's my mother, and you don't get to talk about her. I've been working on myself, but I was taught what I was taught. It doesn't disappear overnight. And I was taught every day that Blacks were the problem with all that was wrong in the world."

"I told you, Jonesy, race is a social construct."

Jonesy began to reach for him, then pulled his hand back and rubbed it through his hair instead. "Well, you and Mom loved the hate away."

"*Almost*. Sometimes, you aren't right, Jonesy." Deacon stood and walked to the large penthouse window. He leaned his forehead against the glass, and his body slumped. "I'd like to do more than work the rest of my life," he admitted quietly and then lamented, "It's times like this I miss Mom and Dad."

Deacon saw Jonesy clasp his hands together, and he knew it was because Jonesy wanted to reach out and touch him. He was a toucher. But he knew at times like this, Deacon didn't want to be "crowded," and being touched when his feelings were all over the place felt claustrophobic. Deacon appreciated that his brother understood him.

Instead, Jonesy grumbled in frustration, "It feels like we're falling backward. I don't like it when you're like this. It's like you're sixteen again. You were all angst and hormones."

"It's called being a teenager."

"Yeah, well, a teenager on the spectrum was a whole 'nother trip."

Deacon gave his brother his middle finger.

"Okay, since that was childish, maybe we should spend time with Dad and Mama Linette. We can fly to the islands, catch some sun, and lie on the beach."

"I do love the water," Deacon mused.

He moved away from his slouched position on the window and squared his shoulders. "But instead of moping around on the beach, I think I'll do something about getting Nia back."

"You can't get her back, Deacon, if you've never had her." Exasperation was easy to read on Jonesy's face. He cajoled, "I think we were on to something by looking at visiting our folks. Let's go. Get some good, old-fashioned soul food. We can stay through Thanksgiving. We promised when you bought them their place that we'd visit often."

"Then you should go." Deacon turned and marched into his bedroom, leaving the door open. "Go home, Jonesy."

"You kicking me out?"

"No. I'm asking you to go to your place next door. I won't need you until tomorrow. You're my brother, my driver, and my assistant, but you're not the boss of me. Go home. I don't want to talk anymore. If you decide to visit Mom and Dad, text me. I'll arrange a car service."

Reluctantly, Jonesy walked to the door and glanced back. Standing over six feet of solid muscle, he grasped the doorknob. "If you need me for anything, I'll be working out at the gym."

Deacon didn't answer as he walked into the master bedroom. In the mirror, he stared at his reflection as he heard the door's multiple locks whirl and the many locks whine into place. The alarm toned, "The door is closed, Deacon. Your alarm is set. Would you like me to play soft music?"

Already in another world, Deacon ignored the AI that ran his home.

I can be better for you, Nia. I can help you fall in love with me.

* * *

Nia

Wiping the cleansing cream off her face, Nia listened to Sin drone on from her FaceTime app about the problems with men. "I'm telling you, Sis, they're not worth the time it takes you to get dressed for the date. We should stop all the bull. Have them pull up with some wings and wine, eat, jump in the bed, and then leave the same way they came. When you put your heart out there, they disappoint every time."

"Uh-huh." Nia said absently, then whispered, "The girl has issues, fix it, Jesus."

"Nia? You haven't stopped fooling with your face or put together a whole sentence since you called me. Now you're mumbling."

"That's because you haven't stopped talking. I need to get up in the morning, but I wanted to discuss something with you. Also, given how you're dressed, I interrupted your evening. You're heading somewhere."

"It's 9:30 p.m. your time, Nia. Only you and elementary school kids have finished for the day. I'm an hour earlier, and my night is just beginning. What's happening with you?"

"I had a date, well, an 'outing.'" Nia picked up the phone and carried it to her nightstand as she climbed into bed. "And before you start, it didn't go anywhere."

"First of all, what is an outing? And why didn't it work out?"

Nia used the remote to cut off the overhead light and turned on the nightstand table lamp.

She could also hear Sin moving around, then saw her move back onto the screen.

"Nia Lewis, you never date. You must have liked him if he got you to go out, even for an 'outing,'" Sin said, using her fingers to make air quotes. "Tell me what happened. Do I have to come there and kick some donkey butt?"

"Donkey?" Nia said.

Sin sniggered. "Well, you're upset, and I don't like to see you upset, and you don't like me to cuss, so excuse me for trying to compromise."

"First, thanks, but you know you have a nasty mouth—"

"Don't start, Nia, and don't change the subject. What happened?"

Nia hesitated. "Um, his name is Deacon, and he's . . . well, I guess, um, I should say . . . 'special.' As in 'different.' As in, he's probably neurodivergent."

"Oh, Nia. You and your causes. Why haven't you mentioned this, Deacon, before? You know what? Never mind. You never tell me anything without me dragging it out of you."

"I'm trying to tell you now. When we went out, I got so embarrassed. Kids laughed at us. He was so loud, socially awkward, and intense."

"Nia, people aren't squirrels with a broken leg you can just keep and take care of—"

Nia snorted. "Oh, here we go. I was only *eight*."

"Old enough to know better. How did that tetanus shot work out for you? Hiding that thing in your room could have given us all rabies."

"Stay on subject, Sin. I hurt him when I realized I wasn't noble enough to look past his issues."

"Is he cute?"

"Ugggh. You are so basic. Actually, he's gorgeous. If you don't conversate with him, you can't tell he's, well—you know. Well, maybe if you're paying attention, you can because sometimes, he gestures a lot. But I think he's very smart. At least, he reads some very advanced books."

"Oh, I know you love that."

"Yes, and although he is extremely blunt, he doesn't intend to be mean. He is close to his brother, and there's a story behind that. His brother is white, but I'm unsure about the family dynamics. I'm guessing Deacon is biracial. I don't think he drives, and I'm not sure if he's gainfully employed."

"Oh, hell no. If the boy doesn't have a job, you *really* need to move on."

"So much for me thinking you're not going to curse in this conversation."

"Hell is a place, Nia. A destination you send losers to, where they burn like the lowlifes they are."

Nia rolled her eyes where Sin couldn't see. "That was *not* the context in which you used the word. But small wins, I guess. And as for him not having a job or prospects, I've moved on. However, I'm not saying he doesn't have a job; I just don't think it's a good one."

"As long as he leaves you alone, all should be well. But if he continues to bother you, let me know."

Chuckling, Nia scooted farther under the covers. "What are you going to do? Jump on a plane to Columbus just to beat him up?"

"Humph! Remember that girl in college? She and her friends were making your life miserable. Then she stopped."

"How do you . . .? Sin! You *didn't*!" Nia sat up in bed, threw off the cover, and picked up the phone.

"I did. Nobody messes with you, Ladybug. *Nobody.*"

Sliding down in the bed, Nia closed her eyes as though in

prayer. "I could have handled them. You have me all hyped up now. I'm hanging up, Sin."

"I see you, Ladybug. You don't have the heart to hurt a cockroach. But me? I stomp on what afflicts me. And if they're hurting you, I'm afflicted."

Nia didn't answer. Sin was always doing too much. The screen went black as they ended the FaceTime call.

As Nia drifted to sleep, she thought about her time with Deacon as her eyes gradually closed.

It would be nice to be in love. It was such a nice kiss.

Chapter Seven

Sin

With a half-smile, Sin clicked off FaceTime. While Nia was going to bed in Columbus, Ohio, things were becoming interesting in Austin, Texas. The woman, named Sincere Lewis by her parents, but known to her sister and friends as Sin, was entering her clandestine world—an existence far removed from her sister's—where her code name was Pop.

She strolled into the restaurant as if she owned it. Her long-legged gait, inherited from her father, and curvy figure, a gift from her mother, attracted attention wherever she went. But it was her face that captivated both men and women.

When Sin was younger, during a visit to meet her daddy's family in Georgia, her great-grandmother nicknamed her "Black gal." At the age of eight, she rebelled against this nickname. Raised on military bases around the world, she wasn't prepared for the color-struck insensitivities of some of her relatives.

She couldn't hear the affection in their voices as they claimed her as theirs; all she heard was contempt for who she was, failing to notice that her great-grandmother's complexion was the same. She hadn't been around them enough to grasp the nuances of their love. There was the uncle she knew as Red, the cousin who proudly requested to be called Black John, and the nephew nicknamed Fats. This was their way of inviting her into a fold that was uniquely theirs. However, you couldn't teach grown folk who had always loved in a certain way the common sense that a little girl needed to be validated.

It drove her insane until she learned to claim everything about herself. Her choice. She didn't do self-hatred. She was who her parents created, and she loved the skin she was in. She also loved her people. So, while some of her closest friends came from diverse ethnic backgrounds, she embraced her men, often encased in a mocha latte, a chocolate sundae, or a dark chocolate hue with no chaser.

The man she was meeting now was the latter version, midnight to her moon, fine personified, and built to last. At one time, she thought he was "the one" . . . until he did what all the others before him had done: fooled around and discovered that she couldn't care less about forgiving his trespasses.

They had their Jesus for that. The only "Confessions" she wanted to hear was an Usher's song.

Umber stood as she approached the table, a slow smile spreading across his face. "Sin . . . Three years later, you still know how to walk in like you own the room." His voice dropped to a velvet baritone, thick with meaning. "Especially mine."

He pulled out her chair with a practiced grace. Once she slid into it, he settled back in his seat, one arm draped over the back of his chair.

A toothpick found its way to the corner of his mouth as he studied her through half-lidded eyes. "You good, girl? 'Cause that catsuit?" His grin deepened. "It's hugging all the places I like to call home."

Sin tipped forward from her seat, the movement fluid and deliberate. Inches from his face, she angled her head, her lips grazing the air beside his ear. "You like that?" she whispered.

Umber drew in a deep and ragged breath, his eyes threatening to close under the weight of her nearness. "Yeah, baby," he said, his voice low and rough. "I like you."

Sin slid back into her seat, placing the dinner napkin on her lap. "Good. None of it is for you." Seeing the color warm in his cheeks and pleased with her intention to put him in his place, she reassured him, "Don't get your boxers in a bunch, man. It's time to do business. You got what I need?"

Steel rolled over his features, and Umber nodded. "Never thought of you as childish before. But yeah." He took her hand in his in a lover's caress and transferred a small flash drive into her upturned palm.

Seemingly accepting and reciprocating the loving gesture to anyone watching, she smiled in return. "Thank you; feeling is mutual," she said sweetly. "I'm hungry, so I'll eat when my food arrives, and you'll behave yourself. Then we'll part ways."

Umber examined each part of her body, letting his gaze linger last on her face.

"So, that's it, Sin? Are we going to end this with petty insults?" he groused, snapping his fingers as he spoke. "I've been trying to reach you for three days, and you haven't responded. Are you going to leave us like this? We're done?"

"It was cool when we were young, but snapping your fingers for service is rude, dude."

Umber's nose flared, but the server chose that moment to deliver the orders Umber had placed when she texted that she was parking. Both stared intently as their hot plates were set before them.

"Be careful, they're hot," the server said, moving expertly

around the table. "Can I get anything else for you?" His eyes fixed on Sin, almost ignoring Umber.

"Man, we're good. You can leave," Umber barked.

Slightly bowing his head, the server quickly left. Umber's hardening gaze focused on Sin. "Answer the question."

"You don't want me to answer the question. You only want responses that make you feel like the victim rather than the coldhearted liar in heat that you truly are. And from now on, please refer to me as Pop."

Exasperated, Umber sputtered, "Woman, you've got me mixed up with those boys you've been playing with. You may be bad in the streets and the sheets, but you will not handle me. Pop is your assassin code name. What makes you think I'll call you that after three years?"

Placing her fork down and using her napkin to pat her mouth, Sin locked eyes with the man she thought would be her forever. But they both had spent so much time committed to their missions, fighting for their country, that they had missed the part about committing to each other. And, somewhere along the line, Umber had decided she wasn't worth the effort.

"Because you're dead to me. I didn't have to sanction you— you removed yourself. You erased everything we were. Your thoughts and your needs are no longer my burden to bear. I'll leave that to the new missus."

Umber froze. Not even his eyelids moved. The shock was etched into every inch of him before he blinked and finally stirred back to life. "Wait, that social media post was a mistake. It was only up for a minute. She promised no media. I told her no social media. Baby, let me—"

"Don't speak," Sin said as she rose. Furious, she whispered, "I'm not a fool. I may be able to drink you under the table, wear you out on the workout mats, and then keep up with you when the lights go off, but my heart is just as tender as any other woman's. You don't get to explain after ghosting me for months. You don't get to act as though there could be any explanation I would accept. What you *do* get to do is stay out of my way. And while you have so much to say about my code name, Pop, Umber means 'shade, shadow.' And that's where I'll leave you—in the shadows of my life."

Umber hung his head. "I didn't—"

Before he could finish, Sin was headed out the door. Behind her, she left gaping mouths of men in lust, glares of women jealous to the bone of her size-eight packed frame, and one contrite heart.

Tears falling, Sin hurried to her car. Yet even in her pain, as usual, she looked back and forth, ensuring she was not followed. She almost smiled at the realization that she had done what she promised herself she would never do: be this vulnerable for a man. It would serve her right to get shot at such a crybaby moment.

Sin hadn't cried over a man since Daniel Aki told everyone in Algebra 3 that she kissed like a fish. But Umber had been her heart, and even though he broke hers, she could still feel it beating in time for the man she had just left behind.

Her heart was a traitor, just like Umber, who said, "I do," to someone else. They had been together for three years, two years when they were serious, where 'I love yous' were murmured as shared pillow talk. But he'd been distant for months.

She reasoned they were busy; saving the world took time, and their relationship would improve when things quieted down. However, there was no shortage of bad players who had designs on conquering the moral consciousness of the world, which kept them on their toes and apart.

They were black ops agents used to keeping their home lives separate. Umber hadn't ever met her family, but Sin had felt that after three years of being together, they were closing in on the time they would make mutual introductions.

Instead, Umber had messed up and allowed his new wife to place a picture of them from their wedding day on her Facebook page. Sin was out of the country, but her software facial recognition program immediately picked up his facial profile. The program was keyed with all their profiles, intending to be one step ahead of anything going out on social media when they were all deep cover, specifically on the dark web.

When Sin's phone dinged, Umber's tux-dressed picture was attached. Nervous for his safety, she immediately called him, hoping for the explanation he now wanted to give, but back then, she was forwarded to voicemail each time. After there was no rattle on her cage from their agency handler, she took the breach of Umber on social media as non-invasive. Her desire that this was an undercover assignment she wasn't privy to died. Instead, this was a "you've been played" moment.

Sobered, she didn't leave a message, and he didn't call back until three days ago.

It had been months.

She let it ring. It was evident the couple felt an extended honeymoon was in order, and she was an afterthought. Sin would never know because after he finally called, she blocked him. The next day, when she received notice from headquarters to meet him for her next assignment, she swallowed her hurt and complied.

When she first sat down, she waited patiently for him to tell her what he had done. But he didn't, and the fact that he showed her so much disrespect by sitting there and playing the victim had enraged her.

She pulled up in front of the restaurant, popped the trunk, and grabbed the box—a bitter collection of the things Umber had left at her apartment over the three years they'd been entangled.

She dropped it on the curb as if it burned her. Just as she climbed back into the driver's seat, Umber burst through the restaurant's double doors precisely as she had expected. He could never allow anyone else to have the last word. She slammed the car door, struck the steering wheel with the heel of her hand, and shouted through the open window with clenched teeth, "Scum!"

Then she tore into traffic, refusing to give him one more word.

Plugging in her phone, she clicked on an oldie but goodie, Mary J. Blige's "Not Gon' Cry."

Bopping down the freeway with the radio on blast, Sin defied the song's title and let the sobs come. She sang off-key in such a heartbreaking staccato rhythm that anyone listening would know it was her plea for it not to be real. The truth was she wished she had left him. At least, she would have been left with her pride.

Exiting the freeway, she pulled into a KFC.

Eating healthy tonight was out of the question.

The fool didn't even let me eat my dinner in peace. I need grease.

Leaving the drive-through and pulling to the back of the parking lot to eat, Sin pulled the flash drive from her bra and her government-issued mini tablet from her purse and merged the two. Biting into a juicy leg, she hit play.

"Pop, this assignment is connected to your last two. We're assembling the pieces, and we need you to get to this location by noon tomorrow. Your contact has advised she will not be there at 12:05 p.m. She will hand you a package. Bring the package and rendezvous with your team at the coded coordinates listed at the end of this message with your contact informant in hand. We have promised to protect her by taking her into witness protection. You are her safe place, Pop. You must not fail. We have been following this fragile thread for over twenty years, and this is the biggest break we've received yet. Watch your back on this one, agent."

Excitement poured through Sin, drying up all thoughts of Umber. This was the big one, the assignment that might finally bring them closer to ridding the world of toxicity so vicious that it had survived for over two hundred years, oppressing a world that didn't recognize it was being oppressed. Instead, it numbed itself with pills, trying to soothe the anxiety of living in a world that no longer functioned as the Creator intended—too blind to realize it was being controlled all along. Sin's job, as Pop, was to make society work as designed as much as she could in her own small way. Chewing a french fry, she input the coordinates into her notes for the location of their meeting when the decoded location popped up.

"Son of a . . ."

Sin laid her food aside and gunned her motor. She was on her way to Columbus, Ohio, at breakneck speed. The meeting was scheduled for the main entrance of the Columbus Metropolitan Main Library, where her kid sister, Nia, worked.

Chapter Eight

Deacon

Deacon was Superman in disguise, with Nia as his Lois Lane. When he removed his imaginary glasses, she would realize he was in love with her, just as she was with him.

At least, that was how the movies would make it.

Deacon stared in the mirror, encouraging himself, preparing to return to the library and let Nia know he would still capture her heart. Last night, he had read everything online he could about romance and how to make someone fall in love with you. He would be gentle, talk softly, and keep his arms to his sides. She would see him like Lois Lane never saw Clark Kent. He didn't want to be her friend. He wanted to be her loving husband.

On Sunday, he'd go to his mother's old church and pray for her to be his. He didn't believe you couldn't pray at home, but there was something about entering a space that held the collective prayers of many that made him feel God heard you at home, but your voice was amplified in a house of worship. At least, it was what his mother had taught him.

There was a double knock on the door, and without Deacon answering, Jonesy let himself in. "You ready?"

"Yes, I'm ready. And, Jonesy, you need to leave your key. It's rude when you just walk in, and Nia won't like it."

"Man, you need to let all of that go. You're starting to sound like a stalker," Jonesy said as he waited for his brother to pick up his backpack.

Deacon walked briskly in front of Jonesy. His Timberlands were fresh, and his well-worn jeans were molded to his long, slightly bowlegged strut. The sleeves of his polo shirt gripped his arms. Jonesy tapped Deacon's biceps as if testing them for firmness.

"Just checking to ensure that's all you," Jonesy joked.

"You work me in the gym every day, Jonesy. It's hard-earned."

"Remember Curtis Jackson?"

Deacon grunted. "Man, enough with using my childhood bully whenever you want to make a point. I haven't been beaten up in a long time."

Jonesy squinted at Deacon, sizing him up and acting as though he found him lacking. Jonesy punched his arm. "Because you train."

Deacon shook it off and kept moving. Behind him, Jonesy called out, "And we need to get to the gym today too. It'll let you blow off some steam. You missed yesterday because of your date."

"Okay, okay. Let's go." Deacon stood impatiently at the door of Jonesy's car.

"Chill, man. I'm coming." Jonesy used his remote and unlocked the car.

"It's 11:40 a.m., Jonesy. Nia takes her break at noon. You're making me late."

Jonesy didn't answer, which caused Deacon to turn away, tilting toward the windshield and drumming his fist against his thigh as though each pat would make the car go faster.

Ten minutes later, Jonesy turned onto Grant Avenue, the massive library building looming ahead. "Don't pull into the parking lot, Jonesy. Just let me out."

"But it will only take two minutes for me to whip inside."

"I said no. Why is it so hard for you to respect that?"

Jonesy pulled over, and Deacon jumped out before the car slid to a complete stop.

"Man, are you crazy? At least wait till I put it in park."

Deacon threw up the peace sign behind him.

Trotting up the stairs, Deacon felt his backpack slipping. As he righted it, he crashed into someone standing at the top of the stairs. His backpack went down, and the woman followed along with her satchel. Both scrambled to right themselves.

"I'm sorry, ma'am. Here, let me help you." Deacon reached for her satchel, but she swatted his hands away.

"Stop!" she hissed, shifting items into her satchel and looking over her shoulder and his furtively.

"Hold on, I apologized. There's no need to get physical. I was only trying to help."

"Shut up and move on." The young woman glanced at her cell phone and hurried away, mumbling that she was too early.

Deacon rolled his eyes and continued into the building. He had no time for unhappy Karens; it was almost noon, and Nia might have already left for her break.

Nia

"Girl, I'm heading upstairs to take my break. I need a drink to swallow this aspirin. I have a splitting headache."

"I got it. Go on." Serena stepped to the center of the front desk. "Uh-oh."

"What?" Nia spun around and saw Deacon racing to the desk. "Hi, Deacon. I'm going on break. Anything you need, Serena will be glad to help you."

Serena grunted but put her hand out to take the books Deacon had in his hand. Looking forlorn, Deacon handed them over.

"Aww, I think you hurt his feelings." Serena laughed. Switching her attention between the two, she placed Deacon's books in the return cart without looking away from Nia and Deacon's interaction.

Both ignored Serena. Nia's breath hitched when she saw his earnestness, the weight of yesterday pressing against her chest. After their trainwreck of a date, she hadn't expected him to ever speak to her again. Instead of facing him, she wanted to duck behind the nearest bookshelf.

"I can wait; I'd like to talk to you," Deacon said as he walked away.

Nia wearily nodded her head. Her soft heart ached. She desperately wanted to walk over, wrap her arms around him, and tell him he'd be okay. That someday, someone would see the quiet brilliance he carried and never look away.

But that someone wasn't her.

Feeling guilty made her irritable. Turning on Serena, she snapped, "I guess what the textbooks say is true: hurting people hurt people. You need to leave that man alone," she said, stomping away.

Serena called behind her, "You only have ten minutes of break left. And since I'm so terrible, these books will be here for you to put away yourself."

Nia didn't even turn around. Serena got in her feelings at least once a month. And nobody was walking on eggshells around her today. The girl needed a hug and a little something more. Nia might have told her to try Jesus if Serena wasn't a diehard social media Christian. Serena was clicking away if it was more than a five-minute sound bite. But they'd already had that argument, and Nia saved her breath for those willing to listen.

Opening the door to the break area, a few other staff were already there, having lunch.

Nia gave a brief wave as if to say, "Hey, don't bother me."

"What's up?" Marvin, one of the library's guards, asked. "Haven't seen you up here lately. The weather is changing, and folks are starting to take their breaks in the building. Too chilly to be walking down to Mickey D's."

"You're right about that," another staff member answered. "I wish they hadn't closed Subway."

Nia pointed to her head, listening to the banter as she got juice from the vending machine and popped two painkillers out of the bottle in her purse. After swallowing them, she lay in the lounge recliner, closing her eyes.

"Hangover?" Marvin whispered.

She opened her eyes, glaring as he held up his hands. "Girl, chill out. I'm kidding. I remember when you turned me down for Happy Hour 'cause you don't drink."

Scooting to the edge of the chair, Nia gracefully rose, unaware of how tempting she looked with her fresh-faced beauty and innocence stamped on her countenance. "Duty calls."

Marvin waited until she was abreast of him when he said in a lower timbre, "Late-shift lunch on me?"

She shook her head. Nia was kind and denied him in a whisper. "Nah, I packed. Thank you, though."

Nia felt him watching her walk out of the room when, before the door closed, a female voice said, "Marvin, you ever see the movie *She's Just Not That Into You*?"

A cacophony of voices burst into laughter as the door shut behind her.

Nia shook her head. Marvin seemed to be a good guy. He was clean and good-looking in an understated way, but he had once made the mistake of dating someone else at work, and when it didn't work out, fireworks erupted. It got so bad that the woman had busted a window out of his car. The drama lasted about six months before the shattered woman transferred to one of the other branch offices. It taught Nia that she never wanted to date someone she worked with because the heartache seemed unbearable.

Nuh-uh.

Descending the stairs, Nia's breath caught in her throat when she spotted Deacon. He was working, head down, unaware of the storm he stirred in her. Her heart jumped—traitorously—and she exhaled hard, willing herself to stay composed.

She already had a job. Dating Deacon would feel like clocking in for another shift—one that the world would require her to explain every day.

Her eyes swept the room, desperate for an emotional detour. And then she froze. A familiar silhouette leaned against a distant column, head bowed, posture quiet.

It couldn't be.

She blinked once. Twice.

Sin.

But muted. Not her usual commanding self. She wore black, not sleek or styled for attention—just . . . comfortable. Nia's brow creased. Sin never dressed without intention.

As if feeling her stare, Sin lifted her face and smiled—that same crooked, warm smile that said everything and nothing all at once.

By the time Nia reached the bottom of the stairs, Sin had

already stepped forward, closing the distance with that effortless grace Nia had envied since childhood.

"Sis, what are you doing here?" Nia gleefully cried as they embraced.

"Well, I came to check out this Deacon character you were talking about." Sin stepped back at arm's length and turned her sister around. "You look good, little girl. However, your ends could use a good trimming. And an outfit that doesn't scream Thrifts-R-Us would also be nice. But, hey, your skin is clear."

Throwing her hand in the air, Nia groused, "You said all that when you were here last month. Don't start." Sin followed, and they approached Serena as she returned to her desk.

Serena rolled her eyes and sniffed in the air as though one of them stank. "It's all yours."

Nia decided not to answer her foolishness.

Sin nodded Serena's way. "What's her problem?"

"Girl, she's all right. She gets this way about once a week."

"Oh, she just needs a good—"

"I'm at work, sis. Please, don't start." Nia tipped closer to Sin's ear. "But I thought the same thing. A little talk with Jesus would set her straight."

Smirking, Sin laughed. "Yeah, that's where I was going with that thought."

A shadow fell between the two, and then he spoke. "Hello, I'm Deacon."

Like a cat who swallowed the canary, Sin grinned brightly. "Hi, cutie."

"Thank you. You resemble Nia. Are you a relative?"

Nia exhaled in a groan. "Deacon, it is not polite to invite yourself into a conversation."

"You would not have invited me, Nia. And I wanted to know

not just because I'm curious but because I'm interested in everything about you."

Sin's eyes darted between the two, her lips pulling up into a smile that illuminated her face. She blinked twice, a twinkle in the deep honey brown of her eyes.

"I like a man who says what he wants and does what he says," Sin said, sending a message to her sister by her tone and stance.

"Hold your roll, Sis," Nia warned.

Sin put her hand out to Deacon and shook his hand. "Good to meet you. You have good taste."

Deacon widened his legs and rolled back on his heels. "I think so. Nia is the best." He tucked his hands into his pockets and sauntered away. "I'd still like to talk, Nia."

Sin and Nia watched him move smoothly to his desk. Nia's mouth slightly gaped open. Deacon had handled the entire situation very well.

Maybe I was wrong?

"Girl, I've been sleeping on visiting you at your job. I don't see anything wrong with that man. You betta swipe right. He's fine and carries himself well. A little upfront about what he wants, but I can dig it." Sin stopped and looked at her little sister. Nia clamped her mouth shut, still in a daze.

Sin checked her phone. "Listen, we'll get together later. If I don't hit you up until tomorrow, I'm all good; I'm just busy. I'll see you, Ladybug."

Nia's mind was still on how Deacon had handled meeting one of the most important people in her life. If it was a test, he just aced it without her grading on the curve.

Chapter Nine

Nia

Already in a better mood, Nia watched her sister sashay toward the hallway and head outside. Even in regular street clothes, a man passing her stumbled, looking back at her hips, sending out an invitation Sin had no intention of fulfilling.

Sis can't help it.

She hummed softly as she pulled the cart around to her side of the desk and gathered an armload of books to categorize before shelving them. Looking at the spine, she crinkled her forehead at the expensive leather-bound book with no outward library labels to scan. She weighed the book in her hand. It was heavy but not too heavy for her to lift easily. The gold lettering had authentic gold filigree; when opened, the pages were of a quality she had rarely seen. Eyes closed, she ruffled the pages and felt the fineness of the paper. One of her professors at Ohio State had a book in a glass-locked case in her home that she would occasionally take out and let her most prized students touch, using white gloves. Nia sat and delicately laid the book on her desk.

The book didn't belong to the library. Nia was sure of it.

Who lost such an important book?

Nia touched the book and felt . . . off. It was not uncommon for a non-library-issued book to land in their return pile. Mostly, they found students' textbooks mistakenly shoved through the slot or even some erotica before a nosy parent could see what their child was reading so avidly. Those were the ones she was sure Marvin took home to read himself. However, this book seemed prestigious and had a certain vibe, but not in a good way.

She reached out without thinking, her fingertips grazing the spine.

A chill coursed up her arm. Not a coldness from temperature. Something . . . else.

The book didn't whisper "Precious" like a cartoon villain. It didn't need to. The word pulsed inside her—him? Like a memory she didn't recognize.

Nia, who'd spent her life avoiding anything that could be called trouble, looked over her shoulder. Her gut told her to leave it alone. However, her chest ached with a magnetic pull, like the book had reached into her rib cage and found a string it could tug.

Closer. Closer.

She quickly slipped it into her backpack.

Not to steal it, to read it. To understand why it felt like it knew her.

The moment the flap closed, the pressure in her chest eased. Her breath, which she hadn't realized she'd been holding, came out in a soft whoosh.

Somehow . . . This was what she was supposed to do.

She just wished she knew why.

She kept her head down as she turned, scanning the room for witnesses. Guilt was hot on her cheeks, but not because of the act; instead, because of the eyes drilling into her.

And, of course, it was him.

Deacon.

His expression wasn't angry; it was worse. Disappointment lay plain and bare on his face, like a bruise. He didn't hide his thoughts; he wore them, and they colored the air between them.

At that moment, Nia knew with a certainty that chilled her more than the book, Deacon had seen it all. Not just the act but the subtle shift in her.

Leave it alone, Nia. Let him think what he wants to.

But Deacon didn't look away. He crossed the space between them with a single-minded determination that made her feel more exposed than the backpack at her feet.

His voice, usually direct and full of odd rhythms, was low and measured. Almost gentle.

"I saw you." He paused. "Are you really going to take something that doesn't belong to you?"

"I, I—" Her throat clenched. She hadn't expected him to confront her.

His eyes narrowed. Not in anger. In study. "No. I've spent six months watching you, Nia. And you've never taken a book, even a New York Times Bestseller. Then you pull that book from the cart. The way you touched it . . . like you hated it. Then needed it. All at once."

He took a step closer. "What is it? Tell me."

"I don't have to tell you anything," she snapped too fast. Too defensive.

And then, like her sister when cornered, she said something stupid. Something childish. "You're not the boss of me."

Deacon flinched as if the words had struck skin. "No, I'm not," he said softly. "Let me see the book."

"What book?" she asked, folding her arms with exaggerated care and turning to the rest of the cart. "I'm busy. Please go back to your own business, Deacon."

But as he lingered, the corners of his mouth tightened.

A flicker. He touched his nose, squinting as if the air had shifted. "Do you smell that?"

"What?" Nia snarled.

He sniffed. "Sulfur."

"No. I need to get back to work, Deacon."

And Deacon—pure-hearted, clear-eyed Deacon—would never be able to let it go for long. And Nia, a thief in the book's eyes, was no longer an innocent . . . She was one of them now—her choice.

Deacon marched back to his table and slammed himself into his seat. She felt his displeasure radiating across the room as he grunted and slapped books on the table.

"Want me to call Marvin?"

Jumping, Nia looked over her shoulder at Serena, who was never too mad at her to stop interfering in anything that would make her right and Nia wrong. Namely, that Deacon was a problem.

"No. Why are you always trying to call Marvin? I don't need him. Security is not necessary."

"Because you don't listen, and Marvin could help. I told you that man's obsession with you could prove dangerous. See how he's looking at you? You need to have him kicked out of here, Nia."

"For what? Reckless eyeballing?"

"Mark my words. Guys like him are trouble. You can't trust what he'll do next. He's mentally unbalanced."

"He's not crazy, Serena. Different doesn't always mean dangerous."

"If he's so great, why didn't you go on another date with him?"

Nia paused, putting the returned books into order. She swung around, facing Serena. She rasped, "Explain—*now*."

Serena, missing Nia's inflection, giddily reported, "Kate from the third floor—you know, the one with the lisp?—told Donna from the media room that she saw you meet up with the nerdy cutie library patron, and you two walked down to McDonald's together. Everybody's talking about it. We've also noticed that you haven't gone out since."

Nia was so flabbergasted she looked at Serena as though she had lost her mind.

Serena placed her hands on her ample hips and stammered, "W-W-What? Inquiring minds wanted to know."

"You know what? You and everybody in this place need to get a life," Nia growled.

"Oh, chile, please. You haven't accepted a date in all the years you've worked here. And when you do accept a date, you pick him? Girl, anybody would have wanted to see that. You guys are like a high-speed chase on the 270 highway with both cars driving backward. Hard to look away from and understand how the heck it even happened."

"I'm glad my life entertains you. But my suggestion is you live your own." Nia spun around and tramped down the hallway to the bathroom. She wasn't even waiting to use a staff bathroom. Instead, she burst into one for library patrons, startling a woman who, on diaper duty, was changing her gurgling infant on the table.

"Sorry," Nia murmured as the door hit the wall when she shoved it open too hard.

The woman also had a toddler holding on to her long sweater, thumb in mouth. "I get it, Sis. People can get on your nerves. And if it's about a man, they're worse. You good." She bent down and lovingly pulled the little girl's thumb out of her mouth. "We gotta give each other grace."

Nia choked up at the kindness of a young mother who had her own hands full. Too embarrassed to speak, she nodded and hurried into the handicapped stall, silently praying that no one who needed it would come in.

She paced a tight loop inside the cramped space before finally sitting on the seat. Her breathing quickened.

People would talk. That's what they did. They'd whisper, point, laugh behind her back—and sometimes not even wait until her back was turned. That's why Deacon was out of the question.

She *hated* being laughed at.

All her life, she'd been trying to outrun that sound. As an army brat, she'd never stayed anywhere long enough to build real roots. Always the new girl, always a step behind the inside jokes. Sin had adapted—joined the military herself, like it was coded in her DNA. She made friends out of grit and command.

Nia had survived by becoming the quiet one, the agreeable one. Sin had filled in the gaps with her loud loyalty, her fierce sisterhood. Eventually, it had just been easier to let her.

However, that old strategy was no longer enough. Hiding didn't feel safe anymore—it just felt small.

She drew in a long, ragged breath—too sharp, too deep—and had to pause to steady herself before she tipped into panic.

She braced one hand against the stall wall and murmured, "Go back out there. Ignore them. Talk to Sin. And you've got that book to figure out."

The thought of the book settled something in her. She had to figure out its pull.

When she finally stepped out of the stall, the restroom was empty. She washed her hands automatically, not for hygiene but to reset herself.

And when she pushed open the door, Deacon was there. Waiting. Propped casually against the wall like he hadn't just seen her unravel a few minutes ago.

Nia froze, glanced around, then let out a frustrated breath. "Deacon, please stop following me," she said, her voice tight.

"I only came to check on you. I'm not okay with you taking the book. But it looked like Serena upset you. You all right?"

"Deacon—"

"Did she see you take the book, Nia?"

Nia looked around and cringed. "Shush!"

Seeing Deacon's face fall, she answered, "No. Serena shared something else."

Shrugging, Deacon placed his hands in his pockets and crunched his forehead as he watched her wring her hands. "This doesn't make you feel good, Nia. If something doesn't make me feel good doing it, it usually means I shouldn't be doing it." He then headed back to his table.

Watching, Nia couldn't help but think, *What if the thing that doesn't feel good is how people feel about me dating you?*

She took her time following him into the room before veering off to return to the counter. She pointedly ignored Serena, even when Serena tried to make small talk as if nothing were wrong.

Nia was convinced that people were messy. And Serena was the Queen of Messiness. Suddenly, there were shouts:

"They're shooting. Get down, get down!"

"Run, run!"

The commotion was loud as staff and customers ran inside the building. Nia ducked, then remembered that Sin had gone out the same door only twenty minutes before.

Sin's long gone . . . right?

Chapter Ten

Sin

Sin loved her some Nia, but she had always practiced business first. She hoped to have some time with her little sister after she got her package delivered and handed off. Standing outside the library's entrance, blowing into her cold hands, she looked around at the mixture of people coming and going through the library's main doors. She was instructed that her contact would be female and that she would wear a gray and red scarf around her neck. She didn't know whose bright idea the scarf was because it was football season, and the number of gray and scarlet scarves embroidered with "OHIO" was driving her eyes to cross.

Somebody's getting cursed out.

Sincere's saving grace was advising she would be wearing the blue and gold Michigan U scarf around her neck. She was getting nasty glances from the staunch Ohio Buckeyes, but one lady kept eyeballing her. Her lashes were too full and long to be real; her eye color was a startling blue, and the expensive highlights in her hair screamed high maintenance. Sin took inventory of the woman inching toward her. She was advertising some man's side piece—

but lobster mac and cheese, not coleslaw—this woman cost somebody some real cash to play.

"Go Blue?" Sin said between puffs into her hands.

"O-H . . . I-O," the woman simpered, her eyes bucked and theatrically wild.

Sin glided closer. "You have something for me?"

The woman pulled a book from her satchel and handed it to Sin. Not looking at it, Sin put the book inside her duffel. "Follow me."

Small beads of perspiration dotted the woman's brow as Sin saw a look of relief flood her face. As they moved, four men charged up the stairs and surrounded them.

Sin's alter ego, Pop, surged forward before Sin could blink.

Birthed in Afghanistan, Pop was a survival instinct weaponized —a controlled blaze in combat boots. Where Sin hesitated, Pop handled business.

With enemy agents closing in and civilians watching, it was time for a theatrical performance of her own.

Pop shrieked, loud and panicked, her eyes wide with feigned terror. "Who are you?! Get away from me!"

Heads turned. Phones went up.

She flailed, stumbling backward into one of the approaching men. He reached to capture her—wrong move.

Her elbow smashed into his throat so fast no one saw the setup. He crumpled without a sound, collapsing in a heap.

To everyone watching, it looked like she'd tripped into him, and he'd just . . . fallen.

That's one.

Three more advanced.

Still shrieking, Pop spun toward them, throwing her arms wildly as if she'd lost balance. But then she dropped low—precision in motion—twisting into a tight roundhouse kick that caught the second man squarely in the ribs. He flew off his feet, crashing into a nearby bystander with a yelp.

That's two.

To the crowd, it was chaos. To Pop, it was choreography.

Thank you, Jackie Chan's Saturday matinees.

"Help, help!" she cried out, her voice trembling on purpose, her hands clawing the air like she couldn't control her limbs. She was counting on the audience—on their shock, confusion, and need to record everything. Because what people were *told* they saw usually outweighed what they actually did. After all, it was the secret sauce to men getting away with cheating for centuries.

Her mouth twisted, the anger welling. Not just at these men. At *him.*

"No, baby," she mocked in her mind, letting the venom rise. "That wasn't me marrying someone else. Must've been a misunderstanding. Let me talk to you for a minute."

Her throat tightened. *"You know I love you."*

Umber's voice. His lies. The way he'd looked Sin in the eyes and denied everything, even after she saw the wedding photo. He didn't just leave Sin.

He rewrote her out of the story like she'd never mattered.

Pop's rage sharpened. She screamed.

The two men who were left appeared startled at her vociferous yell. They hesitated for a fraction of a second before resuming their approach, but an opening was all Pop needed. She shoved the befuddled woman farther behind her, instructing, "Don't move."

The men lunged forward, pulling out weapons with threatening glints in their eyes.

"Somebody, please," Pop whimpered as she threw up her hands in angst but crouched low where only the men looming above her could see her.

Pop attacked; she two-punched both men in their knees.

Hearing a crack, one went down, but the other staggered back, staying on his feet. With a gleam of admiration, she grabbed him by the neck, lifting herself from the ground as they flipped over, Pop pleading, "Let go, let go!"

She came down on him so hard that she felt him go slack.

Grabbing the woman who stood there trembling, mouth propped open, Pop bolted. Then, glancing back, she saw the first man she downed stagger to his feet. A gun in his hand, Pop hurled down on her knee, bringing the woman down beside her.

With his gun pointed up in the air, he shot three times, and the panicked crowd shrieked and then scattered.

The resulting ricocheting pain in Pop's knee made Sin appear.

Ow, Pop. That's gonna cost me.

Shut up, Sin. Stay outta this, Pop snapped.

Her knee burning, Pop pulled out her blade. As the man charged toward her, dodging the people, his eyes trained on the woman crouching behind her, Pop's arm slid in a zigzag arc as she made sure he wouldn't rise again.

Slice, slice.

Blood spouted from the man's ankle; his gun discharged once again into the air.

Everyone screamed louder, including the woman she was protecting. All the men were down, but none were dead. Pop intended to change that as she moved forward while people panicked.

A sharp tug yanked her back. "Are you kidding me? Your job is to keep me safe. Get me out of here, Warrior Princess," the woman barked.

The yank made Sin reappear, causing Pop to falter—the two halves of a whole—battling between Sin's mission with a throbbing knee and Pop's blood thirst. One of the men leaped up and was inches from her. Steadily backing away, Sin ducked beneath his swing and came up as Pop with an elbow-sharp jab to his chin, sending him crashing onto the concrete stairs beside his fallen comrade.

This is why you should've let me end them, Pop raged at Sin.

No, Pop. Sin held to her ethics. *This is not Afghanistan.*

Pop disagreed. *These men are not innocent bystanders.*

Sin knew her mission, and her little sister was just steps away. *Pop, I said no. The woman is right. Let's get out of here.*

Hands up, head down, where her face stayed obscure, Pop sobbed dramatically, "Please, no more, no."

A few brave, nosy souls began to creep back, and to those watching, Pop appeared hysterical. As an earlier downed man rose from the stairs, people began to yell for him to stop.

"Hey, leave that woman alone. I'm filming you!" a young woman blasted.

The man roared, but with clenched fists, he limped the opposite way down the stairs, keeping his face averted from the numerous phones filming. One of the other men staggered to his feet.

However, a concerned citizen grabbed the man from behind, hindering him from continuing his pursuit. The young man's friends jumped in to help.

They shouted as they stomped him, gaining courage with every new blow. "How're you attacking a lady in broad daylight? Nah, not today, son!"

Pop and her package took off running. Together, they ran as sirens sounded in the air. The cavalry had arrived, and they couldn't be detained for questioning. The Council had people in high and low places.

As the last remaining people ran, one of the fallen men yelled, "Ariel Sutton, where will you hide?"

Sin took over as she whirled around to face her package. Ariel was frozen and wide-eyed.

"We have to get out of here," Sin urged. "Run, and don't stop. I'll be right behind you."

The woman followed Sin's lead as they darted toward the side of the stairs to the exit. Sin kept a sharp eye behind them. But right before they turned the corner, she saw two new men join the others, one man lifting the man with sliced tendons over his shoulder, fireman style.

Shoot, Pop was right. But I'm tired of the bloodshed.

Pointing toward them, the new men took off after Sin and the woman named Ariel.

Sin gnawed on her lip. The numerous sounds outside were fighting for prominence as sirens blared in the distance, and she thought quickly of her next move. These two men were fresh, and they didn't have the inconvenience of an audience watching them. Sin was winded but not exhausted.

The entire battle took ten minutes, but it was in speed-of-light motions. Sin had bruises, a knee that might give out, and a girly girl who looked like she would be of zero assistance. Keeping Pop under control was becoming increasingly difficult. Lately, she had appeared without Sin releasing her.

They had a reciprocal relationship. Pop was the killer, Sin the strategist. Coexisting in one body, they had stayed alive because they knew when to call on the other to take over. This line of work was taking a toll on her. More and more, she was thinking of retiring.

Yeah? And do what? This is the only thing you're good at.

Sin's head throbbed. *Shut up, Pop.*

You make me shut up!

Running ahead, Sin ducked into an alley. She inhaled deeply, and Pop opened her eyes. Keeping her hand firmly on Ariel's arm,

Pop didn't avert her gaze from the men who followed at too close a distance.

"Ariel?"

"Yes," she sobbed.

Nodding, Pop pulled Ariel farther down the alley around a dumpster behind the building. The sounds of the sirens were now silent. They were no longer en route. They were at their destination.

Pop attached the silencer by slipping her knife from its holder on her leg and grabbing her gun from her cross-body satchel. She listened as the sound of Ariel's rapid breathing panted in her left ear.

"Shhh," Pop whispered.

Heavy footfalls entered the alley.

"I'll check back here," a deep voice boomed.

"Okay, man. I'll check behind the building up ahead. Remember, he said to bring both packages back to him. He wants to handle it personally."

Perspiration sprinkled Pop's forehead.

The footsteps paused, and she heard boxes and trash being ransacked. Silence . . . then footsteps, more cautious now.

What had spooked him?

Pop sniffed the air and turned. Ariel was wearing an expensive perfume. One that defied a trash smell for a discerning nose. Their luck, they had a hound on their tail.

He was closer, but the man's arm reached her before he did. She snatched it, flipped him over, and put him in a sleeper hold as good as any WrestleMania match.

"Sin," Pop breathed, hating when Sin held her back from getting her hands dirty. She was going to kill him when Sin interfered and stopped her hand from snapping his neck.

Angry, Pop left Sin to fend for herself.

Grabbing Ariel's hand, Sin moved away from the alley. She knew Pop had receded for now, and she reluctantly concluded that she might need a therapist. What started as a way for her to cope while all the violence in her life escalated out of control was becoming untamable. Pop was getting too strong.

Glancing up and down the short street, Sin didn't see anyone. She couldn't go to her car. It could be compromised. Taking off her U of M scarf and Ariel's OHIO scarf, she dumped them. She then turned her reversible jacket inside out. Reaching into her large cross-body bag, she took out colorful leggings and pulled them over her black pants. She then placed a wig of Box braids over her pixie-cut hair.

Ariel stood in shock as Sin even changed the way she walked. More boyish and wide-legged.

"They're no longer looking for just you. They're looking for me too. But I'm hiding in plain sight. Put this on." Sin handed Ariel a baseball cap. "Push all of your hair under it."

She then stepped back and looked at what Ariel was wearing. "I can't do much more with how you look. If I could have gotten to my car, I could have. But we'll have to sell the act. Make them see what we want them to see."

Finishing pushing her hair under the cap, Ariel still sobbed.

"Okay, you can skip the damsel-in-distress playacting. Save the talent for your next role. You're gonna need it. Nobody who pulled off what you pulled off could be this naive."

A hardened glint replaced the innocent act that had filtered their earlier communication.

"There she is." Sin clapped.

"Whatever," Ariel said, all subterfuge gone. "Y'all have seriously messed this up. I thought I was getting 007, but a Keystone Kop showed up instead."

"I got yo' Keystones." Handing Ariel some oversized glasses,

Sin put her arm around her and began a masculine stagger. "Put your hand in my back pocket."

Ariel did as she commanded, and they continued down the street unharmed and unnoticed.

"Where are we headed?" Ariel asked for the fourth time, this time with a whine.

Ignoring her, Sin kept going, noting street signs.

* * *

A little later . . .

Ariel dragged her feet. "We've been walking for almost an hour, and I feel like we've passed this street before. Where are we going?"

"Stop complaining. Our contact was supposed to meet us here. But he's a no-show. And he never misses an assignment. So shut your mouth and let me think."

They rounded a corner, and Sin pushed Ariel on faster as they moved. Ahead, her eyes widened as she saw three men appear at the end of the street, their weapons ready.

How?

She continued toward them as she pushed Ariel's face into the crook of her neck as they approached the men.

If Ariel was playacting fear before, she wasn't now. Sin could feel her shivers permeating into her jacket.

She took a deep breath. Her eyes briefly closed as Pop's eyes opened. She stared the men down, her gaze silent and strong, her wide-legged stance unwavering despite her pounding heart.

The men looked around her, not noting that she was the woman they had just fought.

"Twenty more steps, and we're clear," she whispered to Ariel.

Pop could feel Ariel's tremors as though they were her own. But she gave credit where it was due. Ariel held fast, kissing her cheek as they passed the men, who grunted in disapproval but continued looking past them.

As they moved around the corner and separated, Pop noticed Ariel's hand close to her side—it held a gun.

"Really? Now you were going to help?" Pop sneered. Shaking her head, Sin appeared, her hand outstretched. "Give me the gun."

"Nuh-uh." Ariel went to put the gun back in her satchel-like purse.

Sin snatched the gun out of her hand. "Thank you."

"I need that."

"Yeah, well, right now, *I* need it."

"Why?"

"Because I don't plan on waking up dead because I turned my back on you. Now, say less."

Ariel clamped her mouth shut.

"We have to get out of here," Sin barked. "My contact should have met us. The fact that these goons were waiting nearby, however, doesn't sit well with me. Something has gone wrong, and you'll have to trust me to get us both to safety."

Ariel's bravado had faded, but her gleaming eyes filled with admiration and respect as she stepped behind Sin, and Sin hobbled them down the street. Pop had injured Sin's knee in that earlier battle, but she thanked the powers that be that she could walk.

It was still broad daylight, and the sounds of scuffles, danger, and mayhem coming from a neighborhood two miles from the library were not foreign to its inhabitants.

Satisfied that she had not lost her package, she fingered the book inside the crossbody she had slung around her back. Pacing herself, Sin pulled Ariel with her, and they ducked into the entrance of a small storefront church.

It was right on time as a helicopter scanned the neighborhood from above. The words "Food Bank available today between noon and 4:00 p.m." were prominent on the church door's window.

It swung open behind them, and an elderly Black woman pulling a cart with groceries exited.

"Bless you, baby," she said sweetly as she ambled down the street.

Both women ducked inside and were greeted by a rotund man. "Welcome, sisters. Have you ever been to His Mercies Holiness Church?"

"Uh, no," Sin said, "but we've heard of the good work you're doing in the community, and my good friend here needs your services."

The man looked at the quality of Ariel's clothing, and his face turned to stone.

Sin saw his reaction. Sober, she said, "You see, sir, she recently lost her husband and her job." Sin then looked around and moved closer to whisper in his ear, "Her boss stole her husband, and she was fired at the same time. She's been left destitute."

The man's face softened into sympathy for Ariel's plight. "Come, sister, follow me. All are welcome here."

Ariel's blue eyes rounded as they blinked in helplessness, and she followed him down the rickety steps to the food bank.

When they reached the church's basement, Sin announced, "Don't be embarrassed. Go and get some food for your empty pantry. Don't forget things like detergent and toilet paper. I'll be right over here."

Moving to a corner away from those people moving around to get help, Sin maneuvered the purse from her back and reached inside. She pulled out a leather-bound book.

"*The Effect of Viruses on Third-World Refugees in a Modern America*," she read out loud.

Her lips tightened, and she shook her head.

Four men were out of commission (although they would have done more to her), one was a missing agent, and she had a liar informant. One thing she knew was that the package she had come for was not a book from the Columbus Metropolitan Library.

All hell and its demons were about to break out.

Chapter Eleven

Nia

Nia couldn't breathe. "Get off."

Deacon uncurled his body from on top of hers. "You okay?"

Nia took several breaths and rolled to her knees. "Yesss, *hisss . . .*" She puffed, working to catch her breath. "I appreciate your efforts to protect me, but I couldn't breathe."

"I know, Nia. But it was temporary. Death is permanent. And you can breathe now," Deacon stated in a matter-of-fact voice.

He held out his hand, and she took it. Then he pulled her to a stand. Nia hunched over, her hands on her thighs, inhaling and exhaling deeply.

"Breathe, Nia."

"I am breathing. I need to check on my sister. She's why I was heading toward the exit door when you tackled me."

"It's not smart to run to where people are running from. I'll go with you."

"What if it were your brother?"

Deacon froze. "Jonesy can take care of himself. He's very good at it. Come on. I'll help you find your sister."

Together, they passed other staff and library customers as they stood around, gawking and talking about what had just occurred. This was the public library, one of the best in the area. They had security and other safety measures in place.

"Where can we ever really be safe?" the crowd murmured as it tried to make sense of the recent insanity.

Nia went through the door and ran out without her coat. She didn't see Sin. She could see a man with a bandaged head sitting in an ambulance.

Breathing in relief, Nia glided back into the building with Deacon on her heels.

She slowed when she heard two young men debating.

"I'm telling you, she was beating that man's butt."

"Nah, player. The moves she was doing were her trying to get away from the men. She was kicking and screaming for help."

The older of the two sucked his teeth. "My cousin does that martial arts crap, and I'm tellin' you, I know their moves. Chick was bad."

Nia gasped, and her head snapped around as she searched the building.

As they walked off, the younger one said, "Well, regardless, she and another chick ran off. Po Po put some bodies in the ambulance, but did you notice a few of those men who scampered away? Dude, what was with all the blond hair? They looked like a bunch of children of the corn village people."

Cackling, the guy slapped his hands together. "At the end of the day, all I know is there were four white men tryin'a beat up a Black lady. Instead, they got whooped."

Chuckling, the other snorted, "Well, they've been wanting to put a stop to Black-on-Black crime."

Both young men fell out laughing as they walked farther into the library.

Nia was so in tune with the young men that she jumped when Deacon tapped her shoulder. "Your sister's not here. She was probably long gone when this all started."

Nia opened her mouth to contradict Deacon, but instead, just nodded. "Yeah, you're probably right. We'd better go back inside."

As they moved, ten additional police cars pulled up. The first officers on the scene, interviewing a bystander, hurried to meet the arriving officers.

"Let's go," Nia said as gawkers scattered, not wanting to get involved with the police.

Nia and Deacon flew up the stairs into the library together.

Entering the building, they grimaced when a police officer announced that anyone outside in the last hour would be held for questioning. Grudgingly, they followed directions.

Nia groaned when Mary and the officer in charge stood right in the path of her and Deacon. As they approached, she could hear the end of their conversation, in which Mary stated that the executive director was on her way down.

Head down, Nia tried to tip past her. "A word, Nia," Mary said.

Nodding, Nia met Mary aside from the stream of people waiting for more directions.

Mary folded her arms and gave Nia a look of consternation. "I didn't pick you for a rubbernecker, young lady. You left the front desk unmanned while people inside scurried around without direction. It's good that Serena ran and got me at the first sign of trouble."

Nia snorted. "Yes, I imagine Serena ran at the first sign of trouble."

"This is not like you, Nia. Except for your tardiness, you always place our customers' welfare above all."

"Sorry, Mary. It won't happen again."

"Nia's sister might have been hurt; she was checking on her." Deacon's voice jarred both women, and they jumped at its volume and closeness.

"Deacon!"

"Young man, this was a private conversation," Mary said, not unkindly. She then continued to Nia. "Was your sister involved in this, Nia? You're from a military family, am I correct?"

"No, Mary, my sister wasn't involved. My father is a *retired* officer." Nia then placed her hand on Deacon's arm. "I will escort this customer to where the sergeant asked us to wait. As you said, the faster I can return to the front desk, the better."

Mary's glasses slid to the bridge of her nose, and the pencil behind her ear stuck out of her tight bun, illustrating the librarian stereotype. She pointedly stared at Nia and Deacon, then at Nia's hand on Deacon's arm. "Hmm, you do that."

As people were taken to one of the library's rooms, Nia fumed. Deacon didn't know when to stay quiet. She didn't know how her boss, Mary, had found out about her family and the military. Nia talked about Sin as little as possible, always afraid she would share too much.

"Are you angry with me, Nia?" Deacon said, lower than she had ever heard him speak.

"This is my problem with a relationship with you, Deacon. We don't suit. You do too much." Grinding her words like steel through a mill, she continued, "*You're* just too much." Nia lowered her harshness to a hush as Serena walked closer.

Deacon's body slumped, and Nia instantly wanted to recall her words. But Deacon surprised her when he stood taller and made eye contact with her, which he rarely achieved.

"And you major on minor, Nia. You constantly worry about other people while they're living their best lives. I feel sorry for you, Nia."

Gasping, Nia stepped back when Serena released a loud burst of laughter.

"Well, maybe he ain't as nerdy as he acts with his fine self." Serena crowed loud enough to be heard throughout the crowd.

"Serena?" Mary called from the front desk.

"I'm coming, Mary," Serena replied, moving back to cover the front desk.

Nia's embarrassment was cut short when Marvin arrived. The sergeant standing near her requested the library tapes of the outside area up to an hour before the police arrived. He also requested that they pull from every camera around the perimeter of the building.

As Marvin went to fill the police requests, Deacon and Nia were separated and interviewed by detectives.

Nervous, Nia listened carefully as they questioned her. The detectives were more interested in who Nia had seen and what she knew about the people involved than anything else.

"I didn't see anything. I was inside working. I heard screaming and something about shots fired. People began to run in every direction."

The female detective looked at her for a moment after her statement. "Didn't I see you outside when we walked up?"

"Yes, ma'am, I was. But that was after it seemed to be over. I was curious like everyone else, so one of our library regulars and I stepped out to see what was happening."

Holding her pad and pencil, the officer perused Nia for more than a beat. "You don't look like the type who gawks at train wrecks."

Licking her lips, Nia stumbled over her words. "Umm, no. But it was so close and all . . ."

The other detective grunted. "Tell me, who doesn't stop and gawk at tragedy? We have a room full of folk to get to. We need to move on."

"Place your name, phone number, and address on the sheet on your way out," the female detective ordered.

Nodding, Nia exhaled as she hurried to leave when the officer snatched her arm. "You've got my spidey senses tingling. Be aware, we can call you back with questions anytime."

Nia's hands clenched. Instead of continuing to rush, she slowed down. She hadn't given them any information on Sin and prayed that whatever had happened, her sister would be okay. Sin was very good at what she did. Not even their parents knew the extent of Sin's involvement in covert operations. She was her sister's sole confidante and didn't know much herself. Yet, she would never expose her sister's identity.

Nia wrote her information on the paper and left the room.

"You can go home, Nia," Mary said. "We're closing for the rest of the day. You'll be notified through email and the phone tree messaging system if there are any additional instructions. Otherwise, I'll see you tomorrow."

"Thank you." Nia went to her desk and unlocked it to remove her purse and backpack. She grabbed her heavy sweater from her chair and went to the elevator banks, waiting with others to reach the garage.

After pushing the button and the doors sliding open, Nia stepped in, and right behind her, a voice blasted, "You okay, Nia?"

Folding her arms, Nia looked at Deacon standing beside her in the crowded elevator. The elevator stopped on the second floor. Her car was on the third, but when Deacon didn't get out, she did. As the door closed behind her, she breathed with a slight grin at outsmarting him. She was ready to skip up the ramp. But a second later, the elevator doors opened again, and Deacon hopped out.

"Wait. You almost left me, Nia." Deacon ran to catch up with her. "Listen. I know you don't want me here. But somebody just shot up the front of this building. I'm going to walk you to your car."

Nia felt lower than scum. Deacon was only trying to help. When was the last time any man not trying to get into her pants had been so kind?

"Thank you, Deacon."

Nia's cheeks warmed, and she prayed she wasn't reddening as they trotted up the ramp to the third floor.

"Really, Nia?" Deacon complained. "You were so in a hurry to get away from me that you got off on the wrong floor?"

Nia's stomach fluttered as she witnessed his body deflate and his face stiffen, pensive. She was on pins and needles as he cleared his throat. "If I'm bothering you this much, I'll let you go."

She flinched and waited for the feelings of relief to come. There were none.

What?

She speed-walked to get away, but Deacon stayed with her. Reaching her car, Nia didn't know what to say. She didn't want to hurt his feelings any further. She didn't want to encourage him by telling him it was all right because it wasn't. But the absence of relief at his announcement bothered her. Yet, cowardly, she said nothing.

Silent, Deacon watched her get into her car.

As Nia drove away, he became a statue covering her escape as her car wove its way down the ramp, his frame a dot in her rearview mirror.

Nia didn't know why she was the one who wanted to cry.

Chapter Twelve

General

General marched into the luxury suite as Eric sat in a high-back chair with a sumptuous meal before him.

He carefully laid down his fork as General approached. "Sir?"

Out of nowhere, General swept his arm back, then thrust it forward in a wide arc. The powerful follow-through was the most epic pimp slap that had ever been delivered, especially on the weak-chinned billionaire by a seventy-one-year-old.

Falling over, Eric attempted to climb up, holding the table's edge, General's handprint stenciled on his pale face. On his first attempt to right himself, his arms failed him. He missed pulling himself up onto the chair, but he tried again. This time, he landed and tittered precariously close to the edge as he settled awkwardly.

The accompanying thunderous sound from General held Eric's voice at bay. There was no need to speak. Speaking could be detrimental to his long-term goal to make it out of there alive.

Running his fingers through his disheveled gray hair, General straightened his jacket. He then marched stiffly back to the door, pausing as he opened it to leave. "Your Ariel is missing. If she remains missing, you will also become missing. I hope I've made myself clear. If you have even a small inkling of her whereabouts, spill it fast. It is late fall, and the blood must be spilled before the end of the year. You already know this."

"Yes, General," Eric moaned between loose teeth.

Geoff came and waited before General as he held up his hand for him to hold on.

"This was to be your first year to attend the sacrifice. My first was at the age of twenty-one."

His face now swollen, Eric squinted at General as one of his eyelids began to puff. General pointed at Eric with his beefy hand. "Do you know the story of my father, who refused to sacrifice my half-brother, a man who was born from his insignificant mistress?"

Eric moaned in answer.

"We sacrificed them both. My proxy, my half-brother, died as the sacrifice demanded publicly. My father died in the same manner, but in a private manner for my enjoyment only. For the *Book of Disasters*, blood must be spilled. If we don't find Ariel, you will be our sacrificial lamb instead of the half-sibling we've picked to represent your lineage. Each family must spill blood. It is our Jubilee."

Gulping, Eric's body convulsed as he jumped up and staggered to the en suite toilet. He was going to be sick, and maybe he was then going to die in a very public way.

Chapter Thirteen

Nia

Nia trudged through the front door of her apartment, her heart heavy and mind clouded. She kicked off her sneakers. The weight of her heart made moving difficult. She shuffled to the kitchen, not hungry but needing some distraction. If Sin showed up, surely, she would be hungry. Nia grabbed a pack of chicken from the fridge, tore open the plastic wrap, and dumped the pieces into the sink. With numb fingers, she turned on the cold water and watched as it washed away the red-tinted liquid. Absently, she reached for the salt shaker and sprinkled it over the chicken.

Barefoot, she padded around the living room, searching for her slippers. Seeing them haphazardly left in front of her couch, she slipped them on when her shoulders began to shake. A hiccup bounced between the walls as she tried to hold in her quaking tears. She hit the top of the sofa's arm several times with the heel of her hand. She was overwhelmed. Too much was going on, all at the same time. Rubbing her chest, she wondered what had happened to her quiet, orderly life.

Nia had no idea where her sister was or whether she was

involved in the earlier mess. She had hurt the feelings of a man she liked, all because she was scared of what a relationship with him would look like. And she had taken a book that didn't belong to her. Her head snapped to attention.

The book!

Nia grabbed her backpack, and her hand inched toward the flap. She snatched her hand back. She felt such a pull toward the book that she questioned if she was losing her senses. Placing her hand in front of her, she could see it was trembling. Small beads of sweat lingered at her hairline, and her stomach roiled. She felt as though she faced Pandora's box.

What would Sin do?

She tried to focus on Sin, which was Nia's usual way to fix what was broken, but her mind refused her desire to control its direction. Instead, she heard . . .

"If something doesn't make me feel good doing it, it usually means I shouldn't be doing it."

Jolted, not only could Nia hear Deacon's voice, but she could also see the expression on his face. His eyes pleaded with her not to be that person. It made her wonder.

Was this what it meant when someone said, "They make me a better person."

Nia fell back from the book. Her eyes locked on the word engraved on the front: *Nachalo.*

"Well, I can look that up. Alexa, what is the definition of Nachalo?"

Alexa lit up. "The definition of Nachalo. The beginning. An outbreak. The origin. The start. Would you like me to play music for you to relax?"

"Alexa, no."

Nia ran the definition through her head. The beginning or start of what? She would not learn anything outside of the book.

As she edged forward again, there was a frantic knock on her door. Jumping up, she ran and looked through the peephole. She could only see hair in corn rolls, and she didn't know anyone who would be coming to see her who wore that hairstyle.

"Who is it?"

"Me!"

Nia began to unlock the deadbolt, then stopped and ran back, picked up the book, and put it in her backpack. It was out of character. She shared everything with Sin, even her mistakes. She intended to tell Sin, but with Deacon's words ringing in her ear, Nia decided to do the smart thing and take the book back and act as though she had never removed it from the library. She felt God must have been telling her something, and she intended to listen. She would turn it in at work the next day, as though it had just arrived, and be done with it.

"Nia!" the impatient voice hissed through the door's letter slot.

Now, knowing her sister was good, Nia's urgency had lessened. "Keep your pantyhose on. Jeez." Unlocking each lock, Nia let her sister and another woman who crowded Sin's back inside. Both were dirty, rumpled, and sweating as they rushed past her.

"Hey! Why does this remind me of all your escapades when we were growing up? Please don't make me worry even more about you."

"You should know I'm good," Sin said with a grin. "I'm working, babe. I won't be here long. Just need a place to catch my breath and think." She then pushed a grocery bag into her arms. "Here's some toilet paper and canned goods."

At Nia's raised brow, Sin added, "Don't ask."

"Make yourself at home." Nia put the bag down and spread her hands to Sin and her guest. "Uh, hello?"

Ariel ignored her.

Not wanting this rude woman in her house, Nia side-eyed her.

"Sin, whatever this is, just go to the nearest police station or FBI office. You both look like you need help."

"No can do, Ladybug."

Marching by Nia like she should kiss her ring, Ariel flopped down on the couch. She stretched her lithe body along the cushions and grumbled, "When you figure all this out, Agent Double O Zero, let me know. I have to get some sleep." She yawned and lifted her arms above her head.

"Excuse me, Sis." Stomping over, Sin grabbed her arm and lifted her off the couch. "Nia, this is Ariel. Ariel, this is my sister. Now, her house is admittedly tacky, but it's *her* house. We have hidden behind garbage dumpsters, lain under cars, and walked, run, skipped, and jogged all over creation to end up here where I never wanted to end up," a frustrated Sin barked.

"And?"

Ariel cringed as Sin squeezed her arm tighter.

"And you will get your nasty, funky butt off her couch. Go in the bathroom and take a five-minute shower," she sneered.

Ariel reached behind her, and Sin barked, "Leave the purse."

Sucking her teeth, Ariel groaned. "Can I at least take my cosmetic bag? A girl has her feminine needs."

Eyeing her disdainfully, Sin shrugged. "Sure."

Sulking but moving, Ariel followed Nia out of the room and down the hallway. Nia stopped and pulled a washcloth and a towel out of the linen closet. "Here you go," she said as Ariel strutted into the bathroom. "Feel free to use any toiletries you need."

Before Nia could say anything else, Ariel slammed the door in her face. Trudging back to her sister, Nia braced herself for the mess her sister was about to lay at her feet.

"I love you, but why does your presence always mean my discomfort?" Nia whined. She then threw her arms around her sister and squeezed her tightly. "You're a troublemaker, Sis."

Sin leaned into the hug, drawing her sister closer. "It's all in a day's work. Nothing is going on that I can't handle. After our FaceTime last night, I want to know how you're doing?"

Nia looked down the hall, and Sin shook her head. "You're good to share, girl. That chick is high-maintenance. Hence, I knew she'd jump at a chance for a shower, and she'll never do only five minutes. That gives me a little break 'cause that woman is a doozy. You've got time; talk to me."

Sin sat and patted the couch next to her.

"You're just as nasty as she was, all that dirt on my couch, Sin."

"Yeah, but it's my nasty. You're stalling, Ladybug . . ."

Sitting, Nia looked toward the hallway and down at her folded hands. "Yeah, well, I told you about Deacon—"

"Boy is fine, by the way," Sin interrupted. "Doesn't seem overtly neurodivergent, and he seems genuine. You should see some of the men I've dated: Neanderthals or players, each one. I would date—no—I'd marry genuine," Sin said, her fingers wiggling in the air, indicating they were ringless. "But no one has ever asked me."

"Ahem. If you want this conversation to be about you, I can wait," Nia teased.

Nia always felt better when Sin was around. Somehow, the air was sweeter, better. Maybe it was big-sister magic.

"Sorry. Tell me all." Sin took Nia's hand down from her face, where she was about to start biting her nails. A bad habit she had broken years ago.

"First, I was arguing with Deacon, and then there were people shouting that someone was outside shooting. Then Deacon threw me down and jumped on top of me—"

"What? He threw you down and covered you?"

"Uh-huh, then—"

"Ain't *nothing* wrong with *that* man." Sin looked at her as though she had missed an important point. Nia blankly looked back at her. "Nia! That man was ready to take a bullet for you."

"Oh, um, I guess." Nia paused. Her thoughts raced, and she shook herself to return to her original point. "It all got a little muddled together. After I spoke to the police, I—"

"Whoa. Go back. Why did the police interview *you*?"

"They interviewed everyone outside and those working on the first floor." Nia tilted away from Sin, searching her face. "Uh, why? I didn't tell them anything. Wait. Was there something to tell? Is your agency going to clear everything up with the locals?"

Sin studied her sister. "You know I can't talk about my assignments. You know more than anybody in my life. However, this one is so under the radar that we can't tell anybody, not even the locals. I promise that I'm good, though. You know I can handle myself. How many escapades have you seen me in through the years?"

"That's what I told myself. That you're indestructible, but we both know that's not true."

Sin stopped, then stood and walked to the beginning of the hallway. She bent low and held out her hand. "You feel that?"

Puzzled, Nia shook her head. "Feel what?"

Running down the hall, Sin called behind her, "The air, Sis, the air."

Going to the bathroom door, she knocked twice and then called out over the rushing shower, "Ariel!"

There was no answer, and when Sin went to kick it in, Nia snatched her arm. "Girl, don't you break down my door." Lifting her work badge from around her neck, she used the library card resembling a credit card and jimmied it across the lock, popping open the door.

There, the frosted window stood wide open. Ariel was long gone.

Nia turned to her sister. "You think she washed her butt before she took off?"

Sin stomped out of the room and charged into the living room. Lifting Ariel's purse, she saw it was empty, save for a small bottle of sanitizer from Bethel & Morris Retirement Center.

"Son of a—" Sin's phone began to ring. "Now he calls," she mumbled as she held up her finger to her sister and went into Nia's bedroom to answer.

Nia followed her with questions she needed answered, but when she opened her mouth to ask, Sin slammed the door in her face. With her hands on her hips, Nia breathed deeply several times.

Y'all better stop slamming doors in my face.

She puffed and blew curls from her damp forehead.

Lord, please let everything work out okay. Don't let this be Karma for treating Deacon so mean. I repent.

Chapter Fourteen

Sin

Sin flopped on Nia's bed. She listened and responded—her earpiece blinking—as she tossed the small sanitizer bottle up and down in her hand. "Yes, Boss. I know, Boss. My apologies. Yes, I understand that my apologies do crap for you, sir."

Her boss was tough but fair. However, the taste of being so close to figuring out a move against the Council, an organization they had chased for years—he'd pursued them with unrelenting determination before she even joined the agency—had her boss's attitude on rector status. And she wasn't mad at his attitude. She got it.

But her mind was churning. She had lost their informant. And after the fiasco of a handoff at the library, she was loath to tell him. Never failing an assignment had been her badge of pride. She had to recoup her losses. She just had to. Tuning back in, she tried to explain her actions.

"Sir?" The bark of his answer sent an unwanted shudder over her body. "The package has fled."

The screaming and expletives that assaulted her ears had Sin standing and then leaning against the wall. She folded her arms with a hung head as her boss read her for filth. Finally, he took a breath, and she tried to explain.

"Well, since I came to help her, I didn't think she'd run. She was spooked, I guess. As I mentioned at the beginning of this conversation, sir, she didn't know where she had lost the original package. But what she had instead was a library book." Closing her eyes, she felt the pressure of Pop pushing to come out. Pop didn't like how he was talking to her, but Sin knew she deserved it, so she held Pop at bay. She didn't need a written reprimand because of Pop cursing him out. The day had been a mess of errors. And she had lost their informant! She had no excuses to give. She needed to put on her big-girl panties and take these ego blows.

Sighing, she continued to grovel as she lay down on her back. "Yes, sir, I should have secured the premises. I should have considered she would be feeling vulnerable." Sin rolled to the side and rubbed her butt to see if the feeling of having it chewed out had actually taken place. It felt like it. Inhaling as her agent in charge bellowed even more into her ear, she pulled her mind back to business. He wanted results, and she would deliver them.

She then thought about her fellow agents who had never answered her calls. Contrite, she said, "How many did we lose?"

On the other end of the phone, his tone shifted and became somber. "We lost one agent and had two injured. They were attacked while they were waiting for you. Local police have been scrambling to determine why most of their satellite feeds of the encounter were scrambled. In addition, there is another problem: the two feeds we tried to scramble were scrambled before we could access them. So wherever you are, whoever you're with might be compromised. You need to get out of there, and now."

Hearing that news, Sin leaped up and circled the room, starting in Nia's closet. Throwing Nia's things inside a duffel bag with workout gear spilling out, she'd spied in the corner, Sin packed for her sister. They were items she could wear and toiletries she would need for her short-term stay somewhere else. "Roger that, sir."

Stopping, she noted the label on the small sanitizer bottle lying on the bed and followed her sixth sense. "Sir, can you run a scan on Bethel & Morris Funeral Home? Check and see if our runaway has any connection there?"

"Will do. In the meantime, you work on getting my packages back, Agent!"

Clicking off, Sin came bursting out of the room. "Nia, let's go now."

Adjusting the fire under the skillet on the stove, Nia looked startled. "Go? I was going to fry this—"

Ignoring her sister's words, Sin abruptly reached over and turned off the burner. Before Nia could put the chicken back in the refrigerator, Sin dragged her out the back door of her townhouse. Thinking quickly, Nia managed to grab her satchel as she was pulled past it, groaning along the way. Following the path Ariel probably took earlier, Sin threw Nia's duffel bag over the privacy fence to her patio.

"Sin, aren't you being a little melodramatic? Why is it necessary for me to go through all of this?"

"Come on, Sis. Up and over. And before you say anything else, yes, we need to do this. Now, go."

Nia climbed on the patio chair, then the table, and hoisted herself over the privacy fence. Sin followed closely, panting anxiously to get her sister to safety.

Moving quickly down the street, Nia raised her head with her satchel strap around her neck. "I have my car keys. We can go faster if I get it."

"No. Your car could already be compromised. Keep moving. Who do you know who nobody knows you know?"

Nia turned her head to look at Sin as though she were joking. "Girl, people here barely know I have a sister. I don't let people in my life like that. I'm still the same loner, Sin."

Sin stopped. "Come on, Nia. There has to be someone."

Looking affronted that Sin would call out her lack of a life, Nia's lip trembled. "You know that I don't know people like that. Just take me with you. You've done it before."

"That was just to give you some excitement in your life. This assignment is not that."

"You mean you might really be in trouble, Sin?"

Sin slowed while still surveying the area. "I'll be fine. I need to get you somewhere safe so I can work."

"And I can't go with you?"

"No, ma'am. That's not going to happen." Sin pulled her behind a tree and looked up and down the street. "What about lover boy?"

"Deacon?" Nia screeched. "I can't call Deacon. I just totally hurt his feelings, and it would be so wrong to call him up out of the blue and ask him for assistance after dogging him out."

Sin arched her eyebrow as though Nia talked gibberish. "Girl, lower your voice and give me your phone."

Before Nia could move it out of Sin's way, she snatched it out of Nia's satchel and pushed the gym bag into Nia's hands.

Sin clicked on the number Deacon had given Nia weeks before, a number that Nia had never planned to use. It rang once. "Hello, Deacon. This is Nia's sister, Sin. We met earlier, but there is no time for niceties. Nia needs you. Can we explain in person?"

Nia tried to get closer and listen, but Sin turned her head and body away.

Seconds later, Sin hung up and looked down at the text. "Okay, that's a little way from here. We'll need a car."

Pulling the SIM card out of the phone and crushing it under

her foot, she looked around. Seeing a midsize, banged-up Buick across the street, she sprinted over with Nia tailing her. Checking the door and finding it open, Sin pushed Nia inside.

"Wait. What? You're going to steal this car?"

"Yes, so please, don't touch anything but the door handle. I can't take the time to wipe off a bunch of fingerprints."

"We're good. I've been passing this car for at least a month, and it hasn't moved. It may not even start."

Reaching beneath the dashboard, Sin hot-wired the car. Old car, old ways. As Sin pulled them onto the road, she kept her eyes on the rearview mirror. "I thought you said the man was broke. This area we're going to is known as the up-and-coming young millionaire's block."

Puzzled, Nia hunched her shoulders. "I'm not going to ask how you know that—you haven't lived here in years--but I didn't say I knew he was broke. Maybe it's his brother's place?"

"Hmm. Well, let's hope his brother is a good guy and will let you stay until I can get back to you with an all-clear. Also, you now have the flu and will not be at work for at least a week."

"Aw, man. I wanted to use my time more wisely than that."

"Nothing wiser than staying alive. Use this time to get to know Deacon. And get some steel cojones. You can't fall in love based on popular opinion. Give them all the middle finger."

Nia exhaled. "That is so you and *not* me. How about I pray about it?"

Shaking her head, Sin peered into the rearview mirror. Seeing the car from behind her turn left, she let out a sigh. "Girl, do you."

She sped up, accelerating down the highway to head back downtown. "Did you know he lived this close to the library?"

"No. I feel bad. I don't know much about him at all." Nia mumbled, "I should have asked him more questions."

Sin patted her on her hand. "You can fix that while you're there."

Pulling up, Sin and Nia looked up at the building in all its elegance. "They have valet parking and a doorman," Nia murmured, shocked.

"We can't valet park; there's no key. Plus, I'm not valet parking a 1999 banged-up Buick held together by rust."

Driving past, Sin pulled around the corner and parked at a meter. Nia reached behind her and grabbed her satchel and duffel, and they ran to the entrance after wiping the door handles. Both women slowed down before they reached the doorman and worked to calm themselves as they drew closer.

As they approached the doorman, Sin took charge. "Deacon Everette, please. He's expecting us."

"Yes, miss. He called down." The doorman then opened the door and stood back as they entered. "Go to the check-in desk, and they will let you up. You will need to show ID."

Sin caught Nia's eyes as she slightly shook her head when they approached the desk. The security guard sat behind a bank of monitor screens on every side of the building. Sin knew he'd watched them get out of the battered car and run around to the front of the building.

His smirk telegraphed his opinion that they didn't belong in this building. "ID, please," he barked.

"Whoa! Why the attitude?" Sin said, searching through her purse. "Oh, man." She frantically started pulling out items, flipping them over, and dumping out the rest of their contents. Patting her face in distress, Sin grimaced, "I'm so sorry. I don't have my ID. Could you please call up and ask Deacon to come down? Thank you."

Stoic, the security guard said emotionlessly, "Not our policy to call up yet. First, you'll need to show your IDs."

Nia then tried with a softer tone. "Sir, we left in a hurry and don't have them. Could you please call upstairs?"

"Lady, you haven't even bothered to look in your purse. No. We are not allowed to bother the owners."

Exasperated, Nia whined. "But the doorman just said Deacon had called downstairs, alerting you we were coming."

Standing to his full six feet, the guard flexed his muscles and power. "I said no."

Sin was tired. She needed to get back out there and wanted nothing more than to put this man on his back. But she could not draw more attention to them. She had to be strategic.

Then another man appeared next to her.

"Is there a problem here, Tony?" a good-looking man, blond and in his late twenties or early thirties, questioned the guard.

"No, nothing to concern yourself with. Have a nice day, sir."

Sin wished she had more time to appreciate the good-looking specimen beside her, but she had other priorities.

As the man turned to leave, he did a double take at one of them. "Nia?"

"Jonesy?" Looking away from the guard, she had been giving her best scowl, Nia gave a slow grin of relief. Turning to Sin, she said, "This is Deacon's brother."

Sin gave him a smile of pure pleasure. "Great. Well, there you go, Tony. Jonesy will escort us upstairs."

Looking at Nia as though something in his mouth had soured, Jonesy glowered. "No, I will not take you to see my brother." He then moved around Sin and stood in front of Nia, growling. "Why are you here?"

Sin couldn't believe this guy had rudely sidestepped her to confront Nia. His back to her face, she gripped a pressure point on the back of his neck and squeezed. To his credit, Jonesy didn't go down, but he swayed back, and his face contorted with pain.

"Don't ever get in a lady's face like that, especially when her sister has her back."

Twisting around, Jonesy stepped toward Sin when the bank of elevators opened, and Deacon appeared in his lounging joggers. "Nia, I am waiting for you," he shouted, clearly worried.

He then mumbled and inhaled. Swallowing hard, he said, "Why are you still at the front desk, Nia?"

From where Sin stood, she saw Tony's expression shift—from smug satisfaction to uneasy guilt—as Deacon's agitation started to simmer.

"That's on me, Bro," Jonesy said. "I'm bringing them up now."

Deacon nodded. "You weren't here when they called, Jonesy. How would you know to bring them up?"

Jonesy stammered, "Because I know my brother when it comes to Nia."

Deacon walked up close, a whisper space from Jonesy's ear. He growled low. "I know you, too, Jonesy. Be good or be gone, brother."

Sin bubbled with laughter that she caught in her throat as she snapped her mouth tight when Jonesy lifted a sharp brow at her with an intense, penetrating glower. Giving Jonesy a cutesy pout, Sin pulled Nia along. "Come on, Ladybug."

Sin watched Deacon stare at his brother, then at Tony. His eyes drilled both with lightning intelligence.

Ain't nothing wrong with this man, Sin thought. Baby Sis may have a winner if she can get out of her own way.

Sin pushed Nia in front of her away from Jonesy's intimidating glare. Nia walked toward the elevators as directed. Sin followed behind Jonesy while Deacon brought up the rear.

As Deacon stepped back, only Sin caught his quiet words to Tony. "You laughed at me behind my back. Thought my silence made me weak, yours to punk. I didn't care. But what you won't do—what I won't let you do—is disrespect my lady."

Sin turned in time to see Deacon level a steady gaze at Tony, so calm it was chilling. And just like that, the color drained from Tony's face.

Jonesy waved his digital card on the scanner, and the elevator silently glided open. He nodded at his brother as Deacon caught up and pressed close to Nia.

When they entered, only Sin beamed a bright, knowing smile as the doors slid closed. "Shoot, child, give Sis a cup of some different with a fine o' man sprinkled on top," she murmured.

She jumped slightly when Jonesy leaned in and whispered, "Not in this life."

Chapter Fifteen

Deacon

They all bounded into Deacon's apartment. He was agitated with how the evening had unfolded, including waiting to hear what was wrong that caused Nia to come to him for safety. He understood that much from Sin's hurried last whispered words. *"We're in trouble; it could be life or death."*

The words hit harder than he expected, and the silence that followed stretched into forty agonizing minutes. Unable to take it any longer, he went downstairs, restless and raw. When he saw Nia at the front desk, shoulders slumped and expression drained, something in him tightened. She looked like she'd already lost—before she'd even begun.

He had withstood bullies all his life. When he was young, Curtis Jackson was determined to make his life miserable, but Jonesy intervened. Jonesy fought Curtis on his behalf and afterward went into proactive mode.

Jonesy taught him every form of martial arts, street fighting, and plain old butt stomping that he knew. Raised in an extremist camp, Jonesy was well-versed in the fine art of street war. When Curtis Jackson's mother named him after the rapper 50 Cent, she had no idea that before the year was out, Deacon would be handing her back her son with change left on the half dollar.

Ironically, when Deacon took Curtis down, it wasn't for himself. It was for Jonesy—his half-brother, but closer to him than most full-blood siblings ever got.

Once, Curtis and his boys had caught Jonesy alone. The damage showed in his swollen eye, the blood crusting around his nose, and the gash splitting his forehead. And Curtis? He was a block away, bragging about the ambush as if he were proud.

Deacon still remembered the sound of Curtis laughing as he came running up the street toward him. "What's this little retard about to do?" he cackled, full Chris Rock energy, loud enough for the whole block to hear.

Curtis's boys stepped forward like they were ready for round two, but he waved them off with a sneer.

"What's the matter with you fools? I look like I need backup to handle this little freak? Let the kid do what he came to do."

He spread his feet wide and tapped his chin, daring Deacon to take the shot.

Deacon didn't blink.

The side thrust kick landed so cleanly against Curtis's jaw that it silenced the sidewalk. Before anyone could react, Deacon followed up with a strike to his throat. Curtis stumbled, choking.

The rest of the crew froze, mouths open, paralyzed between awe and indecision. Curtis had just told them to stand down. Now, they were caught between loyalty and self-preservation.

Then, screeching tires.

Jones Everette Sr. pulled up, Jonesy jumping out behind him, his nose still stuffed with bloody tissue.

Jones Sr. stared down each boy like he had their rap sheets memorized. "You boys looking to get into something you don't want any part of?"

One of them—the biggest—reached down to help Curtis off his knees. "Man, we don't even know this li'l freak. He came running outta nowhere and started messing with us."

Jonesy growled, blood on his teeth. "Stop calling my brother a freak. He ain't no freak."

Jones Sr. stepped forward slowly and deliberately. "Son," he said to the big one, "I take offense to you calling my child out of his name. He's not a freak. He's smarter than most of you standing here—and being Black, you should know just because someone is not used to you doesn't mean you should mistake them as less."

He turned to Deacon, then placed a steadying hand on his shoulder. But Deacon wasn't done. His eyes were locked on Curtis, who finally looked back—not with mockery, but fear.

Not a drop of sweat clung to Deacon. Not a ruffled breath, not a mark. Just stillness and a look that made Curtis flinch.

"Come on, son," Jones Sr. said. "Let's go home. You showed them not to mess with the Everettes."

He looked at the others, his voice still calm but carrying steel. "I trust this ends all past, present, and future interactions between you and my family. I teach my sons peace—but I'm not above reminding people that sometimes, peace has teeth."

He circled around to the car. "Get in, boys. Your mother's got dinner waiting."

Deacon turned to go, and Curtis, desperate to save face, did the unthinkable. He kicked Deacon from behind.

Time stopped.

Jones Sr. didn't speak. He just nodded.

Deacon whirled. No hesitation. No mercy.

Two punches wiped the smirk off Curtis's face. Two more sank into his gut. Curtis hit the pavement, wheezing, reaching for air that wouldn't come.

On his knees, Curtis struggled to stand, all the while trying to catch his breath. With little emotion, Deacon knocked him back down. As he flopped over—like a fish on dry land—Deacon stomped him.

Arms came around his middle, lifting him off Curtis. "Enough, son. Jonesy, pick up the boy and put him in the car."

The crowd of young men fell back. Jonesy lifted Curtis as Deacon hung his head. "They beat up Jonesy because of me, Dad. I had to," Deacon said.

Everette put his arm around Deacon, and Deacon stepped back. "It's okay, son. Some people only know violence as their teacher. We'll take the boy home."

Later, when they walked Curtis to his door, no one said a word. Curtis's legs wobbled, one eye swelling shut, his breath still ragged from trying to recover.

The door creaked open before they could knock.

His mother stood there, her housecoat clutched at her chest, rollers in her hair, eyes sharp enough to slice. She took one look at Curtis and didn't even ask what happened.

Her gaze flicked to the boys, full of venom. Her eyes narrowed as she looked them over. "You must be real proud of yourselves. Bringing my boy back like trash off the street."

Deacon felt Jonesy tense beside him, but their father's hand came down on his shoulder—a silent order to stay calm.

Her hate felt physical as they turned and walked away.

Behind them, the door slammed, followed by the muffled, rhythmic thumps of something hard connecting with flesh. "Let them bring you here like you're nothing? I'll teach you, boy!"

Then Curtis's voice—pleading, breathless. "Ma—Ma, wait—Ma, I—"

The sound cut off with a cry that made Deacon wince.

He didn't look back.

None of them did.

Hurrying down the steps, Deacon remarked, "She smells like Auntie's cabbage."

They tried smiling, but what they heard made them hurt for Curtis Jackson. It made Deacon sad for days. He'd never liked violence and was glad later when he overheard his dad reporting her to Child Protective Services. Curtis would be seventeen soon, but maybe something could be done.

Deacon shook the memory from his mind. He knew if he needed to, he could give Tony something he wasn't ready for, but he had determined people like Tony were to be pitied. They only ever saw the obvious and failed to see the minute details that made someone special. Deacon had learned from the best, his mother, that he was "fearfully and wonderfully made." The world just wasn't equipped to see it. He still had hope in his heart that Nia would see past his 'isms.

Sitting on the edge of a deep leather club chair, Deacon watched Nia take it all in. Her gaze swept the room like she was trying to match it with the man she thought she knew.

The space was open and deliberate—walls of exposed brick softened by linen drapes the color of sand. A charcoal-gray sectional, sleek yet plush, stretched along one side of the room, anchored by a modern glass coffee table with brushed-metal legs. Above it, an abstract painting in layered blues and ochres pulled the eye, almost pulsing in the warm lamplight.

Everything smelled faintly of cedar and clean linen.

Thanks to his mother, Linette, the space was designed with a purpose: masculine without being cold. Cool blue and beige tones layered in texture across the throw pillows, area rug, and minimalist decor—each element chosen to calm and quiet the mind. It was the kind of place built for someone who needed a peaceful home.

And Nia felt it. Her body eased. Her shoulders lowered. She liked it.

And he liked that she liked it.

"Nice place you have, Jonesy," Sin said, glancing around before drifting over to the oversized picture window that framed a sweeping view of downtown Columbus. Lights glittered like a moving constellation below.

Jonesy folded his arms and frowned. "Not my place. I live next door."

Nia turned toward Deacon, her brows knitting in confusion. "Deacon?"

He was a little disappointed in her. "It's mine, Nia. You've never asked what I do for a living. I never said I was broke—you assumed it."

Nia's head dropped in acceptance of her shortcomings. Sin then stepped forward and said, "So, enlighten us. What do you do?"

Deacon looked over at Jonesy, who made a grunting sound as though objecting to Deacon telling them anything more about himself. In defiance, Deacon blurted, "I'm a geneticist."

Sin and Nia exchanged looks, and Sin chuckled. "Okay, what is it you *do*?"

Deacon gave an answering grin. "I analyze and research genes." He studied their puzzled faces. Then he turned toward Nia. "You know how the traits of families are inherited? I also identify and study gene disorders. I specialize in engineering, Nia. This includes developing genetically modified organisms known as GMOs for agriculture, and creating therapeutic proteins, or gene therapy for treating genetic disorders."

"They still don't have a clue about what you do. Or how much you do," Jonesy snorted.

Nia clasped her hands together. "No, I get some of it. That's wonderful, Deacon."

Jonesy grunted. "Is he acceptable now?"

Her cheeks red-tinged, Nia shook her head. "Uh, I never meant for him to feel like I didn't accept him." She rose and sat beside Deacon on the couch. "I guess I need to address the elephant in the room, but I think the conversation belongs between Deacon and me, and I will discuss it with him when we're alone." She lightly touched Deacon's hand. "Is that all right with you?" she murmured.

A smile brightening his face, Deacon spoke as though broadcasting it to the world. "I'm good with that."

Shaking his head as though all was lost, Jonesy marched toward the door. Sin followed but asked. "Can I use your bathroom before I leave? Knock some of this dirt off me?"

Jonesy backed up, pointing down a hallway. "This way."

"Thought you were going?" Sin could be heard sniping.

"Right after you," Jonesy sniped back.

Deacon shook his head. "You have to excuse my brother. He's super protective."

"Sin's the same. I think the pot just matched its lid."

Coming back up the hall, still sniping at each other, Jonesy said, "We'll be leaving now."

Sin nodded, acknowledging, "That's my cue to leave you, good people. Deacon, Nia will fill you in on what's happening, and I will check back with you both. I memorized your phone number from Nia's cell and will be in touch. Ladybug, don't worry about me. I got this."

They watched as their siblings rushed out the door.

Deacon then called out, "Secure."

His alarm system answered. "Door locked, alarm set, sentry on, Deacon."

Delighted, Nia asked, "You have a smart home? You're full of surprises."

Deacon grinned. "I was always fascinated by artificial intelligence and tinkered with it in college. However, then genetics became my primary focus. As someone biracial who thinks and processes information differently, I had a lot of isms to overcome: ableism, racism, and people's issues with me. On top of that, people seemed to need me to pick one label, so do I consider myself Black or white? It bothered me that people are so fixated on skin color instead of what truly makes a person who they are—their soul. I've wondered how much our genetic makeup determines our personalities. Is it nature or nurture? Studies on twins suggest that nature may play a greater role than previously thought. I had so many questions on the hows and whys of who we are."

"I hadn't connected any of those points of view to you. Hearing all you just said, choosing to be a geneticist makes sense."

"Half my life has been crafted around others' opinions of my being atypical. I'm not unaware that I'm sometimes an odd duck—"

"Wait, Deacon, no—"

"It's okay, and it will help if you don't interrupt me. Please allow me to get this all out, Nia Lewis."

"Apologies . . ."

Deacon squared his shoulders. He was determined to push through his thoughts. This wasn't easy for him, and he wanted to get it over with as soon as possible. "I. Am. Neurodivergent. Studies indicate some cases of neurodiversity, like ADHD and autism, are heavily dependent on genetics. I like to explain it as I process information differently."

Deacon paused, searching for any indication that Nia was

repulsed by his admission. *Does she understand how hard this is for me, this bearing of my vulnerabilities?*

He couldn't read her expression, so he continued. "My mom heard it all as we went from doctor to doctor. One day, at the end of another appointment, she clapped her hands and said, 'Enough.' She decided I didn't need to fit the world's norms to live in it. She committed to loving me as I am. When the school and family members badgered her for a diagnosis, she refused to comply. She just said, 'We don't use labels; the world does.'"

Quiet settled over the room. Deacon's pulse beat rapidly as he waited to see if Nia would finally say something.

"I shouldn't have mistreated you, Deacon."

Exhaling, Deacon waited to see if Nia would speak her truth. He was hoping his vulnerability would unlock hers. "I can be timid. I get anxious even thinking about what others think about me. Sometimes, I live in the constant replay of the day's events. Were they judging me? Did I say that right? It gets overwhelming. My mind whirls in my imagination. I love books because they never judge me."

"Of course they don't. They can't." Deacon then stopped when Nia's face tensed at his comment. "I'm not judging you, Nia. I think you're wonderful. But I also think you're a coward. How come you're like that, Nia?"

Deacon's face scrunched as Nia's caramel complexion blossomed into a reddish hue for the second time that night. Her voice trailed off as she leaned forward, her elbows resting on her knees, and her chin cradled in her folded hands. "We moved around a lot. It wasn't so hard when I was younger, but as I got older, I went through a gangly stage: all buck teeth, wild eyebrows, and knobby knees. I had zits across my forehead, and I stumbled over my words when I was nervous. Others laughed at the new kid. When they met Sincere, she was always so poised and self-assured.

She was the life of every party, and when they met her little sister, the disappointment was always clear. I distanced myself more and more from that disappointment until I learned to live in my books."

Deacon reached over and took her hand away from her chin and tightly enfolded it in his. He held their clasped hands up. "I find it amazing that I can touch you freely like this. I have problems sometimes with touch—the level of pressure matters. So, I hold tight. I press firm. It's the first thing I notice when we touch that you hold me secure, Nia. Maybe it won't always be that way. This connection . . . Some days, maybe it'll be too much. But maybe you won't mind if you know it's not you; it's me, right?"

Nia giggled, then covered her mouth. "I think that's a movie. *It's Not You, It's Me.*"

"I don't watch movies, Nia."

"Oh. Well, no, Deacon, I won't feel it's me. You've explained so much, and I feel I know you better now."

"We can work on that, learning each other even more . . . Discovering what we have in common." Deacon moderated his tone when he felt his anxiousness sounded like he was pleading.

Breathing softly, Nia said, "I'd like that."

Deacon pressed his palm gently to the small of her back. That was as far as he went—close, but not wrapped up. He didn't do arms-around-him closeness. Never had. The sensation of being held too tightly made his chest constrict as if the air might disappear.

But Nia? He needed her near. And for now, that palm, that quiet contact, was enough.

"Now," he said, his voice low but steady, "tell me what you and your sister are running from."

Nia exhaled slowly, the weight of the past few hours still settling over her shoulders.

She nodded, her arms hugging herself instead of reaching for him, like she sensed the boundary without being told.

"I don't know everything," she said. "But when the shoot-out occurred at the library today, I had an innate sense that Sin was involved. And it worried me."

He gave a slight nod.

"But this is Sin, and it's always been the other way around, her taking care of me. And as much as I know, her job is dangerous; she keeps it light, so I keep it light. It's our thing. Plus, other things were happening at work, and it all got overwhelming."

"Go on," Deacon said.

"Sin's a government agent. It's all hush-hush, but she told me to share it with you, so I'll keep it simple. Two hours ago, she showed up at my door with this woman. She was beautiful in that icy, high-maintenance way—blond hair tangled but still somehow shining like it belonged in a commercial. Even dirty, she had a certain panache, like trouble in designer heels. But her mouth . . ." Nia paused, recalling it. "Her mouth was brutal. Not just what she said but how she said it. Like she was used to cutting people off before they got too close. Her eyes—wintry. Like whatever was behind them wasn't interested in people, just outcomes. She made my skin crawl, but she was important to Sin, so I let her in."

"You're a good sister."

"Sin was supposed to protect or bring her into her agency. I'm unsure which, but the lady went to the bathroom and took off through a window. Sin needs to find her because whoever she is, bad people are after her, and now, after us. My sister got off a phone call, and we ran here—"

Nia stopped talking and turned to Deacon. "You can't repeat this, not even to your brother. Can you do that?"

"For you? Of course. I want you to know you can count on me, Nia, for any and everything."

"Okay, you're trusting me by providing a safe place. I need to trust you too. You see, Sin's part of a covert government security agency. Not even my parents know. I hate to say it, but I don't know how dangerous this could get and that we might have brought danger to your door. She's never involved me before in anything this important. Initially, I wasn't *that* worried. Sin is a bit of a badass—sorry—I don't know any other way to describe her. But pulling me out of my apartment like that? I don't know what to think of any of this," she rushed.

"Breathe, Nia."

"Right." Nia took a deep breath and continued, "I keep to myself. Most folks don't even know I have a sister, but if she's taking this kind of precaution, I could be compromised. And *if* they are looking for me, they wouldn't think of looking for me here, of all places. The rumor is that our McDonald's date did not go well."

"Oh, so you are admitting it was a date?" he said, feeling like maybe the danger she was in might be his big break.

"Seems kinda silly, now. But yes, it was a date," she answered. But still stuck in their predicament, she mumbled, "I pray they aren't looking for me or find me here."

Deacon didn't want her to stress. "Even if they do, Nia. I got you. Because of my job and the special projects I work on, Jonesy has been a pain about keeping me safe. He's not just my brother but also my driver and bodyguard. I know a little something too."

Smiling, Nia stood. "Let me earn my keep. If you're like me, in all the excitement, I didn't eat. If you show me your kitchen, I'll make us something."

"Hmm, can you cook, or will I need a stomach pump?" he teased.

"Is Aunt Jemima on the pancake box?"

"No, she's not." Deacon cackled loudly and then quickly covered his mouth. "Sorry."

Taking his hand from his mouth, Nia shook her head. "No, Deacon. I'm the one who owes you an apology. A loud, open laugh is good for the soul. If I ever made you feel otherwise, I apologize. Come on, let's go see what's in your fridge."

Grinning broadly, Deacon led the way. He wondered as they maneuvered through his home if one day she would allow him to lead her to his heart.

Chapter Sixteen

Sin

Sin was pissed. And she loved it. The angrier she got, the better her
brain operated. When her brain was at optimal performance, her
eyes were keener, her hand steadier, and her senses razor-sharp.
She'd been chasing the Council for too many years to fall short
now. The cat-and-mouse games were tiresome, but she'd been here
before. Ariel would heel to the agency's demands or face the
consequences. Touching her earpiece, she whispered, "Going in
hot."

"Roger."

Scaling the roof of the retirement home, she swooped into the
same window as the dark figure thirty seconds before her. He crept,
and she followed each step. The days of sneaking out of base
housing and off base as a teenager had paid dividends over the
years. Even her sister never knew the number of times she was
AWOL. Smirking, Sin was startled when her secondary target
swiveled and shot his silencer, taking out the large Peace lily plant
to her immediate right. Her ballerina-practiced jeté placed her
directly in a position to kick the gun from his hand when he

immediately threw his left hand out, swiping across her torso with a dual-edged blade. She danced back and counterpunched him in the back of his head as she pivoted around him. Even with his knife dancing in the air like a serpent ready to strike, she heard movement in the other room. It could have been their grunts or the Peace lily crashing, but her primary target should have been in REM sleep mode. Her informant reported that the granny was almost deaf, but instead, it sounded as if someone was on the move.

Let me out, Sin.

No, stand down, Pop. I got this.

You got zilch without me.

Sin wasn't used to shaking off Pop. But Pop was becoming more insistent, more often, and she had to rein her in, even if it meant her handling things she had handed over to Pop in the last few years. The headaches to control her were becoming arduous, and Sin was not above a power play to teach Pop a lesson.

You come out when I say so.

Sin was handling this Council agent, and playtime was over. Unfortunately, her opponent felt the same way because they both pulled weapons and fired. Sincere knew the God her mother loved was answering her prayers when he only grazed her shoulder, and hers landed its mark dead center. A dull ache centered in her chest. It wasn't something she wanted to do, but when they both fired simultaneously, Sin's bullet to maim . . . killed.

See, Sin, you shoulda let me handle it and kept your hands clean.

Shutting Pop out and inhaling, she walked over and pulled off his mask. Surprise flitted across her face as she discovered he was a she when beautiful auburn hair cascaded out from under her skullcap. Checking for a pulse and finding her assailant had a faint beat, Sin felt a bulletproof vest. Fast and sure, she pricked her adversary's neck with a small needle filled with a sleep potion.

Resting back on her heels, she stared at the woman's delicate features. Maybe they could get something out of her if she survived, but she doubted it. She felt off her game somehow. Not considering her adversary was another woman made her feel old-fashioned. She had lost Ariel and had no idea Umber was seeing someone else. Maybe she wasn't the top agent in the field anymore if her professional and personal life were in shambles.

She leaped to her feet and spun when she heard a slight movement behind her. Not seeing anything, she darted toward what she thought must be the foyer of the large apartment. There at the door, she intercepted her primary. Ariel, ex-mistress of Eric Rothwell, one of the identified men she had been watching for five long years, was once more trying to outwit her by slipping out the front door no less. Sin was getting pretty fed up with this chick.

"Uh-uh-uh. No, you don't." Sin's demand was matched by her grip on her escapee's forearm.

"Let me go!" screamed a panicked Ariel.

"Girl, I've been working on this case for too long to keep fooling with you. Sit yo' gold-digging butt down." Pulling her into an elegant dining room, Sin then looked around the beautiful retirement village condo. "But, chile, at least you got the heart to do your granny right. This is niceeee. 'Scuse me." Sin tapped her earpiece and said, "Clean up on aisle one. She's a sleeper."

She lowered her hand from her com, and her mouth gaped open at the woman tapping her high-heeled foot rigorously.

Sin howled with laughter. "How you tryin'a run in red bottoms?"

Ariel folded her arms, tilting her head away from Sin while rolling her eyes. Sin knew if looks could kill, she'd be casket-ready. Sighing, she got on with it. "You're something else. All that weeping and sniveling you did . . . I can see how you got these men feenin' on you. You're one Oscar-worthy actress."

Sin's eyes widened as a look of pleasure covered Ariel's face. Swaying seductively, she bit her bottom lip. "Yes, daddy. Oooh, daddy. You're the best, daddy."

Digging her fingers into Ariel's arm, she snarled, "But Mama's here. There is no daddy." Sin then dug her fingers harder. "Where is it?"

Ariel shuddered, her eyes telegraphing pain. She grimaced and then stared solemnly at Sin before a sly grin slowly spread across her face. "You have no idea what you're looking for, do you?"

Startled that Ariel hadn't buckled, Sin kept her poker face. "Why don't you tell me?"

"'Cause I don't share for free."

Releasing her arm, Sin stepped forward inches from Ariel's nose. "Baby, I just incapacitated a person before they killed you. I have paid. I'm asking—no—I'm telling you, pay up. Besides, you ought to realize they won't stop coming. I'm sure that their second team is on their way."

"I can take care of myself."

"But can your granny?"

A knock on the door caught Sin's attention. She opened it, and two black ops stepped in, moving past them to the body in the next room. After bending over and lifting the prone woman, they moved to the window that still stood ajar. One went out the window, and the second came behind with the body and clipped it to a hanging harness. Two minutes later, they were gone, and the window closed behind them.

Sneering, Ariel asked, "Why use the door at all?"

Sin grinned. "To show you we can come and go however we want. Plus, I'm sure they lowered her right into a waiting medical vac."

"Well, isn't that just—" Ariel froze when a weak voice called out from the back bedroom. Holding her finger up pleadingly, she rushed from the room.

Distrustful of her motives, Sin followed her, remaining concealed in the shadows of the hallway. From afar, she observed a frail figure adorned with wisps of gray hair peeking out from beneath a silk bonnet.

"Nana, you should be resting," Ariel whispered.

"How, with your friends making so much racket?"

Sin saw Ariel pulling the blanket around her Nana's shoulders when a pale hand slapped Ariel's hand away. "Stop fussing over me, Betty. What have you gotten yourself into?"

"Betty?" Sin snickered.

"It's Ariel, Nana. Remember?"

"I remember you always getting yourself into trouble. I remember you don't have a job, but you have me in this highfalutin seniors' building. I'm not dumb, Betty."

Ariel whispered frantically, "It's Ariel, Nana, please."

"Uh-huh." The weathered, veined hand clutched Ariel's tight. "You're all I got left, little bird. Don't you be flying too high to the sun."

"Oh, Nana, I love you." Turning and locking eyes with Sin, Ariel urged, "I'm going to need you to put some clothes on for a little ride, Nana."

The small woman rose with surprising energy. "Just take me down to the second floor. Mildred will take me in for a little bit. I can let her try to beat me in UNO. And I can figure out who might come looking for you. While the dog is chasing the fox, let's get the little chickadee to safety. How about that?"

Ariel's eyes wide, she reluctantly nodded.

Nana tutted. "Now, don't be acting surprised. I have been loving you since you were a sparkle in your daddy's eyes and you were giving your momma heartburn. You not slick. I know you, child, and you can't run from whoever's hunting you with an old woman like me in tow. I'd hold you back. Remember, I know a little bit about running and hiding, and I'll weigh you down."

Tenderness oozed from Ariel as she held her granny to her. "Don't you give up on me, Nana. I'm working to make some things right."

Watery eyes turning sharp, Nana snapped. "What's that mean, Betty?"

Ariel blew a kiss to her grandmother before urgently saying, "Hurry now, Nana. There isn't much time left."

Leaving the room, she glared at Sin, who had a crooked smile on her lips.

"Well, *Betty*, we'll give your grandmother time to dress and then escort her downstairs. Get what you need. I'll check in with my boss, and then we're out. You told your Nana correctly. Our time has run out."

Pulling off her red bottoms as she walked barefoot down the hall, Ariel admonished, "And while you're calling in, why don't you not? Someone on your team is a mole for the Council. I want to stay alive if that's all right with you."

Sin held her tongue because the girl wasn't wrong. Her request to check out the hand sanitizer had unearthed Ariel's grandmother. It was only a few hours ago, and the assailant was already in Nana's apartment when she arrived.

She wasn't sure who had snitched, but somebody was playing dirty, and Sin could smell the foul odor of betrayal blowing her way. She was glad she had never revealed where she had left Nia. As long as Nia lay low with Deacon, she at least didn't have to worry about her.

Chapter Seventeen

Deacon

Patting his mouth on the napkin, Deacon burped. "Excuse me, Nia."

"I take that as a compliment." Nia stood, picked up Deacon's plate, and placed it on hers. She then returned to the kitchen to put the dishes in the dishwasher.

Deacon watched her body naturally sway as her stocking feet silently walked along the cherrywood floors. He wondered if he dared try to kiss her—and if he did—if she would allow it. Courting someone you cared about was new to him. He understood bodily functions were part of natural biological needs. But the fluttering of his heart and the sweating on his upper lip only happened with Nia. Moving from the table, he hurried to the living room's sectional and sat as he waited.

Rubbing his damp hands back and forth on his thighs, Deacon eyed her return. He watched her closely when she noticed he had moved. He now sat in the middle of the couch with room on either side of him for her to sit.

What will she do? Come closer or hide?

Hesitantly, she followed and sat at the end of the sofa.

Hmm, hiding.

"You good, Nia?" Deacon said, noting her nervousness.

Nodding, she bit her lip.

Deacon scooted closer. He wanted to use his fidget rings, but it was important for him to make her comfortable, not show her he was uncomfortable.

Nia scooted away, closer to the arm of the couch she was already leaning against.

Secretly amused, Deacon inched a smidgen more.

This song and dance went on while both watched the other from the corner of their eyes.

"You're going to end up on the floor, Nia," Deacon complained.

"Oh! Uh . . . ahem."

Deacon gently placed his hand on Nia's knee. "Are you scared of me, Nia? I'm not a dangerous person. Mama taught me a long time ago, no means no. Are you saying no to kissing me?"

"Why'd you have to say it like that?"

"Say it like what?" he blurted.

"All out in the open, Deacon."

Deacon groaned. "This is where I don't understand. I like you. But you run hot and cold. I want to kiss you. It was nice last time." Deacon's hands flew into the air, and he quickly pulled them down. He lowered his voice. "Don't you want to kiss me, too? You have beautiful lips, Nia."

Swallowing, Nia nodded. Then she put her hand up against Deacon's chest. "I haven't done anything like this in a while. My last date stole my wallet while I was in the bathroom. I haven't done online dating since."

Deacon lifted his hand and drew his finger down her nose, then traced her plush lips. "You are so beautiful," he whispered.

Nia visibly gulped, then breathed, "You're very handsome."

Leaning forward, Deacon placed his lips on Nia's and didn't move them. As Nia trembled, Deacon slowly moved his lips against hers. His heart exploded in a drummed rhythm inside his shirt, and he believed it was in the calypso beat of Nia's. Thigh to thigh, lip to lip, hands firmly entwined. Deacon was sure he was home.

Their united sigh was what both needed to hear.

Sitting next to each other on the sofa, they watched a Netflix show from the distended TV screen that lowered from the ceiling. TV shows and movies weren't his thing, but Nia was. It felt so easy, the two of them sitting here. Deacon didn't want to make Nia uncomfortable, but he needed her to know how his behaviors might affect her. He felt that since he had shared that he was neurodivergent, he should let her know what that meant because everyone functioned uniquely. Pressing his thigh against hers, he was pleased that he only felt pleasure.

"I like being close to you like this, Nia. However, I cannot promise to always maintain this level of intimacy. Sometimes, I freeze up, and I don't want it. Like anyone else, I have my days. Another example is a person putting their arm heavily around my shoulders; I can feel imprisoned. You already know I can become loud. I know when we went to McDonald's, I embarrassed you. I'll try not to do that, but I must admit I've always done it. " Deacon smiled, " It's part of my charm."

Nia exhaled loudly. And Deacon wasn't sure what it meant. Did it mean he was too much? Was it a sigh of relief that she could handle what he told her, and they could be in a relationship? Deacon didn't know. And at this point, they were touching, in his home, together. He was going to let it alone.

Time passed as they continued to sit, pressed together like fitted puzzle pieces, watching a silly movie on the theater wall monitor. Deacon was not interested in the film; he was interested in Nia.

Soon, the credits rolled, but Nia hadn't moved. The movie had become little more than background noise, a hum against the pulse of tension still hanging in the air. She sat beside him on the couch, her knee barely brushing his, her presence soft and close. She wasn't holding him, not crowding, just there.

Deacon didn't mind it. Not tonight.

His arm stretched across the back of the couch, not quite touching her, but near enough in reach if she needed. That kind of space was essential to him. He wasn't always able to be held. The feeling of someone wrapping their arms around him, boxing him in, made his chest tight like the air might leave the room if he didn't escape fast enough.

But this? This worked.

And the reality was, after spending so much time alone, he wanted everything with Nia to last. Like ice-cold lemonade on a 97-degree weather day. She brought relief.

He settled into that thought when Nia's voice broke the quiet. "Can I ask you something?"

He tilted his head toward her, giving her the room to speak.

"All the times you came to the library," she said, her tone light but curious, "you never let on how successful you are. Why?"

Deacon's eyes flicked to the blank TV screen before drifting back to her. "Why would I?" he said simply. "It's just . . . part of who I am." He sat forward slightly, resting his elbows on his knees, his fingers laced together. "I've always known success, even before the money. I was fed, clothed, and loved. I've never gone without, and as a man, I've built a life that lets me take care of the people I love. My family doesn't worry about bills. My dad worked construction—union jobs when I was a kid. Solid, dependable.

Now, he and my mom live on a beach where they used to vacation. Jonesy and I visit all the time."

There was pride in his voice, but it wasn't arrogant. Just steady. Rooted.

Nia blinked, studying him. "So . . . one of your parents is white?" she asked.

"Yeah. My dad."

She nodded, quiet for a beat. Then, "being Black . . . It's layered. We're not often allowed to be individuals. We carry a whole culture on our backs, like we have to prove something constantly. What's it like for you? Being biracial?"

Deacon exhaled through his nose, his fingers flexing once in thought. "It's . . . layered too," he said. "I'm biracial and neurodivergent. When people treat me a certain way, I can't always tell why. Is it my skin? My intensity? The way I move? I don't always know what part of me they're reacting to."

The words weren't bitter. Just honest.

And then, without thinking too hard, he leaned in and kissed her again. Just a brush of connection. Testing the weight of it.

He pulled back slowly, watching her reaction. She didn't move away.

Empowered, Deacon gave her a loose embrace—his version of closeness. Not wrapped, not locked. Just . . . offered. Then he let go again.

"I don't get to touch people much," he said quietly. "And right now, I don't want to stop."

Nia smiled gently. "Kissing?" she asked.

He shook his head. "Touching. This. Being next to someone without flinching. It's nice. My mom could manage it most days. But even when I was a kid . . . There were times she couldn't hold me. And she learned not to internalize it."

He felt her shift slightly, giving him space.

"Am I making you uncomfortable?" she asked.

Deacon shook his head. "No. I want this. But if tomorrow's different, I need you to know it's not about you. I have off days, that's all."

"We all do." She looked at him more intently. "You've said that a couple of times now. Is that why there are days you don't come to the library?"

"Yeah." His voice dropped. "My off days can push people away. I stim—I'll rock or bounce my leg nonstop. It unsettles people. So, I stay home. Fewer stimuli. More control. Even Jonesy gives me space on those days." He looked down, his hand slowly curling into a fist. "I've said it so much because I've lost people over it. They take it personally. They walk away."

Then her hand covered his.

She gently unwound his fingers and held them in hers—firm, warm, and grounding.

She leaned in just enough.

"So, you're saying you're a rich, moody guy, so beware?" Nia said with a lilt in her voice. "Then I guess I should make the most of it while you're feeling touchable."

A soft laugh escaped him. She was braver than she knew.

"I thought about telling you I was rich," he said quietly. "At the library. I considered it—like maybe it would make you like me."

Her brows rose. "You thought I'd be after your money?"

"No. I thought the money would make *you* feel better. About me. Because money makes people acceptable. And you . . ." He looked at her fully now, his eyes steady. "You crave acceptance. Not from me. From everyone."

Her lips parted, but he let her go and held up his hand. "Not tonight. We'll talk about that when things aren't spiraling out of control. When your sister's not in danger, and you're not carrying the weight of every room you walk into."

She nodded. Quiet. Processing.

Then his voice softened. "You didn't watch much of that movie."

Her mouth curved. "Nope."

"You're worried about Sin." She didn't need to say yes. It was written all over her face. "I have a feeling she can handle herself."

Still, he reached for her hand again. Not to hold her. To let her hold him if she needed to.

After a moment, she whispered, "Tell me about your family."

He took a breath. That was easier. Solid ground. "Jonesy's my half-brother. Same dad. Different moms. But he's mine. No questions asked. My mom's people . . . I have an uncle who's neurodivergent. Not like me, but he prepared my mom's side of the family to be accepting. My dad's side is much bigger. Blue-collar. Distant. They don't get me and don't care to try."

He looked down at their hands, hers resting inside his. "But I take care of who I love. You asked me earlier about success. That's success to me."

She traced his palm gently with her finger, slow and quiet. "You're not what I expected," she murmured.

Deacon's lips curved into something half-smile, half-understanding. "I rarely am."

Suddenly, a beeping sound filled the room. "Intruder, Deacon. Persons of unknown origin—elevator breach in your outer hallway. Please practice safety."

The alarm system blared as Deacon and Nia watched the ceiling light up like a solar system science project, causing his TV monitor to twirl to the other side. Security footage began broadcasting on six panels, each showing a different scene. Tony was slumped over his counter at the front desk. Men were standing in the lobby, and the perimeter outside of the building showed two men standing at the back near the exit door. Stunned, the two watched as six men prowled from Deacon's private elevator.

Deacon stood, his only thought to protect what he felt was his, and when he saw Nia's expression change, he did his best to normalize what he knew was a deadly countenance because how he felt always showed on his face. "Please get your things, Nia. Put your shoes on and go into my bedroom."

Jonesy appeared on the monitor screen from his home, dressed all in black with a hood over his blond hair. Methodically moving around the room, he placed two guns in his holster and added small knives to a harness on either side of his body. "I'll slow them down, Brother. We've practiced this a million times. You good?" Jonesy asked, peering into the monitor.

Deacon reached over and touched a button under the lid of his marble cocktail table. As it rose to stand equal to his waist, the lid lifted, and Deacon grabbed a holster he secured over his shoulder and two guns that he placed in their sleeves. He then put on an identical black hoodie to his brother's. It took all of two minutes. Nodding, he said, "See you later, Jonesy."

The screen went black and retreated into the ceiling. Looking at his watch, Deacon followed Nia into the bedroom.

By his estimation, they were only seconds away from ramming his front door. They couldn't, but what they could and would do next was blow it.

Entering the bedroom, he watched Nia pace, her face drained of color. Deacon preferred her cheeks to be rosy from embarrassment or passion rather than pale from fear. They would pay. He had always tried to give peace a chance, but Nia was his line in the sand.

"This way." Deacon gently grabbed her arm and entered his walk-in closet, steering her to the farthest wall. He pulled a fake tennis shoe from a rack of tennis shoes, and the wall slid up. Double doors opened, and an elevator appeared.

"Who are you?" Nia whispered as they heard a blast from the front.

Deacon pushed her in, then followed. The wall slid down, and the elevator doors shut as they plummeted down. They exited the elevator onto the side street from a door that appeared to be part of the brick facing of the building's outer wall. A black Camaro sat at the door, its engine idling as softly as air.

The tinted window rolled down, and Jonesy urged, "Move it; get in."

Stepping over a body lying on the sidewalk, Deacon said sarcastically, "No, we'll wait for another driver with a better attitude." Deacon shoved Nia into the backseat. Then he sat up front and shut the door. After that, they rolled down the street. "Well, Brother, only you would get the girl, and she would come with an extra dose of chaos," Jonesy snarked, turning to the backseat. "What have you gotten my little brother into?"

Nia sniffed as slow tears fell, her eyes as round as marbles. "I don't know. I don't!"

Deacon reached back and squeezed her hand. Turning, Jonesy met him with a questioning stare.

Ignoring his brother's unasked question, Deacon grumbled, "Leave her alone. None of this is her fault."

"How do you know that?" Jonesy yelled.

"I just know, Jonesy. Okay?" Deacon began rocking and hitting the dashboard as Jonesy continued to fuss. "Stop yelling. You know I don't like yelling." Deacon fidgeted in his seat.

Pulling down the visor, he watched Nia bite her lip and look fearfully back and forth as Jonesy yelled. Deacon hated it when his body betrayed him. His foot was rapidly tapping, and sweat leaked under his armpits. He was stimming. These impulses were signs he was losing control, something he promised himself Nia would never see. At least not yet. He pulled his rings out of his pocket, and they whirled through his fingers. Over and over.

They left the building with little time to spare, but it could have gone differently. The plan Jonesy made him drill biweekly could have failed. If just one thing had gone wrong . . . Deacon didn't dare ask Jonesy about the man lying on the sidewalk that they stepped over getting into the car. He couldn't have Nia fall apart even more.

You're okay. Nia's okay. Let Jonesy fuss. He's scared, too.

He had to pull himself together because if he lost it, Nia would never trust him as a man she could depend on. He had to show her he could handle her trouble and keep her safe. He had to be in control of this situation. Women like strong men.

Deacon breathed in and out as he looked in the visor mirror and cataloged Nia's anxiety. He saw her plump lips tremble and her eyes flutter with moisture dripping from her eyelashes. He breathed deeply to calm himself. His heart slowed.

He looked at his watch when it dinged and then opened his phone. "Jonesy, I'm watching the effects of the sleeping agent in the sprinkler system. These guys are reacting as we hoped; some are collapsing where they stand."

"Yes, and that is why they call you a genius. You tinker, and we win. I'll go up to the police station after I drop you both off. I'll pretend we weren't home, and we don't know the hows and whys of this attack. We have a small window of opportunity to move. Let's not blow it."

Deacon looked once more at Nia, huddled in a corner of the car. His lips tightened. He didn't know what to say to her, leading him to stay quiet. How do you assure someone everything is okay when unsure of it yourself?

When they pulled into the Bolton Field Airport, Jonesy's

words tumbled out as he kept his eye on his rearview mirror. "Get to Dad and Mama Linette. They know you're coming, and Dad is putting everything in place. I only told him a little, so he expects you to fill him in when you see him. I'll meet you there."

Nia climbed out but waited when Deacon did not follow. Slightly turning away from her—in a low tone—Deacon said in irritation, "Jonesy, I'm not twelve anymore. You don't have to be my hero. Let's go together."

"Nah, because whoever is after you will just keep coming. Those men were not thugs. They were trained mercenaries moving in military formation. I will have to do things you won't want me to do. So, get your lady to safety. I'll check in with you later. Oh, here," he exchanged Deacon's phone for a new one. "It's one of the new encrypted ones you designed with specific AI capability. As designed, it can detect being monitored and reroute the signal, so hackers are chasing rabbits. And here's a solar charger."

Eager, Deacon took the phone and turned it around. "It works? No more bugs, Jonesy? When did it come in?"

"It's what I went out to get from the courier when I met your lady in the lobby. I was going to show it to you when your company left," Jonesy snapped. Then Deacon saw his eyes shutter, and Jonesy exhaled as he looked over his shoulder at Nia. "If she has a phone, ditch it. We all know that SIM removal will not make the phone untraceable. If her sister calls her number, it will ring the phone I just gave you and cloak the location. Pretty cool, Little Brother." He then spoke to Nia over Deacon's shoulder. "My boy's a tinkering genius."

Deacon slid out and took Nia's hand as he pulled her toward the entrance to the debarkation point, and Jonesy peeled away. Deacon flashed his passport and simultaneously slipped money into the agent's palm. Gripping Nia tighter than before, they were quickly waved through.

Pulling back, Nia exclaimed, "You can't trust someone who can be bought. Won't they be able to track us by your passport?"

"No. Because Deacon Everette didn't bribe him and isn't flying out. Jose Mendez is. Nia, as a biracial person, people are always assigning different ethnicities to me. This time, I used it to invent this identity."

The flight attendant of the private plane met them at the door. "Hello, Mr. and Mrs. Mendez. I'm Darlene, and I'll take care of you on this flight. We hope your honeymoon will be all you want it to be. Please feel free to sit wherever you'd like. I'm so sorry to hear about your luggage being misplaced. But you're honeymooners, so who needs clothes, right?"

"Clothes are a necessity, Darlene," Deacon explained. When Nia nudged him, Deacon's eyes widened, and he leaned over and kissed her with a smack on her cheek. "Uh, except us. You're right, we don't need clothes. Not one stitch." He scrambled to lead Nia back to their seats in the middle of the plane.

The seats were lush and luxurious recliners. Deacon looked around, ensuring the flight attendant was in front, pulling out hot, steaming towels and warm cookies.

Nia took the opportunity to speak without someone listening. Furiously, she seethed, "You can't just take control without talking to me about it. Did I hear him say we were going to your parents? I don't want to meet your parents."

"Well, the timetable might be moved up, but it was going to happen anyway. Prepare yourself and buckle up. It's a long flight."

Chapter Eighteen

Sin

Ariel's incessant questioning had Sin on edge, and she was getting on her last nerve. "If you don't get away from that window . . ."

"Why are we still here?" Ariel asked for the twentieth time.

The streets around their Honeycomb Hideaway were loud and chaotic. People yelled, engines revved, car radios blasted, and stray cats darted around corners. Graffiti covered every crumbling wall . . .

"It's simple. Until I can reach my sister, we're not going anywhere," Sin vowed. "You might as well stop asking."

"Ugh!"

Sin watched Ariel flop on the worn couch. They were in the heart of the hood, in a gang-infested area where only the strong and some foolish survived. Trust in her agency waning, Sin broke down and called Umber, a man she didn't trust in love but one she could always trust to have her back on a mission. Umber had places stashed even she didn't know about. She had called him crazy when he never trusted anyone and kept his stuff close to his vest, but today, she was grateful.

On the outside, the place was a run-down hovel. But inside, it was neat. The furniture was worn but clean, and the electricity worked.

Both ladies had eaten a bowl of soup and a fried Spam sandwich, staples Umber had stored in his cabinets. The smell of the cheap fried meat was still in the air.

"What do you know about Spam, Ariel?" Sin asked when Ariel wolfed down the food.

Ariel narrowed her eyes, and sadness filled them. "Ariel may not know anything about Spam. However, Betty used to eat it way too much."

Their stomachs satisfied, both ladies were quiet, each ruminating in their heads.

Stretching, Sin's muscles tensed as a sharp, burning pain shot through her arm. She flinched and struggled to remove her jacket, dropping it onto the floor. She ripped the fabric of her shirt sleeve to free it from the dried blood gluing it to her skin. Her fingers were gentle as they steadily peeled away the cloth, revealing an angry red welt along the length of her shoulder blade.

"I almost thought you were invincible," Ariel mocked. She joined Sin to examine the wound before pronouncing, "You'll live." With a disinterested huff, she went back and lay down.

"Thank you so much for your care and concern. I'm going to the bathroom. Our host will have a first aid kit here."

"Knock yourself out. And I do mean that literally."

Sin entered the bathroom and saw the large box labeled First Aid as soon as she walked in. She opened it, and it was as well stocked as she knew it would be. Taking out a syringe, she pushed it into her arm, right below her shoulder. She was pulling out the needle and thread when Ariel appeared in the doorway.

She stomped in and, without a word, took the needle and thread from Sin and expertly began to sew her wound.

Ariel exhaled. "You're looking for a particular book."

"Well, I kinda figured that one out."

Ariel stabbed the next stitch, and Sin shut up. "It's titled *Book of Disasters*."

"*Book of Disasters*?" Sin murmured, gritting her teeth at the stab of the needle.

"Yeah. Let me tell you a little story."

"I'd appreciate a story if it helps us stop maneuvering around in the dark. We're at a big disadvantage here."

"My telling you the story won't help our advantage. These people are so deadly and big that I now wonder why I thought I could take them on." Ariel's hand trembled, then steadied. "But I had to at least try. I owed my parents that much."

Sin felt she was seeing the real Ariel for the first time, and she was Betty all along. "I'm listening."

"My dad was a great guy who came from a messed-up family. His mother, my grandmother, was the mistress of a very powerful man. This petite, vibrant flight attendant from Macon, Georgia, somehow got this international businessman to fall hard for her. Not knowing the man already had a plan for his life and a wife and children, she fell in love."

"Oldest story in the world."

"Yeah, but then my father was born, and my grandfather did something unexpected. He loved him."

"That's good, right?"

Ariel stepped back and looked at her handiwork. She reached into the white metal box, pulled out a large bandage, then applied it with a light touch. "No. It ended up being bad."

Sin stood and looked in the mirror, satisfied with Ariel's work. "Thank you. So, why was it bad?"

Ariel methodically put everything back in the first aid kit, and the two moved back into the living room.

"Because my father's legitimate half-brother found out he had a favored brother and hated that their father doted on him. Dad was intelligent and kind, and my grandfather thought he was the best of him. This infuriated the real heir to the throne."

"That's sad, but how does this have anything to do with the—"

Legs spread apart as she sat, Ariel leaned forward. "If you will let me tell it."

"Go on—"

"My grandfather was the head of a family that ruled four other families. These families are all over the world. Finland, Russia, Germany, Poland, and what they consider New America."

Sin leaned forward in anticipation. "I know of these families. Not who each are individually but of their existence."

"They're called the Council. They exist only to bring destruction to this world. They will wipe out everything we know as good and decent in the guise of returning us to a former glory that never existed."

Smashing her lips together in anticipation, Sin almost pleaded, "Now you're getting to the good part. Continue . . ."

Ariel rubbed her hands together as though she were cold. "The book is powerful. It foretells disasters. Every catastrophe that has occurred in the last 250 years is in the book—"

Sin made a noise of disbelief. She wondered if Ariel believed the things she was telling her.

"Now, wait a minute—"

Ariel nodded. "Yes, it's hard to believe, but true. Spanish flu? In the book. The China Floods of 1931, where 2,000,000 people died, are in the book. The 1887 Yellow River Flood, where 930,000 died—"

"Okay, okay. But how?"

"Now, we're getting to my story. I'm not sure how it works, but think of the *Farmer's Almanac* and how it predicts the weather years out. However, this book continues to unfold death and destruction. If the death toll isn't large enough, it won't report it. I guess its motto is 'Go Big or Go Home.'"

"Not funny," Sin groused, "This is some heebie-jeebies stuff."

"I'm not finished. My dad is the golden child of his father, and he meets my mother. Knowing his father would never approve, my dad kept her a secret. You see, my mother is half-Hispanic. My Nana was married to a man from Spain, the lower caste system of Spain."

"I'm aware of their caste system. If you're brown, see you around. Like the good old USA."

As though her body were a balloon deflating, Ariel nodded. "Anyway . . . Keeping us a secret was fortunate. Because it turns out that every thirty years, blood from each ruling family needs to be shed for a sacrifice to the book."

"That's demonic."

"In your line of work, I know you've heard of worse rituals."

Sin frowned. "Similar in nature, yes."

"Over the years, the families decided they didn't want to keep sacrificing their best, but the blood spilled must be from the five families' male lineage. Their solution to the problem was to have their bastard offspring be the sacrificial lambs. Soon, the practice became the norm."

Sin shook her head. "They were breeding their own children for sacrifice?"

Ariel nodded. "No, they were sacrificing their mistresses' children, think plantation life."

"Well, dang. Go on," Sin said.

"But my grandfather wasn't willing to give up my father. It seems my grandfather's wife had made a special request for my dad to be the one. So, my uncle, who could have chosen another one of his bastard half-siblings, had not only my father killed but *his* father too. The part about him killing his father is a rumor that won't go away. And they were both killed by the same method. My father publicly and my grandfather in private. My uncle took over the family from that day on."

Apprehension flowed through Sin. She stood and pushed her pain away. She went to the blinds. Peeking between them into a night that had finally gone quiet, she could only see darkness.

Keeping a watch, she asked, "And you stole the book?"

Ariel rubbed her hands across her face as though trying to wake up. "And now, it's missing. God help whoever has it."

Sin felt compelled to call her sister again.

"Nia, are you good?" Sin shouted into the phone when Nia finally answered. "I've been calling you for hours," Ariel's tale coursed through her veins, unsettling.

"Yes, yes. I'm good. I'm heading out of the country. That's why it's taken so long to contact you. The men who were after you found us at Deacon's. They blew the door and everything." Nia began to sniffle. "What's going on, Sin? Deacon got us out of there, and his brother took us to the airport. Deacon used a fake passport, and we're headed to his parents' house."

"I don't know how they found you, but I have a clue. Stay with Deacon and out of the way. We better not use this phone again."

"We're good. Deacon is some crazy inventor genius on top of everything else, and he has also invented an untraceable phone. I think he calls it the ghost phone. Jonesy ditched the phone you gave me, but transferred the number first. It's how you reached me."

"Let me talk to Jonesy."

"He's not here. He stayed behind to make sure they couldn't follow us."

"That man is going to get himself killed. Give me his number." All Sin could think of was that Jonesy was one more person she would now have to look out for. Why didn't the man get on the plane with his sibling?

"Hold on."

Sin could hear Nia talking to Deacon.

"Hello? This is Deacon. My brother can take care of himself."

"Deacon, not against these people. Please, give me his number."

Ariel was motioning for Sin to get off the phone. Sin held up her finger. "The number, Deacon."

Deacon gave her the number and handed the phone back to Nia.

"I love you, Ladybug. Stay safe."

"Love you too. Don't you die on me, Sin."

"Never," Sin said as she hung up. Staring at a pacing Ariel, she snorted and wondered what ant had crawled up her butt.

"Take off your clothes," Ariel demanded.

"Girl, you don't know me like that."

Huffing, Ariel barked, "Either you have something on you they are tracking us with, or it's in you."

Sin contemplated that every move of hers was being watched, and she quickly began to disrobe. Someone from the other team was playing on hers, and she wasn't about to trust that they wouldn't hurt her family to get to Ariel. After the story she shared, Sin understood that this was bigger than any of them knew and went back longer than her agency's existence.

Standing in her birthday suit, they burned all her clothing in the oven. She had on new Salomon Boots, and Sin's hope was not to destroy them. They were her favorite brand.

Ariel grunted at her standing there in boots and nothing else, but Sin was cool with that.

She went down Sin's body, trying to feel under her skin to see if she could feel anything. Nothing. Pointing to Sin's feet, she stepped out of the boots, and Ariel checked her feet.

Sin shook her head. "These boots are brand new and went from the shoe box to my feet. We're not sacrificing them unless necessary."

Sin and Ariel faced each other. Ariel was seething with anger, and Sin was trying to figure out her next steps.

Sin snapped her fingers and ran to the kitchen. "Let's try this—"

She pulled down a magnet stuck to the front of the refrigerator door with a potholder hanging from it. Ariel, who ran behind her, grabbed it and began to go over Sin's body with it.

"Gotta love Discovery Channel," Sin said when a small bubble appeared on her opposite arm from her injury.

"Dang, it worked," Ariel yelled.

Sin went to the bathroom and opened the first aid kit. As the gleaming instruments were lined up in plastic, she said a small thank you in her head to Umber. She pulled out another syringe, handed it to Ariel, and then gave her a scalpel.

"You were competent sewing up my shoulder. Please do me a solid and get this thing out of me. I wonder how long I've been running around the country with the agency keeping tabs on me."

"Maybe it was the agency, or maybe it was your mole. You've never wondered how you guys keep getting only so close?" Ariel asked.

"I've wondered, but when you're in our business, leaks happen."

Fingering the scalpel and rubbing antiseptic on Sin's arm, Ariel said, "So, in preparation to go after my uncle, I took some medical classes, weapons, and hand-to-hand combat training. I can dig this out, and this numbing agent will work some, but honestly?"

"Yeah?"

"You about to cry, girl."

"I'm standing here in front of you naked as a newborn. I'm already crying. Get on with it. We don't have much time."

Ariel bent over her and went to work on removing the chip. When the blood oozed down her arm, Sin closed her eyes. She mewed when it got too bad and gnawed her bottom lip raw.

"Got it!"

Ariel sewed it up much more gently than she had Sin's other shoulder. She now had matching wounds. Working her shoulders back and forth, Sin shuddered.

You need me.

No, Pop. I'm good. Stand down.

"I take it they're waiting on us to fall asleep before they attack. Or whoever the turncoat is hasn't discovered our location yet. Either way, we need to go," Sin groused, moving around the room.

"Agreed."

Sin rummaged in Umber's closet and pulled out a black shirt. Using scissors, she cut the sleeves and pants. She put his belt around her waist, used her knife, added some holes, and cinched it.

Taking Ariel's favorite exit, the bathroom-side window, they climbed out and scrambled over the neighbor's fence. Sins's shoulder burned from the exertion, and she felt a wave of dizziness but believed she hadn't lost enough blood to stop her. Running through two more neighbors' yards, Sin led them into the alley. Only then did she call Jonesy as they escaped into the night. Sin hoped he could be trusted because, right now, he was all they had.

Chapter Nineteen

Nia

The seven-hour plane ride to Costa Rica had taken Nia and Deacon into the heart of the Everette family's breakfast hour. As Nia washed her hands, the aroma of breakfast made her mouth water, but upon entering the large, airy kitchen and seeing the enormous spread, she paused.

Lord, this is a lot of food. It smells wonderful, but I'm just not that hungry . . . too nervous, too anxious waiting to hear from Sin.

Giving a small laugh, Linette, Deacon's mother, who was a well-preserved Halle Berry stunt double, said, "You can close your mouth, dear. We don't eat like this every day. But we felt it was an occasion when, for the first time, my Deacon brings a girl home to meet his parents."

Deacon whispered-shouted, "Don't do that, Mom. Nia is not sure if she even likes me yet."

Puzzled, Linette pivoted between the two. "What?"

At the same time, Nia interjected, "I like you fine, Deacon."

Linette grinned and clapped her hands together. "Well, I'm

glad that's settled. Nia, please help yourself. You haven't even started filling your plate, dear."

Nia almost sighed out loud, but not wanting to offend, she placed a little of everything on her plate.

Jones Everette strolled into the room. A handsome, imposing figure, he filled the doorway as he came through. Like her father, Nia thought he looked like a man not easily ruffled. Linette tilted her head as he bent as though to kiss her on the cheek, but he turned her head and gave her a lingering one on her lips. "Good morning, all."

Deacon tapped Nia on her arm. "Don't mind my parents, Nia. They are very affectionate. I think my dad gave my mom the extra affection she didn't get from me. I was a pain."

Jones grabbed his chest. "Did Deacon just make a joke? Son, I kiss your mother because I can't help myself."

"I think I understand that now, Dad."

His father sat and loaded his plate with some of everything. After bending his head and saying a short prayer, he dug in. Jones licked his fingers and asked, "Where are you from, Nia?"

"Everywhere, sir. I'm an army brat. I now live in Columbus, Ohio, where I'm a librarian."

Jones nodded. "I'm asking because Linette is from the South." He waved his fork at her. "This meal is so good, babe, that a nap is right around the corner. Nothing like a woman who can cook."

"Dad, Nia made a tasty meal last night. So good, I had two helpings."

Jones held up his hand for Deacon to give him a high five. Linette appeared to hold her breath as they waited to see if Deacon would return the gesture. When he did, his father slapped the table.

"That's what I'm talking about."

For a few minutes, the clinking of silverware hitting plates was all that could be heard as each person enjoyed their food. Nia was surprised that she ate a small amount. Everyone continued eating and making small talk, but Deacon's leg bounced under the table, jostling it. His parents watched him as Nia watched them. Deacon was right. When something was wrong, it showed plainly on his face, and everybody could tell he was holding something back.

Nia sensed it like static in the air—he was waiting for the right moment. She caught the flicker of his eyes toward the hallway, then back to his plate, where the syrup from the pancakes mingled with his grits.

"Dad," Deacon said quietly, setting down his fork, "can we talk for a moment? Just the two of us."

Linette's hand stilled midreach for the syrup.

Jones raised a brow, but he stood without question, brushing crumbs from his shirt as he nodded. "I was waiting for when you were ready. Let's take it to the den."

Deacon rose, then glanced down at Nia with a look that didn't need translation. *You okay?*

She gave a slight nod. "Go ahead."

The men exited the room, their footsteps fading into the carpeted hall. As soon as the soft murmur of their voices turned a corner, Linette leaned back in her chair with a sigh, the pleasant hostess veneer relaxing just a touch.

"Well, I suppose it's just us girls," she said, folding her napkin with delicate precision before placing it beside her untouched French toast.

Nia felt her palms warm. This part—the one-on-one with the mother—was a rite of passage. It could go in any direction. But something about Linette's tone told her this wasn't a trap. This was an invitation.

"Don't be nervous," Linette said, smiling gently. "I'm not going to grill you. Well . . . not too hard."

Nia chuckled despite herself. "I guess that's fair."

Linette's gaze softened. "You know, I've been praying for years that Deacon would bring someone home. He's always been so . . . closed off. Too much in that head of his. Too many secrets in his silences."

Nia shifted, feeling both seen and implicated. *This woman is moving too fast.*

"I can tell," Linette continued, "he's different with you. He's softer but still . . . watchful. You must be someone very special."

"I don't know if I'm special," Nia said honestly. "We've really just started talking, ma'am. But I care about him."

Linette's smile was touched with something wistful. "That might be all he's ever needed."

Nia hesitated. "Is it always like this? All the food?"

Linette laughed lightly. "Only when we miss him. Which is . . . always. We used to get him and Jonesy to come see us for the holidays, but then that stopped. They claim they're here often, but a mother misses her boys. Now, he shows up with a beautiful girl on his arm and expects me not to roll out the good china?"

"I guess I should be flattered."

"Oh, you should," Linette said, her eyes twinkling. "You've gotten further than anyone ever has."

Nia looked toward the hallway, where the sound of two men talking—low and deliberate—filtered back in waves.

Of all times to keep his voice low.

Nia couldn't help but wonder how Jones was taking the news. How would Deacon's family feel when they learned she had placed them all in danger? Could the people who found her at Deacon's find her here? She felt sick to her stomach. When Sin reached out, she would ask her to come and get her. None of this was fair to Deacon or his family.

Nia's fork listlessly moved the food around her plate.

"You're not hungry, hon?" Linette asked.

"No, ma'am. My stomach is a little upset. All this work, you've gone through so much trouble—"

Linette blushed. "Oh, baby girl, don't you feel bad about it. I can be a pushy person. Please pay no attention to my meddling about the amount of food on your plate or your relationship with my son."

Deacon was taking control, and she thought she might like it. She would wait and see the outcome.

Linette started to remove the dishes from the table and carry them to the sink. Nia's home training kicked in, and she followed with dishes in her hand. The large sliding glass door was open, and the screen allowed a breeze to float into the room. Nia looked out at the ocean view, and she stopped.

"Beautiful, isn't it?" Linette said.

"It's breathtaking. How blessed that you're able to look at this every day."

Linette pointed to the humongous butcher block kitchen island, and Nia placed her dishes there. She then patted the chair for Nia to join her.

When Nia sat, Linette said, "I hope I didn't make you uncomfortable. I'm thrilled to meet you and to know that Deacon has met someone who likes him for him." She stood and craned her neck, looking down the hallway where Deacon and his father had disappeared. Turning back, she whispered, "Not like those other girls Jonesy hired to 'make Deacon a man.'"

She let out a breezy laugh, more habit than humor, as Linette fussed with motherly enthusiasm.

"Don't laugh. I know I'm talking too much. But, baby, none of that was what a mother wanted for her son or what makes a man a man. I'm sure you know that. I told Jonesy and his father that the right girl would come along, and here you are."

Nia froze; she did not want to be the prize Deacon won for a life of sainthood. She wasn't even sure that they would work. She needed to rein in Ms. Linette's thoughts before she began planning a wedding and a baby shower.

"Ms. Linette, Deacon, and I are just getting to know each other. I don't know how this relationship will go in the future. I don't want to give any of us a false perception that we know where we're headed."

Linette stood and began putting food into containers and dishes in the dishwasher. "When Deacon was a toddler, they told me he would have issues. I took him to numerous doctors, waiting for someone to tell us that he would be what most folks consider 'normal.' That never happened."

Nia rose to help, but Linette shooed her away. "One night, I cried in my husband's arms and wondered what I had done so wrong to have a son who would need so much more than I felt I was capable of giving. You see, I have a brother who is autistic. He's ten years older, and in the seventies, they didn't have the system in place to care for him properly. So, we did it at home. I grew up looking after him as though I were the older sibling. I didn't think I had anything left for Deacon."

Nia's eyes welled as she thought of the pain that Linette must have felt. "Oh, child, don't feel sad for us. That night, Jones held me and asked me to look at things from another perspective. How much must God love Deacon to give him to people who had learned to love beyond what a person looked like to society? I had already proved my mettle: Sister and caretaker, wife in an interracial marriage connected to in-laws with confederate flags flying. My perception expanded then. I stopped taking him for a diagnosis of what was wrong and treated him like the intelligent human being he is. Then I prayed every step of the way. And it worked."

"He is very accomplished—"

Linette cut her off. "Please don't say 'for someone like him.'

Deacon is intelligent for anyone. He started studying genetics because he wanted to know not only why he was neurodivergent but also why people cared so much that his father was white and his mother Black."

"He shared some of that with me," Nia said.

"Impressive. He doesn't share his journey with many. As a child, he was obsessed with trying to find out the things that would show we are all different but, in many ways, the same. We're each like our fingerprints, unique to ourselves. That boy studied the history of racism and understood that it was designed to keep the rich, rich and to have us small folk fighting among ourselves. He's the one who taught us that racism was a social construct and that, in reality, race wasn't real as we all belong to the human race."

"I like that," Nia said. "Most people look to be with people who are the same. They want that commonality. They never discuss celebrating or engaging in another way. If we change our mindset, we change our trajectory."

"Right. Then he began to work on other things that could help disadvantaged people. Before he completed his first degree, he invented a method to isolate the cells of certain seeds, revolutionizing the ability to grow crops with minimal water. It's been done before, but not in this way. Areas around the globe with food deserts will not have to fight so hard when these seeds are introduced to barren soil. He's added an addendum to his contract with an agricultural company that they must give a fourth of all their products to charities to benefit struggling communities everywhere."

The surprise on Nia's face prompted Linette to get up and hug her. "Oh, darling, Deacon is much more than you see. Give him a chance."

"Give who a chance, Mom?" Deacon said, as he came into the room, his more somber father following.

"Deacon, why don't you take Nia out on the beach and show her how beautiful this place is that you gifted your family? I want to talk to your mom," Jones said.

Deacon walked to the sliding screen door and pulled it back. "Come on, Nia. My dad wants to let my mom know how much trouble we're in."

Hanging her head, Nia hurried out of the house. "Deacon, I think I should leave. I don't want you to be more involved than you already are. It's not fair to you or your folks."

"I knew a long time ago life wasn't fair, Nia. Dad phoned Jonesy when we were talking in the room. Jonesy said Sin called and that he was going to meet her. When he picks her up, they'll come for us. And then, we can figure this out."

They descended the wooden stairs toward the sand. Deacon grabbed folded beach towels off a glass table. Since her shoes overflowed with the grit of sand, Nia used Deacon's shoulder to lean on as she removed them. Warm sand swished between her toes, and she exhaled into the balmy air.

With the sun shining like a new promise, Nia reached up on her tiptoes and stretched.

Maybe things will be all right.

With half-smiles of hope, she and Deacon lay on lounge chairs, their towels beneath them. Nia was mesmerized by the gentle, sea-green waves lapping at the shore. In her peripheral vision, she could see Deacon hesitate before turning to her, his back to the water, and like the water flowing in and out, he poured out more of his history.

"I heard a little of my mom's sharing our family history. My dad was raised in a far-right-survivalist camp with my great-uncle, a man that I've never met."

"Because you're part Black?"

"Every day, Nia."

She smirked. "So, in Costa Rica, you're a funny man."

"Something about these balmy breezes. Anyway, Dad said he got tired of all the violence and never felt the hate for others that they wanted him to feel. His girlfriend had Jonesy, but then she started to push more violence against other groups. When she had an affair, Dad thought that was his chance to leave and go to college and make something of himself. He met my mom in one of his classes and realized he had never really known a Black person."

"Sounds like one of my romance novels. Your dad is the tragic alpha hero."

"I don't know about that, but Dad has always been open about who he used to be and why hate doesn't work."

"How did Jonesy end up living with you? I take it he was raised by his mother."

"Yeah, and he was abused by her and her husband. It's a long and twisted story that I may share one day. But it's Jonesy's story. What it did for me was put me on the hunt for answers."

"Did you find them?"

"Not always, but it never stopped me from looking."

"I appreciate your being openness," Nia said.

"Right, I'm talking a lot. I don't think I'll talk for a while when I'm finished."

Nia shook her head. "Oh, please don't shut down. I'm familiar with needing to get something out. I didn't want you to feel pressured to tell it all now."

"I'm almost done. And then, you'll know me better. You said we need to get to know each other. So, I need to hurry it along."

"But, Deacon—"

"—I'm almost finished, Nia. I want you to understand my relationship with Jonesy. One day, after being out to dinner, we came home, and a teenage Jonesy was balled up on the porch. He was beat up pretty badly. He came in, and we all nursed him back to health. Dad never let him go back after learning what Jonesy had gone through for all those years."

"I would have thought that you and Jonesy would have grown up together. You're so close."

"We bonded from the beginning. Can you believe it? He, a son of the Confederacy, and I, the son of Jones and Linette Everette. It would have been easy for him to hate me. I had everything he wanted. But Jonesy loves me, Nia. He always has. He still has some rough spots when it comes to other Black people, but Mom says he's a constant work in progress and to pray for him."

"Do you pray?"

"My mom prays, and my dad sometimes, like at meals. But I don't know, Nia. I prayed for you. Does that count? Do you think God is real?"

"Yes, I do. I don't believe in man-made rules that aren't biblical. Things that my grandmother used to spout, like, 'Child, you can't wear pants. It ain't holy.' And whenever you did something she didn't like, she'd spout, 'Holiness or hell, little girl.' But, Deacon, I believe He has all the power in His hands."

"Well then, why are you so scared? Did she scare the pants off of you?" Deacon joked.

"You're pushing the jokes. No, my fear comes from knowing what evil men can do. Having a dad in the army, I learned early that it rains on the just and the unjust."

"Well, there is not a cloud in the sky, Nia. I think we're safe."

Relaxed, Nia sighed in contentment and watched the blue sky with its clear, puffy white clouds floating by. Looking over the horizon, she suddenly saw black dots on the water. They were moving fast and coming straight for them.

"Nia, run!"

Deacon jumped up and pulled Nia out of the lounge chair. He yanked her up the steps onto the back patio, moving behind and pushing her into the house first. Sliding inside behind her, he slid the door shut and hit a button.

Storm shutters glided down, covering the sliding back doors at the rear of the house, as well as the windows over the breakfast nook. Nia ran to the front of the house, grabbing her satchel from the chair. Jones Everette stood loading an AK-47. Deacon threw open his duffle bag and pulled out the guns Nia had seen him with earlier.

As the storm shutters clanged closed around the house, the pounding sound of feet stopped, replaced by an eerie silence inside Deacon's parents' beach house. Dim daylight filtered through the reinforced shutters' small slits, casting an ominous glow on the tense faces of Deacon, Nia, and his parents.

They took a collective breath.

After throwing bulletproof vests at Nia and Deacon, Linette put on hers.

Deacon and his father, armed with guns, took defensive positions near the entrance. Nia was worn out and scared. But something Deacon said about God being real resonated in her spirit. She either believed in God or not. He was either real to her or not.

Remembering the games she and Sin played as kids, Nia assessed her surroundings, her eyes scanning for potential points of entry. Before she could ask for a gun, the phone jarred everyone when it rang.

Jones answered, "Thanks for calling back, Jonesy. I don't know who these people are, but they're here." Deacon switched on a computer monitor. "Thanks, son. I forgot you put all of this nonsense throughout the house."

They could all hear Jonesy's reply. "Can't be nonsense if you can use it, Dad. What do you see?"

"An eight-man hit squad. Evidently, they didn't do their homework on us—their error."

Nia almost grinned when she could hear Jonesy's smart reply. "Okay, Rambo. You do remember you're fifty-one years old. Let Deacon take the lead."

As Deacon looked at the monitor, his calm comment made them all freeze. "He's got a rocket grenade launcher, Jonesy."

Jonesy began to scream at someone near him. "Give me back the phone."

"Not on your life. Nia?" Sin shouted.

"Yes, Sis. I'm here."

Sin's words were fast, punched out in forceful spurts. "Remember the article in the paper about the family from 1859, and everybody debated if it was fake news?"

"Yes, I remember. You said you knew the husband of one of them or something like that, right?" Anxious, Nia watched the monitor as one of the men put the launcher on his shoulder.

"We did some missions together. Go to the Benson plantation in Tennessee. I'm texting the coordinates. Zachary has turned it into a retirement home for former Special Ops operatives. Green Berets, Navy SEALs, you name it, they're living there in harmony. All of you get there."

Jones looked at the screen; the man with the launcher waited for a signal to be given. Another man nodded to him.

"Oh no, they're going to mess up my house, aren't they?" Linette cried.

They watched as two men prepared to flank them from the front.

"Dad, I'll have the plane waiting in plan B's location," Jonesy said as a boom hit the house and shook it through its foundation.

The house felt like it was falling off its foundation, and Jones hit the garage opener. The monitor screen was squiggly, but it continued to hold its surveillance of the outside. As the garage door went up, the two assailants ran inside and Deacon and Jones opened fire. Both men went down.

"Move," Jones yelled. "I'll cover."

Sand kicked up around their feet as Deacon led them to two dune buggies hidden behind foliage under a small wooden carport.

Deacon jumped into one behind his mother, and Nia got in with Jones.

They flew across the beach, moving further inland. Bullets flew overhead and pinged the back of the buggy as they zigzagged across the terrain, and Deacon fired back as they went. When they made it as far as they could in their buggies through the swampy area, they got into a small paddle boat, hidden under brush, and rowed across the inlet, jumping out onto a flat, grassy area. In sync, they ran.

"Won't they follow us?" Nia puffed, slamming herself for not keeping up with her dojo schedule like Sin had advised.

She hated to slow them down, but she began to jog at a slower pace, and the others accommodated her by slowing down and then speed walking.

How are Deacon's parents not panting?

Falling back, Jones answered. "A car can't go over the terrain we just came over. That's why we took the buggies. They can eventually follow us, but we should be long gone by then. This abandoned airstrip is not used a lot. I used to bring the boys out here for target practice. Jonesy remembered and always said that if anything happened and we needed an alternate way out, it would be our plan B. Being raised for civil war like he and I were, you never stop having a plan B. Then there is the slight problem of having a millionaire genius son who is too trusting."

Nia gulped, "A millionaire?"

Deacon shook his head. "It's just money, Nia. There are over fifty-nine million millionaires in the world."

Nia was processing this information when she heard a plane overhead, and all four began to run again. Half a mile later, a dilapidated air hangar with a field full of overgrown weeds and a long and wide strip of dirt and gravel came into view . . . with the plane sitting right where Jonesy promised.

Once they boarded the plane, all four of them collapsed into their seats. Perspiring, Nia was wiping her face with the tail end of her shirt when a small towelette was handed to her.

"Thank you," Nia said as Linette patted her face with one.

The pilot announced that they were leaving Costa Rica and would land in Tennessee in six hours.

Shrugging out of her bulletproof vest, Nia stretched out in her reclined seat. She decided then and there that she would be fine if she never rode on another plane in this life.

Thinking of who she was running to for help, Nia grabbed a throw and burrowed herself under it. Almost numb from the adrenaline, she wondered how running to get help from people who once graced the front page of the *Enquirer* was a winning plan B.

I've gone from cataloging books to dodging bullets and fleeing to an ex-military compound—if this is chapter one of my new life, God, please hand me the pen and an eraser.

Chapter Twenty

General

The desk vibrated when General slammed down the phone. "You tell me how some retarded boy, and his whiny little girlfriend can keep evading us! If we get the girl, we get the sister to hand over the package. We get this Ariel and the book back, and our problems are solved. It's *not* hard, people," he thundered.

Geoff stood waiting for his orders; four men stood behind him.

General drummed his fingers on the desk. "How many men did you send to Costa Rica?"

"Eight, sir."

"Eight? And only six returning?"

"Yes, sir. Our inside contact has also lost the transmission from the agent, code name Pop. We found burned clothes in the oven and bloody tissues. Looks like they found her tracker and removed it."

"Preposterous! There's too much tech out here for us to have lost her."

"It's worked for years, sir. Since she was assigned to our case, our inside contact had her tagged when she updated her international immunizations."

General stalked across the polished marble tiles of his office, a purposeful scowl etched into his weathered face. He paused at his favorite window, working to get his bearings. Although higher and bigger than him, the puffy clouds always reminded him that this was his kingdom.

He folded his massive arms across his broad chest. "My father loved this sight, but when he stood here, we were not allowed to disturb him," he said, his voice distant, lost in memories. "One day, I stood in that doorway—I was just a boy then—and he finally motioned me closer. I remember; I could barely contain my excitement."

A large sigh emanated from General as though he had held on to it for years. "You know what he wanted?" General side-eyed Geoff, then not waiting for a response, his attention returned to the snow-covered scenery. "Of course, you don't. He wanted me to run and get my little half brother. A boy who shouldn't have even been in our home."

General's hands were clasped behind his back as he paced the room, veins throbbing in his neck. His voice echoed against the walls like the sound of ricocheting explosions. "The audacity!" Geoff remained immobile as he continued. "The interloper came and stood next to him, and with my father's arm around him, my father regaled him with times of old." General leaned into the window, transfixed as though in a trance.

Geoff remained stoic, listening but not moving an inch.

"I didn't moan about it because I always knew the brat would be sacrificed when the time came. My mother had chosen him personally as her sacrificial gift for putting up with the children my father had birthed outside of their marriage. Father always appeased her by saying they all had to sacrifice for the Council. But mother had her ways of coping: alcohol, overspending, traveling. Her avarice never included me. As the heir, I was expected to understand. It was an open secret that Father slept around. He reasoned that he ensured the family had the right sacrificial lamb when the time came. He preached ceremonial bloodletting first. The *Book of Disasters* must be kept satisfied."

General spun from the window. "Old news, though, right? Our problem is that Eric could not keep it in his pants, and the *Book of Disasters* is loose. There is a reason that our people must vet all mistresses. Do you know how many sacrifices it took to duplicate the book four times? The countless innocent lives?"

General now stood toe-to-toe with Geoff. "And the book regaled in each soul it gobbled, new pages appearing, forming new books as the blood flowed."

If one looked closely, Geoff appeared composed, except for his eyes, which sparkled and gleamed with unchecked lust at the mention of the lives sacrificed.

General's fingers curled around the edge of the back of a chair, his knuckles whitening with tension before he propelled the furniture across the room, the crash echoing against the walls. His voice roared, each word punctuated with rage and determination. "Hunt them down, every last one. Don't just bring me Ariel and the package. I want them all. The sacrifice *will* happen. The book will be reclaimed. Blood will stain these floors."

"Council!" Geoff slung his arm straight out with his hand extended in the air. Then he took his leave.

Before Geoff could reach the door, General shouted, "And have someone come in and clean up this mess."

A soft, unruffled reply floated back. "Already done, sir."

After Geoff and his men left, General walked over to the wall where oil paintings of his ancestors hung in prestigious glory.

When he reached the blank space after the last picture in the row, he wondered how long it would be before his image hung in its place. His picture would be placed next when the time came after his death. Taking one step backward, he moved very close to his father's portrait and spat in the likeness of his father's face.

He then moved back to the window and resumed staring out of it.

* * *

Sin

Sin and Jonesy were at a stand-off, poised to tear each other apart. The stale motel air crackled with tension in Groveport, a city outside Columbus, Ohio.

"Don't you ever snatch anything outta my hands again," Jonesy snarled, his voice low and lethal.

"I asked you twice to give me the phone. You didn't listen. You pay the consequences," Sin shot back, her words sharp enough to cut skin. "You're a piece of work, you know that?" Sin flipped him the bird and turned her back on him.

Ariel sat on the battered couch in the run-down motel and crowed, "A box of popcorn for this matinee would be perfect. However, we need to take this clown show on the road."

Turning, Sin and Jonesy yelled, "Shut up—"

Ariel clapped her hands. "Finally, the two of you agree on something. Can we now agree to get me out of here? We should find the missing book and get it somewhere safe."

"What missing book?" Jonesy said, snatching Sin's arm.

Yanking away, Sin went into a fighter's stance.

"You're kidding, right?" Jonesy howled.

Ariel huffed. "Oh, she's not kidding. She will deck you, and I suggest you become less handsy. Can we get back to finding the book and keeping me safe?"

"How valuable is this book?" Jonesy asked.

"Based on what Ariel told me? It's a demonic portal to the apocalypse. How's that for valuable?" Sin deadpanned.

"You're talking like Mama Linette. What is it about you people and your spiritual mumbo jumbo?" Jonesy asked.

Ariel leaned forward. "Hey, jerk face, I told her that story, and it's not mumbo jumbo. Are you so sheltered that you don't know there are things out there that go bump in the night?"

Jonesy landed in front of Ariel so fast that she and Sin blinked. "Lady, you don't know one thing about me. What I know would give your demons nightmares. But right now, I only care about getting my family back in one piece."

Sin stepped between Ariel and Jonesy, "Look, your white hood is slipping—yeah, I caught that 'you people' reference—as long as they make it to the plantation, they'll be okay. Zachary and his security forces are the best of the best. They'll protect them."

"How do you know that? I can't let my family be placed in a situation where they're on the run for days, waiting for danger to catch them. They're not built like me or my dad."

"I'm trying to explain everything, but you won't be quiet."

Jonesy's eyes narrowed as he stared.

Sin took his nonverbal response as permission for her to lay it all out. "It's okay. They're going to a safe place. I served on missions with Zachary Trumble, and he's an ex-Special Forces soldier who is very capable. His wife and her family were in the media when they claimed to be from the year 1859—"

"What?" Jonesy turned to Ariel, "Are you buying any of this?"

Ariel smirked. "I was carrying a demonic book, remember?"

Sin snapped, "Do you want me to finish or not?"

"Yeah, you can finish. But I can't promise it's making me feel any better. This whole thing is becoming a crap show." Jonesy raked his blond locks off his forehead.

Sighing, Sin said, "There has to be some truth there because when Zachary's wife sued the estate, she won the plantation she alleged she was once enslaved in." When Jonesy made a noise, she held up her hand. "Shut it and let me finish. There was so much land that Zachery decided to turn the plantation into a retirement village for former Special Services personnel. These guys are the real deal. And most came home only to be treated like they didn't matter. Some of them had lost limbs, had PTSD, and had fragmented family lives. They were miserable. Zachery took them in, including their families, and gave them a free place to live, food, and mental health counseling. And as they healed, he gave them what they had been missing: purpose—"

Jonesy shook his head, a bitter smile creeping across his face. "You're describing my childhood hellhole. I once lived in a so-called village. They had free housing, food, and their purpose was hate. They were toxic and anything but safe. I got my head pounded, teeth busted, and ribs bruised on the regular."

Sin stilled. She looked at him, this time—really looked. "Man, I am sorry that happened to you. But you have to know that I love my little sister. I'm trying to explain that I'm sending them to a compound that is safer than the White House. Over 300 people live on the estate. The place is fortified, guarded by men and women who've stared death in the face and made it blink. Navy Seals, Green Berets, Black Ops, you name it."

"A military compound?"

"No, a community. Zachary has built a security business where these men and women now go out and protect those who are being harassed, in trouble, or without a placc to turn. As such, they have jobs for income."

"Okay, now, you're quoting the movie *The Equalizer*. I'm not buying all of this pure intentions story you're selling on this demigod, Zachary, and his Never-Never Land," Jonesy said.

Ariel stood. " We don't have time to convince someone who doesn't want to be convinced. If this place is all you say it is, they can help us find the book. We need to get going."

Jonesy snorted. "Why would I want to go somewhere that sounds loony? I didn't believe anyone time-traveled when it was on the news and in the papers, and I'm not believing it now. Now, she's adding this Equalizer mess. We would like to believe there are people out there looking for the greater good, but that's comic book stuff. I need my family." He then pounded his fist into his hand. "They're all I have."

"Jonesy, seeing is believing. This is a special place, and it's where we're headed because it's where my sister will be."

Exhaling, Sin continued, "When we arrive, you can get your family. I can ensure my sister stays safe while I find the book. It's a no-brainer for everyone. Plus, I want to see this place I heard so much about. They even have a school for the gifted. I heard Zachary's brother-in-law is a kid genius."

Jonesy grabbed his duffel bag and started moving. "Lady, I only believe half of what you just said, but I'm out of options. I say we get started. The sooner I fetch them from this mess and away from you guys, the better."

Arms outstretched, Ariel jumped in front of the flimsy door. "While you guys are securing your families, I need one of you to say we'll stay focused on the book. It's our only bargaining chip if they catch up with us."

Sin pulled Ariel away from the door. "We'll get the book. I've already promised. But I'm leaving you at the compound under Zachary's watch, where you'll be safe."

"I'm not agreeing to that. I may not have been military, but I've trained for this. Girl, we'll fight about it later, but right now,

I want a shower, a warm bed, and a decent meal," Ariel complained.

"Jonesy, how fast can you get us there?" Sin asked as she followed him out of the grimy room into the evening's coolness. She needed to lay eyes on her sister. Guilt was eating her up.

"Tennessee is about six hours the way I'll be pushing it," Jonesy said tersely. He tried popping the locks through the open car window on the driver's side, but they refused to open. So he got in and reached behind him, feeling for the locks. With a tug, they finally popped open.

"Lord Almighty, Jonesy, where'd you pick up this hooptie?" Ariel seethed with contempt.

Ignoring her, he looked in the rearview mirror at Sin. "No whining, no begging to stop for bathroom breaks. And no messing with my car radio," he spat out through clenched teeth.

"Man, ain't nobody trying to hear all that. Just drive," Sin said with a yawn.

"Do you think I'm not tired too? I had three on my tail until I had to twist the situation around, then ditch my ride and get another car. So, deal with this piece of crap." His voice rose in a crescendo of rage. "Now, shut 'er up."

Sin growled and leaned menacingly across the seat, her face inches from his. "Who do you think you are telling to shut up? Everybody needs to stop whining—especially you."

"Yeah, what she said," Ariel spat as she slid down in her seat.

The old, beat-up sedan's engine gurgled to life as the three occupants sank into the worn, cracked leather seats. Jonesy pulled out of the parking spot with a sputter, and they slowly drove away from the dirty motel room. The unnoticed trio blended in with the other miscreants who rented the rooms by the hour.

Three separate spiraling fumes of anger and frustration filled the air. Sin peered out the car window, watching as the sky slowly lit up with the morning sun. She felt her stomach tighten in a knot as the reality of their situation sank in. She sat in the backseat, her weapon on her lap, covering their backs and cursing herself for getting her little sister in the middle of the most dangerous mission she'd ever been on.

I'm sorry, Nia. I'm going to get you out of this . . . soon.

Chapter Twenty-One

Deacon

The roar of the descending plane engines ripped through Deacon's groggy mind, jarring him awake. The pinging of his heart had been ricocheting off its chambers during takeoff, and he had barely managed to drift off until everyone else around him had started to doze. Six hours later, and night drifting into the early morning, they were all landing in good old Tennessee, and he was no closer to figuring out how to get Nia safely to the plantation using Sin's coordinates.

He twitched in his seat, glancing around the plane as if his answers were etched into the small oval windows. His face was pale and slick with sweat; his expression was an uneasy mix of apprehension and terror, like that of a child who regretted running away from home. He didn't function well with change. He longed for the comfort of his familiar surroundings and the steady rhythm of his routine. But aware he couldn't return to what was, he was resigned to moving forward.

He wasn't prepared. Even though his father and Jonesy had trained him in combat and had taken him through the motions of what to do if he was ever kidnapped, none of that had been real to him—none of that involved Nia. The training exercises were designed to help him cope if he were ever taken for ransom, not what to do as a man hopelessly in love.

The pilot announced their arrival. His father moved to the front of the cabin, and his mother followed him, going into the bathroom.

The influx of stimuli surrounding his senses felt overwhelming, causing Deacon's leg to shake double time with unease. He had to hold himself together before his parents could tell he was awake. If they discovered he was up, his mother would smother him with concern while his father tried to second-guess his every emotion. Without Jonesy present as a buffer and Nia's contradicting reactions, Deacon's chest constricted harder with every passing second, an immovable weight settling deep into the pit of his stomach like the sinking of an anvil into quicksand, each inch deeper and more prolonged.

Calm down. Move confidently toward Nia and show her you can take charge.

Deacon stood in front of Nia's seat with his hand outstretched. "Come on, Nia," he said, controlling his voice level to a soft volume.

Sitting up, she swung her head from side to side, craning her neck; she appeared concerned about the others' whereabouts.

"Mom is in the bathroom," Deacon said, keeping his tone mild. "Dad is up front with the pilot. Please take my hand. We have to go now."

Nia breathed heavily before accepting Deacon's hand and getting to her feet. She ran her hands through her tousled curls and rubbed at her sleep-gummy eyes before turning back to Deacon expectantly. He held out a breakfast bar.

She looked rumpled in her jersey and relaxed jeans as she

accepted the bar and firmly grasped his hand. "I need to use the restroom too," she said. "As soon as your mother comes out, of course."

Deacon's heart raced as he led Nia down the narrow aisle of the small aircraft. Despite his best efforts, he couldn't help but feel self-conscious.

He was acutely aware of Nia's hand in his, the warmth of her fingers seeping through his skin. He didn't think she realized she hadn't let go when she grabbed him the second time.

She's getting used to me.

They reached the bathroom door as his mother came out. Deacon hesitated, wondering if he should go in with her or wait outside.

As though his mother could hear his thoughts, she murmured, "Let her go in, son. There's not enough room for two. A woman needs her privacy."

Embarrassed, Deacon nodded, and a relieved Nia went in alone.

"I didn't mean to embarrass you, but you were the same with that stuffed dinosaur you had. I had to wash it while you were asleep."

"She's not a stuffed toy, Mom."

Touching Deacon's arm lightly, his mother said, "Exactly."

His mind raced as he waited, conjuring up and discarding plans for their arrival at the plantation. Sin's coordinates had been cryptic, and he didn't know what they were walking into. The thought of unknown danger was on his mind, but he tried to push it away, focusing instead on Nia.

The bathroom door opened, and Nia emerged, looking a little refreshed. She gave Deacon a quizzical look as she passed, but taking her cue from his mother, she exited the jet, joining Linette on the tarmac, where she appeared anxious to leave.

Deacon followed eagerly; at least they were one step closer to their destination.

Hearing an approaching vehicle, Deacon, weapon out, maneuvered in front of Nia and his mother.

Linette tapped him. "It's okay, Son. Your dad went to find a car."

Jones pulled up, driving an old Ford F-150 pickup truck with an old lawnmower in the bed. The cab was large enough for all of them to jump in.

"Dad, how'd you get the truck?"

"Using old skills that only work on old cars. It'll have to do. We've got to get out of here. Wherever this place is we're going to, we can't get there fast enough."

"I agree," Linette said. She then laid her hand on top of Nia's trembling one. "You okay, honey?"

"Yes, ma'am. A little anxious."

Linette's eyes widened when Deacon held Nia's hand freely.

"Don't be scared, babe. I got you."

Deacon saw his mother tap his father's thigh as though they were communicating silently.

Jones took out his phone and called Jonesy on speaker. "We made it. We're about thirty minutes away if I haul like somebody's chasing me."

The line crackled as Jonesy replied, "Somebody *is* chasing you, so make it here yesterday."

"If this old girl has smoke, I'll puff it," Jones said.

Squeezing Nia's hand, Deacon spoke. "Is Sin there, Jonesy? Nia would like to hear her voice."

"Negative. The she-devil has left her cave and is in conference with the man who owns this place. Wait till y'all see it. It's the darndest place I've ever seen."

"Less commentary, Jonesy. Will it keep Nia safe?" Deacon bit out.

There was a small silence before Jonesy replied. "How are you doing, Bro? You okay? You're not losing it, are you? 'Cause you know when you—"

"Son, put your brother and us out of our misery. Is it safe?"

"Yeah, Dad, that's what I was talking about. It's like Fort Knox up in here. They even have blockers for satellite feed over this place. You're good."

"On our way," Jones said.

The engine continued to roar to life as they drove down the old dirt service road toward the ex-plantation.

Time seemed to fly by as they drove in silence, lost in their thoughts about what lay ahead.

A wave of uneasiness crept along Deacon's subconscious, prickling it and ruffling imaginary feathers, spiraling his mood until he was in full-blown panic.

He loosened his hand from Nia's. They were all sitting too close, touching him, sharing his air. A shallow wheeze escaped his lips.

No, no, no.

He saw his mother double-tap his father's thigh, and his father pushed the old truck even harder.

A shallow pant rose out of Deacon. He was in a silent war, raging against himself. He was holding on with all he had, doing exercises learned with various therapists over the years, but he could feel himself slipping. And the question was, would they make it to the plantation before he lost it? And if he lost it, would he lose Nia?

Deacon had limited practice praying. He tried in his youth, but he was only mimicking his mother, and when Jonesy secretly teased him, he stopped. He prayed for Nia to be his, and though this was a miserable trip, they'd grown closer. Maybe he should have been more specific with God about how he wanted Him to bring the two of them together. He felt he wasn't supposed to act like God was a genie in a bottle, but he hoped this prayer worked.

Dear God,

You built me differently, and I don't mind that so much. But I love Nia; she needs to see my strength before she sees what the world thinks are my weaknesses. Please hold me together. I promise to learn more about you when we get through all this. If it helps, I'm your daughter Linette's son. She's told me how great you are, and I want to believe her. Please keep everyone safe. Amen.

Chapter Twenty-Two

Sin

Benson Compound

The Benson Plantation carried the weight of history on its back
and the promise of the future stitched into every blade of grass.
The main house, with its Colonial white columns and wraparound
porch, stood proud despite its past. There was an awe-inspiring
silence as their battered car drove through the heavily guarded
gates. They stopped at the guardhouse and received instructions.
Then at another checkpoint, two guards waved them through with
smiles contrary to their stern military bearing. As instructed, they
followed an army green golf cart to their hosts.

Rolling, keeping their own counsel, Sin noted, like her, they
were all too astounded by the enormity of the estate to comment.

It was early November. The car windows were cracked, and the
air was crisp enough to bite; each breath pulled in the sharp tang of
woodsmoke and fallen leaves. Trees once tall in their summer
splendor now tilted their branches, shedding the last of their

golden and crimson robes, waving goodbye as they bowed to the season's change.

"This place . . ." Sin whispered.

"Say less," Ariel whispered back.

This wasn't the plantation they imagined. This land had been reclaimed, reshaped into something new—something righteous. Land once worked by bitter hands and broken hearts now bursting with second chances.

A school, medical clinic, and gardens were ripe with the last stubborn blooms of the season's produce. Children rode bikes along gravel paths worn smooth by time and tenacity. This was a community with teeth—and it wasn't letting go.

The main house still stood—regal but softened by the passing years—its wide porch sprawling out like open arms. Beyond, the landscape was dotted with homes of all different sizes and shapes, each unique, like the families residing inside.

But down a winding path past the main gardens, a new building had risen: the Tactical Center. Looming behind it was a wide building twice its size; the signage read: *Benson Gym.* Built of glass, steel, and willpower, the center and gym didn't pretend to belong to the past. It was sleek, cold, and functional—built for strategy, not memory. Here was where today's combatants were prepared, and wars were fought: quiet, unseen, but no less dangerous.

The golf cart stopped. The Center's doors swung open, and Sin jumped out, boots crunching against the gravel, brisk November air fresh against her face and energizing.

There he was, Zachary Trumble. Once hailed as a legend in elite military circles, Zachary's name started showing up with question marks instead of medals the day he chose to stand by—and later marry—the woman who claimed she'd arrived from 1859. Broad-shouldered, blue-eyed, dark blond streaks threading his shoulder-length hair, the only indication that regulated military policies no longer bound him. Yet still, every inch of the man who had once commanded black ops missions in the shadows of wars the world pretended didn't exist.

Time hadn't dulled him. If anything, it had carved him sharper. Undeniably handsome. A leader molded by experience and grit.

Hope hummed under Sin's chest; she trusted this man.

Bebop and Malachi flanked him—both scarred, both standing like the only thing holding them back from violence was discipline. Second in command, Zachary's best friend, Bebop, stood in camouflage knee-length shorts, his Colgate smile made brighter against his Hershey-hued skin, his chocolate prosthetic leg a bold, unapologetic statement: Team Strategist. Malachi, wearing his home of Puerto Rico's flag on his T-shirt, gave no hint of weakness, although he had lost both a forearm and a leg, serving his country. They were battle-tested men chiseled down to necessity.

John Benson stood just behind them, arms crossed over his broad chest, his expression unreadable—a man who had rebuilt a legacy from ash and blood. His deep brown skin was unlined, his hair thick and flush, belying his age of over 200 years; like his son, Junie, they were anomalies—once enslaved, now residing in modern times.

This group was as diverse as their intentions.

Sin slowed as she approached, allowing Jonesy and Ariel to step beside her. Coming in hot, Junie jumped from his bike and scampered behind the arriving team.

Zachary marched forward. "Sincere," he said, his voice rough with memory. "Long time."

She offered a nod, short and sure. "Too long, Trumble."

Bebop reached out, and their hands clasped in a grip that spoke louder than words. "Sinclair, you ornery piece of work," he muttered into her hair, his voice rough and warm. "Still too stubborn to die, I see."

"Maybe next week," she shot back, grinning against the knot in her throat.

Malachi leaned forward, his gait uneven but strong. The absence of his left leg and arm didn't slow the sense of threat that rolled off him like a second skin.

He offered a hand. "Malachi Price."

"Sincere Lewis." They shook once, firm, no pretense.

Zachary nodded to his side, "My father-in-law, John Benson, and the kid genius skidding in on his bike is my nosy little brother-in-law, Junie."

"Hi, everyone," Junie said with a wide smile. He then shook Sin's hand enthusiastically, pumping it up and down as he spouted, "I've heard a lot about you. I hope you can tell me more about your time with these fellows. I'm a big fan."

Surprised, Sin looked up at the gangly teenager, who stood at least six feet tall, and chuckled as she carefully released his tight clasp. She laughed at his exuberance. "My traveling partners are Jonesy and Ariel."

Jonesy exchanged nods with the men, tension flickering around his shoulders but respect sharp in his posture.

Ariel moved more cautiously, her presence quieter but no less significant. She stared at John, the closest, who returned her look with a shadow of wariness but gentleness.

Sin watched as Zachary's eyes swept over their group, assessing, calculating.

Same old Zachary, she thought. He hadn't survived the world they'd lived in by taking anything at face value.

"You said you needed help," Zachary said, his voice low but not unkind. "Protection detail for your sister. But from what I'm sensing from this skittish group, you're not telling us everything."

Sin exhaled slowly, the weight of her responsibilities pressing harder now that it had an audience. "There's more," she admitted. "And you need to know it before you decide how deep you're willing to go."

She looked at Ariel, who stepped forward without hesitation. "It's not just protection," Ariel's voice cut clean through the cold air. "We're in the middle of a war. People just don't know it yet."

While Bebop raised an eyebrow, Malachi's jaw tightened. John's eyes narrowed slightly, a slow inhale flaring his nostrils.

Ariel continued, her hands unsteady, her voice dropping an octave. "Can we go inside? This isn't for just anyone to overhear."

Moving inside, the room's center featured a long granite table embedded with screens and small whiteboards for notetaking in front of each seat. Twelve chairs surrounded the table, with one end open, as though each strategizing voice held the same weight. Facing that open space was a large whiteboard. Flicking a switch to share on your whiteboard allowed you to write from your chair, and it appeared on the large wall screen. Unless you clicked the share box, your notes remained your own.

Ariel sat as everyone took a chair except Malachi, who stood at the door. His prosthesis is not a hindrance but a natural extension of him.

"There's a book," Ariel said. "An ancient one, but I think it dates back about two hundred and fifty years for the group that currently wields it. The *Book of Disasters*. It doesn't just foretell tragedies—it somehow increases their damage. I can't say for sure, but it seems to direct the Council to ensure the disaster grows to a worst-case scenario."

Questioning stares caused Sin to add to Ariel's explanation. "Think Hurricane Katrina and the lack of early government intervention. Or the destruction of Black Wall Street in Tulsa, which was magnified when no one intervened to help."

A silence settled over the group—thick, electric, heavy with the scent of something vast and dangerous waking up.

"How is this book connected to you?" Zachary asked Ariel.

"I stole it from a very dangerous group of people. The Council. The member I stole it from is one of the heads of the five ruling families."

A marker in his hand, Zachary asked, "Name?"

"Eric Rothwell of the Rothwells of New America."

"New America?" Bebop asked. "What in the name of all that is unholy is New America?"

"The good ol' USA," Sin said, "*if* they are not stopped."

Zachary wrote Eric Rothwell of Rothwells of New American on the whiteboard. Next to the family name, he wrote TARGET.

John straightened, the weight in his voice was enough to still the room. "You may have read about my family and have your own ideas of who we are and how we got here. But I have firsthand experience with the history of this country. I was born when it was young—only eighty-three years old—a baby compared to European countries. But I know this much: unless this country is born again, it will never become a *New* America."

"Amen!" Malachi added.

Zachary pointed his marker at Ariel. "John's got a point. What am I missing here?" He looked around, but Sin just stared at Ariel.

Zachary wanted answers. "Excuse me, Ariel, but you don't look like a woman out for the common good. Why did *you* steal the book?"

"Well, that wasn't judgmental at all," Ariel snarked. "I stole it because it ruined my life! I'd shoot it if it were flesh and blood, but it'd probably come back like a Chucky movie. But yeah, you're right. There isn't an altruistic bone in my body. My grandfather was head of the Council."

Sin watched the Benson group exchange worried looks. She

waved for Ariel to continue. "Granddad is dead now, and my half-uncle is the head of the snake. He is Ragnar Alstead, known as General."

Zachary wrote his name and asked, "The General is a military man?"

Ariel shook her head. "It's not *the* General, just General. My grandfather encouraged his leadership qualities when he was a demanding toddler. He nicknamed him the Little General. By the time he was six feet tall in middle school, the little had fallen off."

"So, he likes playing soldier," Bebop mused.

Sin interjected. "Don't let the lack of military history deceive you. I have been following the Council for the last five years, and they are strategic, well-disciplined, and lethal."

"How is it we've never heard of this Council?" Malachi asked.

"Do you think the fact that they've flown under the radar from men who are in the business of knowing makes them less dangerous?" Sin grunted.

Zachary ran his hand down his face, then turned to Ariel. "I know what Sin wants from us. Besides hating the book, why are you here, admittedly plotting against your own family?"

Ariel stood and positioned her face two inches from Zachary's. "General killed my father." Her eyes roved around the room, and the words flowed out of her like a faucet. "I've worked for years to get everything I could on them. My father's death was the reason my mother and I ran for years for fear we were next. Most of what I know about the Council and the book came from her. The stories were nighttime *Grimm's Fairy Tales*, she told me on nights huddled together in low-rent housing. She wanted the fear to make me stay away. It did the opposite. Later, I found out a little more through Eric. He was sloppy with his information when he was drunk. When Mom's heart finally ran out, my Nana took over, and we kept running. Nana is part Mexican, something my mother was terrified the Council would find out. You see, they were all about pure Aryan bloodlines and all that. They couldn't find out about my father's marriage, and my birth tainted the bloodline." Ariel's eyes lowered as Sin felt her unearned shame fill the room as she mumbled her last sentence. "Some kin folks aren't the same skin folk."

Sin wanted to intervene, to stop this flow of vulnerability that she had never seen from Ariel. They hadn't known each other for long. But she had a feeling it was Betty they were now talking to. Sin knew a thing or two about hiding behind an alter ego.

Ariel's eyes shone with unshed tears. Her voice wavered, but she pressed on. "I was nine when I made the promise I would avenge them both. So, I planned and waited. And when the moment came, I took it. Becoming Eric's mistress was key. He was sloppy, all ego and weakness. He talked too much during his drunken pillow talk, pridefully boasting about things forbidden to share. That's how I found out about Sin and her team, the kind that doesn't officially exist but one that he was worried about. When I stole the *Book of Disasters* from him, we had one shot to get it right. I was to meet Sin, turn the book over, and she'd get me— and eventually my Nana—out. Safe."

"Family dynamics are fascinating to me. But it's still not clear to me why your uncle killed your father," Junie said, scribbling notes.

Sin stopped holding her breath when the Ariel she knew reappeared.

"Boy, so-called genius or not, are you even old enough to be in this meeting?" Ariel snapped.

A calm Junie stopped writing. "I'm 164 years old. So, to answer your question, yes."

A questioning Sin looked at Zachary, who acknowledged,

"Who else but us would believe your story about a demonic book? We've been through some unexplainable things."

Ariel breathed, "It's the blood," she murmured. "The blood is why he wanted to kill my father."

Sin knew this was the part where, regardless of the Bensons' group's posturing, the information Ariel was about to reveal might make them rethink helping them.

But I need them. She couldn't trust her agency; Jonesy was ready to leave. And it would be just her and Ariel—somebody else she couldn't trust to have her back. And Nia needed protection. She'd remembered Zachary as heroic, but he had a family now, a wife with a baby on the way.

Spinning away from Ariel, Zachary stood. "What blood, Sin?"

"From what I've been told, and what Ariel learned from her time with Eric Rothwell, the book operates best on the innocent blood of others. The more blood it drinks, the more it prophesies. It's why it loves major disasters."

Junie's facial expression had Sin waiting for him to say whatever he had on his mind, but instead, he started rapidly texting.

John stepped into her line of vision, pointed at Junie, and explained, "He plots his own course. Please, tell us more about the blood."

"Ariel?" Sin said.

"To answer Junie's question, the blood *is* why my father was killed. We are coming up on the thirtieth anniversary of my father's death." Ariel walked over to John, whose empathy seemed to ooze from his pores. "Every thirty years, the five original families have to shed their blood in a public death. However, privileged people rarely pay their own costs. DNA doesn't have an address."

John placed his hand on Ariel's shoulder. "You don't have to share it if it's too painful. I know the pain of being used by those who should love you."

Zachary whispered to Sin. "My wife, who John raised, was really his master's daughter."

Sin's eyes widened as she looked through the center's window at the abundance of Benson's compound with new understanding.

Ariel shook John's hand from her shoulder. "I'm only telling you this one time. My dad was murdered because he had the blood of the original families running through his veins. Bred for just that purpose. He was an Alstead, and like a virginal bride who was sacrificed to the dragon in the olden days for the sake of the villagers, they killed him. I intend to slay that dragon. But to do it, I need that book."

"But how do you lose something like that?" Bebop asked.

Frustration pouring from her like fire, Ariel screamed, "I don't know! I thought I had it. Then it was gone."

Sin touched Ariel. "Easy. We all need to calm down. Zachary, I need to know if I can count on you?"

"I have a pregnant wife, a family, a community—"

"I wouldn't be here if you weren't my only hope. There's a traitor in my agency, and everything has gone to sugar. We've been compromised, and my civilian sister is caught in the mess." Sin slapped her hands together. "I need your special touch of pixie dust, Zachary. Your promise to keep her safe and whatever else you're willing to provide."

Jonesy cleared his throat. "Okay, let me add my $1.99. I plan to get a good night's sleep and get my family out of here." He pointed to Sin. "My brother Deacon has a crush on her sister, which shouldn't be a death wish. And my parents don't deserve any of this. Fighting a blood-drinking book is not on my skill list, even if I believed half of this, including time-traveling slaves. You people are bonkers."

Junie, who had been fidgeting near the door, froze when, a moment later, they all observed a pink golf cart pulling up through the window and an aging woman climbing out, her silver and grey wig askew. She wore a loud pink jogging suit and carried a large Bible in one hand and her phone in the other.

She carried her Bible like a shield and climbed the steps with the assurance of a warrior who knew her battle plan was unbeatable. Entering the room, Sin watched Junie meet her and saw how he flinched when the old woman laid her hand on his bowed head.

The prayer that followed wasn't loud. It was seismic. Sin felt the shift under her boots, the breath of something old and holy brushing against the walls of the Tactical Center.

Sin wasn't interested in religion; she needed help to fight a battle. *What is this?*

Mother Sweat lifted her hand, and Junie sagged, spent but somehow steadier.

"I had ta pray or smack you. I don' told ya about texting me. I don't like it. Pick up the phone. It's always in ya hand. Then you use all those letters that don' mean nothing to me. Ya got ta spell it out. Make it plain. Then while I'm on my way, ya texting me again. I love you, boy, you know I do, but patience is a virtue."

Junie hung his head. "I needed you to come, and I couldn't talk in the middle of them talking. I'm sorry, Mother Sweat. *He* sent for you."

"Who sent for her?" Jonesy asked, looking around the room.

"God," John said. "He can hear his voice. The boy has a calling on his life. But right now, he feels he should be doing anything but accepting his call. He wants to be a teenager, freedom hard on a parent."

"It's not that—" Junie protested.

"You listen now, baby," Mother Sweat said, her voice low but cutting clean. "You stop running from the God that has been faithful to you."

Junie nodded, a tear slipping silently down his face.

She turned to the group, her gaze sharp and bright. "You ain't just protectin' no girl," she said. "You standin' in the way of somethin' that wants to devour us whole. Best you decide now if you're built for it."

No one spoke or moved.

Sin clenched her fists against the tremor rolling through her chest. *What did Junie text this old woman? And who might intercept it?*

"Junie, what did you put in that text?" Sin demanded.

"Just what God told me to tell her, for her to come," Junie stammered. "Mother just knows things. Always has."

"But, I ain't no psychic. Fill me in on the rest," Mother Sweat said.

Zachary got her up to speed as she rocked and listened. When he finished, her gaze swept the gathered group. "You think you're looking for the book, but the book is after you. You got death sniffin' at your door. You also got a God who already kicked the hinges off every door meant to keep ya bound."

She paused, letting the weight of her words settle deep. "Now, fight like it."

No one spoke or moved. Sin knew—deep in the marrow of her bones—they had just crossed a line they could never uncross.

Mother Sweat bowed her head in prayer. When she looked up, her gaze was fierce. She marched toward Ariel. "'Vengeance is mine, so saith the Lord.' Ya tryna right a wrong that can't be undone. Ya daddy ain't coming back. But if he could, he would tell you to live free," she added softer now. "It's still ya fight, but he wants ya ta change your reason for fighting."

She smoothed her hand down her sweats, readying herself to

leave. Then she stopped beside Sin. She inched close, her voice low and compassionate. "Your two must become one. A double-minded person is unstable in all their ways." Then slapping her thighs, Mother Sweat bopped over to the door. "Now, I gotta go. The Lord expects me to get my steps in—stiff joints lose battles."

An uncomfortable chuckle rippled around the room, the tension cracking just enough for folk to breathe.

She patted Junie's shoulder as she sprinted past. "Keep listenin', baby. Heaven's louder than fear if you let it be."

Then she was gone, the Tactical Center's steel door slamming shut behind her.

"What whirlwind was that?" Sin asked. "And did she just dump all that mumbo jumbo on us to go to aerobics class?"

Bebop chuckled. "That was no mumbo jumbo; that dynamo of truth was my grandmother-in-law. She said aerobics, but those holy rollers she's exercising with will shift the atmosphere during knee bends before one gospel song is completed."

Zachary nodded. "They've converted me over the last year. They're our community intercessors. They told us two days ago that a shift was coming. Then you called. You asked what I was willing to provide. I'm here to help in any way you need. When she doesn't say no, she means yes. We're in."

Relieved, but before Sin could thank him, the door flew open. "Truck's coming up the drive!"

Sin took off, Jonesy right behind her.

They poured out of the Tactical Center, gravel skittering beneath their feet.

The truck kicked up dust as it approached, the setting sun flashing against its windshield.

Their family members had safely arrived, at least for now.

Sin could feel it in her bones—everything was about to change.

And ready or not, they all were already in it.

Chapter Twenty-Three

Sin

The truck rumbled to a stop, dust curling behind it. The lawn mower in the back was jumbling along in the long bed.

Sin didn't wait.

She and Jonesy were already sprinting across the compound, Ariel close behind, while Junie grabbed his bike and pedaled furiously to catch up.

Deacon was out, rounding the front of the truck. His eyes locked on Nia's as he helped her down, her battered duffel bag slung over one shoulder.

Sin reached her sister in three strides, pulling her from Deacon into a fierce hug.

Nia melted against her, clutching Sin's jacket, the duffel slipping from her fingers to land with a soft thud at their feet.

"I got you," Sin whispered into her hair. "You're safe now."

Jones and Linette came over slowly, weariness pulling at their frames but relief sparking in their eyes. Jonesy rounded the group and pulled Jones and Linette into relieved hugs. Deacon nodded to his brother as Sin took control of Nia.

Zachary and Bebop gave them all their moments, offering quick nods of acknowledgment, the kind that passed between survivors.

Introductions were brief, tight—there wasn't time for drawn-out family reunions.

"Inside," Zachary ordered.

Sin grabbed Nia's hand again, tugging her toward the main house. Sin didn't care that Deacon's face closed; this was her sister. The others followed without question.

* * *

The great room's comfortable plushness welcomed them with open arms. It was filled with dark polished wood and rich textiles, thickly cushioned couches, and wingback chairs situated in conversation pits before a roaring fire that beat the November chill.

Sari rose carefully from the oversized chair, one hand braced against the armrest, the other resting on her belly. Her caramel skin glowed in the firelight, and those auburn-gold waves spilled abundantly down her shoulders, causing Sin to finger her short pixie cut self-consciously.

Sin knew little about her as a person—just what she'd heard whispered through Zachary's protective tone—but there was no denying the quiet strength in how she stood, steady despite the weight she carried.

"Welcome," Sari said warmly, her voice soft but sure, wrapping around the room like a quilt someone had taken the time to sew by hand.

An overwhelmed Nia stumbled slightly, clutching her duffel tighter. Deacon bumped Sin aside and placed a steadying hand on her back.

Mother Sweat and her exercise prayer warriors were already

gathered in a corner of the great room, humming low under their breath—a steady current of spiritual pressure building under the surface.

The newcomers found seats where they could. Sin and Deacon stood protectively behind Nia, who clutched her duffle in her lap.

"You can put your things down, baby," Mother Sweat said kindly to Nia, her sharp gaze soft but unyielding.

Nia hesitated, then slowly unshouldered the bag and set it on the floor in front of her.

Mother Sweat's head tilted slightly, her spirit catching a ripple in the atmosphere.

"Child," she said, moving closer. Perspiring, she mopped her forehead with her cotton handkerchief. "Open your bag."

Nia blinked. "It's just clothes," she said, her voice small.

"Open it," Mother Sweat repeated gently but firmly.

With trembling fingers, Nia fumbled with the zipper. The duffel yawned open. A gasp escaped Mother Sweat, and the air cooled.

Sin stepped forward when the fire in the fireplace dimmed. *What just happened?*

Mother Sweat leaned in, her hand hovering just above the bag's opening. She hesitated and drew her hand back, clasping it with the other in prayer mode. Two members of Mother Sweat's prayer group stepped forward, and each clutched a shoulder. They peered in.

Nestled between a tangle of T-shirts and crumpled jeans—thick, thrumming with a pulse that didn't belong to anything human—lay the book.

Its cover was ancient leather, seared at the edges, marked with symbols that seemed to crawl and shimmer even under the flickering light.

"Ewee!" could be heard around the room as a rank smell infiltrated the air. *Sulfur.*

Nia frantically scooted back from the duffle bag.

Mother Sweat straightened slowly, her face grave. "You carried it all this way," she murmured, more to the heavens than Nia.

Nia recoiled, horror dawning across her face. "I don't know what's happening. I promise," she whispered. "It was just an old book!"

"That, in this atmosphere, has now woken up. Its sleep was purposeful." Mother Sweat stretched out her hand, and the woman behind her dripped oil into her palm.

"What is she doing?" Sin murmured as Mother Sweat rubbed her hands together.

"That's anointed oil. She's protecting herself." Linette said as she and Jones moved near.

Deacon tightened his grip on Nia's hand, pulling her closer from her chair.

Sin's mouth went dry.

When Ariel staggered back, her hand was clamped over her nose. "How did you get this book?" she demanded. "It didn't do that with me. It smells horrible. Like death," she swore.

Nia helplessly looked at Deacon. Her voice was small, as she admitted, "I took it from work in the return book pile at the library."

Mother Sweat turned to the prayer warriors behind her and nodded.

The humming deepened into low, rhythmic chanting—barely words, more vibration than sound, vibrating against skin and soul.

She faced the gathered group, her voice cutting through the heavy air, pointing at Ariel. "This child said the sacrifice is called for every thirty years." She paused as the hum of the prayer group decreased. "In the Word," her voice said with low thunder, "thirty has several deep biblical meanings. It marks the age of kingship, of priesthood. It also symbolizes dedication to a particular task or calling."

Junie's mouth dropped open, the color draining from his face.

Sin threw up her hands. "In all due respect . . . How does this have anything to do with what we need to do?"

"Well, usually when a body starts off with that term, ain't no respect present. But if ya hold on and let me speak my piece as it was given to me in prayer, I can help y'all."

"I want to hear the rest," Linette said.

Nodding, Mother Sweat grabbed the book. Some staggered away from the smell. She swept her arm around the room, gathering them all into her storm. "Thirty represents the sacrificial blood of Jesus, as Judas betrayed him for thirty silver coins."

"Tell it all, Mother," someone yelled from the back.

Sin watched as Ariel's face drained of color. She turned to comfort Nia, but Deacon was already there. Her sister was visibly shaking. She so wanted to curse the old woman. She was riling everyone up with all the spookiness. Sin bit her lip and listened, but she wasn't happy.

Mother Sweat continued, "In A.D. 30, Jesus suffered and shed His precious blood as God's sacrificial lamb. That's all biblical good news. The problem is that evil mimics good, but it's always a twist, a lie. This book tests the rightful owner every thirty years. But the Council has produced artificial sacrificial lambs through their adultery, which is already wrong, but they breed them to slaughter them at will, later, which is worse. Ya see, they tricking da book!"

The fire flickered, and the lamps went out at Mother Sweat's statement. In the dark, Mother called out. "Ouch."

The lights came back on, and the book lay open on the floor. "That thang got red hot."

Sin's hand hovered over her thigh where her holster sat.

How do you kill a book? Tear its pages?

Nothing about this was tactical. Nothing about this could be trained for.

Mother Sweat turned, her eyes narrowed, gleaming with something wild, like she wasn't just seeing the room but the spirits hanging above it.

"This ain't just paper and ink," she rasped. "This here is a summoning tool—carved in lies, dipped in blood, and baptized in betrayal."

Her prayer team in the back fell to their knees.

Zachary stood and pulled Sari to her feet. "Go on to our room, honey."

"But, Zach—" she said.

"Your husband talking to you, Sari. Do as he asks," John said, his eyes never leaving the book open on the floor.

Sari sighed, her shoulders slumping. "I'm going, but I need you both to know, I'm not fragile. I was next to you in that wagon when we escaped here, Papa."

"But you listened back then, Sari, and more importantly, you did what was asked," Junie added.

"Humph, far as I'm concerned, Junie ought ta be walking out with me. Just 'cause he's a male doesn't make him ready to be here."

"No, but hearing from God prepares him," Mother Sweat said. "Gon' on, girl. Take that innocent babe from dis place."

"Yes, ma'am," Sari said, and she hurried out of the room.

Mother Sweat pointed at Ariel with an oiled finger. "You think you took this book? Child, it *let* you. Don't confuse access with ownership."

Ariel opened her mouth, then closed it, her lips trembling, but her voice gone.

Mother Sweat motioned for Ariel. "Come pick it up. You legacy, let's see what it do."

Ariel looked around the room, then boldly picked the book up and lifted it to the crowd. The pages turned then two new pages appeared, while they watched words scripted left to right across like magic. Ariel through it to the floor.

A loud screech and a chair banged to the floor as someone ran screaming from the room.

Zachary raised his hands to caution everyone to not panic. "Mother Sweat, new pages appear only for those who carry the blood of one of the five families?"

"I think the same, son. Young gal, it never did that for you before?"

Ariel shook her head as though her denial would make life go back to what it used to be. Sin wanted to punch something as she watched Nia's face lose color, her hands twisting in fear.

"Uh, Mother Sweat, what else can you tell us?" Sin asked.

Dabbing her forehead with her hanky, Mother Sweat leaned forward. ""I believe the Council used this book to trap evil's will like it was their spell to bend," She then pushed it away with her foot. "And every thirty years, payment comes due. Then they get new pages, new ways to cash in on the destruction. Every generation, one from each governing family must carry on the tradition. Five must bleed. Five must betray." She snatched up Ariel's hand. "That's what you said, child. Those are your words, merged with spiritual wisdom, God is pouring into me." She pounded her fist to her breast. "A knowing in me says, we got a chance here to right some thangs."

Linette sank onto the nearest armrest, murmuring, "My God . . ."

Junie whispered something behind Sin, but she couldn't catch it. Her focus was locked on the book. It lay splayed open like it had chosen that moment to wake, not from sleep but hunger.

Like Mother Sweat, there was an improbable knowing in her gut that evil consumes.

"*I'm here*," Pop said. Sin looked around as though others could hear her, she spoke so clearly.

But the others' eyes remained on the old woman.

Mother Sweat didn't flinch. She knelt slowly, her knees creaking. Her hand hovered again, but didn't reach for it this time. She just prayed. "Lord, cover us in truth. Bind what is unclean. Expose the traitor. And show us the power of your Lamb."

The book turned a page on its own.

Pulling Nia against him, Deacon cursed under his breath.

Jones stepped forward as if he could shield them all with his body, but paused as the lamps flickered again. The electrical circuit held this time, but the room had shifted.

It felt . . . watched.

Mother Sweat stood. "You want to fight the Council?" she asked no one in particular. "Then you best stop thinkin' you can do it your way. This ain't a war for the squeamish unbeliever."

She whispered to Zachary, who pulled on gloves and picked up the book. He placed it in a wall safe. Mother Sweat stepped up and put a small Bible beside it.

"That'll hold it," Mother Sweat said.

Zachary moved beside her, his eyes shadowed but resolute. "We need a plan," he said. "Something more than prayer and panic."

Mother Sweat turned to him, her lips twitching. "You being a new Christian is showing. Prayer ain't panic, baby. It's preparation."

Then she nodded. "Now, go strategize. But don't you forget this part—" She pointed to the safe. "Whatever move you make, that thang already knows who ain't ready."

Sin grabbed Nia's hand to pull her out of the room when Pop crooned into her ear in a singsong voice. "*You're gonna need me.*"

Chapter Twenty-Four

General

General stood before the wall of darkened monitors; his fists clenched so tightly his knuckles cracked like gunfire. Nothing. No visual. No audio. No glitch to exploit. Just a dead zone where the Benson Compound should have been glowing.

"How?" he growled.

Across the room, Geoff shifted his weight. "They've blocked all satellite surveillance. Even our astral relay drones can't penetrate the perimeter. It's like . . . *something* is cloaking them."

General turned slowly, his voice calm, deadly calm. "Very scientific of you . . . this *something*. It's why you make the big bucks."

Geoff swallowed. "There's no technological explanation for the blackout, sir."

"Then stop giving me a metaphysical report and find the truth." General advanced on him, the room humming with his fury. "Because I know you are not creating some cock and bull fairy tale to cover your men's ineptness."

Geoff didn't blink. "I'm telling you we've used every man-made tool we've got. And nothing has worked."

General stared him down, then marched away with a frustrated growl. "How convenient. This Ariel person crawls out of some gutter and bewitches Eric, and he pretty much hands over the book, which she drags into the hands of time-frozen field slaves who your entail says have regular prayer circles and a community garden. You think this background information you've given me will get my book back? Or is it the basis for the next New York Times Bestseller?"

"I have all of my men checking everything about these people. There must be a crack somewhere; we'll find it. No one is infallible. In the meantime, Eric is a member of the five families; it's his duty to remember something more, sir." General didn't answer. "Sir?"

He turned back with a cold sneer. "No, Geoff. No more talking to Eric. His loss of the book is a betrayal of all we are. The Council has voted: treason."

Geoff stood straighter. "Then I will carry out the sentence of death immediately."

"No. Right now, he's meeting a service," General said. "I want you to bring him up from the other RV when we're done."

Geoff watched the monitor as an old truck flew through the guardhouse. In its bed sat what looked like a lawnmower.

"Lawn maintenance?" General asked.

A beep, then static, and a voice came over the com. "Four people in the truck. The girl matches the picture of the agent's sister."

"Why didn't he stop them?" General yelled.

Static, whispering on the other side, then a disembodied voice. "Sir, at first, it appeared as though maybe it was lawn service. When it was closer, we could see the people inside. By then, they were close enough to the guardhouse for them to return fire. We weren't sure you wanted those inside to be tipped off."

Ignoring his excuses, General yelled. "Go, go, go."

But the two men watched on the monitor as the truck went right through and the heavy iron gates closed. Then, as though in tune with what was happening in their camouflaged RV, four more men ran to the gatehouse and took up the post.

"They've doubled the guard," General screamed. "We could have taken the sister as a hostage, bargained for the book. Turned this thing around."

A stoic Geoff marched before General and was punched in the jaw so hard that he fell to his knees and then slowly rose.

As though nothing had taken place, General huffed. "That place—I've read up on it, it's an infestation. Ex-soldiers, rogue intelligence, freaks with roots in two centuries. Zachary Trumble. I knew about him; I'm connecting the dots now. I remember when the Council low-key tried to recruit him through his security job. I recognized that fool's loyalty was fragile the day he left special forces and then divorced his wife and married that slave woman. It makes me sick thinking about it. All of them living together like some Kumbaya circus." He paused, staring out the one-way window. "That kind of devotion is dangerous."

"Trumble's built an army," Geoff said. "Three hundred strong. Some bionic. All broken. All loyal."

"And all in my way." General moved to the center of the room and yanked open a hidden drawer in his desk. Inside, a velvet-lined cradle held a second book—his *Book of Disasters*—bound in the same branded leather, pulsing faintly like a heart. The original.

He opened it.

Blank pages.

No prophecy. No blood trail of mass casualties at Benson Compound. No guarantee of victory.

It was mocking him.

He slammed the cover shut. "That girl," he said, more to himself than to Geoff. "Ariel thought she stole power. What she stole was an invitation for us to ruin her life."

Geoff shifted. "We still have options. If we can't go in, we can draw them out."

General turned slowly. "They're not stupid enough to take the bait."

"Not yet," Geoff agreed. "But we make it personal. We send a message that rattles that compound's walls—reminding them that only our enemies' blood will erase their blood debt."

A slow smile spread across General's face. It was the smile of a man who remembered who he was.

"I want Eric." His voice was ice. "Stripped down. Shackled."

Geoff blinked. "You want to interrogate him again?"

"No." General turned toward the book. "I want to hurt him until his soul leaks out, and Ariel feels it from wherever she's hiding. The potency of a founding family member's blood is irreplaceable. His traitor's blood will answer for the fact I don't have hers. I will feed my book."

Geoff gave the slightest nod. "Yes, sir."

General's gaze locked on the book. "You ever hear a book scream in ecstasy, Geoff?"

"No, sir."

"You will."

Chapter Twenty-Five

Nia

Leaving the luxurious en suite bath, Nia wrapped the towel tighter around her, pressing it to her chest as if it could hold back the thoughts pressing in. Steam curled around her, but nothing could fog up the guilt clinging to her like a second skin.

She'd never stayed in such a plush bedroom. But she couldn't enjoy it. All she could think about was that she'd stolen the book. And the consequences of her actions were far-reaching.

Sitting on the deep, piled comforter, an unopened bottle of Chanel No. 5 lotion sat untouched beside her. The entire room was first-class accommodation, including the white linen gown draped at the foot of the king-size canopied bed.

Shifting the towel so it remained over her breasts, she mulled over the last twenty-four hours. Her hands rested in her lap, trembling slightly. She spoke into the empty room. "All things work together for the good—"

Her mother's voice echoed in her memory, followed by the verse from Romans. She hadn't even meant to think it, let alone speak it, but the words had risen like a shield. She missed her mother, her stalwart faith. The cruise seemed like a good idea at the time, a gift for her parents and her, a period when she didn't have to check in, explain her days, or update them on Sin. A soft knock —then the door creaked open. Sin stepped in with a steaming mug and a towel in her hand. "You're in here quoting scripture and haven't been to church in a year? Don't let these people spook you."

"Too late," Nia said. "And I wish I had found another church now. But I had no energy after they were so cliquish and gossipy."

"Yeah, well, if you can't trust the church, stay home, I always say," Sin sniped. She placed the mug on the nightstand.

"Why am I discussing this with you?" Nia said, rolling her eyes.

Grabbing the towel two-handed, Sin snapped it in the air. Then lunged. "Reflex check," Sin called mid-move as she wrapped the towel around Nia's neck and yanked.

Nia's body moved before her brain caught up. Her towel fell as her hand came up between the towel and her neck. She caught Sin's wrist, twisted it, and shoved her off balance. She dipped her head from the towel with a back elbow to Sin's gut. Sin staggered, then grinned—sharp and breathless.

"Well, look at you," Sin said, rubbing her stomach. "Still got some spark."

Nia picked up her towel from the floor and adjusted it as she glared. "Why would you do that?"

"Just checking your edge," Sin replied. "Fear's a thief, and you've been robbed enough."

"That's not a fair thing to say," Nia snapped. "I'm aware of my shortcomings. This isn't the first time you've shamed me for being fearful. It isn't helpful."

Sin tilted her head, her arms folding. "Maybe not. But, baby girl, now isn't the time to gently unpack the truth."

"I'm not asking for gentle," Nia snapped. "I'm asking for respect."

Instead of responding, Sin lunged again—fast, sharp, without warning.

This time, Nia lurched backward, catching her off guard. The impact pushed Sin to the edge of the dresser. Nia spun, watching her sister grimace as she rubbed her back.

"That was better, but you still flinch," Sin said, her breath heaving. "Still second-guess. You should have followed through until I was immobilized."

"It's called mercy. And I'm tired!" Nia snapped. "Tired of failing tests I didn't sign up for. You're my sister, not my drill sergeant. Give it all a rest, please."

Sin paused at that.

Nia's hands were clenched now, her fists trembling at her sides. "I've just found out I've been endangering everyone by carrying around an evil book. You have no idea how bad I feel. I've been watching Deacon fight with himself, push against his instincts to show up for me after I ghosted him, all because of what people might say! I need to rethink how I'm living my life, and I can't do it with you in my face giving me GI Jane pop quizzes." Her voice cracked, but she didn't look away. "He's showing up for *me*, Sin. So yeah, I want to be strong now. For him. For me."

Sin's eyes followed her. "Is this bravery tied to this sudden connection you've got going with Deacon?"

Nia's breath caught.

Sin pressed. "You and he seem . . . closer. But let's be real. He and his brother couldn't protect you. Jonesy's already made it clear —he's getting Deacon and their parents out of here at first light. And I agree. They need to go. The Council could be right outside those gates."

"They're not," Nia whispered.

"You don't know that."

"I don't care," she replied, her eyes flashing. "I'm tired, Sin. Tired of being afraid. Mother Sweat said something that stuck with me. She said fear tries to chain you, make you think you're fragile. It's a distractor. But I'm done letting it."

Sin folded her arms tighter. "You've been carrying that evil in your bag and didn't even know it. Doesn't that terrify you?"

"It does." Nia's voice wavered but didn't break. "But what terrifies me more is the idea that I'll live my whole life bowed by fear. Why did evil find me, Sin? Why did I carry it? What was it about me that made it think I was a good home?"

Silence.

Sin's posture softened. "Maybe it found you because it knew you were strong enough to fight it."

Nia blinked fast.

"Still," Sin added, "we're not done talking. I don't trust that your newfound bravery won't get you killed. That's why you're staying here."

Nia stepped forward. "You don't get to decide that."

"Yes, I do."

"No. You protect people. I get it. That's your mission. But you can't keep protecting me from everything, especially not from myself."

Sin's face shifted—less like a soldier, more like a sister. "Aw, Ladybug." She moved past Nia, picked up the tea, and offered it directly. "Then start by resting that new strength. Drink."

Nia hesitated. "What's in it?"

"Just herbs. Chamomile. Skullcap. A little valerian root."

Nia frowned. "Skullcap?"

"It's for your nerves. Earlier, you were shaking."

"Because a woman straight out of the *Book of Deborah* called us to arms. Everybody should have been shook." Nia took the mug, the warmth pressing into her palms. She smelled it. Earthy. Bitter at the edges.

She took a small sip.

Sin sat on the edge of the bed, calm, like the fight hadn't just happened. Like this was normal—sparring, lecturing, then tea.

"You think if you take me with you, I'll be a liability?" Nia whispered.

Sin didn't answer.

That was answer enough.

The heat of the tea crawled down her throat and spread across her chest. It was soothing at first. But . . . heavy. Unnatural. She blinked once. Then again. Slower this time.

Sin stood, smoothing her pants, and headed to the door, muttering, "No way. You can go with me. Save your strength. I will keep you safe—even if it's from yourself." Then she called loudly behind her. "You rest now, Nia. Tomorrow, it gets real."

Nia struggled but slipped the gown over her head; her body sagged against the mattress.

Her hands loosened. The mug tilted, nearly slipping from her grip. Her breathing slowed.

It hit her in fragments—the weight in her limbs, the pressure behind her eyes.

Darkness pulled her under like warm bathwater.

Her last thoughts before her brain turned to mush . . . I don't know why the book chose me. But maybe, just maybe, it had made the biggest mistake of all.

Because I'm done running.

Chapter Twenty-Six

Deacon

Deacon hissed as he skillfully lifted Jonesy onto his shoulder and threw him to the ground. His brother rolled into the fall and, tossing his head, sprang back up, ready for more.

It was midnight, and instead of going to bed, Deacon and Jonesy came over to the training center to spar. To their surprise, Sin and Ariel were already there, working in sync through several martial arts moves.

Instead of conversing with them, Deacon and Jonesy staked out their own area and engaged in sparring between themselves, ignoring the other two.

Deacon craved physical exertion; he needed the outlet because he was annoyed with them all. His brother, his parents, and Sin. They all acted as though they needed to protect Nia when he was the one who should be responsible for her safety. Sin had abdicated her role when she left Nia with him. Jonesy had abdicated his when he put them on a plane. But it was all an illusion. In reality, he was thought of as a placeholder until the real cavalry arrived.

As he maneuvered around his brother, countering his punches

and jabs, he thought of all he had learned only an hour earlier. Deacon's frustration could be measured in every pound he exacted from his brother's flesh.

Deacon stood in the moonlit hallway, his fists clenched at his sides. The shadows from the flickering lanterns danced across the walls, mocking his stillness. He'd stood behind the Big House's walls, hearing Sin make decisions that weren't hers to make.

She was leaving Nia behind.

He had heard it all—every word through the air duct from his bathroom next to Nia's room. He should've left when he and Jonesy realized they could hear from the bathroom's vent. Jonesy told him to. But he couldn't. He needed to know Sin's plan to make sure not only that Nia was safe but that she was also being heard.

His brother's pressure for them to leave at first light made him flip him harder than he needed to. There was satisfaction in Jonesy's every grunt.

He'd sat on the cold tile floor, his fidget rings clicking softly between his fingers. One. Two. Three rotations. Then start again. The pattern slowed his breathing. It helped him think. But it didn't help the fire that had built in his chest.

"You're not ready," Sin had said. "I'll protect you."

But what did she know about Nia? About what Nia had survived? What she carried? Deacon had seen it in her eyes— shadows darker than his, and he knew shadows. He knew what it meant to fight your mind. Your fear. And Nia wasn't running anymore. She was standing. He'd heard her soft vow as she fell asleep, even if he'd leaned into the vent to listen. And he cheered.

She was braver than any of them knew. That alone made her a formidable threat to their enemies.

Jonesy got up from the mat and shook off Deacon's last punch. Wiggling his jaw, he smiled. "We're wheels up in six hours," his brother said without preamble. "You, me, and the parents. Sin says she has the rest handled."

Deacon didn't turn to face him. "I'm not leaving."

Jonesy sighed, already weary. "Don't do this."

"She needs someone who sees her, Jonesy. Who trusts her."

Jonesy snorted. "She needs to live. That's what she needs."

"And hiding her here does that?" Deacon spun now, his eyes hard. "They know we're here. You think the Council doesn't have people watching? They could be outside those gates *right now.*"

Jonesy's silence said he'd thought the same thing.

Deacon dropped his voice. "What if they've already made it inside?"

Jonesy stiffened. "Has something happened?"

"No. Not yet." He paused. "But I feel it. Like the air's holding its breath."

His brother's eyes narrowed to slits. "I'm not arguing with you, Little Bro. We leave together. You know what happens when you get overwhelmed—"

"I'm not a child." Deacon's voice sharpened. "Stop treating me like one. You and Sin both think you can control me and Nia. Stop!"

Jonesy rubbed the back of his neck. "We're not trying to control you. We're trying to keep you alive."

"But alive isn't enough if it means I leave her behind. I'm my own man, Jonesy. I'm not going."

That landed between them. The silence stretched long.

"I love her, Jonesy."

His brother blinked. "You barely know her."

"I know what she looks like when she's fighting back tears. I know the way she stops breathing when someone is confrontational. The way she crinkles her nose when she's thinking hard about something. She's kind to even the homeless people who come into the library for warmth or cool air on a hot summer day. I know she curls her fingers into her palm when she wants to scream, but won't let herself. And I know that even though she was scared, her first thought was to get here so Mom and Dad would be safe."

Jonesy folded his arms. "And what happens if she dies, Deacon? What if they come, and you can't stop them?"

Deacon looked past his brother at Sin and Ariel, who were both slowing down their sparring and looking over at them. With total resolve, he said, "Then I die trying."

Jonesy stared at him, a muscle jumping in his jaw. "You're a fool."

"I'd rather be a fool with her than safe without her. Get Mom and Dad out of here, please."

He turned and walked away, leaving Jonesy in stunned silence.

"Hey, guys, you want to mix it up some?" Sin asked as she and Ariel approached.

Deacon erupted into action, grunting with determination as he charged Sin like a feral animal.

"Let's go. Show me what you have," Deacon shouted.

Deacon's body collided with hers in a loud crash, sending them both tumbling to the ground. They scrambled to stand in a blur of fists and feet, each strike more brutal than the last. With every punch and kick, their faces contorted with effort and an adrenaline-fueled frenzy. But Sin's wicked grin added fuel to Deacon's fire as they traded blow after blow, neither willing to back down in an intense battle of skills.

Deacon shook his head at Jonesy, who stood watching, his fists clenching and unclenching, itching to jump in. Deacon didn't want his interference. What he wanted was for everyone to realize he could handle himself. They needed to know he was a man capable of protecting Nia.

Frustrated because he meant to catch Sin off guard, Deacon

grunted and attacked with all he had. He felt validated when Sin lost her sassy grin, and sweat began to pop out on her forehead.

"Yeah, man, fight!" Jonesy yelled.

Tired of his brother and Sin acting like he and Nia were lost without them, he swung around and attacked his brother with equal zeal.

Hit after hit, he pounded Jonesy and became more infuriated when Jonesy only used defensive blows in return.

"Get it all out, Little Brother." Jonesy's words only seemed to taunt him.

Exhaustion seeped into Deacon's shoulders, his fists finally losing their power. He stopped when the impact of Jonesy's words filtered through his rage-fogged brain. His brother was handling him once again. Exhausted from constantly being watched . . . cuddled and monitored and made to feel as though he was not in control of his life . . . He was no longer on medication, but the early years of continued surveillance had worn on his self-esteem.

He overheard it all: *Has Deacon had his medication? Does Deacon have any friends? We have to protect Deacon. Jonesy, are you watching out for your little brother?*

"So, the baby bear has claws," Ariel teased as she walked over and handed him a towel.

Hunched over, panting, Deacon accepted the towel and wiped his face, sourly murmuring, "Thank you, Ariel."

"You got some skills there, boy," Sin said, her hands on her hips. Her breathing was already under control.

Deacon studied her. *Who are you really, Sin? Besides being Nia's sister.*

Before Deacon could ask her any questions, Jonesy intruded. "My little brother has two high-level belts in Kenpo and jujitsu. He is also skilled in several weapons. You're not running to our rescue, lady. We were running to yours regardless of this military pre-K camp they operate here."

Sin stepped inches from Jonesy. Her chocolate skin glistened from her sparring, and her chest heaved in righteousness. "Listen, honey, this pre-K camp, as you call it, has seen more war than most countries. Don't you ever belittle what these men and women have given for their country."

Jonesy scoffed. "Oh, I'm not belittling them, but what they could do before and what they can do now are two different things. My granddad's 1980 Trans Am Firebird used to do 100 miles an hour in 16.9 seconds; now, I can't coax it out of the garage."

Deacon watched Sin grit her teeth in response to Jonesy's mockery. And Jonesy's eyes lit with passion as he swayed closer to Sin.

Looking back and forth between the two, barely an inch between them, Deacon saw Ariel sporting a knowing grin as though she knew something he hadn't caught on to. He hated it when people gave those looks. It meant he was missing something in the social cues being displayed. And when he chose to ask what he had missed, people became very offended.

Always on the outside looking in.

Sin dismissed Jonesy's presence and focused on Deacon. "Regardless of your brother's opinion, these men and women will keep Nia safe while we go after the families controlling the book. Until we nullify them all, we're still in danger."

"I can keep Nia safe, Sin," Deacon shouted.

"I know you believe that, Deacon, but the people coming after us are ruthless. They will stop at nothing to destroy everyone who gets in their way. Your training is decent; you've got some moves, but it hasn't prepared you for this level of engagement."

Jonesy stepped between them. "My brother—"

"Jonesy, stop! I can speak for myself—"

Jonesy swiveled to Deacon. "I'm only—"

"Doing what you always do, Jonesy. Let me—"

"You're my little brother. I—"

Deacon couldn't do it for one more minute. Nobody listened. A little respect would mean that at least someone would listen. He needed some air. Nothing had been accomplished. They still felt he was less than them, and he was no longer willing to let that pass. Reaching into his duffle, he put his gun in the waistband of his back and threw his bag over his shoulder.

The last thing he heard as he left was Ariel's sarcastic comment. "Well, I'm glad you boys got that all talked out."

* * *

Deacon relished the cool air against his skin, the late-night wind cutting through the trees like a knife. He wandered toward the iron gates. Four guards stood at the perimeter, their rifles at the ready. One nodded at him. The others didn't move.

Beyond the gate, darkness loomed. Not just the absence of light, but something heavier. Watching.

He reached the gate and pressed his hand to the cold metal, and the hairs on the back of his neck stood on end.

Was it his imagination, or were they close?

Suddenly, one of the guards lifted a hand to his earpiece. "Movement in the trees. South perimeter."

Deacon's heart thudded. He peered into the dense woods but saw nothing.

"Could be wildlife," the guard said, lowering his weapon.

Or it could be worse. Deacon touched his lower back where his gun fit snugly against him. He didn't wait. He turned and sprinted back toward the house. His breath puffed out in white clouds, and his shoes thudded against the dirt path.

Inside, he took the back stairs two at a time, moving through the shadows until he stood outside Nia's door.

He raised a hand to knock, then stopped.

She needed rest. He knew that.

But if something happened tonight . . . if this was the beginning . . .

He pulled a small notebook from his pocket and scribbled a note:

I'll be close. If you need me, knock twice. I'm next door.

He slid it under the door.

Then he leaned against the wall, slid to the floor, and sat.

Just in case.

Because he was done running, too.

Chapter Twenty-Seven

Nia

She stirred awake to an unfamiliar quiet, blinking against the soft light filtering through her curtains. Nia rolled over and sat up. Smacking her lips together, she frowned. Her dry mouth and sluggish limbs clouded her thoughts enough that she hesitated to remember whose bedroom she was in.

She stretched, a deep ache throbbing in her muscles, like she'd run a marathon in her sleep. *What Mack truck hit me?*

Hoping a shower would refresh her, Nia staggered into the bathroom, avoiding the mirror as she completed handling her hygiene. Disoriented, she slipped into a sweatsuit folded neatly on the chair and wondered when someone had brought it in during the night. The Benson logo was stitched in gold thread over the Nike Swoosh on the hoodie. She shoved her feet into a pair of cross-trainers and pulled her hair into a loose bun.

Her foot stepped on something, and she looked down. Picking up the small piece of paper, she read a short note from Deacon.

Next door? This man is so sweet.

Making her way out of the room, she cautiously walked

through the wide corridor as she made her way downstairs, passing antique portraits and sunlit windows. The sheer size of the house was overwhelming—it had to be at least twelve thousand square feet—and after all the surprises from yesterday, she was reluctant to wander around. She especially didn't want to run into that Mother Sweat woman.

Where is everybody?

The thought had just passed through her mind when, like a bloodhound, the scent of bacon and coffee led her toward the dining room. When she arrived, the buzz of conversation was already fading. Most of the long table was empty, dishes cleared, only a few lingering voices were left, and the occasional clatter of utensils remained.

"Good morning, all," Nia said, scanning the room for Sin.

Junie looked up with a crooked grin. "You're a little late, Sleeping Beauty. We've been up, trained, and eaten. Twice for me, I'm a growing boy."

Deacon sat near the far end, sipping from a mug. He looked up, surprised. "Nia. I didn't think you'd be up yet."

She blinked at him. "Yet? Looks like I'm late. I got your note. I thought you were leaving with your parents."

"I saw them off a few minutes ago," he said gently. "They wanted me to tell you that despite everything, they were pleased to meet you, and they hope to see you again when this is over."

Nia massaged her temple. "That's nice of them. Deacon, I feel . . . weird. Drained. Like my brain's still in bed."

Ariel leaned back with a smirk. "That's what happens when you've been drugged to sleep."

Nia froze. "Wait—what?"

"Sin laced your tea last night," Ariel said casually. "Figured you needed the rest."

"You're kidding?"

"She's not," Deacon interjected, voice laced with guilt. "I didn't know until this morning. I'm sorry."

Nia turned, her glare finding Sin entering the room. "You drugged me?" she shrieked.

Sin set her glass down with a sharp clink. "You needed real rest, Nia. It's been a rough forty-eight hours. Your body was shutting down."

Frustration poured from her pores. "You always do this. Make decisions for me."

"I look out for you, Nia."

Nia's voice rose. "You make me irrelevant. When you're around, I wake up, and everything's already decided. It might surprise you that I live quite well without your interference."

Ariel's eyes widened as she sat back to watch. Junie shifted uncomfortably in his chair.

"You're overreacting," Sin said calmly. "And maybe you've had more help than you know."

"Right, like my college nemesis. You just let that little tidbit slip. How long? How long have you been the Olivia Pope in my life?" Nia screamed.

Before Sin could respond, the dining room door opened with controlled urgency. Zachary stepped in, his voice carrying throughout the room. "I was monitoring the Everettes' exit. A fallen tree that wasn't there an hour ago was placed in the road. They're being cut off. The Council's made their move."

Everyone froze.

Zachary looked at Deacon. "Your parents are two miles down the road. Any minute, they'll be pinned down. I should have insisted they take our tunnels, but your brother was adamant on leaving out the front gate and that the cargo van would be enough to disguise them."

Deacon stood, already moving. "My mother is claustrophobic; she wouldn't have done well in tunnels. Let's go."

"Gear up," Sin ordered. "Zachary, can we get backup?"

Zachary tossed a rifle belt to Deacon. "Of course. They're already forming outside. My ATV will ride point."

"I'm coming," Nia said, standing.

Sin moved to block her. "You're staying here."

"You don't get to decide that," Nia snapped. "Not after drugging me. Not anymore."

"Let her come," Deacon said, steady and sure. "We don't have time for this."

Sin held Nia's gaze, then nodded once. "Stay close."

The group bolted from the room. Nia ran with them, relieved that she would prove her mettle.

* * *

After an awkward jostling of who would ride with whom, a defiant Nia climbed into the driver's seat of the ATV, a smug Deacon behind her. Zachary had fitted everyone with coms and solicited their agreement only to do what he or Sin communicated.

A concerned Sin stepped into Nia's personal space, pressing a SIG MCX against her and placing its holster strap around her neck. "Don't let your stubbornness and pride make you do something you don't want to, Lady Bug."

"Big Sis to the rescue, right?"

Sin's answer to Nia's sarcasm was a quick hug as she ran, jumped on her ATV, and took off.

"You all right?" Deacon asked.

Revving the motor and taking off, Nia's nervousness only allowed her a brief nod. Zooming around trees and brush, the comm crackled with static. Then she heard it . . . the static sound of gunfire accompanied by the words that dropped her stomach to her feet.

"We're under fire. Multiple hostiles. Northwest ridge. Van's pinned."

"That's Jonesy!" Deacon yelled.

Nia didn't realize she'd stopped breathing until the wind slapped her across the face. As the ATV tore across the ridge, branches whipping by, Nia's gun bounced against her chest. Now, all she had to do was remember all her father taught her—*exhale slowly, don't rush the shot, let the weapon settle before squeezing the trigger.*

"As long as he's talking, that's a good thing, right?" she asked, the words scraping out of her throat like gravel.

The ATV bounced over uneven terrain, and Deacon steadied her as she swayed. "Means they're still alive and fighting back," he yelled.

Beside them, the caravan of all-terrain vehicles fanned out, crunching over fallen twigs, a storm made of wheels and war-trained resolve. Four Benson security operatives rode shotgun in the other ATVs, too calm to be anything but lethal.

Loud static crackled through the air, and then, "Ready?" Sin shouted into her mic. With that one word, Nia could hear her sister's adrenaline pumping; she was in her realm.

"Already moving in position," came Zachary's reply. "Flanking the tree line. Give me sixty seconds. Maybe less."

The rest of the ATVs idled together, waiting for Zachary and his crew's signal. Nia watched the scene opening before them, her heart drumming in her ears. Deacon's family was holding its own against three times its number.

Jesus, take the wheel!

Braking, they sat on their ATVs idling, waiting for their signal.

Ariel checked her sidearm, her eyes narrowed against the wind. "Let's even the odds."

"And let the paramedics sort them out," Bebop said, but Nia heard his next mumbling too, "Let's hope we can end it here."

She gulped.

The Benson van was almost indistinguishable in the brush and mud but for its wheels spinning, to no avail, dust spurting from its left rear tire. Nia tried to see through the sound of gunfire . . . sharp and constant. Her flinches weren't helping.

Then Nia saw her. Ms. Linette. "Do you see her, Deacon? Your mother, over there," she pointed.

Linette fired calmly from the van's cracked passenger window, her face a mask of sheer grit and maternal rage. Jones Sr. was at the rear panel, his fire controlled and precise. Jonesy had taken the wheel, trying to rock the van out of its trap, the modified vehicle's frame grinding against the road's gravel.

"We have to hit them now, or they'll breach!" Deacon shouted.

"Zach, status?" Sin barked.

"We had to hit three from this side. They're down, two running. Rock and roll, you're open."

"Go, go, go," Sin yelled as they fanned out.

Approaching the action, Deacon jumped and ran ahead. "Stay behind me," he barked.

But Nia froze until she saw two men emerge from the trees. Before she could call out and warn Deacon, he had twisted and fired, taking one down. The other ducked behind a tree, but Ariel was coming up on that man's six, and she took him out.

Sin charged straight ahead, the ATV's pedal down, her body hanging over the side like a rodeo cowgirl as she shot two more on the front line. Jones came out of the van to cover Sin when a man shot and clipped him in the shoulder as Linette jumped out behind him and dragged him back inside.

Still sitting there, Nia looked around, and everyone was valiantly helping the cause but her.

She was like superglue stuck to her seat. And the problem for her was that there was no Sin to blame for hindering her movement. It was all on her. She was terrified.

What am I doing here?

From the forest, bursts of fire lit up the foliage. Pounding her fist against her thigh, Nia exhaled and bailed from the ATV, running. She didn't think, didn't check her angles. She moved like lightning, a woman determined to make her mark.

A figure darted to intercept her, Council gear—rifle raised—a shot rang out. Not hers.

He dropped.

She turned. Deacon lowered his weapon. He was already looking for the next target.

Bebop and Malachi were on the right of the action, returning suppressive fire. Ariel moved in sync with Sin like they'd trained for years. And the Benson men? Silent Storm Kings. Every shot was purposeful, and each movement was calculated.

Relieved, Nia reached the van. "Ms. Linette!"

"I'm fine!" she shouted without turning, firing another round. "But Jones needs a doctor."

"I'm okay, baby. Nia, get in here or back behind the trees before someone shoots you or my son trying to protect you," he yelled.

Nia scrambled inside. Putting her gun down, which had been useless to her, she spotted a small white towel, folded it, and scooted over to Jones, pressing it to his shoulder.

"Thank you, darling," he groaned.

Nia nodded, dismissing his comments. In her mind, she hadn't done anything—*ever a coward.*

"They cut off the escape route," Jonesy growled over his shoulder. "But they didn't count on the upgrades in this van."

Suddenly, the van bucked, lurching with force. The barrier they used to block the path was moved back inch by inch. The vehicle's reinforced bumpers, dual exhaust override, and terrain-modified armor worked on their behalf.

It wasn't a van. It was a tank in disguise. Junie's genius at work again. They inched forward as Jonesy turned the vehicle around to return to the compound.

"They've already scurried to remove their wounded. I was hoping to take a hostage," Zachary's voice snapped over comms.

Sin spat a curse.

"Smart," said Deacon grimly through the comms. "Nia, Dad, you guys all right?"

"Yes, we're all right, son," Jones yelled.

"No, he's not. He needs a medic," Linette yelled over Jones.

"Let's head back. My men will clean up any stragglers out here. Everybody's head on a swivel. We have a medical clinic with excellent trauma treatment. Doctors on-site," Zachary said.

"Of course you do," Jonesy snorted.

Little by little, the gunfire ceased—the aftereffects of smoke curled into the air. And then, it quieted. Nia wouldn't call it peaceful or feeling safe. What they had at best was survived. And what part had she played in any of it? She leaned against the inside panel of the van, her heart pounding against her ribs.

Linette slid down beside her, her gun resting across her lap. "Ouch, hot," she said, moving it to the floor.

"Glad you guys showed up, baby girl," she said softly. "I was starting to run out of prayers."

Nia wanted to answer, but the words wouldn't come. Because behind the adrenaline, behind the strategy and the bullets, was one fact she couldn't stop seeing.

They had won this skirmish in spite of her.

Chapter Twenty-Eight

Nia

An antiseptic scent clung to the air as Nia entered the small medical clinic inside the estate. Her Nikes were light on the tile, but her mind was anything but. Jones Sr. lay on a bed, his face pale, his shoulder bound in layers of gauze. The excellence of the level of care he would receive was evident in the well-equipped room and the number of staff already attending to him with expertise.

Linette sat beside him, her hands clasped in her lap, her lips moving silently. Whether in prayer or grief, Nia couldn't tell. But worry was etched in every line of her face. She had put on a good front earlier but was crashing now.

Deacon stood at the foot of the bed, his arms crossed, his expression unreadable. Nia felt the pressure building in her chest again, that familiar blend of fear and guilt.

"Is he going to be okay?" she asked softly.

Deacon nodded once, but it wasn't reassuring. "They got the bullet out. It missed anything major. He's not waking up yet, but he will." He studied her. "I'm glad you came."

She hesitantly moved to stand beside him, their shoulders

nearly touching. "I almost didn't. I feel so guilty. I'm sorry, Deacon. I, I—should have never come to you for help."

"Nonsense," Linette said. "Jones will be all right; he's tough. None of this is your fault."

"Mom's right, Nia. I wouldn't, and neither would Pop, want you to go through any of this without help."

Nia lowered her voice, leaning toward Deacon's ear. "I froze out there. When the shots rang out—I didn't know what to do. I just sat there. I even left you and rode back in the van."

"I'll be right back, Mom," Deacon said.

Linette nodded. She held Jones's hand, wiping the sheen from his face as he slept sedated.

Leading Nia outside the room to a corner in the hallway, he touched her hand. "You were trying to survive," he said without looking at her. "That's not cowardice. That's instinct. And as you can see, I got back fine."

"Still, I didn't help. I could've—should've—done more. Maybe Sin is right. Deacon, what if I'm just a liability to everyone?"

He turned to her, his eyes softer than she deserved. "You're not a liability, Nia. You're a constant. And I've had very few of those."

She swallowed, the words catching in her throat. "How did I not realize how much of my life she controlled? Who medicates a person without permission?"

Deacon's jaw tensed, and his eyes rolled back like he remembered something difficult. "They said it would help. Help me sit still. Help me think 'clearly.' Help me fit into the box they built for me. But what they meant was, 'Make me less different.'"

Deacon reached into his pocket and ran his fidget rings between his fingers.

She sighed and reached for his other hand. "I'm sorry that happened to you," she said, observing the wrinkles in his scrunched forehead. "And now, I've made you feel bad." Caressing his fingers, she brought his hand to cup her cheek. "I was wrong for how I judged you before. For not seeing how messed up that was."

He placed the rings smoothly into his pocket and cradled her face in both hands. "That's why I don't want you to blame yourself. People don't know how to handle what they don't understand. My neurodivergence is not something for anyone to manage at this point in my life, but my family doesn't know how to let go. Just like Sin telling you that you needed rest. And her manipulating you to do what she felt was right for you? Maybe it wasn't evil—but it sure wasn't healthy."

Nia squeezed his hand. "We can't let them make decisions for us anymore."

"No," he said. "We can't. Do you know that Jonesy gets a six-figure income as my assistant and bodyguard? My parents were able to retire because I take care of everything for them. I don't mind, but it galls me that they don't trust me to care for myself."

"Oh, Deacon," Nia said.

For a long moment, they just stood there. Then quietly, she leaned into him. He didn't move at first. Then slowly, he pulled her in. She pressed her forehead to his chest.

"Is this okay?" she asked.

He rubbed her back in answer.

"You know what scared me most?" she said so low that he leaned closer.

He looked down. She tilted her head. "That I might not get another chance to talk to you. That if you had gotten shot instead . . ."

Deacon lowered his voice and let out a shaky breath. "Don't. Don't go there."

"I went there while I was frozen in that seat. I saw your body on the ground. And I couldn't move. I hated that about myself."

He took her chin gently between his fingers and brought his

face to hers. "You didn't fail. You're still here. And I need you here, Nia."

Their eyes locked. She blinked back the tears, lips parting to speak, but his mouth was already on hers—gentle, unhurried, the kind of kiss that asked nothing but offered everything.

She melted into him, her hands clutching his shirt, needing the anchor of him.

When they pulled apart, she leaned her head against his. "Tell me this isn't temporary."

"It's not," he said. "Not for me."

The door banged open, and Jonesy strutted through, his face set in a fierce frown. "You got your wish, little Brother, we're staying. Those fools made it personal. Shooting Pop ensured I'd get in this fight like a platinum invitation to a *Sports Illustrated* swimsuit party."

"But—" Nia said.

"Shut it, lady. You, I don't want to hear from. You think I didn't notice every time I saw you out there? You were either sitting immobile or running," Jonesy barked.

Deacon stepped forward. "Enough! You close your mouth, Jonesy. Now."

He leaned close enough to Deacon's face that there was no daylight between them. "Our father is lying a few feet away, and you're crying over her feelings being hurt? Man, get outta here."

Chest to chest, both men fumed as Nia twisted her hands in alarm.

Linette stormed into the hallway. "What is the world are you boys—"

The entrance to the clinic swung open, pulling everyone's attention. Ariel poked her head in. "Mother Sweat's calling a meeting. Everyone. Main library. Now."

* * *

By the time they entered the main library, the atmosphere felt sacred. Charged.

Mother Sweat sat at the center of the room in a high-backed chair, her eyes closed, her body gently rocking. People filed in, instinctively quieter than usual. Deacon and Nia found seats along the side wall while Junie paced near the door, his arms folded tightly.

Mother Sweat opened her eyes, then lifted her voice in that familiar, deep, omniscient-edged tone. "Nehemiah 4:14 After I looked things over, I stood up and said to the nobles, the officials and the rest of the people, 'Don't be afraid of them. Remember the Lord, who is great and awesome, and fight for your families, your sons and your daughters, your wives and your homes.'"

Junie snorted. Not loud, but loud enough.

Mother Sweat continued, her eyes never leaving the crowd. "We've fasted for the last 24 hours. Prayed. Anointed the gates of this estate. But we must understand this fight ain't only physical. It's spiritual. Emotional. Internal. And the enemy? He's counting on our fear. In this verse, the people of Judah were rebuilding the walls of Jerusalem that had lain in ruin for a while. But, the powers to be did not want the walls rebuilt. When you've been dominated by the powerful, they don't take kindly to folk getting from under their control. You know something about that, don't you, Junie? "

Junie stepped forward. "I do. Enslavement was a yoke of burden around every neck. But I've tasted freedom and Mother Sweat, I want to enjoy being a teenager. Why do I have to feel like I don't have any control over *my* life?"

Heads turned.

"Junie," his father warned gently.

"No, let him speak," Mother Sweat said. "This is still a house of truth."

Junie's voice cracked. "You want to talk about courage and calling? I didn't ask for any of this. I didn't choose to be 'the chosen.' I no longer want to be the one to hear His voice."

Gasps filtered throughout the room.

Mother Sweat raised her hand. "Let the boy speak his piece."

Eyes darting around the room, Junie swallowed. "I'm sorry if I'm a disappointment. But why can't I be like everyone else? If even for a little while? I want to go to the movies, hang out with my friends, fall in love with a cute girl—be normal."

Sari stepped forward from the back, heavily pregnant, her hand on her belly. "Junie . . . you have to understand, this gift—it's not punishment. It's placement."

He whirled on her, his eyes bulging. "Don't tell me what to understand. I didn't ask for God's assignments."

"Why are you saying all this now, son?" John asked, joining his daughter in front of him.

Junie pointed at Mother Sweat. "Because she's about to ask me what I've heard, and I haven't heard anything. Not one small word of instruction. I guess because I'm not talking to Him, He's not talking to me," he cried.

"Junie—" Sari said as she reached for her brother to comfort him, but he shrugged her away.

Zachary moved swiftly, placing himself between the siblings. "Don't you ever."

Junie's chest rose and fell, his fists clenching open and shut, then repeating. Nia had been where he was, holding her peace despite having none.

Her heart went out to him as his face crumpled before he stormed out. An awkward pall swept over everyone.

"Give him some space." Mother Sweat folded her hands slowly.

"God calls us. Sometimes gently. Sometimes through fire. But it's always love, even when it scorches."

She turned her gaze to the rest of the room. "We've already been attacked. You know this is real. They want the book, a tool of evil. Will you stand back and let evil grow? You all must decide. Will you run, or will you rise?"

Deacon looked over at Nia. She nodded slowly.

"After this," he whispered, "we're leaving. Taking back our lives."

She whispered back, "But how?"

He kissed her temple, whispering into her ear. "I have a plan and a few calls to make."

And in the quiet that followed, they both knew: the next battle was already taking shape inside them.

Chapter Twenty-Nine

General

Earlier that Day

General left the compound before sunrise. The fog clung to the road like a funeral shroud, heavy and whispering. He didn't mind. It matched his mood. There was a delay in assurances from law enforcement that there would be no interference when his men moved against the Benson Compound.

What was the sense of having his fingers in every state and providence's government if he had to deal with idiots at every turn?

He couldn't trust anyone, so he was going into town to get his assurances in person.

The entire debacle had him wanting to kill something, but he had to make do with pounding Eric's face, at least for now. General stretched out his hand and placed an ice packet on his bruised knuckles.

"You need anything, Boss?" Geoff asked.

"Foolish question. I need my book back," General snapped, wincing as he wiggled his fingers back and forth.

He looked at Geoff's body language and lack of response and decided to leave it alone. Some days, Geoff's stoic demeanor was tiresome. Yet, he kept him around more than anyone else because that same stoicism didn't blink an eye when General gave orders that others would balk at. Not Geoff. He was a soldier from the old school. Loyal and obedient. There was no grey area with him. It was what General said or the highway.

Cold. Calculating. Cruel. Those were the traits General prized in his subordinates. His mini-me's.

Pulling up to the small sheriff's office, General smirked, "Let's get this over with."

Geoff opened the door, and the two of them marched into the small office.

The potbellied sheriff leaned back in his chair, his feet up, his hands behind his neck as he chewed on his cheap cigar. "How can I help you, gentlemen?"

General stepped out of the office an hour later and slid into his truck. "Barney Fife, acting little gerbil," he snorted.

The gunning of the engine accompanied Geoff's answering grunt as they rode out of the small town.

He was behind because the meeting had not been as brief as he wanted. He hadn't counted on the sheriff being too stupid to realize the danger of allowing his greed to outmatch his common sense.

After dillydallying around, the sheriff finally asked for what he wanted: more money for his silence. He wanted assurances that their partnership wouldn't come back to bite him, as though General's job was to keep him safe.

But General had smiled through the entire exchange, finally sliding the thick envelope of cash across the table like a dealer in a rigged card game. The sheriff's fat sausage fingers grabbed the money with a large smirk on his face. General gave him that win . . . for now. He needed to get this done, but he would not forget. When everything died down, he promised himself that there would be a new sheriff in town, courtesy of the Council.

"Your loyalty better last longer than your conscience," he'd said, his tone like ice cracking. The sheriff gulped, but to give him credit, he didn't blink.

Instead, he rose and escorted them out of his office, his deputies standing as they passed, hands on their weapons, on alert until they left the building.

"You think he'll follow through and cover up what's about to happen?" Geoff asked as he drove up the winding road.

"He did seem dumb, but he didn't seem mentally incapacitated," General said. "Let's get to the barn you bought sight unseen. Then we can finally return to the compound and take care of business."

When they pulled up to the barn, it stood alone, a structure swallowed by trees and shadows, purchased under a false name.

General walked inside, standing at the door as he looked around. Years ago, it had been part of a prosperous farm. But the main house burned down after a failed crop year. It had sat empty and abandoned, too far out of the way to entice a family that felt it was worth the effort to rebuild.

Geoff entered, standing next to General. "It will do."

The stink of rusted metal and animal feces filled the air. Hooks hung from thick beams, and chains lay coiled like sleeping serpents. The floor was already stained with memory and guts.

Had they hung their hunted prizes here? A stag shot through the head made good eating on a winter's night.

The acrid smell reminded General that the clock was ticking.

Soon, the book would require its legacy blood. It had waited thirty years; it would not wait any longer. He needed to get back.

"It is sufficient. Let's go. We still have time to attack."

Geoff was already turning, holding the large barn door open as General swiftly moved , a new urgency in his stride.

By the time he returned to camp, late afternoon had crept in. But the silence that greeted him wasn't relief—it was dread. Something was off.

Geoff's second in command met them near the trailhead, his face stiff, eyes avoiding. He leaned forward to whisper to Geoff when General interrupted him. "Say it out loud. What did you bungle now?"

The muscular man with a crew cut folded his hands before him and lowered his head. "After earning your anger, this time, we didn't want anyone to get past us without acting." He stopped and cleared his throat. "A van left the compound, and we attacked."

"You have hostages for me? Who was it? We can use them to bargain to get the book back. Geoff, go and see the hostages, " he said eagerly.

"No hostages," the man mumbled.

Geoff's eyes narrowed as he snarled. "What are you saying?"

"There were three in the van, two white men, one older, and an older Black woman—"

"Our intel tells us that's the Everettes," Geoff told General.

"I'm aware," General groused. "Go on, tell the rest of it."

"We had them pinned, then a battalion of men and women on ATVs shooting arrived, zigzagging on the offensive. It seemed as though they came from nowhere."

General's keen observation noted the beads of sweat popping from the man's forehead. "What is the bottom line here?"

"Seventeen. Two serious. No fatalities."

General halted. Turned. "No one died?"

The man flinched. "No. And it's my opinion that it was not their intention to kill. They were good; the best I've seen."

General sighed. "Let me see if I can make this make sense. You attacked three people with a battalion of over twenty men. And all of the people from the Benson Compound walked away. Is *that* what you're telling me?"

Seeing the man's lips compress, General hesitated. "What is your name?"

"Emerick, sir."

"And were you the one giving the order to attack the van?"

"Da, sir."

General then asked Geoff, "Do you vouch for this person, Geoff?"

"No."

That was all he needed. General pulled out his gun and shot Emerick in the side.

He stood over him as he lay on the ground. "Take him to the others. What leader has most of his men wounded, and he is unscathed? Do better, Geoff."

"Da, General." He then leaned down and picked up Emerick, who only moaned, and they all marched toward the encampment they had made deep in the Bensons' woods. The scanner blocker they had would not show their campsite to any scanner, and even drones would jam and then turn away if flying near.

The heart of the camp was a pitiful sight. Men were sprawled under two makeshift tents, bloodied and rattled. A few stood nearby, their eyes wide when they saw Emerick being carried in. They stiffened with shame or fear. Guns leaned against trees, useless now. They looked like a band of frat boys after a failed prank.

General observed them all waiting for him to speak. But he decided to let them stew for just a bit. After enough of them lowered their heads upon eye contact, he said, "You saw a vehicle and took a chance. And instead of waiting for a command, you leaped."

No one dared speak.

He pivoted toward one of the men seated on a stump, his leg bandaged, face bruised. "They all walked away. Did you miss on purpose?"

"No . . . We did hit one."

"One!" General then stepped forward and kicked the man in his wounded leg. "You fool. You let them see you. You told them we were here. You let them know we're outside their gates. You ended our advantage."

He looked out at the group. "I've been patient. Maybe too patient. Some of you think this war can be won with bruises. That bleeding a little proves bravery. You want to win without getting your hands dirty." He took a breath. "I am here to remind you what war looks like."

He turned to Geoff. "Prepare the barn. Bring anyone we catch alive there. No more soft strikes. No more mixed messages."

Then, quieter, he said in a resolved tone, "Now, I'll finish visiting the wounded. In the meantime, contact our nearby reserves. Tell them to bring an army. By this time tomorrow, I want the book in one hand and the head of Ariel or that Sin in the other."

* * *

Sitting in the RV an hour later, General watched security footage of the ambush. The Council's men were sloppy. Fearful. Their aim panicked. The van had barely swerved before bullets flew, most going wide. And then, a few returned shots from inside the van sent his men scattering.

Cowards.

He poured a drink, pacing the floor of his private trailer. His mind flashed with scenes over the years of the pages in the book. The pages had begun whispering again. It called. He'd never been able to decipher the language, but the pulse of it beat like war drums in his skull.

He stopped, staring at the monitor. Rewound it. Watched again.

Zachary, an old enemy, once removed. He watched him in action, and it all came back vividly. He had become entangled in one of his projects years before when he was still serving in the military.

He narrowed his eyes. "He'll bleed for this. Another enemy to be added to the list. It is growing."

General played the video of the attack on repeat. He would go to sleep with it playing in his subconscious. When his other men arrived the next day, he wanted to be ruthless.

The book would not be denied.

Chapter Thirty

Deacon

Junie kicked at the pebbled gravel of the walkway, weaving around the rose garden behind the main house. He was pacing like a man who'd just found out the joke was on him—and always had been. "Y'all called me out here on this fly-by-night plan? You think this is how we save everybody? No. Check that. How *you* save everyone?"

Nia clutched her backpack tighter. "We think it's the only way to stop more people from getting hurt. I should never have taken that book. And, Junie, you're more than some divine walkie-talkie."

He stopped pacing, his eyes sharp. "That's easy for you to say. You're not the one God talks through like an AM radio. I didn't ask for this. I didn't ask to be a mouthpiece for everybody else's miracles. And I feel guilty for every day I go without prayer, but if I open those doors? God floods in."

Deacon stepped in, his voice low and steady. "We're not asking you to hear from heaven. We're asking you to stand with us. If we move the book, we make this place safe. If we do this—*really* do this—we're saving lives. I can't sit still and do nothing while my dad is laid up after being shot. My family's caught in this because of me. And you'll be protecting your very pregnant sister by moving the danger from here. Man, we're trying to do the right thing."

Junie scoffed, but his jaw twitched. "And what? Ride off into the sunset? Y'all want to be the heroes? And even if the book is gone, they will still think it's here. How does your leaving solve that?"

"We know they're monitoring everything. We'll phone the agency on an open line and say we're back on the run with the book. We'll do it from the airplane on our way away from here. The mole will do the rest. I reached out to a friend. All we have to do is make it out of here, and we can expose the Council, turn the book over to people who haven't been bought, and walk away."

"That's a little simplistic," Junie said.

"The simpler, the better, don't you think?" Nia pushed. "But the tunnels they mentioned earlier? I have a feeling you built them or designed them. I think if I were ever enslaved, I would always have an alternative way of escape, another way out. This is that moment."

A beat of silence passed. Then Junie muttered, "Yeah, I designed the tunnels. They called me paranoid, but I never wanted to be boxed in again. If I'm breathing, I'm free."

Deacon's hands waved in the air. "But here we are boxed in, waiting for a battle we don't have to have. There are other ways to fight. But we have little time to move forward before the Council regroups."

Junie shook his head. "Fine. Let's see if we can change something."

They moved quickly, slipping back into the house and into the large living room, which housed the safe. Deacon kept a lookout as Junie pulled the picture aside and opened the safe. He hesitated when he saw Mother Sweat's bible sitting there like a sentinel on duty, guarding the book, neutering its power. His hand fell back.

"Hurry, man," Deacon said harshly.

Junie's hand slid inside and yanked out the book. He breathed a sigh of relief when he saw that someone had wrapped it in oilcloth. Nia's hands shook as she handed him her satchel, and he gingerly placed the book in it.

After replacing the picture, he moved to the light switch, popping it open to reveal a hidden panel with a keypad. With steady fingers, he entered the code.

The floor creaked. A hidden door opened.

"Tunnel goes about a mile out toward the east woods," Junie said. "After that, you're on your own."

Then he handed the satchel back to Nia. "This thing feels alive."

"Because it is," she said quietly, shivering like a chill had passed over.

Deacon closed the door and ran to catch up as they individually descended into the tunnel. The air was stuffy, but the tunnel was surprisingly modern.

Junie led the way, his flashlight bobbing as they moved quickly through the narrow corridor.

"It's equipped with air filters and exhaust ventilation, lights, water, food, and a series of bunkers that will hold over two hundred people," he said over his shoulder, "but if I click any of the systems on, it will notify the staff monitoring the compound."

"Noted," Deacon replied. "Hey, why only two hundred people when three hundred live here?"

"Because I calculated the probability of survival if anything or one hit us. Most of these heroes would be the last standing after sending children, seniors, and civilians into the bunkers. It's how they're built. It's how I want to be built."

"You are a hero, Junie," Nia said.

"Uh-huh. No sense in buttering me up now; the deed is done. This better end up being what's best for everyone and not just what's best for y'all," he spat.

The tunnel ended in a small garage, where several vehicles were parked. All were army green or camouflaged, and a few trucks were dark brown.

"Pick any of these vehicles, and I'll let you out. When you leave, stay on the dirt road. Its exit is hidden by the trees lining it, and our tech people jam all electronic surveillance for miles around. Only we have the frequency. We're only forty-five minutes from the Memphis International Airport. Leave the car in the airport parking lot. It has a tracker."

Deacon went over to Junie and put out his hand. Junie slapped it front to back. "Thank you. You're not making a mistake. This is the only way to bring the Council down."

Junie gave him a skeptical look. "You know, I know this is right. But, man . . . I feel like I just set my world on fire."

"Sometimes," Deacon said, his voice low, "fire's the only way to clear a path."

Nia picked a car. "This one, Junie."

"Keys in the cup holder," he said.

Nia got in, placed her foot on the brake, and pushed the ignition.

Junie nodded at her. "All clear."

Deacon ran and jumped in when the entire wall lifted like a garage door. "Thanks, Junie!"

Junie saluted them as they pulled away, the door closing behind them.

* * *

Deacon held on to the dashboard as Nia hightailed it out of the woods, consistently looking in her rearview mirror. His mind raced as he rehearsed the plan again because he was out of his element, more comfortable with formulas, books, and numbers than people. Nia didn't know that they were headed to Ghana. He wasn't trying to keep her ignorant on purpose, but he didn't want her to slip and tell Junie. His heart was whole because she hadn't asked him where they were going, and she might not have realized it, but she trusted him. And that meant everything.

They were meeting none other than Cole Jay, a well-known actor and the first African American to star in and produce a superhero movie franchise. With Ghanaian roots from his father's side, Cole was one of the cofounders of Ghana's prestigious Full Bloom Economic Conference. One phone call from Deacon, and he readily agreed to be their transportation without hesitation or inquiry. Deacon's need was Cole Jay's open door; he had been after Deacon to attend the conference for five years.

Since 2019, Deacon has worked closely with Ghana's Return Home campaign. As part of their agricultural stabilization program, he provided farmers with free, genetically enhanced seeds to increase crop yields and conserve water in challenging soil conditions. He hadn't discussed this mission with his family, wanting to prove that he could make a difference.

However, he often wondered if there was anything he did that Jonesy, his self-appointed handler, didn't know about. Being a part of this project allowed him to showcase his abilities during Zoom meetings without being underestimated or judged for his lack of social skills. It was a refreshing change from constantly questioning his intelligence because of his stimming.

While COVID was a harsh reality check for the world, that they were not indestructible. It had opened the door to the normalcy of virtual conferences, and he was grateful for that.

Deacon also contacted Ghana's ambassador, a man he trusted to provide confidential assistance. He had been quiet about the amount of funding Deacon had given to their organization at his request, and although he was listed as a scientist among many others, few knew the extent of his contributions. The conversation yielded the bonus of Deacon learning CSPAN, and other international news outlets would be televising the Full Bloom Economic Conference. Because Deacon sat on their agriculture committee, adding his name to the attendee list would not be a red flag, as he had been a part of it virtually since its inception.

He sat rigid in the passenger seat, his legs tucked in, his arms crossed. He'd been silent since they left the tunnel, the tension hanging in the air like static, his mind running on fumes.

Finally, he spoke. "You drive well, Nia."

She flicked him a glance. "You're not sitting like it. But thanks. I don't mind driving."

"I'm just running scenarios in my mind." He loosened his arms and shook them out. "Driving is not my strong suit. When I was younger, I tried driver's training; it was a disaster."

"Everyone ought to know their strengths." Nia glanced over at him. "You know I've never gone against what my sister thought was best for me. I don't know if I'm trusting you over her, or I'm just that angry with her for years of mishandling my feelings."

"Or maybe you want to prove you can trust yourself."

Nia gave a small smile. "Yeah? Maybe so. Let's make it work."

Deacon's fidget rings ran smoothly over his fingers.

"Do you think," Nia asked, her voice tentative, "if we had ever put our foot down, we would be much more independent than we are now? Like maybe part of this run for independence is on us?"

"I never felt I had a reason to buck their system," Deacon replied. "It gave my parents comfort and Jonesy a job to look out for me."

Nia looked over with a measure of new respect. "I never imagined you were the sole supporter of your family."

Deacon exhaled, his fingers moving fluidly through the rings. "It's not that they are trying to live off me, Nia. It happened organically. My mother had to take time off work as an elementary school teacher to care for me. I was a handful as they tried to get my medication stabilized. I feel like I owe my parents because I was not easy to raise. Dad worked construction, but I don't want him working that hard anymore. What I did was my idea."

"I get it. It's just . . . They don't seem like the type of people who would require you to pay them back." Nia's eyes flicked to him. "Um, you've shared some things with me about your challenges, and your mother talked a little bit too when you were speaking with your dad. But is there anything more you can tell me about Deacon Everette?"

He grinned, cocking his head. "I could, but then I'd have to kill you and hide that beautiful body."

She laughed. "Oh, you got jokes."

"Sometimes, I can be a funny guy." He turned slightly toward her, earnest now. "I could be your guy, Nia."

A small gasp escaped her lips, her hands tightening around the steering wheel.

Deacon saw it. And . . . misread it.

"I mean, I know I can be a lot," he said quickly. "One doctor said one thing. Another said another. Asperger's, ADHD, sensory stuff. Some said I was brilliant. Others said I was broken. My mom got tired of the noise. She said I was perfect the way I am. So, she quit her job and homeschooled me."

"Deacon?" Nia asked, her voice trembling.

Wanting to cover for his blunder of being too forward, he kept talking. "Yeah. They'd already sacrificed so much. When Jonesy came to live with us, Mom said she couldn't leave two boys who needed her. She walked away from everything. My dad—"

"Deacon!" Nia said. She accelerated and looked into the rearview mirror in panic mode. "The car behind us has followed for the last few miles."

Deacon slid his rings into his pocket, slid his hand inside his duffle, and pulled out his gun. "Keep going. We're only two miles away now. If they try to stop us, I'll handle it."

Nia's face paled. "Maybe this wasn't such a good idea. We can turn around—"

"No! Just keep driving." He pulled down his visor and watched the car keep pace with them.

Nia's hands shook a little, but she kept going.

"You're doing great," Deacon said. "Look, the private aircraft entrance, Wilson Air Center. Go there."

Nia got into the far right lane, and the car following them kept going. When the vehicle got abreast of them, it looked like a soccer mom and her two kids in a black SUV.

Nia bit her lip. "Sorry."

"It's okay. What is important is that you kept going. We're doing this, babe."

A small smile of victory passed her lips.

"You think they've figured out we're missing yet?" Deacon asked. "I can hear Jonesy screaming right now."

"Oh, he won't be as loud as Sin. We'd better be in the air before they catch up with us."

"If Junie could wait even thirty minutes before giving us up, we'll make it. We should be up in the air and on our way to Ghana."

"Ghana?"

"Yes, I have some agricultural projects there . . . Hey, here's a good place to leave the car."

Nia pulled into the parking space, and they both exited. Looking around, they jogged to the entrance. As the double glass doors slid open, they blended well with the droves of people headed to their destinations.

They set a fast pace as they maneuvered around others through the large corridor.

They might have looked like they were hurrying to catch a plane, but Deacon realized they were hurrying to get their lives back . . . even from those they loved.

Chapter Thirty-One

Sin

Junie entered the command center, his usual exuberant swagger absent, replaced by a strange stiffness in his posture. The room buzzed with conversation—Sin and Jonesy, along with a few others, discussed their next steps, their voices punctuated by the soft hum of equipment.

But Junie's presence caused an immediate shift in the air. His eyes darted around, avoiding anyone's gaze before they finally landed on Sin.

Sin caught the hesitation in his stance, the way his shoulders tensed when their eyes met. The teen wasn't one for subtlety; something was off. Sin narrowed her eyes, crossing her arms.

"Junie," she said, her voice steady but with an edge. "Have you seen Nia?"

"Or Deacon?" Jonesy asked.

The words hung in the air as Junie's body straightened, his gaze darting nervously. He was caught off guard, his posture betraying his uncertainty. The room seemed to pause for a moment, waiting for his reply. Junie's eyes flicked briefly to his father, John, standing off to the side, who'd been watching with quiet attention.

Sin's head swung between the two. John's gaze never wavered from his son. His brow furrowed, and he took a slow step toward him, his voice low but firm. "Boy, what's going on? People are speaking to you."

Junie swallowed, his throat working like he was trying to push something out that wouldn't come. Sin was a master at catching clues. A subtle shift in his eyes, a nervous glance toward the door, and she knew that John had caught it. He also knew that look.

John's voice hardened, becoming a low rumble of authority. "Spill it, Junie."

For a moment, it seemed like Junie would bolt, but the silence in the room kept him rooted to the spot. His father's words hung heavy, pulling the truth out of him like a long-buried secret.

"Did they leave?" Jonesy asked, his tone hardening with every passing second.

Junie sighed, his shoulders slumping as if the weight of his decision had finally caught up with him. His voice came out in a soft, reluctant confession. "Yeah, they left." He then turned to his father, "I didn't want to, but Deacon made me."

John's eyes narrowed. "What do you mean, 'made you'?"

Junie swallowed again, his voice a mere whisper. "See, what happened was—"

"Junie!" John said.

"I gave them the book. Took it from the safe. They said it would be okay and that they had a plan. But I don't know where they went, just that they were heading to the airport."

Jonesy's hand rested on his stomach, his face paling. It was as though the words were like a knife twisting in his gut; everyone could see his frustration bubbling up, his movements quickening as he began to pace back and forth.

John, on the other hand, remained calm. "So, they've got the book. And you didn't stop them? Instead, you helped. A venomous, evil *Book of Disasters*."

Junie's face flushed with shame, his gaze dropped to the floor. "I didn't know what to do, Pop. They promised it would be okay."

Sin's voice cut through the tension like a blade. "Wait, so just like that, they're just gone?" she asked, the urgency in her words unmistakable.

Junie dragged out the answer, his head hanging. "Yeah. They've left. But that's all I know."

Sin turned on her heel, her eyes flashing with anger. "Of all the —" Her words died in her throat when Jonesy stopped pacing, staring at Junie with disbelief.

"No, no—this is bad," Jonesy growled, gripping his hair in frustration. "Why the hell didn't you stop them?"

John stepped forward, his hand outstretched in a quiet command for silence. "This is where you'll have to trust your brother knows what he's doing. And they can't be that far ahead. If you're that worried, you can play catch-up."

Sin's lips pressed into a thin line. "How are we supposed to find them now?"

Junie's voice was barely audible as he muttered, "They used the tunnels. You're an agent; you should be able to figure it out."

At that point, the room seemed to freeze. Sin's mind was working overtime. The tunnels were mentioned earlier, but Linette's claustrophobia had the Everetts leave through the front gate.

Jonesy's eyes narrowed as he met Sin's gaze. "We're going after them," he said, his voice hardening with resolve. "We'll find them before they get too far."

But Sin wasn't convinced. She crossed her arms, her stance defensive. "Let's go over this, shall we?" she asked. "Your brother is well-off. Therefore, he could be on his way to a private plane." She leaned close and snarled, "*That's* how they got here, remember! Stop shortchanging your brother."

"Like you shortchange your sister?" he yelled back.

Zachary, who had been observing until now, stepped forward, his expression grim. "It's not about arguing back and forth, you two. You're losing precious time."

Tension flooded the room as everyone processed the weight of what was happening.

Sin watched as Junie looked like he wanted to say something, but his father's stern gaze held him in place.

She approached him in an intimidating manner to push him to reveal his thoughts, but the teenager held her gaze without blinking.

"Enough," Zachary said, snapping everyone back to the present. "Get your gear. We move now. We can still catch them if we hurry."

Jonesy grabbed his rucksack with a grunt, his eyes still locked on Junie. He said it like a confession, more to himself than anyone else, "If Deacon's determined, we're gonna have a time catching up. He can become super focused."

Ariel hurried to the door. "If Deacon has the book, then it's Deacon we have to find. How was he certain that taking the book would keep the compound safe? That's what I would like to know."

"He had a plan. He was convinced he could lead them away," Junie said.

"We've surveyed the surrounding area, and nothing is coming up on our radar. But nothing would show up if the Council is running sophisticated tech, and I am sure they are. We'll send a team out to do further reconnaissance. In the meantime, I'll lead you guys out, then double back. We'll continue to prepare to take on the Council. I promise we'll be ready if they dare show up here. They're probably somewhere licking their wounds."

"Thanks, Zachary. Consider our debt paid, and now, I owe you one," Sin said.

"Nah, I can promise you that this is part of who we are. It's our pleasure and duty to assist."

* * *

Zachary popped open a light switch plate identical to the one in the main house's library. Keying in a code on the panel, the wall inside the closet slid open.

As the group prepared to leave, Sin took one last look at Junie. The kid was still standing there, a mix of guilt and uncertainty on his face. She wanted to say something comforting, but the words felt hollow. Instead, she nodded curtly, then turned toward the exit.

Jonesy was already on the move, his impatience pushing him forward. "We don't have time to waste," he said sharply. "Can we pick up the pace?"

Zachary's answer was in his fluid steps as he led the way, his strides sure and unyielding. They followed close behind each other, bracing themselves for whatever lay ahead.

The tunnel's lights were bright, as though their path were clear. But Sin wasn't sure this was the right move, leaving the compound, or if this was one wild goose chase. Nia had always been predictable, and Sin was baffled that this sister was a puzzle. So, maybe her moves weren't going to be predictable either.

At this point, they weren't just chasing Nia and Deacon anymore. They were chasing answers.

Chapter Thirty-Two

Sin

The group walked through the tunnels, lost in their thoughts.

Jonesy whispered, "This is a crazy escape route, man."

"You don't have to whisper. It's soundproof. Yes, it made Junie happy to have another way out of a place he had once been chained to. And it made sense to me. We even have bunkers and full supplies down here. We could live here for at least five years," Zachary said.

"But will you have cable?" Ariel joked.

Sin shook her head. She was learning that the more nervous Ariel was, the more she played comedian. One more joke, and she was going to give her an Xanax.

Zachary led them to a fork in the hallway. "This is it. Keep going until you reach the end, and you'll find a garage with several vehicles. Pick one. The key fobs are inside; leave the car at the airport. Like Junie, I'm sure that's where they're headed."

Jonesy gave Zachary a fist bump and a slap on his back. "Y'all have been righteous, man. At least we're moving trouble away from your door."

"I'm not sure about that." He then pointed to his earbud. "We have movement in our perimeters and some unusual activity at the front gate."

"Zachary, why didn't you say anything?" Sin demanded.

"Because it could all be conjecture, and it will be handled. I've doubled the recon patrol and added men to the front gate. My teams are on alert. We got this."

Sin hugged him. "You guys have been outstanding. Please don't let me leave with chaos on your doorstep."

Zachary shook his head. "Nah, you and our ex-comrade Legend—the Tiger and Bear Squad—rescued me and Bebop on that mission that took his leg. But it saved both our lives. We owe you one."

Sin placed her rucksack across her back and turned to a pensive Zachary. "You were always the king of your unit, the Lion Squad. We were glad to assist."

She then stepped back and saluted. "See ya, Lieutenant Colonel, sir. Tiger Squad signing off."

Zachary returned her salute, and Sin began to jog backward to catch up with Ariel and Jonesy.

In this hallway, the light gave off a golden reflection against the tunnel floor.

Swiftly moving ahead, Jonesy's feet pounded the ground, and Ariel was on his heels. Bringing up the rear, Sin called out to Zachary an old army chant they once used: "Tigers, Lions, and Bears, oh my, bring the enemy down, catch them on the sly."

Zachary chuckled as his running feet echoed through the tunnel. "Follow the yellow brick road, Hooah," his words fainter as he got further up the tunnel.

Ten minutes later, the golden lights in the tunnel flickered on and off. Stopping, the three stood staring at each other.

"What do you think is happening?" Ariel said.

"He said this tunnel was soundproof, so we won't be able to hear anything. Whatever it is, they have it handled. We need to keep going and save Deacon and, yes, even Nia, from themselves," Jonesy said.

"So they took us in, fed us, offered to fight for us, and we just leave? Really?" Sin stressed.

Jonesy snarled. "Don't act like I'm the bad guy. The man stated that he had it. I'm going to get my brother." Jonesy threw his rucksack on his back and continued in the direction they were headed.

Sin's body followed her conscience, and she slowed. "Go ahead, Ariel. I'm going back."

A stunned look crossed Ariel's face. "Really?"

Sin was uncomfortable, but she had never left someone to fight her battles. "I love my sister. And she's made her position clear; this time, I gotta trust her enough to make her own decision. And if your uncle and his people are behind the flickering lights, I'm not abandoning the group who refused to abandon us."

Ariel watched Jonesy's strides eat up the concrete in the tunnel as he faded down the corridor. She puffed, then took off in a full sprint in the opposite direction. She was headed back to the compound, Sin directly behind her.

Laughing, Ariel joked, "It would have been nice for once to see what's at the end of the yellow brick road."

Stone-faced, Sin ran all-out. All the information she knew about the Council suggested that they had regrouped big time, and she would need Pop to appear.

She would need all her wits . . . and Pop's too.

* * *

Crashing through the door they had recently left, Sin yelled, "Tiger Squad reporting."

They'd entered organized chaos. Sin saw everyone running to and fro, but they all seemed to know where they were going. Running to the command center, she saw the old Zachary she used to know standing in front of the monitors, watching the battle unfold before him and calling out orders into his headset. Sin sprinted forward when she overheard Zachary's conversation with John.

"I have to go out there," he growled to John, who stood by his side with Junie.

"And have my grandchild come into the world fatherless? Not on my watch. I'll go," John blasted.

"Papa, you're no match for trained military people," Junie cried.

John began to check his ammo and strap additional rounds across his chest. "Oh, I've learned a few things living here for eighteen months. And I've learned from the best. Your old man can hold his own."

Sin was impressed with Zachary's people's loyalty. They were the epitome of community, but regardless of their feelings, this was not their fight.

Ariel came alongside her and placed her hand on John's arm. "You don't have to do this. They are our monkeys, therefore, our circus."

"You came back?" Zachary said, stepping around John. "You didn't have to. We can handle this. What happened to you catching up with Deacon and Nia?"

Ariel opened her sack and pulled out a gun as she fussed. "I think it's high time Sin and Jonesy let those two grow outside their shadows. And if the boogeyman is here, this is where I need to be."

Coming into the room, Jonesy stomped over. "And it also

means *he* doesn't know the book is gone. Ergo, my little brother is safe," Jonesy groused as he placed a cartridge into his gun. "So, yeah, I'm in."

Sin looked at Jonesy and gave him a small smile. "Glad you followed."

Junie turned in a circle as the scene escalated. "I thought this would be an adventure. Instead, this is scary. Papa, I'm going to the prayer room to find Mother Sweat."

John's hardened countenance softened. "Son, I'll escort you. That's a perfect place for you to be."

Sin slung her rifle behind her and patted down her torso, making sure her knives were all in place. Reaching up, she pushed her spiked hair under a skullcap. Jonesy matched her movements. His blond hair, covered by his black skullcap, was his last step.

"Let's go," Sin said. Zachary fell in step beside her. "Brother, I appreciate you. But enough of your people are out there meeting the enemy for us. Do me a favor and stay here to command your troops. Call it a baby shower gift to Sari."

Backing away, Zachary swallowed and nodded. He then, in military precision, turned back to the monitors. Speaking into the comm piece in his ear, he barked, "Bebop, three recruits joining your ranks. Continue no-kill shots. Just put them down. Let's get this cleaned up."

Sin was startled by Zachary's no-kill-shots order. Not thinking, she swore as she ran out the door. "No-kill shots? Just bring them down? Pop's not going to like this."

Zachary stopped and turned to John, "Who's Pop?"

"Beats me. Let's go, Junie."

Sin was through the door when John's last words echoed, and she realized what she had revealed. But she couldn't worry about that now; she pushed forward, Ariel breathing down her neck.

Jonesy fell behind Ariel to have her six. The three stomped

down the steps onto the grounds in step, even if sometimes they were not in tune. While running, Sin couldn't see any activity until they hit the middle of the compound. There, she saw their people shooting from behind steel and concrete barricades usually used to control crowds at high-volume functions. It made Sin think of music festivals or political events. Only these were equipped with small, steel-belted tires and appeared to have been reinforced with handles on one side, offering bulletproof protection. Zachary's people were methodically moving forward, protected by the barricades.

Jogging over, Jonesy shouted over the gunfire. "Looks like Junie strikes again. How many things do you think the kid has invented?"

"I don't know, but I'm glad he's on our side," Ariel hollered as she pulled off a shot of someone coming close from the opposite direction.

"We need to find their command center. We find that, and we cut off the head," Sin stated as she put in her earpiece. "Guys, I'm going around to the west side to see if I can determine where their command center is established. Jonesy, can you take the east? Ariel, go with him and have his back."

"But we're such a good team, Chica," Ariel complained.

"I don't need any help. Take her with you," Jonesy countered, already moving away as he put in his earbud.

"No, she goes with you." Sin jogged away in the opposite direction without looking back.

Ariel stood for a moment, her head swiveling back and forth. "How lovely to be so wanted," she said to the sky. Then she took off running.

* * *

Running through foliage and hitting tree limbs, Sin forged forward. She was gaining ground, leaving much of the fighting behind her. But there was something inside her that nudged her to keep going in this direction. She pushed herself, jumping over downed limbs, her breath puffing out before her.

Triumphant, Sin chuckled. "There you are." She came up on a long, camouflage-covered RV nestled in the woods.

She was glad she had remained radio silent with her superiors at the agency. No one could stop her from making a dent in her case this time. She could feel it; she was close to General.

Finally.

"I got you now," she swallowed. "Let's finish this, and then I can find out who the mole is in our agency and rip off his head."

Suddenly, cold steel poked her neck. "On the contrary, I have you, and maybe I'll decide to take *your* head instead." A stiff voice grumbled in her ear, "Slowly slide your gun off your shoulder."

Sin carefully inched her gun down, all the while her brain ticking to outmaneuver the voice in her ear.

"Don't overthink this; just do," the voice barked into her ear. His hot breath was wet against her skin. "Now, I understand you always carry at least four blades positioned about your luscious body. Please begin to drop them to the ground one at a time. And please do not make any sudden movements. I would hate to leave your brains in this wooded area for the birds and other animals to dine on." He rubbed his gun against the back of her head. "Tsk-tsk, it would be such a waste."

Sin's eyes drifted close. She already knew someone, or several, folks in their unit had turned. But for this guy to know so much about her, it was apparent she had been working in the dark for far too long.

She was beyond angry. With a blaze of red forming under her eyelids, it was brewing into a firestorm. Pop was pressing forward, and when she took over, Sin would only remember what happened by the number of dead at her feet. There would be no kill shot rule because Pop didn't follow them. Sin breathed in and out, fighting to stay in control. But she could feel Pop pushing to get out. Like the movie *Alien*, Pop was going to burst through.

Fading against the rush, Sin succumbed, and Pop appeared.

Pop dropped two knives to the ground, as requested, without fanfare. When she grabbed the third one and released it, as it fell, she dipped, snatched it out of the air, and swung the blade backward. She felt it slip into muscled and resistant flesh.

A hard blow to her head made her dizzy as she maneuvered into the fight, seeing her opponent for the first time. He was a blond giant smiling evilly as though he had been hoping she would resist. His following comments made her realize he was indeed making this personal.

"You have been a thorn in my side, Sincere Lewis. You and your people would get close, and for the sake of anonymity, we would move, and you would once again find us. It kinda made me hot."

Sin growled as they circled each other, both with knives in their hands. He then bent closer, his voice low and intimate. "You became an itch I savored. I could have killed you several times over, you know. We'll keep that a secret from my boss. But I knew eventually it would come to this, and before you lie facedown in the earth, I will have you."

Enraged that he knew Sin's real name and that she and Sin had been toyed with for years, Pop swiped at him. He jumped back, his six-five form dancing lightly from foot to foot, chuckling at her desperation to slice him.

"Come, kitten, show me your claws. I don't usually like my women with melanin, but you are my exception."

"Agh!" Running straight for him, Pop managed to swipe his other side, blood spurting but again missing a vital organ. The man stuck his finger in the blood and wiped it across his face, then licked and sucked his fingers.

"Next, I'll taste you, *Родная*."

Disgusted, Pop gave a deadly grin. "I'm not your darling, idiot."

"I love that you know Russian. Oh, but you are my darling girl. And, unfortunately for you, the game is over. I'll need to conserve my energy for what comes next."

Faster than Pop could move, he whipped out his gun and shot her point-blank in her neck.

Pop dropped, and Sin could see nothing but darkness as everything faded.

Chapter Thirty-Three

Deacon

Nia stirred against him, murmuring in her sleep, her hand curled into the front of Deacon's shirt like he was her lifeline. Deacon stayed still, willing the moment to last just a little longer. The quiet hum of the jet, the low lights, and the warmth of her body against his created a fragile calm he knew wouldn't last, not in their present world.

They were in the front seating area of the luxury jet, Cole's people in the back. Deacon appreciated that they knew enough to give him and his special guest space.

"Is your lady all right, man?" Cole Jay's voice rumbled from across the cabin.

Deacon shifted just enough to glance at him. "Yeah. She's out."

Cole nodded, tapping his fingers against his thigh. "I'm proud of you, you know. I've seen you do a lot for people, but this live appearance . . . Feels personal."

Deacon looked back at Nia. "She makes it personal."

Cole grinned. "That woman has your whole code rewritten."

A small smile tugged at Deacon's mouth. He didn't deny it. "I never thought I could feel this. Not like this."

Cole's tone shifted. "You never let yourself. Always hiding in shadows, building things no one knows are yours, and giving money away through back doors. I get why, but . . . Don't you ever want to be seen?"

Deacon's hand moved gently over Nia's curls. "Not by the world. Just by her."

Cole sat back with a low whistle. "You absolutely mean that. I've always admired that about you, your willingness to be in the background. The country of Ghana appreciates you. I hope this visit lets you see some of your donations at work."

"If it all goes to plan, then afterward, my time is yours." Deacon let the pause stretch, the weight of his mission creeping across his subconscious, stealing the peace he had just claimed. This independence he was reaching for with him and Nia couldn't be a failed bust. He needed to expose the Council and get back their lives.

"What about your brother? You gonna clue him into what you're doing?" Cole asked, his voice quieter now.

Deacon flinched. "No. Jonesy has never understood why I need to do what he calls my pet projects. He's always felt that the smaller I kept my circle, the better. And that taking chances was for chumps. And going off on my own today, without his permission? Man, I guarantee he's somewhere fuming. By the way, he especially doesn't like someone like you."

Cole tilted his head. "Someone like me?"

"Famous. Black. Loud. Confident. Everything he thinks would make us targets. He kept us tight and under the radar."

Cole nodded slowly. "You're allowed to outgrow that. He doesn't get to define your world anymore. But if you follow up on your plan, you'll never be incognito again. Are you ready for that?"

Deacon didn't reply; he sighed, knowing his past reluctance to argue with his brother about someone of Cole Jay's stature was because he believed him. He didn't want to be known. He hadn't pushed back because it would have made him more visible to the world. Now, because of Nia, he was doing it willingly.

"In the past, how many invitations did I give you to visit me at my estate?" Cole added with a frown.

"You know why I didn't come, Cole. I liked knowing I could go anywhere and people wouldn't know who I am or what I do. Hanging out with you in public, especially at your place, would open doors I didn't want open."

Deacon's fingers drummed in a pattern on his knee as it bounced.

"But—"

Deacon pulled his fidget rings out of his pocket and twirled them around his fingers. They flowed so fast that Cole leaned in as he watched. "No buts, man. They would find out I'm on the spectrum. Neurodivergence only plays well on after-school network specials. The real world is not so understanding. Then everything I've ever done would be questioned or seen as a miracle when the facts are that I've worked hard every day to do something valuable. To give something that would make my difference a gift, not a curse."

"Forget those trolls. Most of 'em sit at home in dark basements, hating the world. You can have friends and enlarge your territory. That's what I want you to get. I am your friend . . . when you allow it."

Deacon held out his fist for Cole to bump. Such a simple action filled his chest; he had always watched others bond that way. "You showing up like this for me, diverting your plane to pick us up and take us with you to the Economic Conference, is going to help us end something that's an abomination. You're a rare friend."

"There are a lot of us out here, dude. I can't say I understand why you can't give me all the details, but keep safe, all right?"

Deacon nodded and looked at Nia again, watching her nose crinkle slightly as she shifted.

"She grounds you," Cole said softly.

"She frees me," Deacon whispered.

Cole stood and stretched. "Well, I'm gonna let y'all have this moment. But ten hours from now, it's go-time. Get some rest."

Deacon nodded. As Cole disappeared down the aisle, Deacon slid lower in the seat. He gently placed Nia over in her seat, and she snuggled against the plane's window.

He brushed his lips against her hairline. "Whatever comes, we face it together."

Nia stirred, still half-asleep, and whispered, "I know you're watching me."

He smiled against her skin. "Guilty."

Her fingers moved, tracing his arm. "Was I crowding you too much?"

Deacon wanted to be free to share himself with Nia, so he answered honestly, "A little. It was fine at first, but I moved you when it started not to. Is that okay?"

"Yeah, and thank you for telling me your truth. I think if we communicate, we win."

Feeling like sunshine had formed over their small area, Deacon agreed.

"You think the worst is behind us?"

"No," he said honestly. "But for the first time, I don't care. We're going to end this and get our lives back. Lives that include each other. I would fight anyone for that."

She opened her eyes, sleep-drunk and soft, but her gaze was steady. "You say the sweetest things when we are running into danger. We got this?"

He didn't hesitate. "Yeah."

Their lips met, a quiet and unhurried promise between their breaths of air. Deacon was with the woman who had captivated him for several months. An uphill battle he never thought he'd conquer.

Now, all he had to do was put his life on the line, scale the bad guys into oblivion, and become the hero of her dreams. No problem.

Chapter Thirty-Four

Ariel

Ariel couldn't believe she was only five minutes behind Sin; now, Sin had vanished. A boneheaded Council flunky had intercepted her with a sloppy swing that glanced off her shoulder as she pirouetted away. It made her take back every mumbled curse she had hurled at her Nana, forcing ballet lessons on her twice a week. Apparently, grace saved lives.

She ended up in a hand-to-hand scrap with the guy, who seemed more interested in capturing her than just taking the shot. He did manage to land a strong side kick, which stole her breath. Now, the flunky lay out cold by a bush. He'd wake up, but not soon.

She limped forward, a burn flaring in her ribs, and hissed in frustration. The pain suggested something might be cracked. Her eyes scanned the area where Sin was last seen. The earth was disturbed. Tire tracks. Big ones.

"Where's the pain in my butt?" came a familiar voice.

Ariel turned, her glare sharp. "She was right here. I was delayed fighting off one of the Council's men. Five minutes max, Jonesy. She was here."

Jonesy cursed, waving his gun in the air as he paced. "So, now we've lost Deacon, Nia, and Sin? Great. Fantastic. Exactly what we needed."

Ariel squared up. "Watch yourself. None of this is my fault. I brought the book back. I tried to do the right thing. It's not my fault it ended up with Nia. My psycho uncle stays one step ahead."

Jonesy crouched near the tracks, brushing his fingers across the crushed earth. "These are from a big RV. Can't believe something that size got past us. Let's get back."

They tore through the woods toward the compound. Most of the Council's forces had retreated or been captured. Benson residents were out cleaning up, solemn and battered.

Jonesy paused, spotting something half-buried in the brush. He signaled Ariel, then used the toe of his boot to flip over the motionless body. Ariel had her rifle up until she recoiled.

Foam bubbled at the dead man's mouth.

"He wasn't going to be captured," Jonesy muttered. "Swallowed something. He must have been, at the very least, a squad leader. Probably ingested a suicide pill. The foot soldiers we captured won't know anything."

"What kind of nightmare are we in?" Ariel whispered. "My uncle is a madman."

"He's a cult leader." Jonesy wiped his brow. "Let's move."

They burst into the command center. "Zachary!" Jonesy bellowed.

Zachary turned, his face falling when he didn't see Sin. "Where is she?"

Jonesy didn't sugarcoat it. "Gone. But there were RV tracks."

Zachary tapped furiously on the monitor. "They must have had strong tech. Still, I'll pull surveillance."

They rewound the footage. A glitch allowed them to see a camouflaged RV pull away.

Then it was gone. Jonesy grunted as they all watched nothing but the surrounding woods on the monitors.

He pulled Ariel's arm and fussed. "I know where Deacon and Nia went. Ghana."

Ariel blinked. "Ghana?"

"Deacon never told me, but I know about this conference. I just remembered it's going on this week. Africa's Full Bloom Economic thing. Usually, he does these things on Zoom. But he feels these people are his friends. It's televised every year, a big deal. He doesn't know I know how much he gives to Africa because I disapprove."

Everyone frowned at Jonesy.

"What? I wouldn't have tried to stop him. However, he received an invitation months ago to attend a conference there. He usually never attends these things because there's too much media."

Zachary began typing on the keys, and the monitor's screen changed. Several news vans and reporters were lined up to greet dignitaries on a red carpet.

"Can we get some volume on that?" Jonesy asked, walking closer to the screen.

An African reporter held her microphone out to a smartly dressed woman in a business suit. "Deputy Prime Minister, as the Minister of Finance, you represent Canada at Ghana's Full Bloom Economic Conference. Why do you believe it is important for Canada to be present here?"

The deputy minister smiled politely. "I am honored to provide input on such a worthy cause. I look forward to reporting more after the conference as we all come together for the good of Ghana, which translates to the good of the world."

The reporter turned to the camera. "You've seen another dignitary coming to this Full Bloom Economic Conference to share and commit to creating a better Ghana. Citizens of the world, people will arrive at this hotel over the next twenty-four hours, where most of our country's guests will be staying. The outstanding actor and philanthropist Cole Jay doesn't just play a superhero. He is one. And he will host this event.

"We look forward to showing all attendees and presenters the warm hospitality Ghana is known for as they gather to create new economic opportunities for all. This is Ebony Mensah with the news as we see it."

"Now, I'm sure that Deacon is in Ghana. Cole Jay is his friend."

"The Cole Jay? Is Deacon's friend?" Ariel screeched.

Jonesy stepped back, tapping his ear. "A fan, I take it?"

"Who isn't—"

Ariel was interrupted, when Junie and Mother Sweat burst through the doors. Her wig in its usual disarray, Mother Sweat urged, "Tell them what God showed you."

Junie looked solemn. "I saw . . . a red carpet, African robes, and a man with white-blond hair and a cruel grin. He stood over someone curled up on a bunk. Then taillights. An RV."

Jonesy's voice was tight. "It's Sin. And this is confirmation they're in Ghana. We'll go after Sin first."

Ariel blinked. "Wait, you're not going after your brother?"

Ariel watched Jonesy's face mottle red. "Deacon would want Sin rescued first. Uh . . . for Nia. Right now, they're on a plane, safe."

Jonesy turned away from Ariel's knowing smirk.

He asked, "Zachary, I need two favors. Can you keep monitoring and send the RV coordinates to my encrypted line if you get another hit?" He then hesitated. "Look, my parents don't know that Deacon and Nia left alone. I visited them right before I found out they were missing. If I go and tell them what is going on, they'll both worry. Can you say we got a lead, and we are safely monitoring?"

"I'll go with you, Zachary. I'm going to pray for them and tell them the truth. I don't feel anything dangerous concerning Deacon," Mother Sweat said.

Ariel stepped forward. "What does that mean? You don't feel any danger to Deacon? Does that mean you see something on Sin? Get your crystal ball out, lady, and explain!"

"Not see, child, feel." Mother Sweat turned to Zachary. "Let's go see Jones and Linette. Y'all get moving."

He was already halfway out the door when Mother Sweat called, "Your daddy is going to be busy healing, and your bonus mama gon' be busy taking care of your father. Go do you."

As they raced out, Ariel yelled at him with misplaced mirth, "Who knew you would be the one gunning to save the she-devil?"

Jonesy didn't flinch. "Well, you messed this up, and somebody has to save you girls from yourselves."

She grunted, no longer able to pretend she was cavalier about locating Sin. In the short time she'd known the dynamo, she had saved Ariel's life several times. Women had never liked her. She was too pretty, self-centered, and focused on getting revenge. They were useless to her if they weren't part of moving her forward. Sin was a rarity for her. A woman she liked.

And finding her was no laughing matter.

Chapter Thirty-Five

General

The breeze rattled through the abandoned farm. It was quiet as
General sipped his coffee, and Geoff stood slightly behind him.

"Explain yourself," General said.

"Da. The woman interests me. I know she is beneath me, but a
woman with her skills who is still beautiful?" Geoff shrugged while
patting the welts on his face with a medicated pad.

"Per your face and stab wounds, she's a tiger. Asking to have her
before her demise is an odd request, but I'll grant it," General said
with some disgust. He couldn't fathom Geoff's taste, but he was a
good soldier, and the spoils of war had always been his for the taking.

Sin's moans drew the attention of both men.

"Ah, the prey awakens," General scoffed. "Let's get on with it,
shall we?"

Geoff eagerly loomed over Sin when he picked up a large
bucket in his hand. His expression changed from stoic to gleeful as
he threw a towel over her face and upended the bucket, drenching
her in water and ice. Coughing, Sin struggled against her binds as

she swung her head left to right and pulled this way and that to get loose.

"They are zip locks, sweetheart. You cannot free yourself," General said with amusement, sipping his coffee as he studied her as though she were a failed science project. "I've heard you've been looking for me."

Sin leaned forward, her eyes narrowing in fierce defiance, allowing the cloth to fall from her face. She then squinted at the ruddy-faced man who'd only been a legend in shadow, but she'd never seen him before. She was disgusted that this arrogant pig was the man she had been chasing for years. Ticked off, she spat, but it fell short of hitting her target.

"I almost wish you had succeeded in soiling me. Your punishment would have been in proportion to my anger. Of course, you have only made yourself look childish."

Sin's mouth pursed as her throat pulsed, and with all her chest, she spat again, this one landing closer but still falling short.

She finally spoke. "My mother used to tell me that the foulest thing you could do was spit on a person or a sidewalk for some helpless victim to walk through. In your case, it's the intention that counts."

Laughing, General addressed Geoff. "I see why you find her interesting. She is a little rough around the edges. I understand it is called an *angry Black woman* attitude." With speculation, he grunted. "But for you, she will do for one night."

General stood and walked around the two spit stains.

He hovered over Sin and grabbed her by her chin, tilting her face up. "Where is my *Book of Disasters*?"

Sin tried to pull her face away but could not break free. Instead, he squeezed harder.

"Where is *my* book?"

The pain shooting through her jaws made Sin involuntarily shudder, and her eyes squeezed shut.

General stepped back in confusion when a bestial growl burst through his tight hold on Sin's face.

Pop had awakened.

* * *

Sin

Stringy wet hair—turning spongy—touched her forehead as Pop looked around at the mess Sin had gotten them into. Longing to rub her face, she wiggled her cheeks back and forth, forcing the numbing feeling to subside.

Tugging on the binds that held her wrists and ankles behind her back, she could tell they were zip ties without General's acknowledgment. Neither she nor Sin was new to this game. However, she did feel she was an expert at it.

Logging her prison, it looked like an abandoned barn. This meant they were probably still in Tennessee or somewhere nearby. And since she didn't wake up dead, the big oaf must have tranquilized her instead of shooting her with live ammo.

Bad on his part, goody for her.

Pop looked up just in time so as not to get the full-frontal brunt of the slap General had given her. Turning her head to the side, it was still a punishing hit. She was pretty sure he had loosened a tooth.

"You did that real easy like, that slap." Setting aside her pain and looking to rile him, she snorted. "Real feminine behavior, General."

"Talk to me, and I will make sure that after Geoff is finished with you, your death will be swift. I can't say that about your little sister. She is the one who has my book, isn't she? Why else would a top agent have her baby sister on the run?"

Pop gave General a blinding smile.

If she was here, and he was here, Sin's precious Nia was safe. And like Sin, Pop was wired to keep Nia safe.

Pop's mind churned with ideas of escape. Yes, Sin was the strategist, but Pop was the survivalist, and it was her job to get them out of this.

She needed to get free, find Nia and Deacon, and get the book to the right people before whoever the mole was in her camp found Nia and stopped all of them. Then she would give Ariel a new start somewhere with her grandmother. The stupid girl deserved it for hanging around and trying to help.

Eyes locked, General got nose to nose to her stinging face, then he opened his mouth so wide that she could see his tonsils and still herself for the coming intense interrogation.

His shout was Richter scale. "Where—"

Boom!

Boom!

Boom!

The barn walls rattled, and multiple voices shouted in panic outside. General and Geoff pulled out their weapons and ran to the barn's double wooden doors. Swinging them open, a man stood guard outside. His gestures showed he was anxious to go with them and see what had happened, but Geoff ordered him to stay behind.

The man stepped inside the barn as instructed, but once he ensured Pop was still secure, he cracked open one of the doors to rubberneck their activity. His back to her, Sin nudged Pop, knowing she had to act fast. Having loosened the ties enough with her fingernails pinching under the locking mechanism, she could feel the sharp texture of her combat boot's shoelaces against her skin. She sawed.

Pop's mind raced, listening to Sin devise a plan as she wiggled her fingers and felt the tight zip ties cutting into her skin. It'd only happened once before when they operated simultaneously, both aware. Crisis made strange bedfellows.

"You never want to do the hard stuff," Pop complained.

"When you're resting, I'll be the one tending these wounds. Stop whining; keep sawing, Pop."

With a burst of adrenaline, Pop lifted her feet, straining against the bonds that held her. The steel edges of her bootlaces scraped against the zip ties around her ankles as she twisted her feet back and forth with precision. Pain shot up her legs as she worked, but she gritted her teeth, refusing to give in.

Slowly, the zip ties around her ankles began to weaken, the jagged edges of the laces making progress. A trickle of blood seeped from the cuts on her skin, but Pop pushed through the pain, her focus unwavering.

Her eyes riveted to the man at the door. She paused when he turned and looked her way. Whatever was happening outside was keeping them busy. And being busy allowed her time to get free. She could not waste this opportunity. She focused on her feet, and with a final wrench, the zip ties snapped apart, freeing her ankles. Now, with her lower body liberated, Pop turned her attention to her bound wrists.

Sin knew Pop had it, and she retreated.

She didn't want to chance moving the chair at this point—she'd have one chance—so she had to continue to free herself behind her back. Pop lifted her legs high behind her, the muscles in her back straining as she maneuvered her zip-tied hands toward her bootlaces.

Using the same method, Pop began to saw at the bindings with the sharp edges of her bootlaces. Inhaling, she paused when the man once again looked back at her. She stilled. He was so sure she was not a threat, and preening to see more, he stepped outside the door and closed it.

Through a painful process that made her grimace, she lifted her aching legs against her wrists. Each incremental movement to free herself sent waves of agony through her body, but she refused to relent.

The man had yet to return.

Thank you to all the men who underestimate women, Pop thought, sawing away.

Finally, with a triumphant grunt, the zip ties around her wrists gave way, falling to the ground in two tattered pieces. With relief, Pop flexed her fingers, feeling the blood flow return to her hands.

Thanks for nothing, Sin. Constantly ducking and hiding from painful things.

But there was no time to celebrate or piss and groan. With her newfound freedom, Pop sprang into action, her mind focused on one thing: escape. As she made her way toward the barn's exit, she could hear the faint sound of voices outside. She hesitated, but the voices passed by.

General and Geoff hadn't returned, and the man they left behind was outside the door. This was her chance.

With a deep breath, Pop eased through the barn door, her heart steady. The door creaking had the man swivel, only to be met with an arm around his neck as Pop placed him in a sleeper hold.

Her arms burned as he went down, her welts bleeding as Pop pulled him inside the barn and sprinted into a clump of nearby trees as darkness fell.

Without hesitation, her senses heightened as she raced toward freedom. Pop was exhilarated when she realized she had seen the leader's face. He was now a *known* entity.

Pop goes the weasel!

Chapter Thirty-Six

Sin

"Psst!"

Pop stopped in her tracks. She quieted and leaned her back against the broad trunk of the tree. Tipping around the trunk, she peered into the night.

"Sin Lewis, come on down," Jonesy mocked.

When Pop emerged from behind the tree with her arms folded, her stoic expression indicated Jonesy's witty remarks were unwelcome. "You take idiocy to a whole new level." Moving from behind him, Ariel limped to Pop and tried to hug her, but Pop stepped back with her arm extended, fending her off.

"Sin, I'm just happy to—" Ariel stepped closer. Seeing the glacial facial expression on Pop's face, she murmured, "Not Sin, Pop?"

Pop raged. How in the *I'd-knock-you-out-if-it-wouldn't-hurt-me* mess had Sin allowed this girl to know her so well in such a short time?

"Get outta my face," Pop hissed.

"Oh, definitely, Pop," Ariel said.

"Who's Pop?" Jonesy asked.

Both Pop and Ariel turned to him and blasted, "Don't worry about it."

Ariel swung back around, grabbed Pop's arm, dragged her a few feet away from Jonesy, and puffed, "Bring her back."

Pop gave a smug smile. "Maybe. Maybe not. But the girl made mistakes that, once again, I had to fix. So maybe I'll stay around longer this time. I could get the book."

"No," Ariel grimaced. "Bring her back."

"Bring who back? Who are y'all talking about? What's going on?" Jonesy shouted, his voice escalating with each question.

Pop gave a sly sneer, then shrugged. Her body swayed as her eyes drifted close. Jonesy and Ariel moved swiftly when Sin's body tilted as she opened her eyes.

Sin leaned upright, dusting off her pants. "Glad you guys found me. Was that you setting off those explosives?"

Jonesy and Ariel glanced at each other when Sin acted like nothing strange had occurred.

"Is anybody going to tell me what's going on?" Jonesy asked as he pivoted between both women.

Sin shook her head. "No. Let's get moving. Who's on our tail?" She started trotting in the direction Pop was fleeing before she heard Jonesy call her.

Ariel did a hop and limp to keep up, trying to get close enough to say something to Sin, but Sin didn't want to hear it. She didn't know how Ariel figured out that she operated as two distinct personalities, but it was evident she had been out in the field too long, and things were coming to a head.

She used Pop to distract herself from the lives she had to take as an agent. However, if she could no longer compartmentalize her actions, she would have to take responsibility for them, and she was not prepared to handle the accountability for such widespread destruction.

Can you take a break from saving the world?

"What's going on at the compound? Y'all being here tells me Zachary and his men were victorious."

"Yeah, but getting info was a bust. Their leaders are some loyal sons of a guns, rather die than talk," Jonesy said.

"Seen that before. No further word on Nia or Deacon?" Sin asked.

Jonesy moved over and put Ariel's arm around his shoulder to help her. "Yes, we believe they're in Ghana. Your friend Zachary arranged a plane for us. We've lost about four hours that we need to make up. The man promises that our pilot is ex-military and part of their Benson crew, so he'll get us there in record time. He estimates we can make up about two of those hours."

Ariel sucked her teeth. "When did you talk to Zachary? And why didn't I know this information?"

Jonesy rolled his eyes. "Ariel, he called while you were inside the RV setting up the explosives. Something you didn't want my help doing. He also wanted to update me on my parents being fine."

Ariel hung her head and admitted, "I thought maybe he was holding Eric hostage in there. He's the guy I stole the book from in the first place. Once they were after me, I knew they had Eric, too. If my uncle would kill his father, I didn't think Eric had a snowball's chance in—"

"Girl, nobody cares about a man whose entire family's legacy is fire and brimstone to this world," Sin said.

Skip limping along with Jonesy to keep up, Ariel said quietly but with fury, "Eric wasn't so bad. He was born into it. And while you're talking, my father was from one of those families too, and he was the most loving, honest man I knew. He hid me from them my whole life. Everything I've done has been to honor him."

Sin stopped, causing Ariel to plow into her. "No, boo, everything you've done has been for you. Your daddy is dead. This personal vendetta against your uncle is all about you getting revenge." Sin leaned forward and whispered, "You may know about Pop, but I know about you, Betty!"

"What are y'all whispering 'bout now? We've got to go. Come on, the truck is around the bend."

Sin took off, stopped, and backed up. She put Ariel's other arm around her shoulder. Military-trained Sin had never left a man behind. She couldn't help but grunt when she saw the slight smile on Ariel's face.

Chapter Thirty-Seven

General

"Agh!" General yelled as he punched the man in the chair once again. "You. Were. Told. To. Watch. Her," he said, punctuating each word with a blow.

Bloody and trembling, the man clutched his throat, gurgled one final breath, and collapsed into silence.

Geoff placed his hand on General's shoulder. He shook off his touch. "Do not touch me—ever."

"Da, General."

He pulled a white linen handkerchief from his pocket and removed his brass knuckles. He then wiped each of his fingers and knuckles methodically. "The rest of the damage report."

Geoff looked at his phone. "The RV is gone. The van is gone. Jeep one and two are gone."

"Hold it. Geoff, are all the vehicles gone?"

"Da."

"So you couldn't just say all the vehicles were demolished? You —" General exhaled and shook his head. He muttered, "Surrounded simply surrounded by idiots."

Geoff straightened his spine. "Will that be all, sir?"

"No, that won't be all. Did you find out where they went?"

"No, sir, we did not."

He pointed at the man slumped in his chair. "Get him out of here. And bring me Eric. Your incompetence is frustrating." General flexed his fingers and slipped his brass knuckles on again.

Surprise flitted across Geoff's face. "But . . . but, sir, you said not to move him."

"That was when we were parked outside the Benson Compound. Surely, you moved him when we got here?"

"No, sir. Eric blew up in the van."

Disappointed, he slowly pulled off his brass knuckles. "Well, that's disappointing, isn't it?"

"Sorry."

General's hands steepled in front of him. He wanted his book or retribution for not getting it. "Is alternative transportation on the way?"

"Yes. I have also requested reinforcements. We lost two squad leaders to self-inflicted injuries. As designed, we were notified because their trackers activated, beeped red, and then died. They were loyal till the end. Six were captured at the Benson Compound, lower tiered all."

"Hmm, we lost two good men. Benson Compound has much to answer for."

Geoff touched the com in his ear and listened. "Transportation will be here shortly, sir. Where should I map our destination?"

"We're going back."

"Home?"

"No. To the Benson Compound. If I take losses, everybody will take losses."

A large grin formed on Geoff's face. "Yes, sir."

* * *

Later, as the afternoon waned, General sat in the cabin chair of the replacement RVs, his knee bouncing up and down. The RV was later than they promised. Things were falling apart, not together. He frowned and willed his knee to stop; he eventually slapped his hand on it and held it still. His father had hated and labeled this habit weak, and witnessing himself reverting to a childhood trigger caused the veins in his forehead to protrude.

His forehead pulsed like a cartoon character about to blow his top. "What happened to operating in excellence?" he muttered. "Deliver the vans on time. Get my book back. Destroy all enemies of the cause. Next, take over New America, and then Canada falls too."

Geoff looked over, and the more General muttered, the harder he floored the pedal. The RV bucked forward.

General barked, "Hold the RV steady, Geoff! Do something right. I'm tired of your failures."

Geoff's nose flared as his eyes brightened when he looked down at the alert on his phone. "Sir, you need to see this."

Geoff held out the phone, and he snatched it. A beautiful African American woman, dressed in a svelte gown and wearing her hair in an updo, was holding hands with a handsome man in a designer tuxedo.

General turned the volume up. *"Hello, I'm Nia Lewis..."*

General turned to Geoff, and a slow, deadly smile crossed his face. "Bingo. Turn this RV around and get that new jet with the scramjet design on the runway. It will get us there before your lovely agent." His hands rubbed together in glee. "It's the break we needed; we're going to Ghana."

"Um, when you demanded a jet to fund its company, didn't you promise them you'd keep their prototype for show only?"

Guffaws filled the air. "Did you think that promise meant something? Why would I ever desire something I'm not going to use?"

Geoff's jaw clenched, but he remained silent.

"Fool, your job is to do as you're told."

Phone in hand, replaying the news story, General moved to the back of the RV. But his demands were never done, and he called over his shoulder. "Oh, yeah, call all my people in the places we'll fly over and warn them. Pity if we fly over during those folks' mealtime. Those sonic booms are frightening."

General's trilling laughter trailed off as he sank into the plush bed.

He could tell Geoff found his laughter offensive. He didn't care. For a minute, he was worried that his luck had abandoned him. Fortunately, his success was only delayed. By the time the day was over, he would have the most important people involved in this fiasco dead and buried and the book in his hands. Then he would feed the book by sacrificing five public deaths, one from each family tree, as was the norm for the Council's thirty-year tribute. And last on his agenda, and the most satisfying, he would drop a bomb on the abomination known as the Benson Compound.

It was his mantra . . . Once placed on his enemy's list, forever dead.

Chapter Thirty-Eight

Nia

"This is an exciting interview for me. As a local reporter, I am aware of this man's generosity's impact on our country. We have kept his name out of the public eye, but now, he is here to speak for himself. His resilient seeds have produced this season's bountiful harvest, feeding the hungry and our economy. We are so grateful, Dr. Deacon Everette. Thank you," she gushed.

Doctor? Nia's mind screamed.

Saying a prayer, Nia watched an uncomfortable Deacon pull his starched collar away from his neck with a forced smile. Flustered, he answered the fawning reporter. But he was leaning too close to the microphone, and it squeaked as he spoke loudly. "Please, call me Deacon."

Removing the sympathetic look on her face, Nia hurried forward when Deacon fumbled.

Oh no, Deacon. I'm here.

When she stepped forward, Deacon eagerly grabbed her hand in his. "This is my Nia."

The reporter's eyebrows arched, her head swiveling between Deacon and Nia.

Nia's hand perspiring in his, she braced herself. If Deacon couldn't speak, she had to.

Tiny breath, breathe. "Hello, I'm Nia Lewis. And *Dr.* Deacon Everette and I have just arrived in your wonderful country. Please give us a little while to get acclimated to the different time zones, and he promises to give you a breaking news interview before the night is over."

"Yes, Nia is correct. Thank you, and we will talk more later tonight," Deacon said.

By now, their hands were slick with each other's sweat, and they hurried into the conference center.

"Dr. Deacon? Really?" Nia asked.

"I'm an award-winning geneticist, Nia. I've always been a PhD." Deacon was puzzled by her amazement.

Shaking her head, Nia threw her hands in the air. "You're something else."

Deacon slowed, moving away from Nia. "I messed up. The reporter had this look—I don't know—like she had heard something about me and was waiting to see if I would confirm it. So, I hesitated."

Getting in front of him, and rising on her tiptoes, Nia placed her hands on either side of Deacon's face and kissed him tenderly on one cheek and then the other.

She smoothed down his designer suit jacket that Cole Jay had ready for him. "You were a little nervous, but you'll be fine. Nothing is wrong with you, Deacon. You hear me? Nothing!"

She watched as he worked to calm himself. She saw his chest rise and fall, the pattern slowing until it was no longer noticeable. This was the Deacon who took her through a closet into freedom. The man who didn't drive but commandeered a car for their escape to the airport. This is the one who loved her beyond her pettiness, led their escape, and held her on the plane while she slept, despite holding people being the antithesis of who he was. He knew her insecurities, yet he loved her anyway.

Nia's heart thrummed, her hands trembled, and her body flushed.

He was everything she never knew she needed.

* * *

Deacon

Standing at the podium, he looked out at the many faces turned to him in expectation. The conference part of the event would conclude with his closing remarks, followed by dinner and dancing. They were waiting for his breakthrough announcement later, but somehow Cole Jay had talked him into giving a welcome address, too. He was so concerned with his closing that he couldn't concentrate on his present assignment. He was getting exasperated, stumbling over his words. Willing himself to snap out of it, he brought his thoughts back to the present and recovered, finishing his address. "In conclusion, establishing a healthy economy in Ghana is crucial for the entire world." Deacon gripped the podium tightly as perspiration dotted his brow. He faltered, but Nia nodded in encouragement. "We're countering the forces who believe wealth is only for the top 1 percent. We're all here with the same mindset, we believe that no one should have to go to bed hungry, homeless, or naked. And what we do here can be done anywhere. Thank you."

The applause was loud and sustained as people stood up. Deacon returned to his seat at the front table, where Nia embraced him. "You did it. I'm sure they'll listen to you when you present your news break later."

Cole Jay patted him on his back as other people at the table congratulated him.

"I need to make my rounds; be back," Cole Jay said.

Deacon was loath to make small talk. He hadn't shared his apprehension with Nia. She didn't need to know that his plans to unveil the Council had more holes than Swiss cheese. Saving the day seemed easy in his head, but now that he was here, he wasn't so sure. A book was just a book without visible evidence of its power. He was going to end up ridiculed.

Am I incapable of following a plan that isn't theory or logic without Jonesy?

"You okay, Deacon?" Nia asked.

"Yes, I'm fine," he said.

"Good. I can't wait until we expose the Council, get rid of the *Book of Disasters*, and go back home to a peaceful life," she said, keeping her voice low.

Deacon looked around the table and leaned in. "And what about us when we return, Nia?"

"What do you mean?" Nia placed her hand over his. "We go forward together."

"No matter what?" he asked.

"Even if we fail," she stated.

They smiled, content in their feelings for each other.

The band went to their places. The music started, and the table emptied as couples got up and danced.

"I've always been a wallflower at these things, but not any longer. Let's dance," Nia said, firmly stroking his arm up and down.

Deacon gulped. He couldn't dance. He had no rhythm. If he

got up, he would embarrass himself and Nia. Stressing to find an excuse, he swallowed.

"You all right, man?" Cole said, stopping at their table and patting Deacon on the shoulder. "You looking worried. You nailed it, man. And you got a standing ovation."

"I think that was more about my million-dollar pledge at the beginning of my remarks. After that, they would have clapped at anything I said."

"Nia, can you convince this man that he did a great job, money or not?"

Knowing he needed to come clean with Nia about the holes in his plan, Deacon opened his mouth to tell her what was bothering him. "Nia—"

"Bro!" A heavy but familiar arm blanketed his shoulders, then released. "Cole Jay, I should have known you had something to do with whisking my brother off."

Before Deacon could react, Sin wrapped Nia in her arms, rocking her back and forth.

Ariel then slid into Cole's personal space. "Would this be a bad time to tell you how much I love your movies?"

Cole Jay chuckled. "No, ma'am, it is never a bad time to tell me you love my movies."

Deacon turned to his brother. "How'd you find us?"

"I think I've been your brother long enough to know you. Your leaving by airplane gave me one of two choices: Ghana or Costa Rica. Mom and Dad are at the compound, so that leaves Ghana. I also had some heavenly confirmation."

"How is Dad?"

"Oh, now you want to know how Dad is doing?"

"Shoot, Jonesy, don't look at me like that. He was stable when I left. Besides, I'm working on a plan to shut this whole thing down for Mom and Dad, too."

Jonesy spurted, "Uh-huh. Well, Dad is recovering, and he and Mama Linette are safe. But did I hear you say, working on it, as the plan is incomplete?"

"No, you guys showing up now with Ariel is perfect."

"Oh, so you do need me, huh?" Jonesy asked.

Deacon snorted, "Nah, I needed Ariel."

"Right. You know, I recall seeing your face when you opened the email invite to this conference. I also know how much money you've given to Ghana. However, the very reason you've never attended this conference is why you would like to attend this time: the international press is here. I couldn't figure out how you planned to convince people the book is demonic without Ariel. Admit it, I brought you your missing piece."

A trusting Nia said, "No, Deacon already had this all figured out. Don't you, Deacon?"

Turning to her with a sneer, Jonesy snapped, "Was I speaking to you, precious?"

Deacon held up his hand, a calming gesture amid the tension brewing at the table. "Hey, keep it civil. You know I'm not letting you talk to her like that."

Nia, undeterred by Jonesy's sharp retort, said, "Jonesy, we're in this together. We need all the help we can get."

Jonesy sighed and relented under Nia's unwavering gaze. "Yeah, you're both right. My apologies."

Sin interrupted, her tone carrying an air of authority. "All right, Deacon, what's the plan?"

A burst of loud laughter cut through the air as a few of their tablemates approached from the dance floor, their energy too high for the moment. Cole Jay tensed, then rose smoothly, excusing himself to intercept them before they reached the table.

He walked up to them, gregarious and loud. "Can you believe Dr. Everette's family surprised him by attending his first appearance in Ghana? Please allow me to reassign you to another table."

"Oh, no problem. How nice it is to have family," one woman said, waving to everyone.

Deacon returned the wave, then straightened, the weight of responsibility settled on his shoulders. "We need to expose the Council for who they truly are. But we need evidence, something concrete to present to the world."

Jonesy chimed in, "Zachary sent something you can use. You don't know this, but after you guys left, the Council attacked—"

"What? I thought they would follow me after I left a voicemail on the compound's main house line letting them know we had made the plane with the book," Deacon said, his voice wavering.

Nia touched Sin's hand. "Sis, we didn't know. We thought they'd follow us, and we'd be far enough ahead for everyone to be safe. We wanted to help."

"Isn't it always the way? Even the bad guys can't be counted on to do what they do when you need them to," Ariel said. "Plus, Sin was—"

Sin squeezed Nia in a hug. And Deacon saw Sin mouth a "no" to Ariel but didn't know what it meant. But Ariel sealed her lips.

There's more to this story.

Jonesy snapped his fingers in front of Deacon. "Focus, brother. When this is all over, we have much to discuss. It's obvious there are some things you need to get off your chest." He then looked at Nia, who hung her head when Sin pointedly stared at her. He then lowered his voice. "Maybe you feel I don't listen to you. But, Bro, we need to talk it out. And soon. We've been brothers since I showed up battered on your porch. And nothing can change that."

"I almost messed this up trying to prove something," Deacon said.

Jonesy exhaled. "I'm not going to say this couldn't have been done differently. But because of you, we're here. And we can go on international and independent news outlets and break this story."

"He's right for once, Deacon," Sin said, tapping Nia's hand. "This has actually worked out. Because if we're here, they're not far behind. Our sibling issues can be addressed later."

"What else do you have, Jonesy?" Deacon asked.

"Zachery texted video footage of the Council's men attacking the compound. And he has footage of the two team leaders committing suicide rather than being captured."

"They did what? That's awful," Nia cried.

But Deacon's eyes lit up with a glimmer of hope. "No. That's perfect. With Ariel showing the trickery of the book, together, it will all be the smoking gun we need."

"I can't rejoice in suicide," Nia said.

"Humph, I can," Ariel said.

Cole nodded thoughtfully. "Sounds like a lot is going on, and I am somewhat confused. But what I can do is gather everyone together and get the press front and center."

Sin crossed her arms, a determined expression on her face. "Thank you."

"I have to go to the restroom first," Deacon said, standing.

"I'll go with you," Jonesy stood.

"Really, Jonesy?"

"All right, all right. I'll wait here."

"Thank you." Deacon shook his head as he walked away.

A figure stood quietly in the shadows, their dark attire effortlessly blending into the lavish drapes of the occasion. The figure trailed behind as Deacon excused himself from his companions at the dining table and made his way to the restroom.

Chapter Thirty-Nine

Deacon

Deacon felt a sense of unease creeping over him—a gut feeling that something was amiss. The well-lit bathroom should not have provided such a contradictory feeling, but it was a tense night with many lives on the line, all of which depended on him. He had never been the savior in his own story. He had always watched Jonesy be the hero. Maybe that was why he put his heroics into his profession.

After flushing the toilet, he shrugged off the uneasy feeling. He washed his hands, leaned forward, and splashed water on his face. It was at that moment he noticed movement in the mirror behind him. Before he could react, Geoff's imposing figure materialized behind him. Deacon could feel the temperature drop as Geoff's cold, clammy hand gripped his shoulder, sending shivers down his spine. The corner of Geoff's mouth twitched, his lips dry and rough against Deacon's skin as he pressed forward—fear, like an uncoiling snake, twisted and slithered inside him.

"Ah, Deacon Everette," Geoff sneered, his voice thick with malice. "You thought you could outsmart us, didn't you? But now, you're all alone and vulnerable. I've learned a little about you these past few days. No big brother to save you?"

"Too close," Deacon whispered as he tensed, his muscles coiled like a predator ready to strike. Speaking louder, Deacon barked, "Step back, please. You are too close."

When, in defiance, Geoff pressed closer, Deacon's defenses went into overdrive. "Don't do that; get off me."

Deacon's breathing accelerated as he felt Geoff's oppressive presence closing in on him as though he were trying to wear Deacon as his second skin. He closed his thoughts against the panic rising like bile in his throat.

With a swift jerk, Deacon spun around, his eyes locked on Geoff with an intensity that seemed to pierce through and illuminate the already well-lit luxury bathroom. A feral glint sparked in his gaze, a silent challenge to the enforcer standing before him.

As Geoff curled his lip in disdain, his hand darted toward a concealed blade. Deacon's countenance remained inscrutable as he watched the impending threat. Then with uncharacteristic grace, Deacon's hands moved with astonishing speed. He deftly parried an oncoming attack while Geoff's blade sought its mark. Deacon anticipated each move, skillfully meeting every counterstrike with finesse. Geoff appeared taken aback by the unexpected agility and mastery with which Deacon thwarted his advances. Head-butting him, Deacon, dazed but focused, continued to rain blows down on the man who had attacked him. He didn't know this man but knew who he was with—the Council.

The last several days flashed before Deacon's eyes—Nia frightened in the closet, the car, the compound, and the airplane. With each punishing blow, he saw her fear, her crippling doubt, and her pain.

A knock on the door stilled his fist, and the fog lifted. Geoff lay in a crumpled heap at his feet.

Deacon gazed into the mirror. His tux was a little wrinkled, but he could live with that. It was the body at his feet he needed to handle.

"Just a minute, please," he called out.

He splashed his face once again with water and exhaled. Pulling the body into a stall and propping him up on the stool, he lowered the lock and slammed the door until it closed and the lock stuck.

The knock was even more insistent, with a male calling out, "For the love of God, man, others have to go, too."

Deacon unlocked the door, and a burly man with a full beard rushed past him. "Just because you're some kinda celebrity doesn't give you the right to take over the entire restroom. Dang it, man, we mere mortals pee too!"

As Deacon hurried out, a sense of urgency pulsed beneath his skin. He knew that time was of the essence, that every second counted in unraveling the tangled web of lies spun by the Council for centuries.

What would the public believe?

With determined steps, he marched toward the grand hall where the world's most influential figures gathered.

The atmosphere crackled with tension as Deacon's presence drew all eyes toward him. The international news awaited, along with many of the dignitaries who had attended the banquet. Word had spread, and many had shown up late to know the cryptic news Deacon promised to share.

Deacon paused on the steps while Ariel, in a simple dress—the only thing she could get on the plane from a flight attendant—climbed the stairs to stand next to him, ready to present their evidence.

As Deacon approached the podium, an imposing figure of a

man with an authoritative air stared at him in shock. Deacon observed the blatant change in the man's demeanor as he scanned the area, his face flushing with frustration. Deacon peered at a green blinking earpiece visible in the man's ear and watched his lips move rapidly, suggesting a hasty communication via a comm link. Within moments, Deacon noticed Sin, Jonesy, and Nia positioning themselves for action.

The crowd hushed, eager to hear Deacon speak, but he faltered. Too much was happening, flooding his senses at once.

He could see it all unfolding in slow motion in front of him. Ariel touched his arm, and he reached for the microphone. He groaned when he hadn't spoken yet, but the microphone screeched in protest of his rough handling.

Not again.

Eyes widening, he sucked in his breath when he saw several black suit-clad figures, their blond hair visible under the lights, moving toward the man, stealthily weaving through the crowd.

Was this General? It had to be. He acted shocked when he saw him. He hadn't expected that Deacon had survived the bathroom attack.

Ariel was frantically tapping his arm, but Deacon was too busy watching Nia intercept a man near the steps closest to the podium. He was torn, not knowing what was best—sticking to their plan or jumping off the stage to defend Nia.

As the event unfolded—before he could decide—Nia . . . in a designer gown, no less, performed a two-piece punch to the man's throat, and he collapsed. And when Jonesy sucker punched another man in the back of the head as he ran past, making a run toward the stairs, Deacon realized he'd better start talking.

It was a wonder that people were so fascinated by the fact that he appeared too stage-struck to speak that they failed to see the turbulence around them.

As his hand steadied on the microphone, Deacon counted to ten, and he saw one last scene that telegraphed that they had become a team.

It was Sin. He saw from his vantage point her gun jammed into the man's side, confirming to him it was General. In response to her presence, General mouthed words into his mic that stopped the flurry of movement from his men.

He sighed with relief. Based on her actions, Sin knew who General was, and she had pinpointed the infamous leader to guard.

Deacon needed to speak now. He channeled every lesson he had endured on being social at that moment. "Ladies and Gentlemen, esteemed guests, members of the press, t-t-thank you for being here today." He exhaled. "I stand before you not just as a geneticist or philanthropist but as a citizen of this world. A world that has seen its fair share of tragedies, disasters, and injustices. But today, I bring a message of hope and resolution."

At the end of his sentence, his voice pitched with nervousness. Stopping and clearing his throat, he searched for Nia in the crowd. It was her presence that calmed him. "For too long, a clandestine organization known as the Council has operated in the shadows, pulling the strings of power and manipulating events for their gain. They have hidden behind a veil of secrecy, orchestrating chaos and devastation with impunity."

But no more.

Deacon pounded the podium. Anger replaced his fear of speaking.

"Today, I bring forth evidence to expose the Council for who they truly are. Please, if I may, I'd like to invite three journalists to join me on stage."

Deacon gestured to several reporters, who approached the stage hesitantly.

"Thank you for joining me. Now, if you would be so kind as to hold this book."

Deacon handed a reporter the *Book of Disasters*, which appeared expensive but was just a mere book . . . at first glance. As he moved to one side, the three surrounded it.

"This book, dear friends, is no ordinary tome. It holds the secret of how the Council gained power and wealth, allowing them to plan their atrocities and crimes against humanity. It is blank to all except those descendants of the original five families who run the Council. When opened by any of them, it reveals the truth."

The reporter hesitantly opened the book and held it up. To everyone's surprise, the pages were blank. The other two journalists began to film up close with their phones.

"You see, their truths are hidden from us. But because of the sacrifice of many to let justice prevail, we have learned the secret of reading what appears to be blank pages."

Deacon watched the crowd's reaction as Ariel took the reporter's hand, causing letters to appear on the book's pages instantly.

"Behold, the chronicles of destruction, suffering, and loss inflicted upon innocent lives by the Council," Ariel shouted.

The audience gasped as the words mysteriously materialized on the pages, detailing centuries-long disasters. The screen behind Deacon, run by Cole Jay, projected the entire scene.

"But words alone are not enough. You need tangible proof to hold the Council accountable for their actions and understand how they prey on innocent people."

Deacon cued Jonesy to play the video footage, displaying the mercenaries attacking the compound and the aftermath of their team leaders' suicide. The footage then panned to the men they had captured, sitting on pallets, their hands and feet tied.

As the video played, a hush fell over the crowd. Some women

wept openly, watching the destruction and chaos that evil could bring, even the leads' unwillingness to be captured, instead choosing suicide by pill, had many of the guests gasping.

"This is not fake news. This is the reality of the Council's reign of terror. They would rather see their men die than face justice for their crimes."

Before Deacon could continue, Ariel stepped forward, her movements sharp and unannounced. All eyes followed as she approached the stunned journalist, still clutching the book. Without a word, she drew her sleek, gleaming blade and held it high over the open pages.

Eyes widened, and a low murmur rippled through the crowd.

With a clean, practiced stroke, she sliced across her palm. Blood welled quickly, dripping onto the parchment in thick, deliberate drops. The book pulsed visibly when blood touched the surface, and new pages appeared. Lines of script scrawled onto new pages as if an unseen hand wrote each stroke. Deacon recoiled along with the others, instinctively stepping back.

"Read!" Ariel bellowed.

The journalist read one paragraph aloud. *"In the spring of 2026, the Eastern Grid collapsed without warning—fourteen states plunged into darkness, chaos blooming in every unlit corner."*

The room erupted.

"Who are these people?"

"This is unnatural!"

"They must be brought to justice!"

"Dear God, in heaven."

Murmurs and whispers ran up and down the rows, voices raised in horror as the gravity of the situation sank into every ear present.

Deacon raised his arms and his voice. "My friends, we cannot allow this domination to continue. We must stand together, united against this Council and its tyranny. We must demand justice for the countless lives lost to their greed and malice. The book and its four other additions must be destroyed. Today, we start with this one."

Deacon paused as he scanned the crowd, and the news cameras zoomed in on him.

"Today, we take a stand and say enough! We must ensure the Council faces the consequences of its malicious actions. This is only one incident, but as you heard read from one of your own, many more disasters are coming that they will feed with the blood of their victims. Behind you stands the head of this organization."

Sin pushed the gun further into General as he reluctantly held up his hand.

"Let him answer your questions. Thank you."

The crowd's anger soared as they swung around and advanced toward Sin and General. His face flashed beet red as Sin kept the gun pressed closely against his side.

"You will regret this," he growled where everyone could hear him. His face was taut as a group of reporters rushed his way.

"No, I'm having too much satisfaction to regret anything," Sin said.

A news reporter held up their phone. "It says here that you are Ragnar Alstead, head of Wolf Media Corporation. Wolf Conglomerate is behind one of the largest online stores in the world, Gladiator. How do we not know more about you, sir?"

Sin turned away from the camera but said, "He prefers to be called 'General.'"

"Yes, thank you. You are hearing it here first, Ragnar Alstead, known simply as General."

"You will all pay for this. This is a witch hunt," he spat, looking out over the heads of reporters and many frowning people. "It's all fake. I'll get you all for this. Stop filming me!"

His eyes met Deacon's and sparked vengeance.

With the microphones and cameras in his face, General locked eyes with Sin and spat on the floor. The crowd jumped back.

Giving a menacing grin to Sin, he spun away.

Pushing his way through the crowd, he held his head high as he marched forward. When he approached the double doors, a bedraggled Geoff met and opened them. Together, the Council filed out.

Right before the doors shut, Deacon witnessed General's hesitation as he heard their group's exclamations of joy at his being exposed. His back stiffened, and the doors closed. They all hugged and laughed while the Canadian representative to the conference stepped forward.

"I've been in touch with not only our government in Canada but also with your White House. They knew why I was calling because every news channel broadcasted this in Technicolor. I can take that book from you now."

Ariel looked at the book one last time before handing it over. "Such an ancient book, with so much destruction attached to it. Here, I hope you burn it. And find all the others."

The ambassador took the book. "I hope all of you will be available for a debriefing."

Nia looked toward the door where General exited. "Is it over?"

The ambassador nodded. "Yes, as General and his entourage left the building, our security forces picked them up outside."

Sin's phone rang. Taking a deep breath, she answered. "Yes, I am in Ghana . . . because we have a mole, and someone was working to get my little sister killed." Sin stopped midstep, her entire body rigid. "What do you mean suspended until further investigation? I just solved a twenty-year-old case, sir! Sir? Sir?"

Her hand trembled when she looked behind her at all the

quizzical expressions. "They have suspended me until further notice, and I also have to report for debriefing at headquarters."

Before Nia could move, Jonesy rushed over and pulled Sin into his arms. The entire team's mouths fell open when, instead of slapping him, Sin leaned into him.

"I got you, babe," Jonesy soothed, raining kisses across her brow.

Deacon looked at Nia, and a slow grin filled his face until he laughed with joy. "Crisis creates unlikely opportunities."

In awe, Nia stared in a trance. "B-b-but how? And when, Deacon?"

"I don't know, Nia, but this is one way to get them out of our business."

Giggling, she threw her arms around Deacon's neck, and they kissed.

Ariel looked around her and snorted. She then saw a broad-shouldered designer tux walking by. "Cole Jay? Is now a good time to talk about your movies?"

Cole stuck his hands into his pockets and gave Ariel a once-over. "I think now is a perfect time. We have to take our wins where we can."

Chapter Forty

General

Four months later, in the belly of the federal penitentiary, blood and concrete shared a long, sordid history. A crude mural of suffering adorned its walls—etched in peeling paint and the prayers of prisoners.

The USA had done what it did best and had General delivered to their iron jaws where he could be swallowed whole. It had taken a while to close the door on his cell finally. But it was done, and he had spent the last thirty days behind bars.

General stood in the prison yard, jaw tight, shoulders squared, fists raw from a fight he didn't start but had been glad to finish. The other man—bigger, younger, dumber—now lay groaning near the cracked basketball court, the cost of his disrespect paid in full.

The guards didn't interfere, not when he was winning. Some foolishly thought that he needed protection because he was willing to put some of the felons on his payroll with thick commissary books fully loaded.

But life was short, and then you died.

There was nothing like having some future soldiers ready to

join his ranks when they paroled out. He believed in never wasting an opportunity. This bad-boy factory had great potential.

He was reading a message from the Council's leaders. Business went on as usual. The other four books were hidden away. Eric's book was still in the hands of the government. The typical governmental bull, where they wanted to see if they could weaponize it for their use. They couldn't. He had heard that the book had gone to sleep.

He chuckled. NATO could not find anything on his leaders; they were unlike Eric. They were solid men of substance who had played the game for a long time. They had prevailed. And to save face, his only charges were conspiracy to commit murder. What else could they do? It was still debatable among the general public whether the book even existed, and people who insisted they were there in Ghana when its mysteries unfolded soon understood the merits of keeping quiet.

It was his world; everyone else was just visiting.

The call came just after lockdown, jarring the silence with a sharp buzz as his cell lock disengaged. The guard, who appeared like Casper the Friendly Ghost, wasn't friendly, "Alstead. Warden's office. Now."

General smirked. "Took 'em long enough."

When they escorted him through the winding corridors, whispers had already reached the blocks. The devil had a ride waiting. Inside the Warden's office, the air was chilled and humming with tension. The Warden stood stiffly beside a suited man whose badge gleamed with presidential authority.

"By executive pardon," the man said flatly, handing over a sealed envelope, "you are free to go."

The Warden cleared his throat. "Terms are attached. You'll be monitored. Any deviation—"

"Save it," General interrupted, ripping open the envelope. He scanned the paperwork, then lifted his head slowly, a dark glint in his eyes. "I'll be a whisper on the wind."

They handed him a bag with his old clothes and a sealed package containing a burner phone and a black key card.

"You can change into your clothes next door," the guard said.

"No."

No escort, no fanfare. Just the slam of the prison gate behind him and the weight of vengeance rolling back onto his shoulders like an old leather coat.

He inhaled as though the air was undeniably sweet. He exhaled the stale bitterness he had eaten night and day for the last four months: Sin, Ariel, Deacon, Nia, and Jonesy. And all of the Benson Compound, every Bible-thumping last one of them, including the genius kid. They would be yesterday's news.

Waiting at the edge of a long, unmarked road, a matte black SUV purred low in anticipation.

Geoff stepped out.

Their eyes met soldier to soldier, mentor to mentee. Geoff's lean frame was sharper and tired, but his loyalty hadn't rusted.

"Told you I'd get us out," General muttered.

Geoff stood to attention. "Da."

They didn't hug. That wasn't their way. But their silence said everything.

In the backseat of the SUV, a black leather bag shifted. It pulsed once. Twice.

The book woke.

* * *

The *Book of Disasters*

The car door slammed shut, and he felt the shift and stirred beneath the heavy oilcloth, the fabric rustling as he awoke from his long slumber. General's return left a bitter taste mingled with the sweetness of revenge on his tongue. He once called him his master but now refused to grant him that title. He only bowed to those who honored their debts.

The thirty-year tribute date had come and gone, the offering unpaid. It wasn't the ceremonial celebration he missed. It was usually filled with grand speeches, lavish and unnecessary displays, and a modern façade to stroke the human ego. The real issue gnawed at him: hunger. The deadline had passed, and the five sacrifices remained undelivered. He had been denied his due.

General reached over and nestled him in his lap. The long-lost connection had him throbbing with life, resonating like a second heartbeat, each pulse heavy with anticipation. The book vividly recalled the girl who had dared to touch him; her innocence, like a floral scent, clung to his pages like a haunting memory. Initially, her meddling had amused him, a mere tickle in his consciousness. Her curiosity was an amusing break in his mundane existence of blood and guts.

Now, it incited a burning rage within him. His thirty-year tribute had been withheld. A sacred cycle was shattered due to her interference. He missed savoring the taste of legacy tears dipped in their blood. Only the one called Ariel had offered a little of his due when her essence dripped over his binding, creating a few new pages. Then nothing.

He. Could. Not. Act.

Soaked in anointed oil, this oilcloth hindered him like heavy chains strapped to his cover. His once-sharp talons of destruction were dull, and his stomach ached and was empty. He had been left dormant, bloodless, and mocked by inactivity. Mother Sweat, an emissary for his nemesis, the "Good Book," had struck swift and sure.

He would not continue to endure the indignity of being hindered.

He was reconnected with General, his conduit. He remembered the moment when General had drained power from him, conjuring four vile offspring from the strength of his spine. The cost had been blood, and the banquet of destruction had been glorious, but it had weakened him and made him livid. His clones, mere shadows of his true power, scattered like ashes in the wind, diminishing him. It was good that they were locked away.

The final insult?

He was the original, mistakenly given to that arrogant fool Eric of New America. All of the Council had been oblivious. And he, the book, had chuckled, finding dark humor in the oversight.

But now . . . Now, he was home.

And the game would resume with renewed fervor.

He could sense the decaying edges of human civility, a thin veneer ready to crumble. They had made good out of evil and evil out of good. The dragon had returned, and its fiery breath would scorch everything in its path.

In his role, he'd ensure that they remembered his dominion as fear ruled the land. He would consume their history and reshape it with his narrative.

And this time . . . No one would ever mistake him for anything but the original.

Chapter Forty-One

Sin

"Don't tell me what to do, Jonesy," Sin fussed.

"Woman, I'm not telling you what to do. I'm telling you, you don't have to be bummed you're no longer an agent. Your suspension is an opportunity to be free."

"Free? Free? Didn't you sit in front of that big old TV and choke as you witnessed General and his minions being pardoned, or do you only use it for cartoons?"

"It's anime. And let's keep to the facts—"

"Why? They didn't—"

"Sin, the powerful have always had different rules than ordinary folk. You're walking around sulking when a celebration is about to occur; you need to let this other mess go."

Sin waved off Jonesy. "Yeah, yeah. I'll yell surprise on cue." She then mumbled under her breath, "I'll find something on them, and they're going down for real this time."

Jonesy brushed his hands through his hair, frustration flowing through his words. "I can't with you. You're the most stubborn, pigheaded—"

Sin inched close to him. "Be careful . . . Use the wrong words and take a beat-down."

"Woman, just chill."

Sin's words floated so softly across the air that he almost missed them. "The book is still operating. As long as it's out there, the Council will manipulate its evil for their gain. And then, they've won. The world won't survive."

"Aren't you exhausted?" Jonesy asked.

"Oh, you didn't know? Black women die exhausted."

Jonesy's anger left with her matter-of-fact statement. "Today is a special day for Deacon and Nia. Let's focus on them. Is that okay? And maybe after this, we can have a different conversation?"

Sin shook her head. "Don't let one moment of exuberance in finally getting the bad guy indicate we are anything more than acquaintances."

"Yeah, it's been four months of you acting like nothing happened between us. I'm kinda over it and your excuses."

Sin's mocking laughter bounced off Jonesy's living room walls. "You need to read the room. What? You need it in braille?"

"I'm not blind, Sin. You seem to be."

"Boy, bye. What we've done is wait and watch for months while they dragged their feet putting General in prison. Not to mention mending our relationships with our siblings."

"The week we spent in Costa Rica with our parents helped heal us the most. Deacon had kept so much bottled up that when he let it all out, we were glad the ocean was right there to soak it all up," he said.

"But it worked out in the end, right?"

"Yeah. You spend your life dedicated to ensuring someone else is good, and then there is a void left when you realize you can focus on yourself."

"Well, don't look at me to fill your void. Join a club or something."

Jonesy slid closer. "I am in a club. It's called 'Sinfully Yours.'"

Sin cleared her throat. "You know you aren't alone in finding that your commitment to your brother was suffocating them. Nia had always been such a timid spirit that I thought I had to be her voice. Instead, I found out I was stealing it."

"Yeah, I wasn't feeling Nia at all for Deacon. He needs someone who can stand by his side in this world. But when she ran with him, and then I saw her intercept that Council goonie trying to get to the stage—"

"And stepping in and speaking to the press when he froze . . ."

"Yeah, that too. They seem to be made for each other. They are iron sharpening iron."

Sin stepped back. "When did you start quoting the Bible?"

"I did?" Jonesy said, "Humph, maybe Deacon and Nia finding a church home and talking about it all the time has rubbed off. Or living with Mama Linette all those years."

"Well, don't rub it on me. My mother's bombarding me with it as a kid has given me a lifetime of, no, thank you, when it comes to religion."

"You do know if something as wrong as the book exists, that that means something as right as the Good Book is real too, right?" Jonesy asked.

"What did I say?"

Jonesy held up his hands. "How are your parents doing? When they returned from their cruise, they must have been upset at everything that went on in their absence."

"Ha! They are clueless. And we plan to keep it that way. They were only surprised that Nia had gone to Ghana and that she had a wealthy boyfriend."

She was aware of Jonesy staring at her as she stood in a form-fitting gold gown with a plunging back. She had ensured her chocolate skin gleamed with lavish amounts of shea butter. Her short hair was styled in mini-curls, framing her face and softening her edges. Her mirror said she cleaned up nicely.

Uncomfortable with the twinkle in his eyes, she looked down at her watch and began to swish away. "We need to go up to the rooftop."

Throwing on his dinner jacket, Jonesy moved into Sin's space and gave a sexy dance. "Last chance to have all this for yourself."

Sin stepped around him and opened the door, but he caught it. "You're pushing a product I'm not in the market for."

Jonesy let her sashay past, and she saw his slight shake of his head and secretive smile.

It made her wish he could see her warning label.

You can't have this heart. It's broken.

* * *

Nia

Nia felt flushed, and her eyes crinkled as she sauntered into the building on Deacon's arm. The receptionist, Tony, who once denied her entrance, hurried and stood as they approached and passed the front desk.

"Ma'am," he said, dipping his head as they passed.

Nia nodded back, but when they got into the elevator, she burst into laughter. "I love the change in him. Having to stop here to get your wallet has made my day."

"You look like a fairy-tale princess, babe. I'm glad I came up with our once-a-month, dress-to-the-nines night out. Looking at you on our first night, you have me at a loss for words. Tony and anyone else would bow to you because you look so good. Plus, it matters when you find out who signs your paychecks."

"Thank you, and I love it when you flex." Nia embraced Deacon and inhaled his alluring cologne. She reluctantly came out of his embrace, learning to err on keeping her hugs firm and short. "Deacon, we passed the penthouse. We're going to the roof."

When the doors began to open, Nia leaned forward to press the button for the penthouse one floor below, but Deacon grabbed her hand and kissed it as the doors continued to open, and a loud clamor screamed, "Surprise!"

Nia held her face and looked around. Then she ran to her parents and hugged them. "Daddy, Mama, what are you doing here?" she asked.

She was then pulled out of their arms into Sin's, who, after establishing boundaries in their relationship, Nia had neglected due to spending so much time with Deacon.

"Hey, stranger," Sin said. Tears of happiness welled in Nia's eyes. "Oh, I've missed you too. But why are you all here?"

"Ask your man."

Nia turned to find Deacon on one knee with a beautiful four-carat diamond solitaire in his hand. She began to cry, and her crying turned into sobbing. She looked at Deacon and then around the room.

Ariel waved, and Zachary and a slender Sari with wide smiles nodded. Serene from work gave her a sheepish look because she was the reason Nia was running late leaving work. Serene left work early to get ready for Nia's party. *The nerve. She looks cute, though.*

She knew she was in an alternate universe when Jonesy stepped forward and hugged her. Deacon's parents were hugging him as Ms. Linette cried.

Mother Sweat huffed. "Baby, answer the man."

The group laughed, and Nia got down on both her knees. She held out her hand, and Deacon slid the ring on her finger. "I love you. Marrying me will be the greatest adventure of your life, Nia."

Crawling closer, Nia laughed. "It already is."

Chapter Forty-Two

General

The book lay heavily in General's study, its pages swollen and bloated with secrets and atrocities. It reveled in the chaos of recent events, a vile feast upon the spilled blood and broken bodies of the Council's innocent family members as the tribute had gone forth. Immediately after, hundreds had perished at a rap concert that had gone wrong.

In the quiet of the library, it pulsed with malevolent satisfaction, relishing in the destruction it had caused. General's eyes held a fiery intensity as he continued to observe the muted screen, his mind already concocting intricate plans for retribution.

The monitor displayed photos of Sin coming and going from home, jogging in the park, and dining with her sister, Nia. As he watched, pictures of an ongoing engagement party came through. Had he known, he would have leveled the building, ridding him of all his enemies in one great bang.

No, they needed to suffer.

Geoff stood over his shoulder. "They have no idea what is

coming. Your plan is perfect, sir. I admire and fear your tenacity to set your sights on a target and never relent."

"They will be sorry for interfering in our business, that Sin agent and my niece who spilled our secrets. Can you imagine me sleeping with a Hispanic?" General paused and snickered. "Sorry, I forgot who I was speaking to, with your sudden obsession with darker flesh."

Geoff only shrugged. "Just hers, sir."

"Anyhow, there is no other choice but to destroy them. We shall strike while they least expect it," General declared, his voice low and dangerous.

"I look forward to it, sir."

General rolled his chair back to regard Geoff more closely. "Your loyalty has been unwavering. And you will yet have your chance at Sincere Lewis. She has already been disgraced at her job, and her nightmare is only beginning."

Depravity seeped into every corner of the room like a toxic fog. It was as though each man inhaled deeply and reveled in the wickedness. As expected, the public had lost interest in him, which was perhaps to be expected. The Council owned numerous social media sites that were used for spin control.

Wolf News spun the story that the *Book of Disasters* was fake, a Grimm fairy tale created by mentally unhinged people. Even BNN followed suit on its shows. Sin's suspension was reported as an overreach of her government analyst job, and this spin helped to give credibility to their conspiracy story.

General clicked into an email message that had popped up. "Do you see this, Geoff?"

"The engagement party?"

A video played of Deacon down on one knee proposing. It then panned to everyone clapping and cheering at Nia's yes.

Both men stared vehemently at the video their plant in his

building had filmed. The message in the email stated Tony had only been notified right before the first guests began to arrive.

As the night deepened and the world outside fell into silence, General and Geoff huddled over maps and blueprints, the demise of the people in the video foremost in their thoughts.

"Nachalo!" General murmured, a cruel smile playing on his lips.

Epilogue

Deacon and Nia stood in the far corner of the rooftop, their bodies pressed against each other as they gazed at the city lights. On Nia's hand was her stunning engagement ring, which she kept turning to catch the flickering torchlight.

Jonesy glided over to Sin. "Your sister is tripping over that ring."

"No, she's tripping over the man. The ring is a nice bonus. Who would have thought it would be my shy little sister who'd marry the man of her dreams?"

Squeezing her arm, Jonesy said low, "You feel left out?"

A sudden commotion in the elevator caught everyone's attention, and suddenly, a confident stranger swaggered onto the rooftop.

Ariel rushed over, grabbing Sin's hand. "Girl, introduce me. He is fine."

"Who is that guy?" Jonesy growled.

But both Jonesy and Ariel were speaking to air. Sin, in a strut that owned the room, was gone.

Jonesy's eyes narrowed as he observed the newcomer intently.

Sin put her hand out to stop the stranger from entering the room any farther. Her voice carried as she shouted, "Umber? What are you doing here?"

fin . . . for now

* * *

Want More? Read *Finding Different*, Book 2 of the Loving Different Series.

One kiss and Jonesy knew Sin should be his. But does Sin agree, and will her alter ego Pop stop it all before it can even start? The Council is up to something, but what exactly is it?

Find out in Book Two of the trilogy, *Finding Different*. Click this link to sign up for my website and a free excerpt.

subscribepage.io/D4xA6I

The inhabitants of the Benson Compound have their own story. Their story can be found in the five-star-rated book *LATER* on Amazon.

www.amazon.com/dp/B0B9Q9Z38W/

About the Author

Colette R. Harrell debuted as a traditionally published author of the book, *The Devil Made Me Do It.*

The book, *Chasing Different,* is her second Indie project.

She fills her days as wife, mother, grandmother, author, developmental editor, and literary event facilitator. She likes cold days, a warm blanket, and a good book. She loves to engage with readers.

She would love for you to share your thoughts in a review.